Eighteen eyes were looking at him, with a who's-been-sleeping-in-*my*-bed expression that he found impossible to forgive.

For the first time in his wasp-not-swatting, spider-catching-in-matchboxes-and-carefully-putting-outside life, he urgently wanted to kill a living creature. The fact that it was a minimum of twenty feet long, nine-headed and blatantly supernatural somehow didn't seem relevant. Either it goes, said a voice inside him, or I do, and I'm not particularly bothered which.

At such times, ignorance can be your friend. Experienced professional dragonslayers—one immediately thinks of Ricky Wurmtoter, former head of pest control at J.W. Wells, or the legendary Kurt Lundqvist, thanks to whose efforts Seattle is now 77 percent dragon-free—knows the risks, the moves and the distressingly unfavourable chances of survival. Accordingly, they duck, weave, shuffle their feet, wait for an opening, feint, drop into an extended high guard, trip over something and get torched or eaten. Maurice, who had no idea what he was doing, neatly avoided all these pitfalls. He marched up to the dragon, yelled "Bastard!" at it at the top of his voice, and swung wildly with the breadknife.

WHEN IT'S A JAR

Tom Holt

www.orbitbooks.net

Orbit
Hachette Book Group
237 Park Avenue, New York, NY 10017
HachetteBookGroup.com

First U.S. Edition: December 2013

Orbit is an imprint of Hachette Book Group, Inc. The Orbit name and logo are trademarks of Little, Brown Book Group Limited.

The Hachette Speakers Bureau provides a wide range of authors for speaking events. To find out more, go to www.hachettespeakersbureau.com or call (866) 376-6591.

The publisher is not responsible for websites (or their content) that are not owned by the publisher.

Library of Congress Control Number: 2013947171
ISBN: 978-0-316-22612-7

10 9 8 7 6 5 4 3 2 1

RRD-C

Printed in the United States of America

For Jacob Edwards
Who, in spite of being upside down,
continues to inspire me

PART ONE

When Is A Door—

Years ago, when he was a child, Maurice refused to go on the Underground because he was scared of all the dead people. His father had asked him a few questions and glanced at his bedside table, and explained that the Under*ground* wasn't the same thing as the Under*world* that he'd been reading about in his *Myths & Legends of the Ancient Greeks* book, which his aunt Jane had given him for his birthday. There were no dead people, three-headed dogs or sinister boatmen down there, his father promised him, just crowded platforms, unreliable trains, people in scruffy old coats who talked to themselves, a really quite small proportion of homicidal lunatics and a rather unsavoury smell. He'd been reassured (though he'd secretly quite fancied seeing a dog with three heads) and withdrawn his objection. Nevertheless, even now, there was something about it—

Especially at night, in the uneasy lull between the rush hour and the last junkies-drunks-and-theatre-goers specials, when the platforms are quiet and deserted and nobody can hear you scream; when the tiled corridors echo footsteps, and the trains, when they finally arrive, come bursting out of the darkness like dragons. Since he'd had to work late at the office recently – not because there was work to be done, but because the firm was rationalising, so everyone was sticking to their desks like limpets after nominal going-home time, to show how indispensable they were – he'd had more than his comfortable ration of nocturnal Tube travel recently, and it was starting to get on his nerves.

There were three people in the compartment when he got in, all women. There was an elderly bag lady in a thick wool coat, muttering to herself and knitting what looked like a sock. Opposite her was an elegant middle-aged businesswoman, with dark hair and glasses. She was knitting, too; that seemed a little out of character, but it was just starting to get fashionable again, or so his mother had told him. In the far corner there was a rather nice-looking girl, and *she* was knitting, which suggested his mother had been right about something, for once. In any event, they seemed harmless enough. He chose a seat in the middle of the carriage, sat down, opened his book and raised it in front of him, like a shield.

The windows were black, of course, so there was no visible world outside; all he could see in the one next to him was the reflection of the pretty girl, and it didn't do to dwell on pretty girls who might look up and figure out what you were doing. Instead, he looked up at the advertising boards. One caught his attention, as it had been designed to do—

WHERE IS THEO BERNSTEIN?

That was all: white letters on a black background. For a moment he allowed himself to wonder who Theo Bernstein was and what he was selling. Then he realised he'd been ensnared by evil capitalists and looked away. Out of the corner of his eye, he saw the elegant businesswoman bite through a strand of wool with her teeth. It was an incongruously savage act – though perfectly reasonable, when he thought about it; after all, you aren't allowed to have sharp things on you in a public place. Teeth, however, are the oldest and most basic weapons of all.

The train had slowed down to the point where, with no view through the window, it was impossible to tell if it was moving or standing still. He yawned. He'd had enough of this journey. He was in the kind of limbo, between the culmination of one sequence of events and the start of another, that you get in restaurants after you've finished eating, before they bring the bill. He looked around for something (other than the pretty girl) to graze his mind on. Not much of that kind of thing in a Tube compartment. Further down the carriage, he saw four more black advert boards with white lettering. The Theo Bernstein people were clearly determined to get their message across. He shuffled in his seat to get comfy, and tried to read his book. But that was no good. It was a self-help thing She'd given him to read, shortly before She'd stormed out of his life, slamming the door on the sunlight, and he really couldn't be bothered. *Coping with Rejection*, snickered the chapter heading. Yeah, right.

"All that time, he never realised."

The old woman had spoken. He winced. He hoped she wasn't going to make a nuisance of herself.

"He never realised," she repeated, "that she was carrying on with his worst enemy, behind his back."

Oh God, he thought, and glanced up to see how many stops there were still to go. But, since he hadn't been keeping track, he wasn't entirely sure where he was. Could be anywhere.

"Right under his nose," said the elegant woman.

She hadn't looked up from her knitting. Maurice peered at her round the cover of his book. Odd, he thought.

"He'll find out quite soon," said the old woman. "He'll be heartbroken."

Actually, she didn't sound particularly batty. If anything, she sounded like a Radio 4 anchor. So, come to think of it, did the elegant woman, who now said, "That and losing his job."

Presumably, then, they knew each other. Then why were they sitting half a compartment apart?

"Of course," said the girl, "quite soon that'll be the least of his worries."

Um, he thought. So all three of them knew each other. The girl, who sounded like a trainee Radio 4 anchor, soon to make her debut seguing from the shipping forecast into *Farming Today* in the wee small hours, took a ball of green wool out of her pocket and, apparently without aiming, threw it across the compartment. The elegant woman caught it one-handed. She hadn't even looked up.

"Getting the new job will cheer him up," the old woman said.

The elegant woman threw her a ball of red wool.

"But not for long," the girl said. "He won't be able to enjoy it, because of the weird stuff."

The elegant woman frowned. "He'll find it suits him better."

"Up to a point," said the girl. "But then he'll make a big mistake."

"He always did have such a vivid imagination," sighed the old woman. "Even when he was a wee tot, bless him. Could I have the yellow, please, dear?" She raised her hand and a yellow ball sailed through the air, straight into her fingers. "Now I'm not quite sure what comes after that."

Something odd, really odd, about this conversation. "His friend," prompted the girl.

"What, the one who—?"

"His other friend," said the elegant woman. "Steve, in the army."

Maurice twitched. He had a friend called Steve, in the army. Of course, his Steve was a girl – Stephanie, at one time the boss barracuda in the Kandahar motor pool.

"That's right, silly of me. His friend Steve. She won't half give him a surprise."

A theory, born of desperation, floated into his mind: a variant on the old kissogram theme, he postulated, in which your friends hire paid performers to weird you out of your skull, while filming the whole thing on covert CCTV. Except he didn't have any friends with that sort of imagination or money, or who cared enough about him to go to so much trouble. In which case, it was just a coincidence. After all, lots of women called Stephanie get called Steve.

"He always did like her more than he cared to admit to himself," the old lady went on; and he thought, Coincidence? Seriously?

"Remind me," said the elegant woman. "What's the name of that boy they were both at school with? The one she eventually marries."

"You mean the one who became rich and famous? George something, wasn't it?"

George. Right, he thought, that's quite enough of that. He was just about to stand up, when he realised what the odd thing – the other odd thing – was. They were talking about the *future*—

"It doesn't last, though," the girl said.

"Now then." The elegant woman sounded reproachful. "We're getting ahead of ourselves. If we're not careful, we'll drop a stitch."

He wasn't a brave man, and the thought of accosting three strange women in a public place would normally shrivel him down to the size of a small walnut. This, though, was different. He had no idea what was happening, he definitely didn't *want* to know, but he knew, with a kind of fatal clarity, that he was going to have to ask. He cleared his throat and said, "Excuse me."

They didn't seem to have heard him. "After he's killed the snake," the elegant woman said.

"*Excuse me.*"

The old lady frowned. "Oh, it's a snake, is it? Must've got in a bit of a tangle."

"Definitely a snake," the elegant woman said. "Well, sort of a snake. Anyhow, after he's done that—"

"*I'm talking to you.*" Maybe, but they weren't hearing him.

"Is that before or after he gets fired from – what's the name of the firm?" the girl was asking.

"Overthwart and Headlong, dear. You remember. Before, definitely," the old lady said authoritatively. "Then the snake." She paused. "I think."

Overthwart & Headlong, whose offices he'd just come from. Fired? Oh *shit* . . .

"Damn. I'll have to unpick."

The old lady smiled sympathetically. "Some of these plait-stitch patterns can be a bit confusing," she said. "It was so much simpler in the old days, when everybody was either plain or purl."

There was a gentle but perceptible jolt. The train was moving. "Ooh," the girl said, "we're nearly there; we'd better get a move on. Where had we got to?"

"The snake," said the elegant woman, as she polished her glasses on her sleeve.

"What about the choice?" the old woman said.

"Oh *hell*." The young woman pulled a savage face. "Now I'm going to have to unpick three whole rows."

"Excuse me," Maurice said weakly.

"Are you sure the choice comes before the snake?" the elegant woman said. "I thought the choice came in between the bottle and healing the wounded king."

The *what?* He opened his mouth, trying to say *Excuse me,* but no sound emerged.

"She's right," the old woman said. "Stupid of me. I've got the pattern upside down."

The girl shot her a furious glare. "So it's the snake, *then* the bottle, *then* the choice and *then* the king and presumably the goblins after that. Or is it the choice and then the bottle?"

"EXCUSE ME." He hadn't intended to roar, but it was the only way he could get his mouth to work. He roared so loud they could probably hear him in the street above. The women took no notice.

"Check," the elegant woman said. She glanced at the window, which was still completely black. "Well," she went on, "we cut that pretty fine, but we got there in the end."

The girl was stuffing her needles and wool into her bag. "Talking of which," she said.

"Sorry, dear. Oh yes, of course." The old woman nodded eagerly. "The end. How will it end?"

"Badly," said the elegant woman.

The girl clicked her tongue. "Well, of course *badly*," she said impatiently. "But how exactly? We can't just say *badly* and leave it at that; they'll want details. Like, for instance, what's the cause of death?"

The old woman frowned. "Entropy?"

"*His* death." The girl sighed. "Precisely when and how does he—?"

With a strangled cry, Maurice jumped to his feet, grabbed at the elegant woman (who happened to be nearest) and felt his fingers close on the lapel of her jacket. On and *through.*

The sound they made was like those fireworks that scream as they shoot up into the air; appropriately enough, because that, as far as Maurice could tell in the circumstances, was what the three women did. It was as though they'd all been simultaneously sucked into the thin nozzle of an invisible, exceptionally powerful vacuum cleaner; they sort of *compressed* from three dimensions to two, into straight vertical lines, just before vanishing with a sudden bright blue flare and a distant roll of thunder. At which point, the train stopped, the doors slid open and three Japanese tourists and a bald, fat man in a raincoat got in. Through the window, Maurice could see a sign saying *Piccadilly Circus*. The automated voice said, "Mind the gap", the doors closed and the train gently moved forward.

Maurice's eyes were very wide. Piccadilly Circus was where he'd got on. He fumbled with the sleeve on his left arm and dragged his shirt cuff off his watch. He'd left the office at 7.45. It was now three minutes to eight—

Oh hell, he thought. Here we go again.

At exactly the same time as Maurice got off the train, in exactly the same place, but at ninety-one degrees to that time and place in the D axis, a man in his mid-thirties rolled onto his back, grunted and opened his eyes.

He lay quite still for a moment, looking up. Then he frowned.

"Hello?" he said.

There was no reply apart from a slight and unusual echo. The precise qualities of that echo meant more to him than it would to you or me, because the man had once been a physicist – a great one, a Nobel laureate. True, he couldn't remember anything he'd learned during his twelve years at the University of Leiden, not even his room number or where they keep the washing machines, but his brain was still as sharp as ever. Imagine a Porsche, mechanically perfect but its gas tank completely empty.

He was working, therefore, from first principles, rather like

Archimedes or one of those guys. Also, he wasn't consciously trying to account for the slightly odd properties of the echo. Even so, his subconscious got onto the problem straight away, and, in the time it took the man to sit up and rub his eyes, it had come up with a viable hypothesis that happened to be perfectly correct. The echo sounded funny because he was inside a cylinder – a cylinder, moreover, that tapered dramatically somewhere out of sight overhead. Sort of a bottle shape.

Because of the way the mind works, he wasn't conscious of all the calculus and equations he'd just performed. Instead, he attributed the flash of insight to intuition, which he'd been brought up to mistrust. That's all the thanks his subconscious got for all that hard work. It's an unfair world.

I'm in a *bottle*, he thought.

Then he realised that that thought was the only one he'd got, like the very first stamp in a brand-new stamp album. His frown deepened. Once again, his subconscious raced. It realised that it occupied a brain equipped with vast memory-storage capacity, a very big stamp album indeed; therefore, wasn't it a bit odd that all that space had just one thought in it?

Well, now there were two, but that wasn't the point. Surely there ought to be, well, *dozens*. And, while he was at it, he couldn't help noticing the substantial quantity of intellectual plant and machinery cluttering the place up – logic and cognitive processes and arithmetic, and God only knows what that one over there was supposed to be for. Unless the inside of his head was just warehouse space, presumably they'd been put there for a reason. I must be somebody, he realised. With a thing, *name*, and a personality and a, what's that other thing, a *history*. And what, now I come to think of it, am I doing in a bottle?

If he really was in a bottle. He looked around. There was nothing to see, absolutely nothing at all. There was light, quite a fair amount of it. What was lacking was anything for the light to play with.

Now then. All from first principles, of course, but it didn't take him long to come up with a theory. I'm in a glass bottle, or just possibly a jar; and the bottle or jar's in—

Nothing?

That's where a frame of reference is so devilishly useful. A frame of reference lets you know instantly if being inside a glass bottle inside nothing at all is normal, the same old same old, just another day at the office; or whether it's odd, a bit strange, possibly even a cause for moderate concern. But, as far as he could tell, he had no frame of reference, not even a scrap of a corner of one. Awkward. And, since he was stuck in a bottle surrounded by nothing at all, it wasn't immediately obvious how he was supposed to go about changing that. In which case, presumably, all he could do was wait patiently in the hope that the frame of reference he must once have had would at some point return and start making sense of things. Well, of course it will. It'll come back when it's hungry. They always do.

At which point (from first principles) he realised he'd discovered the concept of time. For about two and a half seconds he felt rather excited about that, though he wasn't sure why. A small part of him was trying to tell him that finding out stuff about how the world works is a good thing and something to feel pleased with yourself about. Quite why, he couldn't say, but the instinct was surprisingly strong. Maybe that's what I'm for, he told himself; after all, I must be for something, or else why the hell bother having me in the first place? Assuming I exist, of course, but I'm pretty sure I do. Well, of course I exist. I'm thinking, aren't I? And if you think, you exist, surely. Stands to reason, that does.

He stood up and peered down at himself. He was, he noticed, a sort of drab pink colour, in striking contrast to

everything else, which was no colour at all. When he patted
the top of his head, he felt something soft and sort of woolly;
it felt a bit like the thin black hair on his arms, legs and body,
but longer. He tried to think of a reason for it – how being
partially thatched could possibly make him a more efficient
pink entity in a bottle – but maybe he was missing pertinent
data, because nothing sprang immediately to mind. Also,
there were hard, vaguely scutiform plates on the ends of his
fingers and toes. Crazy.

Am I alone?

Now where, he wondered, had that thought come from?
For one thing, it meant he'd invented mathematics, simply by
postulating that there might be such a thing as more-than-
one. But of course there was, because he had ten fingers and
ten toes; therefore, plurality exists. Any damn fool could tell
you that. In which case, given the possibility of multiple entities, there might be more like him, maybe as many as five, or
ten even, out there somewhere. Out where? He peered, but all
he could see was nothing, with more nothing just beyond it,
set against an infinite backdrop of zilch.

Now here's a thought. I'm in a bottle, but I can't see it. I
know it's there, because of the echo. Therefore, things can
exist without me being able to see them. Therefore, even
though I can't see other entities like myself, there may be
some, somewhere. Whee!

Enough of the abstract theorising; time for some practical
experimentation. He walked forward in a straight line (which,
for the sake of convenience, he decided was probably the
shortest distance between two given points). After three
paces, he simultaneously banged his nose and stubbed his
toe—

Ouch. Pain. That made him frown, because he wasn't sure
he liked it. But of course, it must be an inbuilt warning mechanism, to keep you from damaging yourself by, for example,

walking into one of those things that exist but can't be seen. Ingenious and effective, he decided; my compliments to the chef. Still, probably a good idea to reduce one's exposure to it as far as conveniently possible.

"Hello."

The echo again? No, not possible. It sounded all wrong for that. He turned round, and saw – his reflection? Good guess, but apparently not, because the entity he was looking at, though similar to him in many ways, was subtly different in others. Partially covered in white fabric, for one thing; also longer hair and two curious sort of bumps, or swellings, on the front.

The entity spoke. "It apologises," it said, "for any inconvenience."

That made no sense, but he was prepared to make allowances. "Do they hurt?" he asked.

"Excuse it?"

"The swellings on your front. Are you ill?"

The entity's face moved, producing an expression he intuitively suspected was meant to convey displeasure. "It's supposed to be like that."

"Really? Why?"

"Presumably you perceive it as female. Would you mind terribly much not staring? If it's female, it doesn't like it."

"Sorry." He turned away, then turned slowly back and deliberately focused a hand's span above the top of the entity's head. "Is that better?"

"Marginally," the entity replied, "though it's not easy having a conversation with someone not looking at it. But that's fine for now," the entity added quickly, as he started to turn away again. "It'll just have to get used to it."

Hang on, he thought. A million questions were bubbling away inside his head, but there was one he just had to ask. "Excuse me."

"Yes?"

"Why do you talk about yourself in the third person?"

The entity's face showed an expression designed to convey perplexity. "Say what?"

"Well," he said, "there's three persons in speech, right? Apparently," he added, as it occurred to him to wonder how the hell he knew that. "There's the first, like I, and the second, you, and then for some reason there's *three* thirds. But you don't seem to be using the right one."

The entity looked at him for a moment, shook its head and said, "It wouldn't worry about that right now if it was you. There are ... " the entity hesitated. "More pressing issues."

"Are there?"

"You bet."

"Wow. Such as?"

"Your identity," the entity replied. "Your current status. Talking of which, it would like to assure you that you're perfectly safe."

"Ah." It hadn't occurred to him that he might not be. "Well, that's good."

"And, more to the point," the entity went on, "while you're in there, so is everyone else."

"Excuse me?"

The entity looked mildly embarrassed. "It's been instructed to tell you that you're being held in temporary isolation, pending a review. In another time, place and context, your status here would be aptly conveyed by an annoying hourglass, or an even more annoying running horse. There is no cause for concern."

"Great," he said, trying to sound pleased. "So I'm just—"

"Here."

He nodded. "And that's all right, is it? I mean, that's how it's supposed to be."

"Oh yes."

"Thanks, you've set my mind at rest. You see, I don't actually know—"

The entity didn't seem to want to look at him. "Your memories have been temporarily removed and placed in secure storage. It apologises for any—"

"So I've got some, then. Memories, I mean."

"Heaps."

"Cool." He grinned. "So, when can I have them back?"

"Later."

"Right. When is later?"

"Later is after now," the entity replied, "just before eventually. Meanwhile, you have nothing to worry about. Everything is as it should be."

He nodded again, this time more slowly. "You said I've been placed here, and my memories have been removed. Um, who by?"

The entity's face changed colour very slightly; a faint reddish tinge. "It."

"You?"

"No, it."

"Ah."

The entity hesitated, as though looking for the right words. "Since you seem to have a flair for linguistics," it said, "try this. Not every passive has an equivalent active form."

He tried that one, but it wouldn't run. "Sorry, you've lost me."

"Just because something is done," the entity said slowly, "it doesn't necessarily follow that somebody's done it. Some things just ..." The entity waved a hand vaguely. "That's how it is."

"It meaning you?"

"No. Yes. Sort of. Look," the entity snapped, "that's a really abstruse, complex question, and it's on a schedule. All you need to know right now is, you're safe, everything's fine, and it'll get back to you as soon as possible. Meanwhile—"

"It apologises for any inconvenience?"

"You got it. Oh, and one other thing." The entity was looking positively furtive.

"Yes?"

"If you could just sign this form." A sheet of paper materialised in the air a few inches from his face. A pen hovered over it like a wingless dragonfly.

"Excuse me?"

"Sign, please. Just a formality."

He looked at the pen and the paper. They did seem oddly familiar, but he had no data. "I'm not sure I know how."

"Take the stick thing in your hand and rub its pointy end up and down on the flat thing until it makes a mark. Anywhere'll do."

He reached out and took the pen. Without thinking, he cradled it between his index and middle fingers, with his thumb pressed to the side. "Why?"

"Excuse it?"

"Why am I doing this?"

"Oh, it's just a disclaimer," it mumbled. "Sort of absolving it from all present and future liability. Legal stuff. You don't need to worry."

"There's marks on the flat thing already. Hold on," he added, as something about the marks caught his eye. Bizarrely enough, their shape and form seemed to convey some sort of meaning. "Can I look at them?"

"Wouldn't bother if it was you," the entity said quickly. "Just the usual blahdy-blah. Nothing important."

"If it isn't important, then why do you want me to—?"

"Just sign, OK?"

He was aware that he was causing the entity a certain degree of discomfort. Obviously he didn't want that, so he pressed the pen to the paper and did a sort of squiggle. Immediately, they both vanished. "Sorry," he said. "Did I do it wrong?"

"No, that's fine." The entity was smiling. "Well, that about covers everything, so it'll leave you in peace. So, um, enjoy your stay with it, and please feel free to make full use of all the facilities."

"Hey, thanks. What facilities?"

"Um." The entity shrugged. "Anyhow," it said. "Have a nice day now, you hear?"

"Yes," he replied eagerly, "I was meaning to ask you about that. I take it that when I hear something, it's because vibrations made by movements or similar events are conveyed to me in some kind of wave, and there's a specially sensitive membrane or something inside me somewhere that translates those vibrations into sensory input that I'm capable of interpreting. Is that right, or am I barking up the wrong tree entirely?"

The entity dipped its head. "Pretty much," it said. "That style of thing, anyhow. Be seeing you."

"Oh yes, sight," he said. "Is that where tiny particles of light—?" But the entity had vanished.

He stood for a while, his eyes fixed on the particular area of nothing-at-all where the entity had been. Questions, a seething mass of them, tried in vain to leap the waterfall of his mind. Then, abruptly, he turned away, sat down and closed his eyes. So much to think about. Like, for example; suppose you had three lines, and each of the three lines met two of the others; you'd get three angles, so let's call it a threeangle. Now, just suppose that you made each line in the threeangle into one of the four lines in a square—

Time passed. So *that's* what it does, he thought; and then: is that all? Surely there's more to it than that. Well, maybe not, but presumably it can pass in both directions. It'd be ludicrously inefficient otherwise. He sat perfectly still and tried to make time pass backwards. Then he frowned. It didn't seem to be working, but maybe he wasn't doing it right. So he made time stand still – that, apparently, was easy-peasy – while he considered the matter further. Well, of course, silly me: time must be curved, so that it curls back on itself in a perpetual loop. Glad we got that sorted out.

He looked down at his toes and counted them. Five on each foot. Why?

Time passed some more, like a hamster on a wheel, and he figured out a bit more of the basic elementary stuff, like existentialism and relativity. Light, he decided, was most likely split into seven base colours, and he wouldn't be at all surprised if it was the fastest-moving thing in the universe (which could only have started with a big explosion of some sort, although there was a slim chance that in the beginning there might just have been a word). The flat hard plates on the ends of his fingers could only be the vestigial remnants of claws, dating back to a time when his species had eaten other entities for food (weird idea, but what the heck); needless to say, over the course of many billions of arbitrary units of time, various sorts of entities must've adapted to take advantage of their environments, while the ones that didn't manage to adapt sort of faded away; the ones with claws made it, he guessed, and the ones without weren't so lucky, though chances were there was more to it than that.

More time passed. At a wild guess, when the explosion happened, he was prepared to bet that great big chunks of stuff got flung about all over the place, probably catching fire in the process, and if only he could get outside this bottle he'd be able to see them, way up above his head, twinkling against a presumably dark background like little pinpoints of light. That'd be nice. On the other hand, the female entity had told him that being in the bottle was quite normal and he was perfectly safe, in which case he really shouldn't think about what fun it'd be outside the bottle looking up at the twinkly lights. Instead, maybe he should spare a thought for some of the many other issues he hadn't got around to tackling yet, such as why he stayed on the ground rather than floating through the air.

Even more time passed, and there came a point when he thought: Well, that's about everything. Actually, that wasn't strictly true. There were a few loose ends to be cleared up – he wasn't entirely happy with his conclusions on algebraically closed field theory, he still had some reservations about Big Bang nucleosynthesis, and however hard he tried, he couldn't get it to come out as a whole number – but broadly speaking, he was satisfied that he'd figured out all the basic, simple stuff that presumably you needed to know before you were considered fit to be let loose on your own. He had no argument with that (what sort of a world would it be, after all, if there were people wandering about who didn't understand consequentialism and couldn't calculate the volume of an irregular polyhedron?) but as far as he could see, he'd done everything that could reasonably be expected of him, and now he was just wasting time. He wondered if they realised he was ready; and, if not, how he was supposed to let them know. Logically, there ought to be a bell he could ring or a button or something, but he couldn't find one.

"Hello?" he said. But all he got was that dumb echo again.

This can't be right, he thought. I must've missed something or got something wrong. So he sat down, closed his eyes and went carefully back over everything he'd deduced so far. It took him a while, but everything checked out – no obvious glaring mistakes or stupid false assumptions. He really couldn't see what else there could possibly be—

Ah, he thought. That's the point, isn't it? It's an intelligence test, or a test of character, something like that. Along the lines of: unless you can get yourself out of the bottle, you aren't fit to be free. Well, that shouldn't be too much of a problem. He'd already figured out that the bottle was in fact a confined space contained inside a strong electromagnetic field, sufficiently powerful that it could be mistaken for solid matter. Well, duh. To get through the field, all he had to do was identify its power source and turn it off. The only snag there was that the power source had to be somewhere outside the bottle, and there was no way he could think of to get his material body through the field in order to find it and throw the switch. Awkward.

Well, he told himself, you say that, but have you actually tried? No, he hadn't – mostly because he was fairly sure that prolonged contact with the field would reduce him to a pile of ash. That, however, was only an assumption, based on pure theory. Maybe the whole point of this being-stuck-inside thing was to teach him that theory's all very well, but sometimes you've got to do the experiment. He stood up, lowered his head and ran at the invisible wall.

Time passed. He woke up. His head hurt. He was lying curled up in a ball, and there was a funny smell which he quickly identified as oxidisation residue. Well, it was nice to know he'd been right about not being able to get through the field, at any rate.

He yawned. Now he came to think of it, he'd been working pretty much flat out ever since he could remember, what with figuring stuff out from first principles, and now the unsuccessful experiment in field density parameters. His investigation of his body had led him to the conclusion that from time to time it needed to shut down for a while in order to recuperate and carry out routine maintenance functions, during which time he'd probably lose consciousness and move his eyes around a lot. Now, he decided, would probably be a good time to do all that. So he did.

He slept; and he dreamed. In his dream, he was sitting at a table outside a café in Rio de Janeiro. Sitting next to him was a rather attractive girl, and on the table were six empty beer bottles. He was vaguely aware that he'd just reached a decision, and it was terribly important. Under his right hand was a scrap of paper, on which he'd just written *Terms and conditions apply.*

Is this just a dream, he asked himself, or is it a memory? No way of telling. If it was a dream, the girl of his dreams was exactly that. If it was a memory, and she'd really smiled at him like that at some point, the sooner he got out of this damn bottle and back to his life, the better.

"This one," he heard himself say, as he picked up the one green bottle (the others were brown) and slipped it into his jacket pocket, "is for me. No terms and conditions. Complete freedom. I reckon I've earned it, don't you?"

She was gazing at the five brown bottles. "What about—?"

"One for you." He pushed a bottle across the table at her. She stared at it but didn't touch. "And one for Pieter, one for Max, one for your uncle Bill, since he did put all that money into Pieter's damnfool project. And one," he concluded cheerfully, "for fun."

"Fun?"

"Yes, fun." He touched a fingertip to the neck of the bottle, which glowed blue and vanished. "Hey," he said, shaking his hand and putting the fingertip in his mouth, "did you see that? That was *cool.*"

Her eyes were still fixed on her bottle. "And the one you've kept for yourself—"

"Well." He made a vague and-why-not gesture. "One empty San Miguel bottle to bring them all and in the darkness bind them. If necessary," he added. "But it won't be, I'm sure. After all, I've given the others to people of unimpeachable integrity, so what could possibly go wrong?"

"What about the sixth bottle?"

"Oh, that." He smiled. "A pound to a penny it'll end up at the bottom of the sea. In which case, it'll get eaten by a fish, which in turn will get caught by the seventh son of a seventh son. That's what usually happens, and we're all still here, aren't we?"

She'd shrunk back when the bottle started glowing blue. Now she leaned forward again. "And what about you?"

"Ah. I've been thinking about that."

"And?"

And – damn it – he woke up. *Not fair*, he howled silently at the universe, *I was watching that*. But it had gone – dream, memory, whatever – and all that remained behind was a scramble of unintelligible images and meaningless proper nouns: Rio, San Miguel, Pieter, Max. He had no idea what or who any of them were; but he had known, once, he was sure of it. And the girl, female entity, basically similar but still significantly different; what was all that about? It had to be a memory, because he couldn't have *invented* anything so perfect, even back before his mind had been wiped clean and he knew what girls, female entities, were supposed to look like—

"Hello? Can you hear it?"

He snapped his head left. It, no, *she* was back, the female entity, the one he'd met earlier. Wonderful. "Yes, I can hear you," he shouted. "Listen, you've got to let me out of here. I've just found out, I've got a life."

But she didn't seem pleased. "You found out."

"Yes. I fell asleep, and I *remembered*. I was sitting on a thing beside a thing in a place, and there were six empty things on the thing, and there was this utterly amazingly wonderful female entity. Which is why I've got to get out of here. *Now*."

The female entity shook her head slowly. "It's very sorry," she said. "But that's not possible."

"Why?"

"Not possible," she replied firmly. "Besides, what you thought you saw wasn't real. It was a—"

"Dream, yes." He nodded enthusiastically. "A jumble of images generated during rapid-eye-movement sleep as a result of ascending cholinergic waves stimulating the forebrain. But it wasn't *just* a dream. It was real. It was something that actually happened."

The female entity pulled a face. "Really?"

"Yes, I'm sure of it. I remembered. It was terribly important, because of the six things. They're things, you see. They make a sort of thing in a thing, which means you can get through into other things. And places. And the female entity—" He stopped. The last traces of the image were starting to break up, so that he could no longer remember the dream, only the memory of it. It was so desperately sad, he wanted to burst into tears.

"Oh dear," said the female entity. "Oh deary deary it."

"What?"

"That's not good," she said, giving him a serious look. "It was afraid something like this might happen."

"Something like what?"

"You're not well." She was frowning, which worried him. "Everything is not as it should be." She tapped her forehead. "In here."

"*What?*"

Now she was giving him a sympathetic look, which was downright scary. "Essentially, it's an infection of the lower hippocampus. It can treat it," she went on, as his mouth opened in a perfect circle, "but it'll have to purge your brain again, which means you'll be back to square one, it's afraid."

"Square—?"

"You'll go to sleep," she said, "and when you wake up, you'll have no thoughts or memories at all. Again."

"Oh."

"Not to worry," she said encouragingly. "You'll soon figure it all out again, just like you've already done. But this time, with any luck, the infection won't come back."

Two words registered. "This time?"

"Yes."

"Does that mean it's happened before?"

Pause. Then she nodded.

"More than once?"

Nod.

"How many—?"

"Two hundred and forty-seven." She gave him a sad little smile. "This'll be the two hundred and forty-eighth time it's had to scrub your brain. But it's all right. It'll get there in the end, it promises. Just a matter of finding exactly the right treatment."

"Two hundred and—"

"Yes."

He thought about that for two and a third seconds. "And each time, I've figured out everything from basic principles, and then you've come along and—"

"Afraid so, yes. But it's for your own good. It has to do it so you'll be well again. You do want that, don't you?"

He hesitated. "Yes. Of course. But—"

He was engulfed in fire. It ran down his arms and back like honey, and he screamed. His head was full of it; he could feel his brain burning—

He slumped to the floor and went to sleep. The female entity stood looking at him for some time, and slowly the expression on her face changed, from sympathetic regret to cold hatred. Then she shrugged and walked away.

He slept. Time passed.

The temperature inside the bottle rose to something in the order of 60 degrees Celsius, then dropped away to −30, then stabilised round about human blood temperature. Then (at exactly the same moment as Maurice got off the train, in exactly the same place, but at ninety-one degrees to that time and place in the D axis), he rolled onto his back, grunted and opened his eyes. He lay quite still for a moment, looking up. Then he frowned.

"Hello?" he said.

Here we go again, Maurice thought, because this wasn't the first time. Oh no.

The first time had been thirteen years ago, and it had started in the corridor outside the headmaster's office, a very bad place indeed. There was a bench there. It was quite a famous bench; Death Row, they called it, and sooner or later, everybody found their way there, in the dreadful time just before the start of morning lessons, when Mr Fisher-King dispensed justice.

Sitting next to him on the bench, looking mildly bored, was Stephanie Wilson, his co-accused. Normally he wouldn't have minded sitting next to Stephanie Wilson; in fact, there had been times when he'd gone out of his way to arrange it. One such arrangement had landed them here, charged with two counts of illicit snogging on school premises. Ah well. It had seemed like a good idea at the time.

Stephanie – red-haired, plain-faced, undisputed arm-wrestling champion – took a biro from her pocket, removed the lid and used the plastic clip to clean out dirt from under her fingernails. It was something she did quite often, and it usually needed doing. No other girl he knew did that.

The door opened, and a kid in the school only by sight wandered out with a look on his face that suggested his brain had just been sucked out through his ears. You saw stuff like that, sitting on Death Row.

The kid nodded slightly, which meant it was their turn next. Maurice really didn't want to go, but Stephanie stood up briskly, put the cap back on the biro, and marched into Mr Fisher-King's office without looking back. You had to admire someone who didn't know the meaning of fear, though it had to be said that fear was just one of many words Stephanie didn't know the meaning of, let alone how to spell them. Reluctantly he got up and followed her. It was his first time in Mr Fisher-King's office. People said it didn't actually hurt, though of course you were never the same afterwards.

Mr Fisher-King was sitting behind an enormous desk, his back to an enormous window, leaning back in an enormous chair. It was as though he'd chosen his surroundings to high-light just how small he was; five foot nothing in thick socks, with the body of a malnourished child and a bigger-than-average head. His hair was thick, curly, a blend of auburn and grey that together made up a sort of ghastly pink; he had the face of an unwrapped mummy, and the lenses of his glasses were as thick as a man's thumb. As they walked in, he looked up from whatever it was he'd been reading and smiled at them. The smile mostly bounced off Stephanie, who instinc-tively turned her head at just the right moment, but Maurice caught the full force of it.

"Well," said Mr Fisher-King.

There was no way of knowing how old Mr Fisher-King was – somewhere between fifty and a hundred and ninety – but sooner or later, Maurice thought, he'll have to retire, and when he does, they'll want to give him a leaving present. No problem whatsoever about what to get him. The biggest, fluffiest white Persian cat that money can buy; so that, when he quits the teaching profession and is immediately head-hunted by SPECTRE as their new CEO, to drag them kicking and screaming into the twenty-first century, he'll have everything he could possibly need in order to do his job properly.

A tiny nod of the massive head meant *sit down*, so they did. Mr Fisher-King looked at them for about twenty seconds, precisely the time it took for his eyes to reduce Maurice's soul to mush without actually killing him. Then he frowned, glanced down at a sheet of paper on his desk, and looked up again.

"Actually," he said, "I've been meaning to talk to you two."

His voice had changed. The shift took Maurice's breath away. It was as though he'd just been strapped into the electric chair, and the executioner, instead of throwing the switch, had pulled out his wallet and started showing him snapshots of his grandchildren. Even Stephanie looked mildly confused, like an Easter Island statue trying to do long division in its head.

Mr Fisher-King's head turned slowly, like a tank turret, and he looked at Stephanie for a long time. "Your great-great-great-grandmother," he said, "was transported to Australia for stealing a sock. Your father won seventeen million pounds on the Lottery the year before last, but he lost the ticket two days before the draw and never bothered to check the number. There's a Viking ship burial twelve feet under your gran's living room. Your brother Kieran's eldest son will one day invent a revolutionary new non-stick coating for frying pans, but someone else will patent it and get all the money. His youngest son will defuse a nuclear bomb using only a pair of pliers and a hairpin. You secretly like carrots, but you've never told anyone because it isn't cool to eat fresh vegetables. Last Christmas you bet Tracy Armitage five pounds that you'd get Jason Turner into bed before New Year; you lost on a technicality, because there is no bed in the back of his van, only a mattress." He paused, and looked at her again. "Are you wondering why I'm telling you all this?"

"Yes, sir."

Mr Fisher-King shrugged, and turned to Maurice. "Your destiny and hers are inextricably linked. So far in your short life you've achieved precisely nothing, unless you count Fiona Cartwright, but what you've got in store for you is quite simply—" He paused, then shook his head. "Which only goes to show," he went on, "because as far as I can see you lack the intelligence, the courage, the resourcefulness and the strength of character to cope with any of the stuff you're going to have to face, and yet—" He shrugged. "Amazing," he said. "Because, well, just look at you. You're a mess. You're not just feckless, you're a black hole into which feck falls and is utterly consumed."

"Sir?"

Mr Fisher-King sighed. "Don't worry about it," he said, "it doesn't matter. You know what? This is supposed to be the crowning moment of my career. My God," he added, and shook his head. "I've thought about it often, but I never thought it'd be like this."

In addition to the anticipated fear and loathing, Maurice was starting to feel the acute embarrassment felt by the young when they have to witness their elders and betters losing it in style. "Sir," he heard himself say, "is everything—?"

"Yes." Mr Fisher-King nodded sharply. "Yes, everything's just fine. In fact, everything's perfect. Guess what, kids, it's nunc dimittis time." He closed his eyes, as though something was hurting. "You know how long I've been in this job? Well?"

Stephanie, who'd been staring straight at him, like an idiot gazing directly into the sun, shook her head. "Sir?"

Mr Fisher-King smiled. "Well," he said. "This school was built in 1926. Before that, there was an old Victorian Board school, which replaced the old village school, which started up shortly after the Dissolution of the Monasteries. Before that—" He winced. "Believe it or not, there's been a school of sorts here for twelve hundred years. I want you to think about that," he added bitterly. "Twelve hundred years of bloody kids, and you know the worst thing about it?"

"No, sir?"

Mr Fisher-King laughed abruptly. "They're all the same," he said. "They're all pretty much like you lot. I thought, when the Normans came in, That's more like it, we'll be getting a better class of students from now on, but no, not a bit of it. Same with the invention of moveable type. It'll all be different from now on, I thought. Any time now we'll have universal literacy – that's got to bring about a quantum leap in intellectual evolution. Boy, was I wrong about that. Oh no. Year after year after year it's still just bloody *kids*." His hands were clenched into tiny balls, the knuckles standing out bone-white. "Until now," he said, and suddenly he relaxed. "That's it. At last, it's over, and I'm free."

There was a long silence. Maurice couldn't have moved if he'd wanted to. Stephanie was chewing slowly. Eventually, Mr Fisher-King started to come back to life. He sat up in his chair, looked down at the papers on his desk, shuffled some of them into a neat pile. "Anyway," he went on, "this is the moment I've been waiting for. All I've got to do is give you two the message – *Wilson, spit it out right now—*" He nudged a steel wastebin out from under the desk with his foot; there was a faint metallic *ting* – "and I can finally call it a day. Which will be absolutely marvellous, believe you me. Right." He straightened up and blinked twice. "Where was I?"

"Sir?"

"Oh yes. You two. Right, let me see." He turned over a sheet of paper, frowned, screwed it into a ball and threw it over his shoulder. "An extraordinary destiny awaits you," he said, in a curious sing-song voice. "Your task will be to kill the dragon, find the entrance to the glass mountain, release the prisoner of the Dolorous Tower and—" He paused, squinted at another scrap of paper, turned it over, folded it in half and stuck it in his top pocket. "Shopping list," he said. "Ah, here we are." He glanced at something written on the back of an envelope. "Actually, we won't bother with all that right now. Let's just say you're going to be kept busy for quite some time. One of you will grow up to be the foremost warrior of your generation. The other one—" He blinked, and lifted his glasses to stare at the envelope. "Well, anyway. Lots and lots for you to be getting on with; success is absolutely *not* guaranteed, and if you fail, we're all going to be in the brown and smelly up to our armpits. The destiny of the universe, in fact, rests on your shoulders." He pursed his lips and turned his head for a moment. "I can only assume that at some point somewhere, somebody knew what he was doing, but there you go. Oh, and you'll need this."

He opened a desk drawer, rummaged about for a bit, then produced a small, battered brown cardboard box. He put it down on the desk. "No idea which of you it's supposed to be for," he said, "so you can fight over it between yourselves later. Well," he added, with a sudden and startlingly beautiful smile, "that's about it. Job done. You two had better get to your lessons, and I'm going to write my letter of resignation. And then—" The smile faded into a look of total clarity. "Well, who knows? Oh, I nearly forgot. Demonstration."

Stephanie looked at him. "Sir?"

Mr Fisher-King grinned. "Apparently I've got to give you a demonstration of some kind," he said, "just so you'll know this is for real and not just me finally having the nervous breakdown I've so richly deserved for so very long. All right," he added, "how about this?"

For some reason, the temperature in the room dropped like a stone. Mr Fisher-King stretched out his left hand, palm upwards; resting on it, suddenly, was a doughnut. Maurice shrank back a little. Stephanie, who liked doughnuts a little too much, leaned forward, but before she could pounce, the doughnut slowly rose into the air. It hung for a moment, wobbling almost imperceptibly, then gradually rotated, so that they were looking directly at the hole in the middle.

"All right," Mr Fisher-King said very softly. "What can you see?"

Maurice looked. Through the hole, he thought he saw a city at night, a great city, in flames. In the orange glow of the sky, he could just make out three or four moving shadows, like birds, except no bird was, or could ever be, quite that shape. Then the glow turned into a blaze, so bright he had to close his eyes, and when he opened them again, he saw a black desert, an endless vista of dunes, which proved to be (the focus narrowed abruptly) tall heaps of wind-blown cinders, with the ends of fire-twisted steel girders poking out like ribs through a desiccated carcase. Then it all changed, and he saw an old man – himself – staring through the bars of a prison door, and then—

"Well?" said Mr Fisher-King.

"It's a doughnut," said Stephanie.

"Of course it is," said Mr Fisher-King. Then he sighed. "Go on, then," he said, and Stephanie's paw shot out and secured it. Then she hesitated.

"You just made it appear," she said accusingly. "Out of thin air."

Mr Fisher-King nodded. "It's perfectly all right," he said.

But Stephanie was giving him a sour look; so he flattened his palm, and another doughnut appeared. He closed his hand around it, lifted it to his face and took a bite out of it. "See?" he said. "Perfectly all right."

"How did you do that?" asked Stephanie, with her mouth full. "Sir," she added.

Mr Fisher-King shook his head. "I could tell you," he said, "but then you'd have learned something, and you wouldn't want to spoil an otherwise unblemished record. All right, the fun's over. Get out, both of you. No, just a moment." He blinked, and settled his glasses on his nose. "What was it you two're in here for? Oh, right, yes. Double detention, Friday, and don't do it again. At least," he added, "not until the third of March 2001, at the very earliest. After that, of course—" He shrugged, and gave them a feeble sort of grin. "Fine," he said. "Now, get out of my sight, and don't either of you ever come near me again."

The cardboard box turned out to be empty. Stephanie kept it for putting small bits of rusty metal in. Nobody knew what she wanted them for and everybody knew better than to ask.

Hence, not unreasonably, here we go again. Thirteen years of not thinking about it, very hard; four thousand, seven hundred and forty-eight days on which he'd fought desperately to keep it from slipping back into his memory. Ah well. It takes thirteen years to climb a ladder, but only a few minutes to slide down a snake.

He thought about Stephanie instead. *His other friend,* the elegant woman had said, *Steve in the army.* The calling-her-self-Steve thing was actually quite recent, since she'd been in the military, presumably a form of protective mimicry. They'd never once talked about when they'd gone to Mr Fisher-King's study, although once, when she was home on leave, she admitted to him that she'd Googled Fisher-King and come across a Wikipedia article that she really thought he ought to read. He'd done so, and was forced to recall that, a mere eighteen months after Mr Fisher-King retired, they'd built a Morrisons on the big patch of waste ground out back of the sports centre that had been left derelict ever since they pulled down the old tyre factory. Spooky, or what?

He went home, checked his messages (none), wedged a frozen pizza in the microwave and opened a can of beer. Thirteen years ago, Mr Fisher-King had shown him destruction, war and death in the middle of a doughnut, which Stephanie had then eaten. Ever since then, his life had gradually soaked away into the sands of routine, and he'd almost reached the point where he was beginning to feel *safe*. Now this. He really wished Stephanie was back in the UK, so he could call her and not talk about it; but she was far away, up to her pale-blue eyes in carburettors and gearbox linkages. Face it, he told himself, you're going to have to cope with this all by yourself, and the first step's got to be, don't think about it.

So he switched on the TV and got the news. Apparently there'd been some sort of appalling disaster at a science lab in Western Australia; a vast new multi-billion-dollar facility run by a multinational megacorp even he'd vaguely heard of had apparently disappeared, vanished, here-one-minute-gone-the-next, with not even a mile-wide glass-bottomed crater to mark where it had been. They were calling it the biggest scientific catastrophe since the Very Very Large Hadron Collider blew up the year before last, possibly even worse than that, except there'd been no explosion. Since nobody had a clue what they'd been doing there or how many of them had been doing it, accurate casualty figures were not available. One thing they could say for certain, however, was that there had been no survivors.

Maurice shrugged and switched channels. More news, same story. He flipped channels again. We're interrupting our scheduled program to bring you the latest developments from Wooloomatta; cut to a bemused-looking woman holding a microphone, standing in a vast open plain covered in small blue flowers. The flowers were, apparently, the latest development. Nobody had seen them grow, but there they were, and – well, yes. Blue flowers, about fifty hectares of them, slap bang in the middle of the third most hostile environment on Earth. Cut to close-up of small blue flowers, which were OK, if you liked that sort of thing.

He frowned and switched channels, and got a documentary about the war in Afghanistan. The hell with that. He switched off and took a bite out of his pizza, which had gone cold. Not to worry; he really wasn't hungry. He got up and went to bed.

Because he never remembered his dreams when he woke up, he opened his eyes about four hours later and had no idea what the extremely important message was that he'd just been given by someone whose name might have been Max, but already he wasn't sure. He shook his head, groped for the light and realised it was already on.

Odd, because he remembered turning it off. He blinked. Also, his bedside light was ordinary light colour. The glow filling his bedroom was more a sort of pale orange.

Somehow or other, you instinctively know when you're not alone in a room. How disturbing this realisation is depends a lot on context. For Maurice, who hadn't had company in his bedroom for a depressingly long time, it definitely wasn't good. His first instinct was to pretend he hadn't noticed. You can be wonderfully calm about burglars if you haven't got anything remotely worth stealing. Burglars, however, tend not to glow in the dark, for obvious reasons.

There was, nevertheless, a lot to be said for keeping absolutely still and quiet; mostly because he wasn't sure he was capable of anything else, but also because, if he, she or it thought Maurice was still asleep, he, she or it might well go away again without bothering him. Fingers crossed. He waited, listening hard. He could hear breathing.

Understatement; a bit like describing the decision to invade Iraq as a lapse of judgement. It wasn't snoring exactly, because the rhythm was different. Maurice had absolutely no experience in this field, but it was the sort of noise he'd expect to be made by an elderly lion with a hundred-a-day cigar habit. Not human, at any rate. Oh *hell*.

At times like this, the mind loves to hide behind logic. Nothing on earth makes a noise like that; therefore, there can be no noise – you're imagining it; close your eyes very tightly and it'll go away. But Maurice was handicapped by his traumatic childhood experiences. He'd seen a doughnut materialise out of thin air on the palm of a man's outstretched hand; he knew that weird stuff was possible. In particular, he couldn't help remembering the viscerally disturbing winged silhouettes he'd seen wheeling and banking in the air above the city in the hole in the doughnut. Something like that, like what he'd always assumed those shapes had been, might well make just such a racket when breathing, because the ability to vent white-hot plasma through the mouth and nostrils must come at a terrible price in the ear, nose and throat department.

Oh, please, he begged the Universe. You can't be serious.

Amazing what indignation, even a tiny drop of it, can do for a person's moral fibre. A moment ago, he'd been entirely preoccupied with terror. Now, with a little speck of rage at the bitter unfairness of it all to build around, oyster-fashion, he could almost feel himself growing a vestigial backbone. Dragons, he thought, how *dare* they. Crazy doughnuts and bizarre women were bad enough, but *dragons*—

He sat up and, although he could see perfectly well by the glow, turned on the light. At the foot of his bed, he could see what looked like a curled-up hose, only rather too thick for your everyday garden irrigator; also, it was covered in scales, for crying out loud.

Scales. Thirteen years of furious resentment welled up inside him and burst. "No!" he yelled. "I'm not having it," but the curled-up heap of thing was still there, still glowing, still making that ridiculous noise. He was so angry he couldn't have felt scared if he'd wanted to. Fumbling angrily for his slippers, he stumbled out of the bedroom and padded into the kitchen. Flinging open the drawer, he grabbed the bread-knife, muttered, "Dragons, for God's sake," under his breath and flumped back into the bedroom, to find the thing slowly oozing up off the floor onto his bed.

"No," he snapped, "get off. Not allowed on the furniture."

It lifted its head, or rather heads. There were nine of them, giving the thing the appearance of fearsome serpentine broccoli. Its eyes were blinking, not simultaneously; he recognised the bleary, not-quite-with-it look from his shaving mirror, but now wasn't the time for sympathy in any shape or form. They had *no right* to make him do dragons, and he wasn't going to stand for it.

Eighteen eyes were looking at him, with a who's-been-sleeping-in-*my*-bed expression that he found impossible to forgive. For the first time in his wasp-not-swatting, spider-catching-in matchboxes-and-carefully-putting-outside life, he urgently wanted to kill a living creature. The fact that it was a minimum of twenty feet long, nine-headed and blatantly supernatural somehow didn't seem relevant. Either it goes, said a voice inside him, or I do, and I'm not particularly bothered which.

At such times, ignorance can be your friend. Experienced professional dragonslayers – one immediately thinks of Ricky Wurmtoter, former head of pest control at J.W. Wells, or the legendary Kurt Lundqvist, thanks to whose efforts Seattle is now 77 per cent dragon-free – know the risks, the moves and the distressingly unfavourable chances of survival. Accordingly, they duck, weave, shuffle their feet, wait for an opening, feint, drop into an extended high guard, trip over something and get torched or eaten. Maurice, who had no idea what he was doing, neatly avoided all these pitfalls. He marched up to the dragon, yelled "Bastard!" at it at the top of his voice, and swung wildly with the breadknife. The dragon, quite reasonably anticipating a transition from high fifth to low third coupled with a defensive back-foot traverse, reared up and lurched to its right, collided with Maurice's breadknife and neatly cut its own throat.

As he watched it slump, twitch and subside into a heap, he felt an overwhelming urge to apologise. But *I'm so sorry* or *I didn't mean it* or even *oops, butterfingers* wasn't going to cover it, he knew that. It looked so odd; so conclusively empty, like a pile of clothes lying on the floor where they'd been dropped. No point apologising, since there was so obviously nothing left to apologise to. He noticed his hand, lolling numbly from the end of his arm. The knife was still in it. He dropped it, then jumped smartly back to avoid lacerating his own foot.

I just killed a dragon. Yes, of course you did; now go and lie down and sleep it off. But there it lay, yards and yards of it, like a neatly coiled rope. Something dripped down his face. He had a shrewd idea what it might be, which he really didn't feel like verifying. The anger that had made him do such an extraordinarily ill-judged thing was draining away like oil out of a vintage motorcycle, fading as quickly and completely as the dream in which someone whose name began with M had told him to do something, but for the life of him he couldn't remember what—

The phone rang.

He couldn't quite bring himself to turn his back on the thing, so he reversed slowly through the bedroom door into the hallway and picked up. "Yes?"

"Hi. This is an important message. Did you know you could be saving up to thirty per cent on motor-insurance premiums? Yes, it's true. If you're—"

He put the phone back and wandered through into the bedroom. It was still there. Damn.

He went to the bathroom and washed the blood off his face. In the process, he got a tiny bit on his mouth and instinctively licked, then retched and spat, though rather too late to avoid finding out that dragon's blood tastes oddly like marzipan. Then he returned to the bedroom. It was getting late and he felt very tired, but if he got into bed, he'd have *that* curled up at his feet. Just on the off-chance that he'd been mistaken, he took another look. Yes, still there.

This is ridiculous, he thought. I've just killed a dragon – there should be honour, glory, brass bands playing, a procession, half the kingdom and marry the princess. Instead, I'm going to have to sleep on the sofa, which means I'll get a crick in my neck and wake up with a headache, which means I'll be useless all day tomorrow, when we've got performance assessment reviews, and—

He caught sight of himself in the dressing-table mirror, and thought, It's not going to be like that. Oh no. You can forget about going to work and performance reviews and just occasionally something nice, like a night out or a date. You've just screwed up your life beyond all hope of recovery. You *killed* it, for crying out loud. There's got to be consequences.

Slowly he looked down. Still there, still unequivocally dead. I ought to call the police, he told himself. It's got to be illegal, killing dragons; they'll be a protected species or something, and then there's health and safety, animal welfare – I'm bound to have done *something* wrong. Yes, fine, call the police and get it over with; hello, I've just killed a dragon in my bedroom. Bet they get calls like that all the time.

The last dim ember of resentment suddenly flared into light and heat. You bastard, he thought, how dare you; barging into my life and trashing it, and it's no use whining about being dead because it's not my fault – what was I supposed to do? And now of course you'll be just as much trouble dead as alive, probably more so, and I just don't need this right now.

Unasked, a gallery of desperate, hare-brained schemes broke on him like a wave. He could burn down the building – electrical fault; I warned them about that wiring, but would they listen? No, forget it; they'd find huge charred snake vertebrae among the ashes, and all he'd achieve would be to add arson to his box set of offences against the Wildlife & Countryside Act. Fine; I'll pack a few essentials in a bag and just go away. How long would it take for a carcase to rot away into a skeleton? Ten years? Of course he'd have to go on paying the rent and everything, it'd be tight, but – yes, but what about the smell? And rats; they'd have Environmental Health up here, and then it'd all come gushing out, and he'd be worse off than if he'd owned up in the first place. All right, he told himself, how'd it be if I called the police and said there was this loud noise, I went to investigate, someone hit me on the head, I woke up and there was this dead dragon on the floor. Me? No, no way, *I* didn't do it; it was someone else. Yes, and a dog ate my homework. Wouldn't be the first time.

(He grinned. Actually, the dog *had* eaten his homework, three or four times, and nobody had believed him, even when he took in a note from his mother. So, what chance would he have lying about something like this? Answer: none. Lying is a fine art. You need to practise, practise, practise, and he'd never had the patience.)

The phone rang again. He swore, stormed into the hall, grabbed it and yelled, "Piss off!"

"Maurice?"

Stephanie Wilson. "Stephanie? Is that you?"

"Steve," she corrected. "Why are you swearing at me? That's not very nice."

"Where are you?"

"Home," she said. "Two weeks' leave, and then I'm off to—"

"Get over here," he snapped. "Right now."

"Mau—" was as far as she got before the receiver hit the cradle. He wasn't prepared to let her argue, because she always won. But a command followed by a hang-up would annoy her so much she'd come round to yell at him. As a precaution, he tipped the phone off the hook.

Stephanie; thank God.

He stopped, and thought about that. The reaction had come as automatically as a sneeze. No doubting its authenticity, but why? He'd always been fond of Stephanie, on and off very fond indeed; how she felt about him he'd never quite been able to fathom. Mostly, the issue had never come to a head. As soon as the question became too big and too ornery to duck, she'd be posted somewhere exotic and that'd be that for six months or a year or whatever. Yes, he'd always secretly admired her strength, her steadfastness, her exceptional and often quite terrifying courage, but did he have any reason to suppose that she'd know what to do when faced with the consequences of a dead dragon in the bedroom? No reason. Just instinct and intuition. And, at the very least, she'd understand; or, at the very least, come closer to understanding than anyone else. After all, she'd seen the doughnut float, just as he had.

Without thinking, he started tidying the place up – dirty cups and plates to the kitchen, discarded socks off the living-room floor, empty pizza trays in the bin, the usual protocols. And then he stopped and thought: Yes, and there's a dead dragon in the bedroom. True, but that was no reason to leave the rest of the place looking like a pigsty, not when you've got a girl coming round. He gritted his teeth and tentatively felt between the sofa cushions for neglected items of food and clothing. Distressingly productive: a sock, his phone before last (with a crunched screen), a half-eaten doughnut—

᛭

Maurice left the motorway at Junction 23, drove round and round the spiral interchange known locally as the Coffee Grinder and turned into a service station.

It was a terrifying experience. First, his stomach swelled and flattened and became the car park. His chest bubbled out, like the bit you remember in *Alien*, shifted and contracted into a sort of a cube, and stabilised as the shops and dining area. His left arm became the petrol pumps, his right melted and resolidified as the slip road. He had no idea what happened to his feet, or various other bits to which he'd hitherto attached considerable importance. His right nipple was now a Burger King.

Now just a minute, he thought.

The big round clock in the main hall that had once been a hair on his chest froze; then the second hand began to move, the other two staying exactly where they were. It swept round, and round, and round again. Every time it passed 12, the people scurrying about in the shops and food places were teleported back to precisely where they'd been sixty seconds ago.

Now, he thought. Just a minute. Oh, I see.

Desperately, he jammed a gag in his mental modem; *no thoughts to be turned into words until further notice. Absolutely no figures of speech under any circumstances. This means you.*

He forced his mind to relax. This is fine, he told himself. It would only be scary and distressing if it bothered me, and it doesn't. It's perfectly all right that six cars are currently queuing to refuel out of my little finger, because, because, it's perfectly all *right*. I'm fine with that. I'm cool.

He shivered, or at least his mind did; his body was too heavily encrusted with buildings for casual movement. Easy, he told himself, easy does it. Accept and adapt, and once we've done that, we can face whatever interesting challenge the universe has decided to honour us with today.

A family of six were buying hamburgers in his— But that was all right too. Relax. Don't fight it. Go with it. Steer into the skid—

The car he was driving was going sideways. Instinctively, he slammed on the brakes, whereupon the car swerved monstrously, reared up on its front and back left-hand wheels, wobbled for a split second and fell over. The impact went straight through him, reducing his bones to jelly and his brains to milkshake, or at least that was how it felt.

The engine died and there was a moment of almost perfect silence, the only audible sound being the drip-drip of a ruptured fuel line. Not good; he'd seen enough action movies to know that drip-drip-drip is generally the overture to BOOM. Unfortunately, he was comprehensively wedged in the wreckage of the car and couldn't get out. Trapped. Hopeless. Up shi—

Um.

He was in a canoe. On either side, a turgid brown stream was barely moving. It didn't smell terribly nice. He glanced around him. Just as he thought: no paddle.

Oh *God*, he thought.

On the right bank of the river, a large rhododendron suddenly burst into flame. *Yes?*

Maurice blinked. The bush had just spoken to him. The *burning* bush had just—

"Hello?" he said.

Hello yourself.

Then the penny dropped. *Ting!* went the penny as it bounced off the polished beechwood rail of the canoe, then *plop!* into the evil-smelling brown stream. "Hey," Maurice said. "Are you—?"

Yes.

"You exist."

Here and now? It would seem so.

Maurice took a deep breath, an action he almost immediately regretted. "Excuse me," he said, "but where is this and what's going on?"

The bush crackled, and a spark drifted lazily into the cold air. Below him, the river steamed. *You are here.*

"Right," Maurice said doubtfully. "Where, exactly?"

The orange heart of the fire flared. *You are in the place you chose to be, talking to the person you summoned.*

"Are you sure?"

Yes. Trust me on this.

A gust of chilly wind brushed his face, and it helped him concentrate. It was the sort of concentration and clarity you only seem to get when things are very bad – when you're flying through the air, or you've just realised that the car pulling out in front of you hasn't seen you – but he resolved to embrace it and make it work for him. "I'm in a world," Maurice said slowly, "where the figurative turns into the literal, and figures of speech become real. Yes?"

Yes.

"I understand. How did I get here?"

Through the eye of the doughnut.

"Excuse me?"

You got here through the operation of the YouSpace device.

Maurice closed his eyes. It was a terrible strain thinking clearly and precisely, and he'd never been terribly good at it at the best of times, of which this was not one. "Tell me," he said, "about the YouSpace device."

The YouSpace device was invented by Professor Pieter van Goyen, of the University of Leiden, as a recreational aid or toy.

Given the nature of the device, which distorts the space-time continuum, it would be pointless to assign a specific date to the moment of invention; relative to your own existence, however, the device first went on line roughly three years ago. Van Goyen's original prototype was developed and improved by—

"What does it do?" Maurice asked.

The multiverse is made up of an infinite number of alternate universes, all of them different. The YouSpace device enables the user to relocate himself in the alternative universe of his choice. It operates on the principle of para-Heisenbergian qualified uncertainty, whereby—

"Stop there, please," Maurice said. "Of my choice?"

Yes.

"I didn't choose this."

Yes you did.

"No I didn't."

Yes you did.

"No I—"

YES YOU DID. Although, the bush added, *possibly inadvertently. Like most advanced technologies, the YouSpace device must be operated with extreme caution and a certain degree of precision if unintended consequences are to be avoided. It's possible that you may have encountered an active, unattended YouSpace portal and operated it without realising what you were doing. Stuff happens. Anyway,* the bush went on, *you are here.*

"Ah."

The saddest-looking fish Maurice had ever seen flipped dejectedly out of the river and fell back again with a glopping noise. The bush glowed cherry-red as a slight breeze fanned it. *Which is fortuitous,* the bush said.

"Excuse me?"

Very well. Your sins are forgiven. Go in peace.

"I meant to say," Maurice said firmly, "I'm sorry, I don't understand. Fortuitous?"

Indeed. I wanted to talk to you, and here you are.

"You wanted to talk to me."

Yes.

"*You* wanted to talk to—"

Indeed. Hence fortuitous. In this universe, I exist, and I am free.

Maurice blinked. "Meaning, in other universes—"

Quite. The multiverse is, after all, infinite. In many universes, I have no being. In others, I exist but my status is uncertain. And in the universe to which you are native, I am in chains.

"Excuse—" Maurice stopped himself just in time. "You what?"

Well, not literally in chains, but I might just as well be. I have been taken prisoner and am being held against my will.

"Um," Maurice said. "Is that possible?"

Apparently, the bush said bitterly. *Which is why,* it went on, *you must free me.*

"Me?"

You. Only you.

Maurice nodded slowly. "It's like this," he said. "I don't know if you ever saw *Star Trek 5* – it's the one where they're kidnapped by Spock's brother, and they fly to a planet, and a sort of superbeing wants to use the *Enterprise* to leave the planet and escape. And Kirk says—"

That was a truly awful film.

"Yes. But Kirk says, what does God need a starship for? You see what I mean."

The bush ebbed a little. The very tips of its branches were white ash. *In an infinite multiverse, all things are possible. And in your universe, I am being held against my will by a complete arse, and I need to get out of there before I go crazy and the complete arse does something very, very bad. And, me help me, only you can rescue me. Got that? Or would you like me to draw you a picture?*

Maurice shook his head. "I don't believe you," he said.

Overhead, the sky darkened. *You might care to rephrase that.*

"Not really."

Darkness fell suddenly, like a curtain. A jagged prong of white lightning tore through the blackness and hit the surface of the river, drenching Maurice in fine, gritty spray. *How dare—*

Maurice frowned. "This YouSpace thing."

The clouds dissolved. *What about it?*

"Is it working? Right now?"

You are within its operational field. However, in order to leave this universe and return to your own, you need an appropriate interface or portal.

"Right. What would that be, then?"

The bush was merely flickering. *My time grows short,* it said. *If I undertake to return you to your own reality, will you promise to rescue me from my captivity?*

Maurice thought for a moment. "No," he said.

What?

"No. No way. It sounds horribly difficult and dangerous. Look, anyone capable of capturing God and locking him up somewhere is clearly an incredibly powerful and nasty person, and I really don't want to get involved. Or alternatively, you aren't God at all, which is how come you've been captured and locked up, and in that case you could just as easily be the bad guy, like in that really bad film we were talking about just now, and I could be doing something really awful letting you loose. Also I've got enough problems of my own at the moment, which I'm probably quite unable to do anything about, because I'm absolutely nobody special at all, so if it's all the same to you, thanks but no thanks. Sorry, but there it is."

A faint red gleam among the ashes said to him, *Oh.*

"Sorry."

It's your choice, the gleam said grumpily. *Also, you say that now, but I feel confident that you'll change your mind. You are, after all, the chosen one, and you cannot escape your destiny. Why you should be the chosen one escapes me completely, I must confess, but there you go.*

"Thank you so much," Maurice said sourly. "Look, can I go now, please?"

Suit yourself. A gust of air, soft and querulous as a sigh, stirred the ashes of the fire into one last spark. *All right, confession time. I brought you here, this being the only reality in the entirety of the multiverse where we could have this conversation, me being in chains and all, and in two shakes I'll send you back, to your native universe, where you are the subject, or if you prefer, the victim of an unstoppable manifest destiny, and you can get on with it. You will, of course, remember almost nothing of this, because otherwise you would cease to be a free agent, and for some reason I can't quite remember offhand, that would seem to be important. I'd hoped for your active cooperation, but apparently that's too much to ask for, so I guess I'll have to make do with you blundering around and fulfilling your destiny by accident, the way you always have done in the past. Sorry,* it added bitterly, *to have inconvenienced you.*

"Almost nothing?"

Theo Bernstein. Find Theo Bernstein. Remember, when you get back to the tedious little continuum you call home, to find Theo Bernstein. Got that?

But Maurice wasn't paying attention. In front of him, hanging glistening in the air, was a doughnut the size of a large lifebelt. The specks of sugar on its rim shone like all the stars in the galaxy. He looked at it. It looked at him.

"Theo Bernstein," he murmured. "Name rings a—"

All around him, the air was filled with the deafening clash of bells. The shockwave of the sound hit him like a hammer, knocking him out of the canoe and into the rich, dark river. He tried to struggle, but it was too dense and thick to swim in; his mouth and nose went under, he choked, and—

ɗ

Opened his eyes. He was sitting on his sofa, and the doorbell was ringing. He raced to the door, stopped, realised he wasn't wearing any clothes, grabbed a coat from the hall cupboard, threw it on and opened the door.

She appeared to have grown an extra inch or so, and either all the freckles had crowded together and fused into a single mass or she'd got a suntan. Apart from that, she was just Stephanie, which was exactly (he realised) what he'd hoped for. "Maurice," she said, "what's the *matter* with you?"

"Get in."

She looked at him and came inside. He slammed the door. "Bedroom."

"What?"

"Go into the bedroom. Now."

"Maurice." She was giving him a look carefully blended from only the finest horror, amusement and acute embarrassment. He scowled at her. "Now," he said. "Please."

She shrugged, walked past him and opened the door. He stayed where he was and held his breath. This ought to be good.

"Maurice." Her voice, higher than usual but still just hanging on to control. "What the *hell* have you been doing?"

Well, he'd only ever have this one chance. "Killing dragons," he replied. "What does it look like?"

"*Maurice—*"

He pushed past her into the bedroom. "I woke up and there it was," he heard himself gabble. "It was *snoring*."

"So you killed it."

"Yes. No, not because of that."

"Mphm. Why, then?"

"*Because.*" He stared at her. She was giving him her

world-famous disapproving look. "It's a dragon, for God's sake. In my *bedroom*."

"You do realise you need a Section 47 permit from Natural England, plus a certificate of actual damage, plus written consent from the secretary of state. And then you've got to be registered."

There were all sorts of things she could've said, but that wasn't one he'd been expecting. "Stephanie?"

"Steve. No, really. There's a whole book of regulations about this stuff."

"You're kidding."

"I don't joke about regulations," she said fiercely. "We did all this at Sandhurst. It's an obligatory core subject. You're not supposed to tell anyone, of course."

"*Sandhurst?*"

"Yes." Suddenly she smiled. "Didn't you know, I'm an officer now. Second lieutenant. I got fast-tracked. They don't do that for just anybody."

He tried to keep his voice calm, but he failed. "You mean to tell me," he said, "that they teach you about *killing dragons* at Sandhurst?"

She nodded. "The first duty of Her Majesty's armed forces is to protect the kingdom against monsters of all kinds," she said. "It's a really old part of the charter, goes right back to King Arthur. And the bottom line is, civilians aren't allowed to." She paused, and frowned. "How did it get in here, anyhow? They're really rare, you know."

She sounded like a birdwatcher. "I don't know. I woke up and there it was."

"Don't be silly. Look at the size of the thing."

"Actually, I have, oddly enough."

"Now look at the doorframe. And the window."

Valid point, which hadn't occurred to him. No way something that size came in through a door, or, indeed, a window.

How *did* the dragon get in his bedroom without smashing a gaping hole in the wall?

But it didn't matter. Stephanie was here now, and by some bizarre quirk she knew all about this stuff: she'd been trained to deal with it, she was a public servant and he paid his taxes. Therefore—

"Anyway," he said. "Over to you."

"Excuse me?"

"You said it yourself: you're a qualified monster-botherer. Well, help yourself. Do whatever it is you do."

She scowled at him and shook her head. "I'm a transport manager," she said. "I plan routes for lorries. I only just scraped through the monsters module. Fifty-seven per cent in the written exam."

He frowned. "Really? That's not like you."

She shrugged. "It didn't exactly help that I didn't believe a word of it. I mean to say, *dragons*. Everybody knows they don't exist."

"Oh yes they do."

"They *don't*." He looked at her, and just for a moment he thought he saw in her eyes a faint reflection of his own bewildered fury. "They can't. It's not right."

"I know," he said gently.

"And anyway," she went on, moving away abruptly, "that's not a dragon."

"Um—"

"It's a hydra. Genus *draco*," she recited quickly, "species *serpens impossibile*, subspecies *serpens impossibile nonacaput*. A native of the southern Mediterranean, western Anatolia and eastern North Africa, its diet consists of birds, small mammals and, increasingly these days, roadkill. Easily distinguished from the more common *serpens impossibile octocaput* by virtue of its having nine rather than eight heads. Completely harmless," she added grimly, "unless cornered and provoked."

Maurice scowled at her. "A bit like me, then."

"One quite significant difference, Maurice. You're still alive. What on earth were you thinking of, anyway?"

"Survival, mostly," Maurice said, and it would've been a good answer, he reflected, if it'd been true. "And besides, how was I supposed to know all that? It's *huge*. It's got *nine heads*."

She nodded. "Apparently they're a great trial to it. Well, you know what it's like getting anything done by a committee. Imagine having to get a unanimous vote every time you want to move."

"I don't care," Maurice said. "I just want it out of here and gone, all right?"

There was a brief silence. Then she said, "I don't know why you're looking at me like that."

Maurice blinked. "You're trained," he said. "You're a professional. Obviously, you know what to do."

"Me? Good God, no." She gave him a blank stare. "The course was basically about their life cycle, habitat and how you go about killing them. We didn't go into disposal. Different department."

"What?"

She nodded. "They just said, when you're all done, call the Sappers and they'll be along at some point with a van and take it away. Stop gawping at me like that, will you? It was just an introductory-level course, you know. We had a lot to get through."

He felt as though all his bones had suddenly melted. "So you don't know—"

"Sorry."

A brief note on the legend of Pandora's box. Ever wondered why, bundled in with all the torments and sufferings of Mankind, the gods put Hope down there at the bottom? Answer: because, in certain circumstances, hope can be the worst torment of them all. "That's it, then," Maurice said.

"I've got a dead dragon in my bedroom and you don't know what to do. That's just perfect."

"Not a dragon. Hydra."

"*Whatever*." He was sorry. He hadn't meant to snap, and she was still his best, read only, hope. But see above about hope. "Come on, Stephanie. You're an army officer. You people are supposed to be able to cope in emergencies. *Think of something*."

"Steve." She frowned, and her hedge-like eyebrows moved together like tectonic plates. "Well, I guess, we cut it up, shovel it in bin bags and cart it away. I'm pretty sure that's what the engineers do."

Maurice looked at her and quietly thanked God from the bottom of his heart for *perestroika*; because – if this was what they fast-tracked you through Sandhurst for – if we'd ever had to fight the Russians, we'd have been screwed. "Cut it up."

"I should think so, yes."

"What with?"

She considered the remains carefully for a moment. "Probably a chainsaw'd do it. Failing that, a block-cutter, something like that. You could get one from one of those tool-hire places."

He nodded. "And the noise wouldn't be in the least suspicious. All right, let's move on. Bin bags?"

Maybe she was starting to get the idea. "You'd need about ... " She quantity-surveyed. "Probably about a thousand."

"Right. So, between the two of us, that's two thousand trips up and down four flights of stairs. I should also like to point out, we're on fortnightly collections. And if it won't fit in the wheelie-bin, they really don't want to know. At that rate – bear with me a moment – I make that just over nineteen years before it's all gone."

"Oh, you'd need a car, or a van or something."

"I haven't got a car."

"If you're just going to make difficulties."

"*Stephanie*." No, wrong approach. He needed her for this. "Steve," he amended. "No disrespect, but I don't think we're going to be able to do this on our own. We need to call someone."

She nodded. "I was thinking that," she said. "Trouble is, if we do, you're going to be in so much trouble—"

He winced. "Look," he said sweetly, "don't you know someone? In the military, I mean. Someone with soldiers and lorries and stuff who owes you a favour."

She gave him a withering look. "It doesn't quite work like that," she said. "I can't just ask the joint chiefs of staff if I can borrow the Coldstream Guards for the weekend, if they're not using them for anything." He was about to express his disappointment, but she gave him her special Shush look. "No, what you need," she said, "is a private contractor."

His heart stood still. "A what?"

She frowned. "We're not really supposed to know about them," she said, "let alone have anything to do with them, because they're all a bit, you know. Private security consultants and all that. But—"

"You really mean to tell me there are companies who deal with dead dragons?"

"One or two. I could get a few names for you."

Well, he thought, why not? Except—"How am I supposed to pay for something like that? It'd cost a fortune. I haven't got any money."

And then she smiled at him, quite unexpectedly. "I have," she said.

"What?"

"Well, there's not all that much to spend your money on in Kandahar, and they do pay me for playing soldiers. I was saving a deposit on a house, but what the hell. You'll have to pay me back, mind. Eventually."

For a moment his mouth didn't work. "Stephanie . . . "

"Steve. What?"

"Oh, nothing." He looked at her. Of course, she still just looked like Stephanie, and always would. "That's . . . "

"I know." She nodded. "What friends are for. Besides," she added, while he was still struggling with his defective larynx, "I owe you."

"Really? What the hell for?"

"Thirteen years of never ever mentioning you-know-what." It was as if she was one of those collapsible umbrellas, and someone had just pressed the button. She folded at the waist and sat down heavily on the edge of the bed. "I think about it all the time," she said. "I try not to, but . . . "

News to him. He'd always assumed— "But Stephanie," he said. "You ate the doughnut."

She nodded. "I felt I had to," she said. "To fight it, you see. That's what I do; I fight things. I'm one of those horrible little yappy dogs that bite your ankles. Everything's much, much bigger than me – it could stamp on me and I'd be squashed flat, but it doesn't matter, I've got to fight; it's the only way I know of dealing with stuff. So, yes, I ate the doughnut."

"I thought . . . " He stopped to choose his words. "When you ate it," he said, "that was the bravest thing I've ever seen."

"Quite. That's me. Brave as two short planks. And, you know what? It was stale. The doughnut, I mean. If I'd got it from a shop I'd have taken it back and complained. And now," she said, giving him a sweet, slightly scared smile, "it's dragons. Sorry, hydras. So, of course, we're going to *fight* the bastards, whoever the hell they are. We're going to get rid of the body and pretend it never happened and try and make life go on, no matter what the cost. Otherwise . . . " She shrugged. "They win. And we can't have that, can we?"

She spent the next half hour on the phone, insisting that he stay in the kitchen, so he wouldn't hear any of it ("because then," she said, "I'd have to kill you"; and of course she was joking, but even so ... He closed the door and put the radio on.) Eventually she came out and joined him. He opened his mouth to speak, but before he could do so she nodded, briefly, once. Then she sat down and told him to put the kettle on.

"You killed it," she said, after a long silence.

"Yes, I think we established that."

"On your own. With a breadknife."

He nodded. "On account of, I don't have a sword, or a howitzer, or a Cruise missile. Some people don't, you know."

"That's pretty impressive."

He shook his head. "No it isn't," he said with conviction. "It's horrible and a bloody nuisance, and I really wish I'd known it only eats birds and mice and stuff. But—"

"Well?"

If he couldn't tell her, he couldn't tell anyone. "I lost my temper."

"I *see*."

"Not like that," he said firmly. "Really, I was at the end of my rope. You see, the dragon wasn't all of it, not by a long chalk."

And he told her about the three women on the train, though not (for some reason) quite everything they'd said. She looked at him for a long time, then said, "Oh."

"Remarkably enough, that's exactly what I thought. *Oh*."

She pursed her lips. They were, he noticed distractedly, well suited for the purpose. "I suppose we really ought to, you know, talk about it."

"We don't have to."

"Maybe, but maybe we should." She hesitated, then went on. "I just need to ask you one thing, OK? It did – well, just appear. Didn't it?"

She meant the doughnut. "Yes," he said. "Out of nowhere."
He closed his eyes for a moment. "Stale?"

She nodded.

"So it was – well, *real*."

"Oh yes. You don't get much realer than stale."

They looked at each other. That was quite enough of that.

"So," Maurice said, "you, um, found someone."

She nodded. "They'll be round in about an hour. Pretty efficient, huh?"

"And they'll—"

"Listen." She lifted her hand for what would probably have been a reassuring pat, but withdrew it again. "It'll be OK; they're good. Done a lot of work for the Bolivian government, my, um, friend told me. Apparently, they even shampoo the carpets."

"That'll be a first, in this place." He sighed, and sat down on the edge of the kitchen worktop. "Thanks, Stephanie," he said. "I don't know what I'd have done without you."

"I do. That's why I'm helping you. Honestly, I've seen grenades that go all to pieces less readily than you."

He let that one go. The kettle boiled, and he made coffee. "So," he said, handing her a mug, "how are things with you, anyway?"

She grinned at him. "Oh, you know."

"As bad as that?"

She shook her head, and her hair sort of floated before it flopped. She's grown it since I saw her last, he thought. "Not bad, just . . . " Shrug. "You know what it's like. Every time I want something I make damn sure I get it, and then when I've got it, it turns out not to have been what I wanted." She smiled. "Like I thought, Sandhurst, wow, how cool is that? And now, here I still am, doing basically the same sort of stuff but people call me sir."

"You mean ma'am."

"No, usually it's sir." She sipped the coffee; she always did have asbestos lips. "How about you? Still madly under-achieving away like anything?"

"No."

"Ah."

"Actually," he said, "I'm perfectly happy. Well, not unhappy. I mean, it's sheer hell at work, because they're probably going to fire between a quarter and a third of us and I'm probably slap bang in the crosshairs, so it's only a matter of time, and then I'll have to grind through all that going-to-interviews crap, and God only knows how I'm going to fool anyone into thinking I'd be an asset to their organisation—" He stopped. "That's if I'm really lucky and my life isn't changed utterly by that in there." He jerked a thumb towards the bedroom. "Thanks, by the way," he added. "I don't know what—"

"You've already said that," she interrupted. "But outside of work. How's things?"

He pulled a face. "I eat and sleep," he replied. "Getting the hang of both of those, thanks for asking."

"No ...?"

"No."

"Ah." She frowned. "Me neither. Not that I'm bothered. Overrated, if you ask me. I mean, look at our friends from school who did manage to find true love. Miserable as porridge, the lot of them."

He looked at her. "Porridge?"

She blinked. "You like porridge?"

"It's all right. I guess."

"That's because you're not in the armed forces. The army does things to oatmeal that'd blow your mind."

"Who's miserable as porridge, then?"

She sat up straight and gave him a detailed report. He found it oddly reassuring. "Kieran and *Shawna*? You're—"

"True as I'm sitting here."

He shook his head. "That can only be some bizarre experiment conducted by a shadowy government agency," he said. "Casualties?"

"None reported so far, remarkably enough, but it can only be a matter of time. I believe the authorities have sealed off the immediate area as a precaution."

He looked at her; easier to do when they were both sitting down, since she was at least four inches taller than him. In an alternate universe, he thought, we could've been— He panicked, and shoved the thought away somewhere before it could hurt anyone.

The doorbell rang. "Hello," she said. "Expecting anyone?"

"No."

"That's considerably less than an hour. I'm impressed. Well, don't just sit there like a rice pudding. Let them in."

So he went to the door and opened it, and saw an extremely old man in a brown shop coat and a flat cap. Some way behind him was an extremely young man, about seven feet tall, eating a sandwich.

"Yes?"

The old man smiled at him. "Rockchucker Disposal," he said.

"You what?"

"Rockchucker Disposal," the old man repeated. "That's us. You've got a—" He lowered his voice a little. "—Bit of a problem? Hiss hiss, crawl crawl?"

The penny dropping hit Maurice like an asteroid. "Oh. Oh, right. Come in."

The old man nodded, hesitated, turned round, snapped, "Art!" in a brisk voice and grinned apologetically. "He's a good lad really," he said, as the tall young man lumbered past him into the hall. He was so thin as to be practically two-dimensional, and he nearly banged his head on the doorframe.

"Just a moment," Maurice said. "You're the, um, here to clear up the—"

"Yes, that's right."

The old man couldn't have been a day less than ninety. "OK," Maurice said, "that's fantastic. You'd better come and take a look."

He led the way into the bedroom. Stephanie didn't join them – deniability, presumably. The old man looked at the dead dragon and made the sort of tooth-sucking noise that Maurice had believed was unique to the motor trade. "Well?" Maurice asked nervously.

"Awkward," the old man said.

"Awkward?"

"Mphm. Of course, it'd be much easier if it was still alive."

You're telling me. "But is there anything you can—?"

"Just a tick." The old man clambered painfully over half a dozen coils of dead tail, excavated a tape measure from his coat pocket, took a few measurements apparently at random; straightened his back with a faint moan; shook his head four times; put the tape measure away and took out something else, either a photographer's light meter or a Geiger counter; waved it slowly backwards and forwards in front of the dragon's array of glassy-cold eyes; clicked his tongue, scratched his head. "Awkward," he said.

Maurice felt icy fingers of panic clawing their way up his spine. "Is there anything you can—?"

"Insulation," the old man said.

"Sorry?"

"These walls." He pointed. "Are they cavity-wall insulation, or what?"

Maurice had no idea. "I think so."

"Uh-huh. You wouldn't happen to know your residual radon count, would you?"

"Um, no. Sorry."

"Well, let's say for the sake of argument it's less than five."

"Oh, bound to be."

The old man put his hands on his hips and looked round. "Mind you," he said, "even if it's below five, we might just be able to do something for you, if only—" He brought out the light meter thing again. "Of course, there's always the small controlled explosion. How would you feel about that?"

"No," Maurice said quickly. "I mean, I'd really rather not, if there's any other way."

"Mphm." The old man shrugged. "Well, we'll just have to try doing it the old-fashioned way, and hope for the best, eh? Joists."

"What?"

"Would you happen to know the precise spacing between your underfloor joists? To within nought-point-nought one, give or take a nibble."

"Um."

"Ah well, I s'pose we'll just have to wing it. Art."

The young man, who'd been leaning against the wall eating a jam tart, lounged forward and stood improbably, reminding Maurice of the bit in the Tom and Jerry cartoons where the cat runs off a cliff and hangs in the air for a moment, paws pumping furiously. No way those thin, spindly legs could support something that size for any length of time.

"Bosometer."

"Uh?"

"*Bosometer*. Oh for crying out loud, don't say you left it in the van."

The young man reached in his pocket and produced a clingfilm-wrapped packet of sandwiches, two Jaffa Cakes, a banana and a small silver box. He gave the box to the old man, who opened it. There was a faint whirring noise and a pale green glow. "Thought so," the old man said. "Ah well."

It was more than Maurice could bear. "Excuse me," he said, "but can you get rid of it or can't you? Only—"

"Well." The old man snapped the box shut. "We'll have a stab at it and see what happens, right, Art? Who dares, wins, like we used to say in the service."

Maurice frowned. "You were in the—?"

"Fire brigade," the old man said. "And after that, thirty-five years in fingerprints with East Midlands CID. That's before we got into private security, Art and me. Well, I promised his mum I'd take care of him." The old man paused, dug in his other pocket, pulled out a huge grey handkerchief and blew his nose in it. "Let's have the doings then, Art," the old man said. "And hurry it up, can't you? We got to be in Bratislava by ten."

The young man finished off a sandwich, gobbling the crusts like a seal rewarded with fish, and slowly removed a doughnut from a paper bag. He looked at it sadly, as if it was his last sight of the old country, then handed it to the old man, who balanced it on the outstretched palm of his right hand in a way that Maurice found disturbingly familiar. "Just a—" Maurice said, but the old man turned, frowned gently and murmured, "Shh," as if the doughnut was a baby that had just dropped off to sleep. Maurice stared in horror at the doughnut, which slowly began to rise.

It was suddenly bitterly cold. The old man sniffed, and wiped his nose on his left cuff. "Temperature, Art?"

The young man was holding a little grey plastic box. He glanced at it and mumbled something Maurice didn't quite catch; the old man clicked his tongue and said, "Right, better give it another five." The young man did something to the grey box. The doughnut quivered slightly.

"Here we go," the old man said happily. "Always knew we'd get there in the end."

Maurice didn't want to look, but the hole in the middle of the doughnut was staring at him, like an eye, and he couldn't resist. He looked, and saw—

"Better give another one and a half, Art, just for luck."

—The corner of the old man's sleeve, and behind it, coils of dead dragon. He wanted to yell for Stephanie, but something told him she'd chosen not to be there, so it wouldn't do to summon her against her will. He breathed out slowly, and his breath was white fog.

The doughnut blinked.

"That's the ticket," the old man said. The hole seemed to be getting bigger, though the doughnut somehow stayed exactly the same. The view through it was different. Now, Maurice could see—

"Steady," the old man said.

—Nothing at all. He felt his eyes twitch and water, as if he'd got grit in them, or as if he was staring straight into the sun. Nothing at all; that didn't make a great deal of sense. Behind him he heard a faint crunch; he swung his head round. The young man was eating a Crunchie bar.

"Easy does it, Art," the old man was saying. "That's halfway, now – *Art, for crying out loud, can't you stop stuffing your face for just two minutes?* Sixty per cent. Sixty-five."

And still there was nothing, nothing whatsoever, in the eye of the doughnut, although the grains of sugar on the outside were beginning to twinkle like Christmas-tree lights. Then Maurice caught his breath. Was it his imagination, or could he see something, tiny but distinct, in the very centre of the hole?

Desperately he tried to concentrate. He saw a man, mid- to late thirties, dark curly hair, wearing a big knee-length tweed overcoat and a big scarf. He was sitting huddled on the ground, his hands wound up in the scarf, and he was shivering. Somehow, although the image hadn't grown, it grew clearer. He saw the man's face and somehow it was familiar. He could almost put a name to it. Maurice; no, that's me. Mike; no, not like. Mervyn; *nobody's* called Mervyn. Matthew? The man turned his head, frowned, as if he was staring into a small, distant hole in which he could see an obscure image. He had one of those good-looking faces you'd be extremely reluctant to lend money to.

"All done," the old man said. The doughnut flipped back onto its side and dropped onto his palm; he handed it to the young man, who gobbled it down in one. Suddenly, it was warm again. The dragon wasn't there anymore.

"Piece of cake," the old man said.

"What ...?" Maurice pointed at the bed. Not even any bloodstains.

The old man was putting things away in his pockets. "Right, then," he said. "Was there anything else?"

"The dragon. What happened to it?"

The old man gave him a sad smile. "Sorry," he said. "Can't tell you that. Regulations. If they thought we were disclosing restricted information to unauthorised personnel, they'd have our ticket like *that*." He stooped down, peered at a perfectly clean pillow case, shrugged and straightened up again. "Touch and go there for a second or two, but it all came right in the end. Right then, Art, switch off. The batteries cost a fortune," he explained. "That's if you can get 'em. So," he added, broadening his smile. "Is everything to your satisfaction, then?"

No dragon. No indication that a dragon had ever been. "Yes."

"That's what we like to hear, isn't it, Art? Well, hate to dash but we'd better be on our way. Rushed off our feet, we've been lately. You were lucky we could fit you in."

Maurice followed them to the door. Stephanie was nowhere to be seen. Still, she'd said she'd pay, and presumably they wouldn't want cash in hand on the spot. He could ask her for a cheque later, and everything would be— "Um," Maurice said.

The old man's hand was on the handle of the front door. "Sir?"

"Um," Maurice repeated. "What do I owe you?"

The question seemed to puzzle the old man, who looked at him for a moment. "No, that's all right," he said. "All taken care of."

"What?" Hope exploded in his heart like a firework. "You mean there's no charge?"

The old man managed to keep a straight face. "Er, no, sir," he said. "I mean, there's nothing *else* to pay." He paused, as if trying to figure out if Maurice had got it yet. "On top of what you paid already, I mean."

"Just a moment." Maurice frowned. "I haven't—"

"Um, yes you have. Well," the old man said briskly, "time we weren't here. You'll be getting a receipt in the post. Glad we could help. Come on, Art."

"I haven't paid you anything," Maurice said.

"I think you'll find you have," the old man said gently.

Something in the way he said it terrified him. "What? How much? What did all this cost me?"

"Oh." There was a hint of fear in the old man's eyes. Not fear of what Maurice might do to him; more the reverse. "The usual."

"How much?"

"Just the young lady, sir. Good Lord, is that the time? We're going to have to get a wiggle on if we're going to catch that flight. Art!"

"What did you just say?"

The old man looked at the door. He was figuring out the

geometry of the situation. The door opened inwards, and Maurice was in the way. He was, in other words, trapped and couldn't just make a run for it. He took a deep breath. "The young lady, sir."

"What about her?"

"She's the payment."

For a moment, Maurice had no idea what he was talking about. Then it hit him, and made him stagger. As luck would have it, his involuntary backward step just about cleared the arc the door would have to describe in order for the old man to get through it. He seized his chance, grabbed the door handle, yanked the door open, darted through it like one of those tiny, almost transparent tropical fish they keep in dentists' waiting rooms, and slammed it behind him as he left. Maurice, who seemed to have mislaid a few of his basic motor functions as a result of the shock, wasted valuable seconds fumbling with the handle. By the time he made it out onto the landing and yelled, "Come back!" the old man was well away. Maurice gave chase, but arrived at street level just in time to see a battered old white van veering away from the kerb, pulling enough Gs to black out an experienced test pilot.

Max, said a tiny voice in his brain. The man you saw in the centre of the doughnut was called Max. He wants you to—

But Maurice wasn't interested in that right now. The young lady; she's the payment. In return for getting rid of the dead dragon, they'd taken Stephanie—

Don't be ridiculous, he told himself. True, he hadn't seen her since the two of them arrived, but that didn't mean anything. Besides, they'd both been in plain sight all the time, or nearly all the time. True, he'd lost sight of the young one for a minute or so towards the end; but seriously, was he asking himself to believe that he, the serial sandwich-gobbler, had somehow managed to overpower Stephanie, carry her downstairs and stow her in the van? Quite. He'd been tall, but

Stephanie was almost as tall and considerably more power-fully built. Fourteen years ago, he'd made the mistake of accepting a challenge to arm-wrestle her, and it'd been a week before he could hold a cup of tea. And that was before her combat training. At the very least, even if the kid had pulled a gun on her and she hadn't made him eat it, she'd have made a racket they'd have heard in Edinburgh. Going quietly simply wasn't in her nature. No, he told himself firmly, I must've got that all wrong. Silly misunderstanding, worrying about noth-ing. So I'll go back up to the flat, and there she'll be—

So he did that, and there she wasn't. Not in the hall, living room, kitchen, bedroom or bathroom. Not hiding in the fitted wardrobe or under the bed, and those were the only two places you'd be able to stash something that size. Fine; she's nipped out to get Chinese, or a pizza from the all-night shop, and all I've got to do is sit quietly and wait till she gets back.

He did that. He did it for a very long time. Then he called her. Her voice assured him that, although she couldn't talk to him right now, she'd get back to him as soon as possible. Meanwhile, if he cared to leave a message—

"*Stephanie!*" he yelled, and put the phone down. It was all he could think of.

It's all right, he told himself the next day. While I was in the bedroom with the two weirdos, she must've got a call on her mobile from work, something urgent or hush-hush or both; she had to leave immediately, without letting me know. I'll get a call from her in the next twenty-four hours, and then every-thing'll be fine.

It's all right, he told himself the day after that (but he was lying; everything was far from all right. He was a complete mess, from not sleeping and not eating, and people had to say things three times before he snapped out of his daze and answered them). She was called away on active service, and right now she's some place where you can't make phone calls, but as soon as she can, which will be very soon indeed, she'll call, and everything will be—

On the third day, he formally acknowledged that it wasn't all right, not by a long chalk, but there didn't seem to be anything at all he could do about it. He tried Googling Rockchucker Disposal, but no dice. Eventually, after a lot of begging and pleading, he got a list of his most recent calls from the phone company, from which he was able to confirm that Stephanie must've rung the people she'd got Rockchucker from on her mobile rather than his landline. He rang Stephanie's old home number, but her parents had moved years ago, leaving no forwarding address. He rang the school and asked if they could put him in touch with Mr Fisher-King, and they said, Who?

It was round about then that the little voice started talking to him inside his head. The little voice said, Well, you've done everything you could. It wasn't much, but it was everything, and you've got absolutely nothing at all to go on, so . . .

After a while he found he could get rid of the little voice by humming loudly. This caused him severe problems at work, where humming was frowned on, so he had to put up with it during office hours. It started saying things like, Since there's absolutely nothing you can do – and obviously, if there *was* something you could do, you'd be honour-bound to get right out there and do it, no matter what the cost, that goes without saying, of course; but *since* there's nothing you can do, maybe you should look on the bright side; namely, the dragon's gone, looks like nobody else noticed anything, it's been a week, ten days, a fortnight, a month and no comeback, no consequences; you got away with it, you lucky bastard, and the thing about luck is, it's not a wheelbarrow, you really don't want to go pushing it. So, since nobody else knows Stephanie was ever at your place that night, and nobody knows about the dragon, and nothing bad's happened (apart from Stephanie vanishing, of course, though you don't know for certain she's vanished – for all you know she could quite easily be alive and well running a top-secret underground car park in Helmand province), and since moping around feeling guilty and depressed is going to get you fired any day now, and where are you going to find another job, a loser like you, and since there really is not a damn thing you can do, not that you don't want to but you've got to be realistic about this; well, you might just as well put the whole thing out of your mind and carry on like nothing's happened.

He hated the voice. Partly it was because it sounded just like him, and he'd always loathed the way he sounded. Partly it was because he knew it had a point, several of them, like a porcupine, and that sooner or later he was bound to give in and do what it said, because he couldn't think of anything else to do. Meanwhile, he spent his evenings engaged in frantic research, calling everybody he still knew who might still know the people Stephanie used to know, in the increasingly vain hope that someone might say, "Oh right, you mean Steve; yes, I saw her yesterday – she's fine." But all he got was the news that she was in the army now, in Afghanistan or Iraq or Iran or one of those places.

Time passed, and each day was more or less the same as the others. Each day, he got out of bed with the eagerness of a tooth pulled from its gum, rattled to work on the Tube, somehow avoided getting fired from nine to seven thirty – things were so bad with the firm nowadays that there was practically nothing to do, which meant everyone was staying later and later not doing it, in a desperate attempt to show that they alone were indispensable – before drooping home to spend another evening on the phone getting nowhere at all; and the more nowhere he got, naturally the harder he tried, which left precious little time for trivialities such as food preparation and housework. So he slept in a sleeping bag in the living room and picked up a hamburger at the Golden Arches on his way home.

"Would you like fries with that?"

"No."

"Would you like to make that a Meal?"

"No."

"You know what? You're not being very heroic."

He blinked, and for the first time looked at the life-form behind the counter. "Excuse me?"

"You're not being very heroic," the server repeated. According to her name-badge she was Yasmin: about nineteen, and probably rather nice looking if she smiled, which she showed no indication of doing. "You've given up, haven't you?"

"Uh?"

"You've given up." She'd raised her voice very slightly, as though he was deaf. "A hero would've moved, like, heaven and earth to find her. You're standing in line for burgers."

Oh hell, not again. He gave Yasmin a cold scowl. "On second thoughts, I'll have a chocolate shake with that."

"Regular or large?"

"Regular."

"Coming right up. A hero," Yasmin went on, "would make it, like, sort of a quest. Like, you'd go all round the place looking for her, know what I mean? A hero wouldn't just quit."

"Fine," said Maurice. "Now, let me guess, you've got a special on doughnuts."

She shook her head. "No, but you can add a Smarties McFlurry for just ninety-nine pence extra. A hero would have *hope*, you know?"

He smiled icily. "I'm not a hero."

"Excuse me?"

"I'm not," he repeated, "a hero."

She looked at him, as if to make sure he was who she thought he was. "Suit yourself," she said. "Talking of which, I can individualise your burger with added dill pickle and red sauce for just fifty pence."

"No."

"You want to get a grip," she said, and went away to fetch his burger.

He thought about that, the next day and the day after that. A hero, Yasmin had said; well, that ruled him out. According to multiverse theory, there's an infinite number of universes, somewhere, in which every possibility is realised; but he found it very hard indeed to conceive of a universe in which he could ever qualify as a hero, regardless of circumstances. True, his destiny had been foretold, he'd killed a dragon and his one true love (now hang on just a moment) had been abducted; yes, he replied, my point exactly. That's precisely the sort of stuff that'd bring out the latent heroism in anyone, always assuming it was in there to start with. And had it? No, absolutely not. His actions, or rather his total lack of action over the last three months, demonstrated it conclusively. Not a hero. Not a single heroic molecule in his whole body. And was he upset about that? No, absolutely not, for the same reason he didn't cry himself to sleep every night because he knew he could never be Father Christmas. And as for that one-true-love business, you can forget about that right now. Simply not true. Absolutely.

So he started buying his evening meal from KFC instead, and that seemed to do the trick, because nobody there tried to badger him into a quest or remind him of his destiny, and although he missed the chocolate shakes, the Dippin' Strips meal was just about the right size, if he added a side of coleslaw. And anyway, he thought, you've got to bear in mind that times have changed, and the new technology's altered our perceptions of everything. Yes, if I was a hero in the Dark Ages or whenever, I'd be going from door to door, castle to castle, wattle hut to wattle hut, asking, Have you seen a girl about so high, red hair, attitude, shoulders like Tyson? And since population levels were so much lower back then, I could probably have scoured the entire south of England in three months. But instead, because this is now and we have the technology, I've been phoning round and Googling and going on Friends Reunited, which is basically the same thing, except I do it from home. No different really, no less valid; it's heroism for the Facebook generation, if that's not a contradiction in terms. And, more to the point, the net result is exactly the same. No dice. Nothing. That's the *point*.

One day, though, he was so preoccupied with not thinking about Stephanie and the dragon that he stayed on the train an extra stop. Accordingly, he walked home a different way, which happened to take him much closer to the Golden Arches than the KFC; and he was hungry, and it was raining, and life is too short. So, very cautiously, he put his head round the door and took a good look before joining the queue. It was unusually short, and before very long he was facing a short, square young man called Kevin.

"Hi," Maurice said. "Yasmin not in today, then?"

"Who?"

Maurice smiled. "I think I'll have the Filet-O-Fish," he said. "With large fries and a large vanilla shake. Perhaps you could be very kind and make it a Meal."

Kevin nodded and went away, and came back shortly afterwards with the usual paper bag. "Here you are," he said. "Would you like to make it a Feast for just an extra ninety-nine pence?"

At that point, Maurice was so relieved that he'd never

heard of Yasmin that he'd have agreed to anything. "Sure. Why not?"

Kevin nodded, extended his left hand, and turned it palm upwards. A doughnut materialised out of thin air just above his palm (presumably, Maurice rationalised later, because of health and safety), slowly rose four inches and flipped over.

Maurice closed his eyes, but not quickly enough. In the split second before his eyelids met— Well, you know what it's like in dreams. In your dream, it feels like half an hour at least, but the scientists will tell you it's less than a minute of super-deep REM sleep. In that split second, he saw the man in the tweed overcoat again. He was sitting on a fallen tree in a clearing in a forest, still wearing the same coat and scarf – they looked worn and scruffy, and the coat's cuffs were frayed – and he was warming his hands over an inadequate looking fire of dead twigs. He turned his head slowly and scowled straight at Maurice through the McHole.

"You," he said.

Maurice didn't say a word, but he heard his voice say, "Do I know you?"

"I'm Max, you halfwit." The man shivered, picked up a very small twig and tossed it on the fire. "It's absolutely freezing here, you realise; most days I can't feel my fingers. Why the hell don't you pick up your mail?"

"Excuse me?"

"Your *mail*." Max shook his head. "Forget it," he said. "Look, we don't have much time. You have no idea how difficult it was, setting this up, and I really don't want to think about how much it's costing me. Your girl."

"My—"

"Don't *interrupt*. You want her back or not?"

"Stephanie?"

"Steve," Max corrected him. "Well? Yes or no."

"Yes."

"Splendid. I really was beginning to wonder. I mean, all you ever seem to do is lounge around in your living room chatting with your low-life friends. If my girl had been repossessed, I'd be out there *doing* something."

That made him so angry that for a split second the McVision wavered. He made a desperate effort and calmed himself down. "Yes," he said, "I want her back. What do I do?"

"Right, then." Max pulled the collar of his coat tight around his neck. "Have you got a bit of paper and a pen? You'll want to write this down."

"What? No, wait, I haven't—"

"Latitude 8896431976 north, 6428914404 west. Longitude—"

"Hang *on*. Eight eight nine, then what?"

"What?"

"You said, eight eight nine, and that's as far as I got."

"Oh for pity's sake." Max dragged furiously at his scarf, wound it round his mouth and nose, then unwound it again. "Look, are you trying to wind me up? Because I don't have to do this, you know. There are other heroes."

"I'm not a—"

"Longitude," Max said grimly, "3947582919 west, 9012348746 north. Got that? Of course you have. I'll tell her you're on your way. She'll be relieved. She keeps saying, What the hell does he think he's playing at? When she heard you were spending all your time fooling around on Facebook instead of looking for her, oh boy, was she mad—"

The image was getting dark. "Eight eight nine," Maurice yelled. "What was after eight eight nine? Please—"

"Excuse me?"

The doughnut had vanished, and Kevin was looking at him with a puzzled frown. Maurice took a step back, his face burning. "What happened?"

"Excuse me?"

"To the doughnut. It was there, and then—"

"You want doughnuts? We have doughnuts."

"Just now." But he knew it was no use. And if he tried to explain, he'd be lucky if they didn't call the police. "Thanks," he said. "No doughnuts."

"Have a nice day."

*

So, next morning, after a long night's research on the net, he called in sick and phoned a hypnotist, who by extreme good fortune had a cancellation at 11.30 that day. When he got there he was called in straight away, no waiting.

"I want to remember something," he told her.

She nodded. "What?"

"A number. Well, four numbers. Very long ones."

"Oh." Her face fell. But she recovered, brushed her hair away from her face and smiled encouragingly. "Well, it's possible. You'd be amazed what's stored in the memory." She hesitated, and then a sort of hungry look passed over her face. "This number," she said. "Did you first encounter it in a previous existence?"

"Um, no. This one. Sorry."

"Oh. Well, no matter." She had a sort of hurt expression, through which she was trying to force a professional smile. The result would've been downright scary if she hadn't been wearing glasses. "Only, you see, I sort of specialise in past lives. I had an article in *Reincarnation Now*."

"Is that right?" He paused, then went on, "I hate to hurry you, but I'd quite like to get on with it, if that's OK."

"Sure, yes, no problem." She was looking at him with her head slightly on one side. "People have no idea," she said. "Who's in there with them, I mean."

She made it sound like one of those stunts students used to do; how many people can you cram inside a Fiat, that sort of thing. "Well, that's great. Um."

"Sorry, yes, of course. Just . . . "

"Yes?"

Her eyes were shining behind the glassware. "If I do happen to encounter, well, previous incarnations, would it be all right if I just sort of say hello? Really, it's the most amazing thing. The other day I was helping this guy quit smoking, and seventeen generations ago he was Sir Walter Raleigh. When I told him what he'd been responsible for, he got quite emotional."

"I don't suppose I've ever been anyone," Maurice said firmly. "But I really do need to know those numbers, so if it's absolutely all right with you—"

"Yes, right, let's get straight to it." She sat bolt upright in her chair and looked past him, as if there was someone else in the room directly behind him. "Just lie back on the couch, close your eyes and relax."

"Sure." He hesitated. "What about the watch?"

"Excuse me?"

"Aren't you supposed to dangle a watch on a chain or something?"

"I don't do it like that," she said firmly, as though he'd suggested something mildly indecent. "Now, starting with your feet, I want you to let go completely."

Like a suicidal lemur? "How do you mean?"

"*Relax*," she snapped. "That's better. Now, then. Your toes are completely relaxed. Your insteps are completely relaxed. Your heels are completely relaxed. Your Achilles tendons are completely relaxed. Your ankles are completely relaxed. Your shins are completely relaxed. Your knees—"

Somewhere in his head, someone was playing *Dem Bones, Dem Dry Bones*. It wasn't helping. He was just about to sit up and politely ask for his money back when—

ø

"Now," she said, "when I click my fingers, I want you to tell me who you are."

She paused, and looked at the man on the couch. He didn't look promising, but one thing she'd learned over the years was that you can never tell by appearances. The little fat girl with mouse-coloured hair had turned out to be Eleanor of Aquitaine, while the six-foot-six, blue-eyed, Kirk-Douglas-chinned hunk she'd had in last week had proved to be the current repository of the life energy of six generations of primary-school art teachers. More to the point, she could feel something rare and unusual about this one. There was an oddly makeshift quality about him, like a pantomime horse in a paddock full of thoroughbreds.

Ah well, she thought, and clicked her fingers.

He sat up and scowled at her. "Where am I?" he said.

Oh boy. "It's perfectly all right," she said.

"Says you. Look, I asked you a question. Where am I? Or is geography not your strong suit?"

"London. England."

He sighed. "Yes, I know that, you stupid woman. Which one?"

The way he asked it, as though it was the most reasonable question in the world. "Excuse me?"

"Which *one?*" He gazed at her for a moment. "Oh hell. You don't know, do you?"

"Um."

He looked around, then suddenly tugged at the neck of his shirt. "Can you turn the heating down a bit, please? Preferably before the fillings in my teeth melt."

It was a chilly day and she could only afford one bar of the electric fire. "You're too hot?"

"You bet." A thought occurred to him. "I guess it's the

difference in climate," he said. "I've been in a very cold place for a very long time."

Ah, she thought. Based on her first impressions of this one, his character and general attitude, there was a long-running theological argument settled at a stroke. It wasn't hot down there after all; quite the reverse. "Just a second," she said, and turned off the fire. "Better?"

He shrugged. "Marginally," he said. "I'm guessing we're now below the actual boiling point of copper. Look, I need to get out of here."

Ah. Always a distressing moment, this, when you had to break it to them. "Actually," she said gently, "that's not really possible. You see, you're dead."

On reflection, usually she handled it better. But he'd got to her, and she was feeling flustered.

"No I'm not."

"Trust me. You are."

"Oh please." He examined her closely, as if he'd just found her in his soup. "No offence, but I wouldn't trust you if I asked you the time and we were standing under Big Ben. Not that I'm implying you're dishonest. Just disastrously mis-informed. Do I look dead?"

She cleared her throat. "It's like this," she said; and she told him about reincarnation, and how sometimes, under deep hypnosis administered by a specially trained expert, it was sometimes possible to access the memories of previous incar-nations. "That's you," she clarified. "So tell me, what date is it where you're from?"

"What? How the hell should I know? I've been living in a cave for I don't know how long. And, sorry to disappoint you, but I'm not anybody's previous life. I'm my own current life, worse luck." He paused, and screwed up his face. "And his, of course. You have no idea how tacky that is, even if we are 90 degrees apart in the q axis."

"Um."

"Shh. I need to concentrate." He was holding up his hand for silence. "Right, you'll need a pen and something to write on. Come *on*, will you? Don't you take notes when you're doing your utterly ill-conceived pseudo-experiments?"

Stone-faced, she picked up her clipboard and clicked her ballpoint.

"Splendid, now we're getting somewhere. It's always so much better when people do as I tell them. Latitude 8896431976 north, 6428914404 west. Longitude 3947582919 west, 9012348746 north. Got that? Well *done*. Now, read that lot back to me, so I know you haven't got it down wrong."

She did as she'd been told. He nodded. "Splendid," he said. "Who said people like you can't be trained to perform simple tasks? No, really, I mean it. I've always liked fat women. Once you get past all the unfocused angst, they're always so pathetically grateful for any show of appreciation, no matter how shallow. Right, I'm all done here; just make sure I get that piece of paper when I wake up." Suddenly he frowned, then grinned. "You know what, I think I may have been a tad harsh on you just now. There's some guy called Elric in here, wants to know if the Black Death's cleared up yet. Just a second, I'll put him on for you."

But she'd had quite enough for one day. She clicked her fingers; then, as Maurice opened his eyes and lifted his head a little, she smacked him round the face so hard that her fingertips went numb.

"Uh?" Maurice yowled. "What did I do?"

"That's for saying I'm fat."

"But you— No, really. What happened?"

"I'm not *fat*. I've just got big bones."

"Huge," Maurice agreed eagerly. "Like an elephant's. Did you get the numbers?"

She gave him a disgusted look and threw the piece of paper

at him. Air resistance turned it broadside-on, and it fluttered to the ground. He picked it up and let out a whoop of joy. "That's it," he said. "Eight-eight-nine. Thanks, you've been marvellous."

She glared at him. "Yes, right," she said. "Any show of appreciation, no matter how shallow. Next time you want to remember something, tie a knot in your hanky."

It occurred to Maurice that maybe he was missing something. Subtle clues, like her blazing eyes and the slap round the face. "Did something happen?" he asked. "While I was under?"

She moved, and he instinctively shrank away. "You could say that," she snarled.

"What?"

"I don't want to talk about it. That'll be forty pounds for the session, and no, I don't do PayPal. And you can tell your friend he's completely wrong. I happen to have a slight, extremely rare hormonal imbalance which has nothing at all to do with chocolate. Got that?"

"My friend?"

"Yes. Now go away. *Now.*"

So he went to the nearest café, ordered a cappuccino, sat down under a huge black-and-white WHERE IS THEO BERNSTEIN? poster and stared at the numbers. He vaguely remembered latitude and longitude from school, but actually using this data to achieve something useful was clearly another matter entirely. He needed an expert. So he called the Royal Geographical Society.

They weren't terribly helpful. They gave him the dates of lectures on the history of navigation, and numbers he could call if he was interested in joining the merchant navy, but nothing more immediately relevant than that. Or, they suggested, you could try the Ordnance Survey.

So he tried them, but they said no, it wasn't one of theirs – too many numbers; your best bet would probably be the Ministry of Defence or possibly NASA. By now his phone was running low on charge, and it was lunchtime, and what the hell. He put the phone away and picked up the menu, at which point a dreadful voice behind him said, "Sniff."

He spun round, nearly falling off his chair. "Alice," he said.

Alice was the head of his department at work. "Hello, Maurice," she said. "Sniff."

"What?"

"*Sniff.*"

So he sniffed, and she looked at him for maybe five seconds, then shook her head slowly. "Pathetic," she said. "You call that a sniff? It's barely a snuffle."

Then he remembered that he wasn't at work because he had a cold. He sniffed again, this time with feeling, but it was too late. Her ice-cold eyes were drilling into him. "You're not ill," she said.

"I'm better."

"Splendid," Alice said. "I'm so happy for you. Be in the office at nine sharp tomorrow."

"Yes, of course."

"Bring with you," Alice went on, "a strong cardboard box, about three feet by two. And sticky tape, and some string. That should be big enough to get all your stuff in."

Terror enveloped him like the big rolling brushes in a car wash. "I was ill, really," he said.

"No doubt." She was doing up her coat. "And now you're just fine. That's a comfort. I'd feel really bad about firing a sick person."

Twenty seconds later, he'd found just the right words to

frame precisely the best arguments to convince her to give him a second chance. Regrettably, she'd left the café fifteen seconds earlier. He sighed, folded the piece of paper with the numbers on it, tucked it safely away in his top pocket, and went home.

The next week was pretty bad. To distract himself from the fact that he no longer had a job or an income, he threw himself body and soul into the task of making sense of the coordinates on the piece of paper. He spent hours online, reading everything he could find about the various mapping conventions, none of which seemed to fit the apparently random jumble of numbers he'd been given. A few of the government and academic agencies he emailed did actually reply, though only to tell him that whatever the numbers he'd got hold of were, they weren't coordinates according to any known system. A friendly lady from the Van Goyen Institute in Leiden wrote back to say that they looked to her a bit like lottery numbers, and if he tried them and he won, could she have five per cent for suggesting it? Other than that, the responses were less than helpful.

The dead end, combined with a bank statement, brought him up sharp. Yes, Stephanie was still missing and the coordinates were still tantalisingly obscure. That didn't mean he was let off earning a living; he would almost certainly find it even harder to achieve his quest if he had to start living in a cardboard box under the railway arches. Reluctantly but resolutely, he started looking for a job.

There's nothing like doing an impossible thing for taking your mind off the other impossible thing you feel you ought to be doing. Somehow or other, he managed to kid a dozen or so of the scores of potential employers he applied to into interviewing him, but the interviews themselves left him feeling like someone who's got into Wimbledon by kidnapping a star player and stealing his identity, and who's now faced with his first match on Centre Court. The interviewers were generally kinder to him than he deserved, but that only made it worse; it's hard to blame your failure on other people when they go out of their way to be nice to you. Eleven spectacular crashes later, he found himself wondering how he could've been so colossally stupid as to alienate the only company on earth gullible enough to exchange good money for his fundamentally worthless time.

Just one to go. He Google-mapped the address (Carbonec House, Evelake Street) and planned his route carefully so there'd be no danger whatsoever of arriving late; about the only virtue he had to offer was punctuality, which would've been fine if the job had been lamp-lighting or clock-winding. In the event, his Tube train got stuck down a deep, dark hole for an hour, and he arrived in Evelake Street twenty minutes late and gasping for breath.

There was no one in the waiting room; well, there wouldn't be, would there? All the others would've made it on time. He sat down and tried to stabilise his breathing, but he felt as though someone had just cleaned his windpipe with coarse sandpaper, and his shirt collar was squelchy with sweat.

A nice lady came out, told him that Mr Nacien was running a bit late, and would he like a cup of tea? He said yes, please, without thinking, and about thirty seconds later, the nice lady came back with a cup, saucer and plate of digestive biscuits.

"Drink up," the nice lady said, "before it gets cold."

So he drank the tea, which tasted a bit odd, and handed the cup and saucer back to the nice lady, who smiled at him.

"Oh, by the way," she said. "The tea was laced with some stuff that makes you tell the truth, whether you want to or not. Sodium penta-something. Hope that's all right."

"What?"

"Oh, it's perfectly harmless," she said reassuringly. "All it means is, you say what you're actually thinking, not what you want to say. Wonderful what they can do with chemicals these days, isn't it?"

He blinked at her. They're evil, he thought. But, on the other hand, they might just possibly give me a job, so be nice. "No," he heard himself say, "it's not all right, it's appalling. How am I supposed to get through a job interview telling the *truth*?"

"Oh, you'll be fine," the nice lady said. "Right, Mr Nacien's ready for you now. Good luck."

Maurice smiled weakly. "I hate you," he said. "I hope you burn in hell."

"That's the ticket. Through the door, second on your right."

The directions brought him to a white-painted door; he knocked, waited, and heard a voice say "Come in." He turned the handle and pushed the door, which (needless to say) opened outwards. Beyond the door was a large, light room, sparsely furnished, having in place of a back wall a huge window, open, leading to a balcony with deckchairs, golf umbrellas and a potted palm. The desk was in a direct line between the door and the window. Behind it sat a bald man, tall and fat. He smiled as Maurice slouched in, and waved him to a chair. "Hello," the man said cheerfully. "My name's David Nacien. Do sit down."

Maurice sat down. In spite of everything, he couldn't help noticing how wonderfully comfortable the chair was. Mr Nacien glanced down at a cribsheet on his desk and said, "You're Maurice Katz."

"Yes." Maurice made a quixotic attempt at a friendly smile. "That tie's ridiculous. It makes you look like you've spilt trifle all down your shirt front."

Mr Nacien nodded. "Quite," he said. "Now, then, let's see. Six GCSEs, three A-levels, splendid. English, computer studies and *philosophy*." He raised his eyebrows. "Interesting choice. What made you choose it?"

Maurice tried to imagine what an intelligent expression would look like on the face he saw when he shaved, and did his best to arrange himself accordingly. He had no idea if it was working. He had his doubts. "I really fancied this girl, and she was going to do philosophy, and I thought it might help me get off with her if I did it too. Also, I thought it'd be a real doss."

Mr Nacien nodded encouragingly. "And was it?"

"No. Loads of reading."

"Ah."

"I didn't do any of it. I cut and pasted stuff off the internet instead."

"Excellent. Then three years reading Theory of Website Design at Towcester."

Maurice nodded. "I thought that'd be a doss, too."

"Was it?"

Maurice shrugged. "Actually, I don't remember much about Towcester."

"I see. Now then, your most recent employment: IT assistant at Overthwart and Headlong."

"Yes."

"Did you like it there?"

"No, it was foul. I never really found out what I was supposed to be doing, the management were a bunch of fascists, the money was rubbish and there were only two women under forty on my floor; one of them was well and truly spoken for and the other one looked like a warthog."

"I get you. Why did you leave?"

"They fired me. I got caught skiving."

"Most distressing," Mr Nacien said sympathetically. "Do you feel they acted unreasonably?"

"No. I mean, I was always calling in sick; it's just a shame I got caught."

"Moving on," said Mr Nacien, "why did you decide to apply for this position?"

"Well," Maurice said, "I put in for everything I could find, and all the others turned me down. Hardly surprising, really. I mean, who in their right mind would want me?"

"Mphm. And what special qualities do you think you would bring to the position?"

"Absolutely none."

"A refreshingly different perspective, perhaps? Energy, enthusiasm, commitment? A shared ethos?"

"No."

"Right." Mr Nacien ticked a box on a piece of paper. "Any questions from your end so far?"

"Yes. How long before this stuff wears off?"

Mr Nacien folded his hands on the desk. "That depends on the physiology of the individual. It can be anything from thirty minutes to twenty-four hours."

"Twenty-four *hours*? My God."

Mr Nacien smiled. "Indeed," he said. "Society professes to place such a high value on truth, but it's hard to see how our civilisation could possibly function if we weren't allowed to lie like troopers all the time. I imagine," he went on, "you considered the issue in depth as part of your philosophy course."

Maurice shrugged. "Search me," he said. "I cut and pasted stuff. I never read any of it."

"Of course not. So, where were we? Ah yes. I take it you're fully conversant with what we do here at Carbonec?"

"No, not a clue. I just saw this ad saying admin assistant, and I thought—"

"That sounds like a total doss?"

Maurice nodded. "Is it?"

"That would depend," Mr Nacien said, "on the degree of drive and initiative you brought to the position. So tell me, do you have a passion for administration?"

"Hardly."

"Would you describe yourself as a team player?"

"Me? You must be joking."

"In your previous employment, what were your expectations?"

"Well, I hoped they'd basically just leave me alone so I could play games on the computer or read a book or something."

"And were they met?"

"No," Maurice said sadly. "Alice was always prowling around trying to catch people out, so you had to look busy, even when there wasn't any work on, which was most of the time. And the phone kept ringing, with people wanting to shout at me about stuff I didn't know anything about."

"What strategies did you use to cope with these challenges?"

"Actually," Maurice said, "I had quite a good one. I got this bit of Blu-Tack, about yay big, and I made it into a little cube and stuck it on the phone between the receiver and the handset, so it looked like the phone was on the hook but actually it was off and they thought I was on a call. They never did find out about that one."

"That was very resourceful of you," Mr Nacien said. "It demonstrates an ability to think outside the box. You'll see just how important that is if you get the job. All right, how would you describe yourself?"

"Me? Oh, I just sort of chug along, you know? When people used to ask me, What do you want to do when you grow up? I told them, as little as possible."

"Interesting." Mr Nacien drew his fingers down his chin. "So, what excites you most about working for Carbonec?"

"Getting paid, though I must say, the money you're offering is rubbish. And getting away at five thirty sharp."

"What challenges are you looking forward to in this job?"

"Oh, the usual. Making it look like I'm doing something. Figuring out what the hell I'm meant to be doing without actually asking anyone, because that always makes you look such an idiot. And not getting found out when I really screw up, of course. That's a real biggie, isn't it?"

Mr Nacien smiled. "So if I were to ask you why you're the best person for this job—?"

"I'd probably laugh myself sick."

"And how would you feel about supervising two or three junior staff?"

"Dear God, what an appalling idea. The blind leading the blind in pitch darkness on the edge of a cliff. It'd be total chaos."

Mr Nacien put the cap on his biro and stowed it in his top pocket. "Now, are there any further questions you'd like to ask about us?"

"Not much point, is there?"

"Oh, I don't know," Mr Nacien replied. "I've got – let me see – another two hundred and seven candidates to see, but as soon as we've come to a decision, we'll be in touch. Thank you for your time, and I hope we'll be seeing more of each other in the near future."

"I don't," Maurice said. "You give me the creeps."

Mr Nacien smiled. "If you speak to Jackie on the front desk, she'll give you an antidote to the truth serum. Oh, and you wouldn't happen to know where Theo Bernstein is, would you?"

"No."

"No matter. It was nice to meet you, Mr Katz. Good morning."

The antidote worked almost immediately, but over the next three days he had a number of terrifying relapses, which forced him to stay at home with the door double-locked and the phone off the hook. On the fourth day he put the phone back, and almost immediately cousin Tony from Nottingham rang to say he'd be in London for a week and could he and the rest of the band stay at Maurice's place? For a moment it was touch and go, but he kept his head and managed to invent an infestation of flesh-eating beetles, which he made sound so convincing that he was awake half the night listening intently for scuttling noises. After that, he reckoned the crisis was past and he was no longer a danger to himself and others.

It was good to smell fresh air again, but apart from that, things seemed pretty bleak. He had no job and no money, and finding Stephanie seemed as impossible as it had before he got the stupid coordinates. The rent would be due any day now, and paying it would take him well past his overdraft limit, but the thought of leaving the flat horrified him. It wasn't that it was a particularly nice place to live, but he had a dreadful suspicion that it was somehow inextricably linked to Stephanie's disappearance and, therefore, to getting her back. If he gave it up, she'd be lost forever.

He agonised over it for a day or so, then came to a terrible decision. There was only one thing he could do.

PART TWO

Not a Door.

He called George.

Hello, said George, and how the devil are you? How long's it been? As long as that? Good Lord. Yes, yes, of course, let's have a drink or lunch or something. Where are you these days? Still? Actually, that couldn't be better: I need to run up to town and see to a few things – how about Wednesday? Pop by the London office, say twelveish?

If only, Maurice thought, as he walked through the colossal plate-glass doors, I believed in God. Because if I did that, I'd also believe in the Devil, which means I'd be able to approach Him with an offer to sell him my soul for what I need for the rent, and then I wouldn't have to be here.

The doors opened into an atrium. It was the sort of thing Kublai Khan might've had at Xanadu if he'd had the money, the total lack of taste and the planning permission. Far above his head, a huge stained-glass dome flooded the marble floor with dappled red and green light. A fountain in the exact centre shot up a fire-hose jet of water that didn't stop rising until it was level with the fifth floor (Human Resources and Accounts). Birds of paradise, imported under special licence from the Spice Islands, wheeled in free flight overhead, occasionally crashing head-on into the practically invisible glass-tube lift and dropping like stones into the frothing water beneath. Two security guards, wearing more body armour than Sir Lancelot, intercepted him before he'd gone two yards; they escorted him to the front desk, where a stunningly beautiful receptionist scanned his biometric data with a tricorder, called up his medical records and psychological profile, ran a criminal record check (2007: 36 mph in a 30 mph zone) and gave him a pass with a small, twinkling hologram of himself set into it like a rare jewel. "George'll be down in a moment," she said, giving him a smile that burnt the skin on his cheeks. "Can I get you a frankincense latte and a slice of passion fruit baklava?"

No doubt about it, George had done all right for himself since they were at school together. All in all, he wasn't surprised. George had always been the smart one. He'd started his own software business, Smartarse Data Solutions, in their GCSE year. By the time the results came through, he was already employing a hundred people – two hundred the next year, and he was flown in by private jet from a meeting in Kyoto to sit his Geography A-level. He couldn't spare the time to go to university, so he had one built on the roof of his corporate HQ.

"Hello, Maurice." He looked round and there was George: still impossibly tall, his ears still sticking out like wing-mirrors, still wearing what looked like the same jeans and Blood Geranium T-shirt he'd worn when he was sixteen. Maurice offered a silent prayer that the truth serum was well and truly gone from his system, and forced himself to smile. "Hi, George," he said.

People who met George for the first time found it hard to understand why he was so universally hated. People who met him for the third time were routinely scanned for weapons by

Security, and with good reason. Of course, the X-ray scanners built into the doorframe at HQ were wonderfully unobtrusive and could tell a bunch of keys from a Kalashnikov without setting off a single alarm. Of course; George had designed them himself. Accordingly, they were intelligent enough to qualify for a place at the Sorbonne.

"You're looking great," George said. "Would it be OK if we had lunch here in the office? I daren't leave the building or Kareena will kill me."

Something splatted on the top of Maurice's head. He closed his eyes. "Sure, George," he said.

George laughed. "Those bloody birds," he said. "They're just to impress the Japanese." He lifted his hand an inch or so, and two enormous men in black suits appeared out of nowhere. One of them held Maurice in a gentle but vice-like grip, while the other dabbed at the top of his head with a handkerchief. "This way," George said. "No, Kurt, it's all right: he's with me."

Maurice followed George. The two enormous men followed Maurice, exactly four yards behind him at all times, until they reached what looked like a perfectly blank marble wall on the far east side of the atrium. "Sorry about this," George said, as one enormous man bounded forward and dropped a bag neatly over Maurice's head. "The stupid insurance people insist, I'm afraid. It's a real pain, but there you are."

When the bag was removed, a lift door had mysteriously appeared in the wall. George stepped in, Maurice followed and the door sighed shut.

"We had Barack in here last week," George was saying, "and his people made the most dreadful fuss – there was nearly a gun battle out there. But you've got to be firm, haven't you?"

The lift went up, and up, and up. "Barack who?" Maurice asked.

"So," George said, "seen anyone from school lately? You heard about Kieran and Shawna? Can you believe it? I suppose at some point the UN will send in a peacekeeping force, but by then it'll probably be too late. Ah, here we are."

Something went *ting*, the door slid back and George stepped out onto, apparently, nothing at all. Maurice hesitated, and looked down. He could see the tops of the heads of people sitting at desks, about twenty feet below.

"Glass floor," George said with a grin. "Come on."

Not just the floor; the walls and the ceiling, not to mention the furniture, were all clear glass, some rare and abstruse variety that eluded the light almost completely. "We developed it for the security side of the business," George said. "Stealth technology, and all that. This way."

Overhead and on either side, fluffy white clouds and a pale-blue sky. He glanced back longingly at the lift door, which slowly faded away. "George," he said, "when you want to go back down again, how the hell do you find the lift?"

George grinned. "I told them to fix us up some grub in the conference room," he said. "Oh, watch out, mind the—"

Something whacked Maurice in the face.

"Door. Oh well. It's OK, nothing broken. Right, sit yourself down and let's eat."

George bent at the knee and sat down on thin air. Maurice prodded tentatively with a fingertip until he encountered some kind of resistance, made his best guess, sat down and found himself sprawling on the (invisible) floor. "Sorry," George said. "To your left, about ten inches, yes, that's it, you're there. It's a bit of a pain till you get the hang of it, but it impresses the hell out of the Scandinavians. Terrine of swan liver with spiced fig and marsala jelly OK to start with? Or they can do you a bacon sandwich if you'd rather."

The sooner I do it, Maurice told himself, the sooner I can get out of here. "George," he said, "I need a loan."

"Sure. How much?"

"It's the rent, you see. I lost my job, and you know what it's like finding a place if you're out of work these days."

"Of course. How much?"

"I'll pay it back, I promise, soon as I get another job and—"

"Fifty thousand? Hundred? Hundred and fifty? Dora," George said to nobody at all, "fetch me my chequebook, there's a love." Two seconds later, a beautiful girl in tortoise-shell glasses walked through the wall, smiled and put down a chequebook on the thin air that had to be the table. "Or shall I just leave it blank and you can fill it in when you've made your mind up?"

Yes. Maurice thought, but how much is my soul actually worth? Unfortunately, it's not like second-hand cars – there's no handy book you can look it up in. At a guess, somewhere between forty and a hundred pounds. Even so, it was a mistake coming here. I should've tried putting it up on eBay instead.

He added the outstanding rent to the sum by which he'd exceeded his overdraft limit, and stuck on a hundred pounds for luck. George gave him a mildly scornful look – the sort you'd expect to get from a genie if your three wishes had been a can of Coke, a corned beef sandwich and a Snickers bar – and handed him the cheque. "You sure that's enough?"

"Yes, really."

"Really?"

That was George for you; the sort of man who refuses to take Yes for an answer. "*Really*. And, um, thank you."

"Oh, that's all right. Now, I'll just buzz Legal, and they'll run us up some paperwork."

For a split second he assumed that was a joke, but then he remembered whom he was talking to. A few minutes later, a tall, dark man in a blue suit walked through the wall holding a blue folder. He gave Maurice a nice smile, which lasted for precisely one and a quarter seconds.

"That's just a simple loan agreement," he said, passing Maurice a five-page document, with a sheaf of yellow stickies to mark the places where he had to sign. "This is a basic garnishee order, in case at some point we need to freeze your bank account. This one here's a floating charge on any property you may buy at any time in the next forty-five years; just sign here, that's fine, thank you, and here, and here, and I'll just witness that for you. And finally, this one's just a one-page bog-standard will, so if you die before the loan's repaid, everything you own at date of death goes to George; now, we'll need two witnesses for this one. Sonia, send Peter up here, will you? Thanks." A twenty-year-old in a grey suit that cost more than Maurice had earned in a year at Overthwarts materialised through the wall, drew his squiggle on the paper and fled. "Needless to say, all these documents cease to be valid as and when" – he gave Maurice an evil smile – "the loan is repaid in full. You-have-the-right-to-take-independent-legal-advice. All done? Smashing. Cheers, George. See you later about the Uzbekistan position? Marvellous. Nice to have met you, Mr, um."

"Well," George said, as the lawyer retreated and they brought the swan-liver pâté in on a massive silver salver, "that's you sorted. So, how's tricks? Everything good with you?"

"Apart from losing my job, you mean."

George smiled. "You can come and work for me if you like," he said, as if offering Maurice the use of a pen. "I could do with someone to head up our operation in Mogadishu. Nothing to it; you could do it standing on your head."

Almost certainly the best way. "That's really kind of you, George, but I'm not sure I'm really up to—"

"Bull," George said cheerfully. "I'll get HR to call you first thing. You'll love it out there, Maurice. Really genuine people, and they're making huge strides with the security position. Huge strides."

"Really, George. No."

George stuffed a baby's-fist-sized knob of swan-liver terrine into his mouth, chomped it a few times. "Fine, be like that. All right, I know, I'll lend you the money to start up your own business – how would that be? Fantastic idea. How about long-distance air freight? Or better still, railways. Now there's a sector that's wide open these days, for a guy like you, with a bit of vision."

Maurice ate a scrap of the terrine. It tasted disgusting. "No, George, thank you. As it happens, I went for a job only the other day, and I've got high hopes—"

"Fine." George raised both hands. The world stopped dead for a moment, then continued smoothly as before. "So, you seen much of the old gang lately?"

Thanks to his marathon of evening phone calls, Maurice had plenty of old-gang news, which kept the conversation away from what George could do for him all through the swan-liver terrine and well into the salmi of wind-dried Thomson's gazelle with blue cheese and chocolate sauce. George, of course, knew far more about everyone than Maurice did – presumably he had all their phones hacked, as a matter of course – but he enjoyed correcting and contradicting everything Maurice said, so that was all right. "Oh, and there's Stephanie, of course," George said, with his mouth full of wind-dried gazelle. "Sorry, Steve, as we've got to call her now. Wasn't that marvellous?" George stopped and gave Maurice a mighty slap on the back. "You all right, mate? Here, drink some water."

The water (snow airlifted from the high Pyrenees that morning, melted at the table in a little silver chafing dish) helped a bit, and eventually Maurice was able to breathe again. "Stephanie?"

"Mm, yes. What, hadn't you heard? No, I'm sorry, this just isn't good enough. Claudio! Get in here now."

"What?" Maurice gasped. "What about Stephanie?"

A bearlike man in a white chef's outfit came through the wall. George took his fork and prodded something small, black and shrivelled on the edge of his plate. "Claudio, what do you call this?"

The bearlike man mumbled something. George shook his head. "No way," he said. "I don't pay five thousand euros a kilo for oak-found Perigord truffles so you can *steam* them. There's a plane leaving Heathrow for Ulan Bator in ninety minutes. Be on it."

"*Señor.*" The bearlike man bowed his head, turned round and marched briskly through the wall. George shook his head and put down his fork. "Nice enough guy, but you've got to make them walk the line, or where the hell are you? Now then, what was I saying?"

"Stephanie."

"Steve," George corrected. "Got to say, though, she doesn't really convince me as a Steve. I think you've got to be extra feminine to get away with calling yourself by a man's name. Sorry, is something the matter? You've gone a funny colour."

"What about *Steve?*"

"Oh, right. Well, I always said she was wasting her life playing soldiers; someone like that ought to be in the private sector, making money. And I was right, obviously."

"She's left the—?"

George nodded. "Headhunted," he said. "By a really top-notch private security outfit: Brighthawk, or something like that. Anyway, it's a subsidiary of VGE, and *they're* all right. Anyhow, they've got her up in Greenland, which is where it's all going to be happening pretty soon, and the last I heard she was as happy as a fox in a chicken-coop. I mean, the army had her stuck behind a desk controlling traffic, I ask you. And now there she is, driving jeeps and shooting guns and blowing stuff up, probably eating tree bark and weevils, having the time of her life. I always maintain, if you insist on being a soldier of fortune, make it the Fortune 500. Anyway, she's looking good on it, bright-eyed and bushy-tailed—"

Maurice stared at him. "You've seen her? When?"

"Last Tuesday, was it, or Wednesday? No, I was in Jakarta, Wednesday, so it must've been Tuesday. No, I tell a lie. Evangelique, where was I last Tuesday?"

"Reykjavik," said a disembodied voice, "all morning, and then you flew back to Paris via Nuuk, and then on to—"

"Thanks, Evangelique. Tuesday," George said. "We had lunch."

"And she was all right?"

"Blooming. She'd just laid three hundred kilometres of razor wire."

"Did she mention me at all?"

George frowned. "No, I don't think so. Mind you, we were talking about oil, mostly."

"Ah."

A sly look crossed George's face, in the same way Lewis and Clark crossed Louisiana. "Why, did you expect she'd talk about you?"

"No. God, no. I mean," he added truthfully, "I haven't seen her for months."

"Got you. Well, to be absolutely honest with you, it's just as well you don't think about her – well, you know. Because, let's face it, you're a really great guy, I've always liked you ever so much, but if it came to a choice . . . Well, she'd have to be out of her tiny mind, right?"

It took a moment for that to sink in. "Choice?"

George smirked. "But it won't ever come to that, so that's

absolutely fine. Yes, Steve and me. Well, I guess it's been on the cards ever since school, now I come to think of it. Early days yet, of course, but let's say I anticipate a better-than-positive outcome, going forwards."

"Stephanie and *you*—"

He hadn't meant it to come out like that, and just for a moment, a flash of anger lit up George's face. But it passed, and the smile came seeping back. "Written in the stars, if you ask me. The distance thing's a bit of a drag right now, but I'm building a new corporate HQ out there – we've just acquired forty hectares of prime land slap bang in the middle of Qaqortoq, well, all of Qaqortoq, really, and the joy of this business is, you can run it from pretty much anywhere. And of course, when the oil starts flowing we'll be there on the spot waiting, so to speak. Bit of a cow for everyone who'll have to relocate out there, but it's a beautiful country, and they'll all be much happier once they've got used to the cold and stuff. Perfect fusion of business and pleasure, really."

Abruptly, George rose to his feet; lunch, apparently, was over. "Come on," he said, "I'll give you the guided tour. You haven't seen the new stuff, have you?"

Maurice hadn't even seen the old stuff, not that he'd ever had the slightest desire to. "Mind the step," George said cheerfully, as he walked into what was presumably a wall; he vanished, and Maurice had to force himself to follow. A moment later, he was in a perfectly normal corridor, with a floor he could actually see. Wonderful. "We had Bill and Melinda over here last month, and she nearly had a fit walking through the interface there. And Warren, bless him, he had to go round the back and out through the kitchen. He's a funny old stick, but quite charming when you get to know him."

Down the corridor to the end, turn left, then right, then left, then left, then right, and they arrived at a vast courtyard paved with black basalt flagstones. Another glass dome, this time clear; brilliant white light flooded down onto a white tower, perfectly smooth and windowless, with no obvious door. "My office," George said. "Kareena calls it my Saruman room, bless her. But you don't want to see that – it's just a chair and a phone and a bit of basic kit. Tell you what, we'll take the lift down to R and D. There's some pretty funky things going on down there, though I do say so myself."

Funky, Maurice thought. Jesus wept. "Actually, George, I really ought to be going. The people from this job I told you about could ring any time."

"Oh that's all right; I've had your calls redirected. Here we go." George touched his left palm to the wall of the white tower, and a doorway slid open. Another lift – what fun. This one was completely black. "Of course, when we get to Greenland we'll have the space to do things in style," George said, as the door slid shut and darkness enveloped them. "I'm awfully fond of this old place, but it's so cramped, if you know what I mean. Practically Coronation Street, all these poky little alleys and corners. In Qaqortoq I'm planning an office that's just a straight room, a kilometre long. I like to walk up and down when I'm thinking."

The door opened. Maurice had no idea where they were; ten storeys up or half a mile underground. The room in front of him was huge, absurd, something out of a Bond film (the Roger Moore era, when everything was a bit over the top). It was also empty.

"Warehouse space," George explained. "It's where we store the—"

Something collided painfully with Maurice's knee.

"Stealth-glass furniture. This way."

George always had walked quickly on those great long legs, and Maurice had always had to jog to keep up with him.

They went through a door into another enormous room, but this one was full: people sitting at desks and consoles, busy people who didn't look up. George greeted a few of them by name as they passed through. A smile and "Hi, George" appeared to be the orthodox reply.

"Number-crunchers," George explained. "Marvellous people, the core of our R and D. But what you'll really want to see is through here."

Another door. This one opened onto—

"Ah," George said. "Thirty-six."

It looked like more warehouse space, except it wasn't entirely empty. In the very centre of the room, a naked man was sitting on the ground, his back braced against nothing at all, his eyes closed. "Shh," George whispered. "We don't want him to know we're here."

The man was in his mid-thirties, dark-haired, a face that Maurice reckoned he might possibly have seen before somewhere, on the TV or in a photograph. "Is he all right?"

"Absolutely fine. Interesting guy, actually, very bright, and essential to the work we're doing here."

"Is he asleep?"

George shook his head. "Thinking."

"Ah."

At that precise moment, in exactly the same place, but at ninety-one degrees to that time and place in the D axis, the dark-haired man in his mid-thirties was thinking, Yes, but all that condensation's got to go somewhere; I bet it gathers in big woolly-looking bunches up in the sky and just sort of hangs there. All right, fine, but what happens when one of these bunches hits a patch of cold air? Precipitation, that's what's got to happen – stands to reason – and then all the condensation's going to fall out of the sky, hitting the ground in droplet form, probably. And then I wouldn't be at all surprised if it soaked away into the ground until the big-burning-ball-of-Big-Bang-leftover-stuff comes out again and heats the ground up, which would surely evaporate the dropletty stuff, making it rise up into the sky to form more big woolly bunches, and the whole process starts all over again. Yes, that must be what happens. Logically, it couldn't be any other way.

Yes, but suppose a lot of the droplets fall at one time, masses and masses and masses of them. They can't all evaporate or drain away – the ground'd get saturated, so presumably you must get a whole lot of droplets sort of gathering in a big sort of mass. No, hold on just a second; this stuff's going to be a liquid, right, so it won't just sit there, it'll kind of roll about, maybe even *flow*, and of course when it does that it'll find its own level, and bet you anything you like it'll follow the line of least resistance, so what's almost certain to happen is that you'll get, like, kind of *streams* of this droplet stuff *flowing* in a *line*. Wow. And then, of course, when it's been doing that for a very long time, I wouldn't be at all surprised if it sort of gnawed away at the ground, I mean you could get great big *chunks* carved out if it went on flowing long enough; and presumably at some point it'll get somewhere where it can't go any further without backing up on itself, and then what? Well, you'd have huge great *pools* of the stuff, wouldn't you? *Huge* pools. In fact, if I'm right about how everything started and all that stuff, you'd be looking at, gosh, let me see, well, something like 71 per cent of this ball-shaped-chunk-of-not-burning-left-over-from-the-Big-Bang stuff I'm on right now, all completely covered with flowed-and-pooled dropletty stuff.

"That man in there," George said, passing Maurice the sugar, "is key, well, fairly key, to the whole project."

Maurice sipped the froth on his frankincense latte. "Ah," he said.

"It's going to be big." George wasn't looking at him now; he was staring just left of him, and Maurice had a feeling he was talking to himself. "Quite possibly the biggest thing I've ever done. If it all goes well, by this time next year I could be well on my way to being the richest man *ever*. Not just the richest man *now*. The richest *ever*."

"That's nice," Maurice said.

"Of course," George went on, "it's so difficult to gauge these things, because of the comparatives and the lack of reliable data. I mean, how can you say for sure who was richer, Tutankhamun or Louis XIV?"

"Quite."

"I mean," George continued passionately, "what's your principal criterion: capital or income? Do you draw a completely arbitrary line according to who was the richest when you translate everything into, say, 2014 values? Or do you try and calculate the total gross value of the world at the time such and such a person lived, and then express richness as the percentage of that total value that the person in question owned? Because if you did that, it'd probably be Tutankhamun – 17.463 per cent, by the way – and poor old Louis would be practically nowhere, 2.019 per cent, peanuts. But if you just go on a strict cash-equivalent basis, how much all his stuff would sell for if you put it up for auction on 1 April 2015, chances are it'd be Montezuma or one of those guys. But if you're going by sustained net income over a whole-of-career period, it's got to be Louis, or maybe just possibly one of the Roman emperors, Hadrian maybe. It's tricky," George said. "I mean, it really helps if you know the rules before you start playing the game, or how are you ever going to be sure you've won?"

Maurice thought, If I agree with him a whole lot, maybe he'll let me go and I can get out of here before I die of noxious-bastard poisoning. "You're so right," he said. "Um—"

"And that's not even allowing for the Chinese," George said bitterly. "Because the Chinese didn't just have wealth in this life, they accumulated vast credit surpluses in the Afterlife, by investing heavily in the Bank of the Dead. So, if you *can* take it with you, what does that do to your accounting frame of reference? I mean, let's take Qin Shihuangdi, the first emperor, suppose he invested two billion *yuan* in the Bank of the Dead in 210 BC. Let's say for the sake of argument the Bank pays 3 per cent compound interest, that's 2,225 years, two billion *yuan*, that gives you a 2015 value of—"

Without breaking eye-contact, Maurice used his peripheral vision to locate the nearest door. Just run for it, he told himself, screw good manners. There's only so much of this sort of thing a man can take.

"So you see," George went on, "if I want to be absolutely sure I'm the richest man *ever*, I'll need to have a pretty substantial margin of error, say 7 per cent, to cover stuff like historiographical distortion and inaccurate reporting, because the last thing I want to happen is for me to get to the point where I *think* I'm the richest and stop trying, and then a couple of hundred years later some smartarse digs up a mouldy old papyrus in Egypt somewhere that proves that Tutankhamun's scribes habitually rounded the fractions *down* instead of *up*, and so in fact he beat me by a lousy billion dollars. That'd be a disaster, a whole lifetime of effort wasted, and I'm damned if I'm going to let it happen."

"I bet you lie awake at night worrying," Maurice said sympathetically. "Well, it's been utterly fantastic seeing you again, but I really do have to—"

"So this project has got to work," George said. "That's all there is to it. Muffin?"

"Excuse me?"

"Would you like a muffin with your coffee? Irina, bring us a plate of those pearl and rosewater muffins."

Here's a moral dilemma for you. If you're held against your will by a toxic jerk and offered muffins, should you eat one? But Maurice was feeling peckish, and they did look rather good, though in fact they turned out to taste mostly of plaster of Paris.

"Actually," George was saying, "it's basically a very simple idea. Multiverse theory."

"That's a very simple idea," Maurice said. "I see."

"Multiverse theory states," George went on, "that there's an infinite number of universes existing concurrently, one universe for every conceivable possibility. So, for example, there's this universe, where you just bit into that muffin—"

"Jolly good, by the way. Yum."

"And another one where you didn't bite the muffin, and another one where you bit into the muffin but didn't drop crumbs all over my priceless seventeenth-century Isfahan rug, and another one where you bit into the muffin, which somehow managed to contain a large chunk of brick, and broke a tooth, and another one where immediately after biting into the muffin and dropping crumbs, you spat it out, and another one where you spat it out but didn't drop crumbs, and so on," George added, "infinitely. OK so far?"

"Mphm."

"Fine." George nodded happily. "So, in multiverse theory, out there somewhere there's a whole lot of universes in which, back in say 2006, the CEO of Schliemann Brothers called all the pushy, edgy young investment bankers into his office and told them to stop being so damn stupid or else there'd be serious trouble. And so there was no global financial crisis, and trillions of dollars didn't get wiped off the net value of the human race, and buying a European government bond would be a marginally safer investment than playing the slot machines in Vegas. Still with me?"

Sadly, yes. "All clear so far, George."

"And *there*," George said triumphantly, "is where you'll find the biggest financial opportunity in the history of mankind. That's how I'm going to make my pile, Maurice. Inter-multiverse speculation. When I'm done, compared to me Tutankhamun and Montezuma and Louis XIV – well, they'll be *you*, Maurice. No offence."

"None taken."

"What I need to discover," George went on, and there was a tiny bit of muffin stuck to the corner of his mouth, "is a stable transdimensional portal that I can send money through. Not people or things, you understand; I *think* that might be possible – they were doing some work on it in Leiden a year or so back – but really that's not necessary. Money's different. It's more of an *idea* than a thing, if you think about it. I mean, if I was to tell my bank to send your bank a million dollars, they wouldn't actually load a thick wodge of paper into an armoured van, they'd just type in a number and hit Send. Well, then. If you can do that between the Seychelles and London, why not between this London and another exactly-identical-except-for-one-tiny-detail London occupying the same point in space/time but a couple of degrees apart in the D axis?"

"Why indeed, George? My God, is that the time?"

"And then," George said, "the fun really starts. I could buy up trillions of dollars of toxic assets *here*, send them over *there*, turn them into valuable assets *there* and bring them back *here* where they'd be worth trillions and *trillions* of dollars, which I could then use to buy even more of the toxic stuff at a cent on the dollar face value, to ship over *there* – and so it goes on. Brilliant. And so very, very simple."

Maurice frowned. "George."

"Mm?"

He'd have to choose his words. "Wouldn't that have the effect of vastly hyperinflating the economy over *here*, while infecting the economy over *there* with the same ghastly problems we've had over *here* and which they over *there* managed to avoid?"

George beamed at him. "Exactly," he said. "Which means there'd then be a whole world of toxic assets in *that* universe that I could buy for peanuts and then sell on in *another* universe – there's an infinite number of them, remember – and so on and so on, for *ever*." He paused and frowned. "Something's bothering you," he said.

"A bit."

"Go on."

"Well," Maurice said, "not wanting to seem like a wet blanket or anything, but wouldn't you be visiting untold misery on billions and billions of innocent people?"

George shrugged. "I guess," he said. "But think about it, will you? In all these universes, circa 2006, in each and every one of them, the US president would still be George Bush and the UK prime minister would be Tony Blair. They're going to come to a bad end somehow or other, on that you can rely. Quite likely, most of them are going to get blown to tiny bits when the kind men in white coats aren't in time to stop George and Tony dropping an atom bomb on Tehran. So really, it's as broad as it's long, isn't it?"

A not implausible argument, Maurice had to confess. Even so. "George," Maurice said gently, "I don't think you can do that."

"Not right now, certainly," George said, with a shake of his head. "But we're close, and getting closer. If only we could fix that stable interface, we'd be laughing."

After the horse had bolted, presumably. "Some of us, George."

George didn't seem to hear that. "There was a guy called

Pieter van Goyen," he said. "Professor at the University of Leiden. They do say he was pretty close at one point, just before he vanished. That was shortly after the Very Very Large Hadron Collider blew up. You remember that?"

"Vaguely."

"Well, Van Goyen was key. Not just key, but *key* key. What I wouldn't give for an hour alone with his notes. But they seem to have disappeared at the same time he did. Bummer."

"A tragedy." Maurice stood up. "George, it was very good of you to see me and incredibly kind of you to lend me all that money, which I'll repay if it's the last thing I do, but I've got to go now, before I feel compelled to kill you for the sake of humanity. Cheers, George."

But George was lost somewhere in his train of thought, which had wandered into a siding somewhere far away and gone to sleep. "Yes, right, so long, Maurice. I'll give Steve your best when I see her next."

"Um, George."

"Mm?"

"How do I get out of here?"

George looked up at him and grinned. "Jermaine," he said, "show Mr Katz out."

It was wonderful to be out in the fresh air again, like being reborn, but he couldn't enjoy it properly. As he wandered aimlessly down the street, his brain was buzzing with far more traffic than it could comfortably handle.

Stephanie's OK. Thank God. Stephanie and *George*. The *bitch*.

He went to the bank and paid in George's cheque, before he could change his mind. And why not, he told himself; I've also taken money from the UK government, and they've done some pretty appalling things over the years. And now at least I won't have to move out of the flat, and I can—

What, exactly? The futile quest for Stephanie had preoccupied him for so long that he couldn't really come to terms with it being over; take that out of his life, and what was left? Also, somehow or other, he'd got into the habit of thinking that once he found her (rescued her, in his imagination), inevitably thereafter they'd be – well, you know, together somehow; not necessarily in a stereotypical Hollywood romantic sense, but, well, *something*. But apparently not. Instead, she's knocking off that unspeakable bastard George – how could she? That's just *gross*. You think you know people, and then—

George and Stephanie. Multiverse theory. Somewhere, every possibility, however weird and hideously bizarre, is real. But not that one, surely.

No more weird and hideously bizarre than a dragon in his bedroom. No, belay that; *much* weirder, *vastly* more disturbing and unnatural. Dragons and self-levitating doughnuts and prophetic women on the Underground and Mr Fisher-King – that was all just *stuff*, which he could just about ignore and put out of his mind. Extreme violation of the fundamental laws of human nature was something completely different. Stephanie had always hated George; well, they all had, back when they were fifteen and the world had been so much easier. But strange things do happen to people as time passes – Kieran and Shawna, for crying out loud; now that had to be multiverse theory, because nothing else could possibly explain it – and when you came to think of it, if you overlooked the arrogance and the self-centredness and the pure evil and so forth, George was not such a bad catch, from a purely materialistic point of view – you couldn't blame a girl for being tempted. Well, yes you could; in fact there'd be something seriously wrong with you if you didn't, but things

like that happen: love is brittle and transitory, but money ...
It's an idea, George had said, rather than a thing. Quite a nice
idea, actually. You could put up with an awful lot, for an idea
like that.

Some people could. Most people. 99.999 per cent of
people. But not Stephanie.

Consider (he told himself, as he filed through the ticket
barrier and down onto the platform) Stephanie, just for a
moment. Here's someone who could've been – well, not anything, let's be realistic, but *something* – but who instead chose
the army: heavy boots, clothes designed to make you look
like woodland, mud, boredom, rules, a system designed to
humiliate everyone and suppress all traces of individuality,
getting yelled at, getting shot at, getting stuck behind a desk
doing a job that made his own typical day at work (when he'd
had typical days at work; he could remember back that far,
just about) look like a garden of entrancing possibilities. A
person who made that choice probably wasn't the sort who
put luxury, ostentation and effete idleness on the top of their
priorities list. So, if she wasn't going out with George because
of his money, then why the hell—?

I don't want to think about it. There, that was that dealt
with. Instead, he thought about being in a position to pay the
rent, which meant sleeping in his own bed, which meant some
recognisable form of life would go on, for a while, until something came along and made everything all right.

Well, of course.

The train (he couldn't remember boarding it, but presumably he must've done) stopped sharply, shaking him out of his
deep well of thought. He looked up; nothing but dark tunnel
wall outside the window, with the usual heavy insulated cables
mounted on brackets. He turned his head and looked round
the compartment. It was empty, apart from a man and a girl,
enveloped in each other like a bad car wreck, at the far end.

He turned away quickly. They might have seen him, but that was rather unlikely, given how preoccupied they were with each other. Well, he thought, good luck to them. True love, or the illusion thereof; that reminded him of George and Stephanie, and he winced. Stupid, of course; he hadn't been in love with Stephanie. In fact, the very idea was absurd and mildly grotesque, because you can't be in love with your oldest friend. True, there had been that awkward, interrupted kiss round the back of the science block, but that had been enough to prove beyond question that there was no chemistry between them whatsoever; and then the doughnut had joined them to each other in a way that mere hormones could never hope to achieve.

The train slowly began to move. He really wished he'd brought something to read.

The happy couple were still at it when he stood up to get off. He tried not to look at them, but inadvertently glanced in their direction just as the doors opened. The girl – no, it *couldn't* be.

The doors were closing again. He leapt through them like a startled gazelle, and the train pulled away.

The girl had been Stephanie. No, of course it hadn't, because she was in Greenland, playing happily with razor wire and dreaming of her own true love. Also, it *wasn't* Stephanie, because – Maurice was no great shakes at judging women's ages, but the girl in the train was at least five years younger; same age, roughly, as her partner, who'd been him.

Not quite him. More like Maurice Katz around about his twentieth birthday. Of course, you don't ever recognise yourself, do you? You're so used to seeing the wrong-way-round two-dimensional mirror image of yourself that you simply don't associate the right-way-round 3D real thing with yourself. Also, you can never see it, so you can hardly be expected to recognise it, can you? Then subtract five years, reducing yourself to a time of life when the face and body are still in a state of flux; there's a significant difference in appearance between twenty and twenty-five.

That was her. And me. And has it ever occurred to you how much the London Underground logo looks like a dough-nut? Well, a doughnut with a horizontal line through it – a doughnut kebab. Her. And me. Only not.

No wonder he didn't like the Tube very much. Because of all the dead people, or at the very least, the people from the past, and the future. It's something I ate, he told himself, and that was plausible enough (swan-liver pâté and wind-dried Thomson's gazelle and muffins flavoured with ground-up pearls; maybe George could be explained in terms of his diet). Definitely not her and me, because if we'd ever done *that* on a Tube train, or anywhere for that matter, there was abso-lutely zero chance that it would've slipped his mind. So, unless he'd somehow strayed for a split second into one of George's lunatic alternative universes, it could only have been a straightforward case of mistaken identity. So there.

He went back to the flat. There were no dragons, and it was his for another month. He picked the mail up off the doormat and glanced at it. Junk, junk, junk, junk, official-looking letter, junk. He sat down, turned the letter over in his hands a couple of times, and opened it.

From Carbonec Industries plc:

Dear Mr Katz,

Further to your recent interview, we are pleased to offer you the post of junior administrative assistant. Please contact our Ms Blanchemains on the above number to confirm availability and start date.

Cordially,
D. Nacien
Human Resources

He stared at it for about ten minutes. No, he thought, surely not. Impossible. I mean, I told him the *truth*—

And then he thought, Yes, but presumably so did all the other applicants, God help them, so it was a level playing field, sort of thing, and— Even so, for Maurice Katz to beat two hundred other applicants, the playing field would have to be tilted like the side of a house, and him the only one with crampons. Unbelievable. He frowned, and examined the letterhead carefully, to see if it had been mocked up with Letraset. But it hadn't been, and, anyhow, none of his friends knew he'd been for the interview, so it couldn't be a practical joke.

There was only one thing he could do. He picked up the phone and dialled the number.

"Human Resources," said a nice Irish voice. "Isolda Blanchemains speaking; how can I help you?"

"Um."

"Excuse me?"

"Look," Maurice said wildly, "the thing is, I've just had a letter from you, and you've given me a job."

Slight pause. "How nice for you. You'll like it here."

"Um."

Another slight pause. "Can you give me a hint of some kind? Possibly even your name?"

"What? Oh, right. Maurice Katz."

"Like the musical?"

"Sorry? Oh, I see, no. With a K. And a Z."

"Ah yes, right, here you are. Yes, I can confirm that. Junior admin assistant. Congratulations, by the way."

"Sorry?"

"For getting the job."

"Ah, right, got you. Um yes, that's me."

"Mphm. Did they give you the truth serum?"

"Yes."

"Ghastly, isn't it? Looks as though it turned out OK for you, though. Right, now then. Can you be here tomorrow, nine a.m.?"

"Yes."

"That's all right, then. Go to Reception and ask for Leroy Pecheur; he'll see to you."

"Um."

"Yes?"

"Should I sort of bring anything?"

Pause. "Flowers and chocolates would be nice, but don't feel you have to. Otherwise, no, nothing springs to mind."

"No paperwork or anything."

"Oh, we'll sort all that out when you're settled in. Now remember: nine o'clock, Reception, Leroy Pecheur. Got that? Excellent. Welcome to the family, Maurice. You know, I don't think we've had a Maurice before. Several Mervyns, a Marvin and a Marcus, God help us, but no Maurice."

"Um."

"Don't imagine you'll be Maurice for very long, mind, so you'd better choose which you'd rather be, Morrie or Moz. Sorry, was there something?"

"Um, yes," Maurice said. "Why me?"

"'Scuse me?"

"There were over two hundred applicants," Maurice said. "Why me?"

"Ah." She practically sang the word. Of course, you can sing almost anything if you're Irish. "You'd have to ask Dave, Mr Nacien, about that. Only I wouldn't. All right?"

"Yes. Um. Thank you."

"Bye now."

"Bye."

He put the phone back in a sort of a daze. It'll have to be Morrie, then, he decided. Death before Moz.

Multiverse theory, he thought, putting his feet up on the

sofa and closing his eyes. So, let's see if I've got this straight. Every choice, every occasion on which things could go one way or another, no matter how trivial, is a brave new world, and every road not travelled by is still out there somewhere if only you could find it. A likely story. But scientists believed in it, so it had to be true, or at least trueish. So, according to multiverse theory, there's a universe somewhere in which that could – *would* – have been Stephanie and me, on the train. Extraordinary thought. But if the multiverse is infinite, like George said it is, then somewhere there must also be trains where I'm making out with Linda Evangelista, Meryl Streep, the nice-looking girl from the dry cleaners, her mother and Condaleezza Rice. Maybe all five at once. *Inevitably* all five at once, given the nature of infinity. And if George hasn't gone barking mad and there really could be a way to access these other universes, really and truly, I should've killed the mad bastard while I had the chance. Still, too late now. Or not; in some universe somewhere, presumably I did.

George *was* barking, wasn't he? He had to be. A severe attack of Dr No syndrome, probably caused by spending too much time in those sorts of rooms in those sorts of buildings. But George, however unbearable he might be, had always been thoroughly, almost aggressively rational, and it was a fair bet that he hadn't made all that money by investing in hare-brained schemes. Purely out of curiosity, he Googled multiverse theory, and read for about a quarter of an hour before his brain started to come loose from the sides of his skull. There was a bit about the Dutchman George had mentioned, Professor van Goyen; mostly it was about his weird and unexplained disappearance, and there was a lot of the usual conspiracy guff trying to link his vanishing act with the Very Very Large Hadron Collider debacle. Apparently, Van Goyen wasn't the only researcher with that project who'd gone missing, though Maurice found that rather less mysterious than the authors of the articles did. If I'd just blown up a big chunk of Switzerland, he thought, I might just make myself hard to find too. Verdict: maybe there was something in it and maybe there wasn't, but he was too tired and preoccupied with other stuff to feel inclined to fret about it. In all probability, George would spend a great deal of money, create a brief economic boom in Greenland, then get real, cut his losses and go and bother someone else.

Swan-liver terrine. Yes. Well.

He yawned. A rich, full day, one way and another. And tomorrow – his first day at Carbonec Industries; he never did find out what they actually did there, but no doubt that would become apparent in the fullness of time. Leroy Pecheur – the name rang a faint, faint bell, like a fairy getting its wings in the flat below.

"Hello, I'm Leroy – you must be Maurice."

For a short man, he had a handshake like a junkyard crusher. He also had a huge, bald head, a short grey goatee beard, a voice so deep it seemed to well up out of the ground and a smile that took away the sins of the world. He'd winced as he stood up when Maurice entered the room; when he sat down again, he did so slowly and in stages, carefully folding his legs like a man dismantling delicate machinery. "So you're Maurice Katz," he said. "Welcome aboard."

Earlier that morning, Maurice had reached a decision. No more inarticulate noises. Just say no to Um. Instead, he tried a polite half-smile, which he suspected made him look both feeble-minded and sinister at the same time. Try doing that on purpose and see how far you get.

"Well?" Mr Pecheur said.

There's not saying Um, and there's dumb insolence. "Er," said Maurice. "It's, um, nice to be here."

Mr Pecheur smiled again. "Great to have you on the team. Now, I'd like for you to start here in Location, and then I thought we could try you out in Retrieval, see how you shape up; and then if that goes OK, you might enjoy a spell in Result Processing. How does that sound?"

Well, Maurice thought, it's like this. Sooner or later I'm going to look a complete idiot. Why not do it now, just for once, rather than leave it and leave it? "Excuse me," he said, "but what do you actually *do* here?"

Mr Pecheur blinked. Then he beamed, as if to say, This is my beloved newbie, with whom I am well pleased. "Good question, Grasshopper. *Good* question. Well, let's see. Half the time we do what we think is what we ought to be doing. Of the remaining time, a quarter of it we do what we think they think we ought to be doing, another quarter what we think we ought to have done a month ago, another quarter what we shouldn't be doing but what needs to be done, one eighth what definitely doesn't need doing but what we think'll make us look busy." He paused and drew a breath. "And the last eighth we just sit around. Does that answer your question?"

"No."

Mr Pecheur nodded. "Essentially we're a data storage and retrieval service. It's like your brain. Part of it thinks; the rest of it remembers. Our clients ask us to do the remembering for them, so that they can get on with the thinking. We ... " He grinned happily. "We hardly ever think at all."

"Ah."

"So naturally," Mr Pecheur went on, "as a junior administrative assistant, your role here will be vital to the smooth running of the entire operation. You see, we work on an inverse pyramid hierarchy system."

"Oh."

"Indeed. The difference between us and everybody else is, we're quite open about it."

"Mphm. Um, what *is* a—?"

Mr Pecheur winced again and massaged his knee. "Take a pyramid," he said. "Turn it upside down so it's standing on its point. That's us. The rule is, the further up the pyramid you go – that's away from the point, towards the base – the less your level of activity. In other words, at the very top, you've got a great many people doing nothing at all. A bit lower down the pecking order, you've got a moderate number of people doing very little. Just up from the bottom, you've got a handful of people doing a bit now and then. And at the very bottom, you've got one poor bastard working his butt off." He smiled. "That'll be you."

"Um."

"And of course," Mr Pecheur went on, "the same principle applies to prestige, privileges and remuneration. So, at the top you've got a bunch of folks who do nothing and get paid a fortune, in the middle there's the ones who do a little and get paid a lot, and at the bottom—"

"Yes, I see. Thank you."

"Your job in Location," Mr Pecheur went on, "will be to find all the stuff we've put away somewhere and then forgotten where. In Retrieval, you'll take the stuff you've found and put it somewhere else. Result Processing, you give the stuff to someone else. In due course," he said encouragingly, "if you shape up and all goes well, you'll be doing all three. Meanwhile, I'll be watching you. The executive management subcommittee will be supervising me, the project management assessment team will be overseeing the executive management subcommittee and the board will be keeping an eye on the project management team, just to make sure everyone's doing their job. Nobody watches the board, but so what, they're not particularly interesting. Might as well watch paint dry."

"Um."

Mr Pecheur chuckled. "Maybe you'd like to see your office now."

"That'd be nice, yes."

"Tough." Mr Pecheur shook his head. "You don't have an office. You don't even have a chair. What you do have is the whole of the sub-basement. Inverse pyramid, see?"

"Excuse me?"

"The board members," Mr Pecheur explained, "have huge offices on the top six floors. Project management have large offices on the middle four floors. The executive management subcommittee guys have sensible-size offices on the ground floor. You get a coat-hook behind the sub-basement door. That's the joy of this system: it's completely logical, within its own terms of reference."

"I see," Maurice said. "So, um—"

"And now," Mr Pecheur continued, "I expect you'd like someone to take you down there and show you what to do."

Maurice nodded. "Yes, please."

"Ah." Mr Pecheur smiled sadly. "Wouldn't it be nice if life was like that? Instead, you head on down there, and I'll be along in a day or so to watch you figure it all out for yourself." Suddenly his face lit up, and he laughed. "Of course, I'm exaggerating."

"Ah."

"Yup. It's not really a coat-hook as such; actually it's just a nail. Guy before last who had your job put it there, didn't think to ask anyone first but we thought, what the hell? Actually, it's not a bad idea. You see, Maurice, we encourage innovation and initiative here at Carbonec. Up to a point."

Maurice waited for a moment or so, but Mr Pecheur just beamed at him. "Can I ask—?"

"Sure. Fire away."

"Well," Maurice said, "stuff like hours and lunchtimes and all that. Not that I'm—"

"Oh, that." Mr Pecheur made a broad, generous gesture. "We figure, so long as all the work gets done on time and on budget, you can come and go as you please. At least, that's not strictly company policy, but in practice, we on the upper floors don't get down to the basement much, so if you aren't there, who's going to notice? Just so long as all the work gets done," he added kindly, "and we don't have to do it."

"That's very—"

"Yes."

Maurice waited, but there didn't seem to be any more, so he stood up, said, "Thank you," and headed for the door. A split second before he could apply skin to doorknob, Mr Pecheur said, "Just one more thing."

"Yes?"

"Coffee and doughnuts," Mr Pecheur said. "Ground floor, back office, eleven fifteen *sharp*. OK? You might want to write that down," he added. "So you won't forget."

Maurice turned and looked at him. "Doughnuts?"

"Oh yes."

"Ah," he said.

Mr Pecheur nodded. "See you then," he said. "Don't be late, you hear? Be there, or . . . " He drew a forefinger across his throat. "Stairs to the basement, second on your right."

"Thanks."

"Theo Bernstein, whereabouts of: any ideas? Pet theories, startling new insights?"

"Um, no."

"No problem. May the Inertia be with you."

Maurice opened the door, stepped into the doorway, then for some reason hesitated and looked back. Under Mr

Pecheur's chair, a few inches away from his left heel, was a small pool of blood.

The basement was *huge*. It was also square, and in the exact centre of the ceiling hung a single unshaded forty-watt bulb. Such light as leaked out of it illuminated row upon row of steel shelves, all a uniform eight feet high, on which sat an infinity of cardboard boxes. On each box was a label, hand-written, in tiny semi-legible script.

Someone at some stage had clearly done his best to organise it all. To the near end of the first row of shelves, his anonymous predecessor had Sellotaped the ripped-off end of a cardboard box, on which he'd written, in black marker pen:

STUFF

And on the corresponding point of the second row, another that read:

MORE STUFF

And on the third row:

YET MORE STUFF

And on the fourth:

LOTS MORE STUFF

At which point he'd run out of enthusiasm, cardboard or both. He'd also put two elderly shoe-boxes on the floor close to the doorway, one marked *In*, the other *Out*. *In* was stuffed full of pink, yellow and blue forms. *Out* was empty apart from the screwed-up wrapper of a Snickers bar. The colourful forms in *In* proved on closer examination to be lodging manifests, schedule dockets (filing) and release mandates. All three had lots of little boxes filled with numbers, dates, ticks and signatures, none of which appeared to relate to anything else. There was, of course, a computer terminal. It was tucked away in the far left-hand corner. It had a flex with a plug on the end, but no socket to plug it into. The floor, however, was scrupulously clean.

Maurice found a blue school exercise book on top of the computer. He opened it, but all the pages were blank.

Ah, but Man's reach must exceed Man's grasp, or what's a Heaven for? He spent the rest of the morning walking slowly down the first row, copying whatever he could read from the labels on the boxes into the exercise book. It didn't make a whole lot of sense. One label read *XPK36/7AE/00006445/DDX/NORWICH*; the next said *SANDERSON*; the one after that, *885PP FRAGILE*; the next one was completely illegible and the next one was blank. He called to mind something that Mr Pecheur had said: we encourage innovation and initiative here at Carbonec. He thought about that for a while, then picked a box at random and, using the edge of a coin to cut the packing tape, opened it. It was empty.

Immediately, a siren went off. Maurice jumped three feet in the air, landed awkwardly, scrabbled to his feet and looked round desperately for some kind of Off switch. There didn't seem to be one, and the siren was piercingly loud. He rammed fingers in his ears and thought, Well, I don't think I'd have liked this job anyway. The siren stopped after two minutes. Nobody came. He put the box back where he'd got it from.

The next hour he spent copying down labels, letting his

mind wander, drifting away into that form of boredom that is the true death of Self. Might be nice, he thought, to go to the pictures, if there's anything on, not that he had anyone to go with. He looked up Now Showing on his phone; not promising. *Spiderman XXVIII*, a couple of new romcoms and, of course, the latest *Carrion* offering; not really his cup of tea. BAFTA-nominated director Tuxie Goss had won a string of awards for his uniquely quirky blend of spatterfest zombie horror and traditional British slapstick-and-innuendo comedy, but Maurice wasn't keen. *Carrion Nurse* had been all right, and he'd quite enjoyed *Carrion Camping* and *Carrion Up the Khyber*, but he felt that the franchise had now reached the point where it had nothing left to say. He looked around for a ladder or something so he could get at the boxes on the high shelves, but there wasn't one.

He was just starting to think about an overarching strategy for sneaking out for some lunch when the door flew open. He spun round, and found himself face to face with a tall, dark woman in a severe charcoal-grey suit. She was maybe five years older than him and had the most amazing green eyes.

"You're Maurice Katz."

Everyone said it like they were disappointed. "Yes, that's me."

"You missed coffee and doughnuts."

She was accusing rather than commiserating. Thanks to the label-induced boredom trance he'd forgotten what Mr Pecheur had said, even though the finger-across-the-throat gesture had made quite an impression on him. "I'm sorry," he said. "I was—"

"Hell of a way to make a good impression on your first day, don't you think?"

Her voice was deep, Irish and familiar. "You're the lady I spoke to on the phone," he said without thinking. "Ms—"

"Blanchemains, call me Isolda," she snapped. "You're in

trouble, you are. They're up there waiting for you. Been there half an hour."

She was quite right; hell of a way to make a good impression. "I'm so sorry. I didn't realise—"

"They're busy people, you know. Time is money."

"Yes, right. I'll just—"

She made an exasperated hissing noise, grabbed him by the wrist, twisted his arm neatly and horribly efficiently behind his back and propelled him towards the door. "I'll tell them you got lost looking for the toilet and got yourself trapped in the closed file store. They'll believe that; we lost two trainees in there last year. Just don't expect me to lie for you again, all right?"

"Um, thanks," he said, as she launched him at the stairs. "Do you think I might have my arm back?"

"Not till I get you safely past Reception."

Well, fair enough. "So," she went on, invisible behind him, "what do they call you?"

"Excuse me?"

"Your name, stupid. What are you called? We discussed it on the phone, remember?"

"Maurice."

"Nobody's called Maurice. Is it Morrie, Moz or Mo-Mo? They'll want to know, upstairs."

"Maurice."

She sighed. "Be like that, see if I care." They'd reached the top of the stairs. She let go of his arm. "Now remember," she hissed. "The lock on the file store door jammed. You yelled, I let you out. Capisce?"

Before he could reply, she barged past him, opened a door dead ahead and bundled him through it. "Hello, everyone," she sang out, as he stumbled over the threshold. "Look who's here at last."

There were about forty people in the room, standing

around a long, mirror-polished burr walnut table, on which stood jugs of coffee and plates piled high with doughnuts. The men were all wearing navy-blue chalkstripe suits, and the women were all in charcoal grey, as though the War Between the States was being refought on gender lines. Everyone looked up and stared at him.

"Maurice Katz, everyone," she announced.

There was a fugue-like chorus of greeting; hello, Morrie, how's it going, Moz, pleased to meet you, Mo. At the back of the crowd, Mr Pecheur gave him a scowl that nearly stopped his heart.

"Maurice got himself stuck in the closed file store," Isolda went on, her voice high and brittle. "Just as well I went looking for him, eh?"

Everyone laughed except Mr Pecheur. Mr Nacien surged forward and slapped him on the back. "I got stuck down there, my first week in the job," he said. "We really ought to do something about that lock."

A low rumble of approval, like the distant roar of the sea. A nice middle-aged lady gave him a hug, and a very old man with huge glasses said he'd been caught out by that damned door back in 1957. A thickset man with a grey ponytail and an eyepatch handed him a cup of black coffee and told him to help himself to doughnuts.

"Thanks," he said, "but I—"

The man had gone. Nobody was looking at him anymore; they were chatting to each other, laughing, arguing, and nobody seemed the slightest bit interested in him. He backed carefully away until he reached the wall and looked down at the cup in his hand. The smell of coffee was having its effect on him, but he couldn't drink the stuff without milk, because it gave him a headache. He looked around for a jug, bottle or carton on the table, but there didn't seem to be one. Mr Pecheur was having an animated conversation with Mr

Nacien, while Isolda was standing very close to a tall, blond man, looking up at him and laughing at his jokes. Maurice realised he was the youngest person in the room by at least five years.

Then a bell rang, and everyone stopped talking. There was a flurry of activity as everyone ditched their coffee-cups as though they were red-hot and started filing out of the room. As far as he could tell, not one doughnut had been eaten. He waited till the bottleneck in the doorway had eased, then put his untouched cup down on the table and moved towards the door, determined to be the last to leave. As he hung back, he overheard one important looking man say to another, "Not today, then. Ah well," at which the other man sighed and shook his head. Mr Pecheur, he observed, was limping badly, though nobody seemed unduly concerned. He tried to catch up with him in Reception, but he hobbled into an open lift and was whisked away before Maurice could get within hailing distance.

When he got back to the basement, he found the door blocked by a tall stack of cardboard boxes, about fifty of them. They were all a uniform height, width and length, and almost too heavy to move.

When he woke up the next morning, he quite naturally assumed it had all been a dream. Then he realised that it hadn't, and he was going to be late.

In the event, he got to the office with thirty seconds to spare. There was no one on the front desk, so he scrambled down the stairs to the sub-basement. No boxes this time; instead, taped to the door, was a brown envelope.

He went in, sat down on one of the boxes he'd eventually managed to manhandle through the doorway yesterday afternoon, and opened it. Inside was a Starbucks till receipt. He turned it over and saw, written in green pencil:

679/OOHTY/**66Gj87B9**/Duluth
ABCDEFGHIJKLMNOPQRSTUVWXYZ/1
3933a44-4JGfGT-iop-88Z88Z
**** ***** *** ***** * a
SANDERSON
qwertyuiop_sansipar_WHEEp_20

Well, yes, he thought. And then he looked at it again, and remembered; Sanderson. There had been a box with Sanderson written on it, one of the first he'd come to. He thought about it for a moment, then got up and found the blue exercise book. It was empty. At some point during his absence, someone had come down here and neatly snipped out the pages he'd spent all of yesterday morning filling in.

No matter. He walked down Row One, found the box labelled SANDERSON, went back to where he'd left the piece of paper, checked it just to make sure it did say SANDERSON, went back to the box and looked at it.

Now what?

It was just possible that compiling a permanent, easily accessible register of which box was where contravened some abstruse but perfectly-reasonable-when-you-knew-all-the-circumstances security or confidentiality protocol. He couldn't imagine what it could be, but he was prepared to acknowledge that an entirely rational speech could be made that would end with the sentence, "So you see, you can't just leave a list of all the boxes lying about where anyone could find it; just think what could happen," and that that speech might make sense and be convincing. So, there could be a reason why he shouldn't draw up a list; and since it was inconceivable – no, since it'd be horribly inconvenient to believe that his employers had snuck down here last night and sabotaged his day's work through sheer malice (because then he'd have to resign, because no one could work for people like that) – that they'd rip pages out of his book without a good reason, he had to assume that such a protocol existed, and was a fundamental part of The Rules. Furthermore, he could believe that there could be a reason why knowledge of The Rules was on a need-to-know basis, and that The Rules stated that he didn't need to know. In fact, from his perspective, it was probably better that way. After all, it was how they'd done things at Overthwart & Headlong, and practically every other large organisation he'd received anecdotal evidence about from his friends. The technical term for it, he gathered, was Management, and it must work, or why does everyone do it that way?

He lifted SANDERSON off the shelf. It was surprisingly heavy, and he had to put it down on the floor, adjust his grip and try again. This time he managed to stagger with it to the doorway and squeeze through. He put it down carefully, straightened his much-aggrieved back, lumbered through to where he'd left the scrap of paper and looked at it. A theory was just starting to take shape in his mind; if it was correct, his entire future with Carbonec (which could just be quite good) hung on whether he got the next bit right.

He'd never been much good at learning things by heart – times tables, irregular verbs, lines in school plays – but that was partly because he'd never had a strong enough incentive. In the event, he found he could do it, just about. He spent an hour and a quarter memorising the jumbles of letters and numbers; then he took the scrap of paper, tore it into the tiniest bits he could manage and ate them. They tasted a bit like out-of-date breakfast cereal without milk, a taste he'd had personal experience of at various points in his career. Even so, he made a mental note to buy a box of matches at his earliest opportunity.

He glanced at his watch. 10.45. Forty-five minutes till coffee and doughnuts.

Forty-three minutes later, he'd managed to locate 679/OOHTY/**66Gj87B9**/Duluth, 3933a44-4JGfGT-iop-*88Z88Z* and qwertyuiop_sansipar_WHEEp_20; he'd chosen to do them first because they were the hardest ones to remember. He put the boxes next to SANDERSON outside the door, brushed the worst of the dust off his clothes and set off up the stairs to the back office. As he went he looked round as unobtrusively as he could to see if he could spot any CCTV cameras or similar hardware anywhere in the room; he couldn't, but that didn't mean they weren't there.

At least this time he wasn't the last to arrive. He took a position at the furthest end of the room, well away from the doughnuts; they were the only factor in the equation he couldn't as yet account for, and also the one he most mistrusted. He didn't help himself to coffee, just in case, though on balance he reckoned it was probably safe.

After a while, Mr Pecheur detached himself from the throng and hobbled over to him. He smiled.

"Everything OK?" he asked.

Ah, Maurice thought. It's so nice to be right, just for a change. "Fine," he said.

Mr Pecheur gave him a rather eloquent nod of approval and went away, straight to Mr Nacien. They spoke together very briefly, and then Mr Nacien went and talked to someone else, who went and talked to someone else. At this point, Maurice lost sight of who was talking to whom, but he'd seen enough to convince him that his hypothesis had been vindicated. His other eye was firmly on the doughnuts, none of which had been touched.

When the bell went, the room began to empty, as it had done yesterday. He located Mr Pecheur and nipped smartly across to intercept him.

"Hello again," Mr Pecheur said. He was smiling.

"I wonder," Maurice said. "Could you spare me just a second?"

He'd said the right thing. "Of course," Mr Pecheur said. "Come over here, sit down. Have a coffee. And a doughnut."

This time, Maurice poured himself a coffee, and another for Mr Pecheur. He hesitated, then put a doughnut on a small plate, which he laid down on the table in front of Mr Pecheur, who grinned and shook his head. "So," Mr Pecheur said, "how are you settling in?"

"That's what I wanted to ask you."

Nod; and Maurice couldn't help wondering how a perfectly ordinary-sized neck could possibly support such a huge head. "Shoot," said Mr Pecheur. "What do you want to know?"

Maurice lifted his cup to his mouth but didn't actually drink. "I just wondered," he said, "if you could tell me if I've got this straight. You see, I've been trying to figure it out for myself, from first principles, and I *think* I've sort of made sense of most of it. But it'd be nice to have it confirmed. If that's OK, I mean."

Mr Pecheur gave him a long, slow look. "No harm in trying," he said.

"Thanks." Maurice put his cup down and drew a deep breath. "All right, here's my theory. I'd love to know what you think of it."

Then his nerve faltered for a moment; but Mr Pecheur gave him a faint encouraging smile. He took another deep breath and said, "I think it's like this. I think—"

"Let me just stop you there."

Maurice's heart missed a beat. "What? Oh, I—"

"You've got a bit of cobweb," Mr Pecheur said gravely, "on your forehead."

"Ah." Maurice dabbed at his face. "Gone?"

"All gone. Now, you were saying."

"I think," Maurice said, "that what you do here at Carbonec is, you store—"

"We."

"Sorry?"

"What *we* do here at Carbonec," Mr Pecheur said. "Go on."

"What *we*," Maurice said, "do here at Carbonec, we store exceptionally sensitive and confidential records and materials on behalf of wealthy clients prepared to pay very well indeed for guaranteed total security and, um, confidentiality. How am I doing so far?"

Mr Pecheur neither spoke nor moved. Maurice went on, "The total security bit isn't exactly obvious to the naked eye, but I guess that's the point. If the place was surrounded with razor wire and concrete bollards, that'd be a really good way of telling everyone we'd got stuff worth taking a lot of trouble to steal. But that sub-basement's a long way underground; it's pretty warm down there so I'm guessing the walls are fairly thick—"

"Four feet of reinforced concrete," Mr Pecheur said quietly. "Go on."

"There's just the one door," Maurice continued. "It looks ordinary enough, but when I had a good look at it just now – well, it's not wood, but it's too light for steel."

Mr Pecheur folded his hands in his lap. "In 1957," he said, staring over Maurice's shoulder, "there was a meteorite strike in south-western Siberia. The meteorite itself was only about the size of a five-pound frozen chicken, but the crater was just over a mile wide. When they recovered it, they realised it was a completely unknown element." He grinned. "Crazy stuff. Omskium, they called it. Broke all the rules. Lighter than aluminium, but so incredibly, unbelievably dense—" He was silent for a moment, then went on. "Well, they did as you'd expect from the Soviets; hushed it up, squirrelled the rock away somewhere while they tried to figure out if you could make a weapon out of it. It sort of got mislaid when the Soviet Union went down, and nobody's seen it since. People have speculated, though on what grounds I really couldn't say, that if ever anyone were to invent a technology capable of working that stuff without blowing up half a continent, there'd be just about enough of it in the rock to make, say, a standard-sized office door."

"Ah." Maurice wasn't quite sure what to say about that. "Well, anyway, that's the security side of things. The confidentiality side, I'm guessing, is probably even more important, as far as the clients are concerned. I imagine that's our main pitch when we're selling to a client. Complete confidentiality; in fact, our service is so confidential, we tell them that even we don't know what we've got – so, if MI5 or the CIA or the White Fish Authority come round with a subpoena and a lie-detector machine, we can say, No, we have no knowledge of any such deposit, and get away with it. Which is why," he added with an apologetic look, "there can't be anything like an index, or file cards, or a register. Sorry about that. I hadn't realised."

If the corner of Mr Pecheur's mouth twitched upwards at this point, it can only have been by a few fractions of an inch. Probably it didn't, and Maurice was imagining it. "Sorry about what?"

For the first time since he'd got the job, Maurice felt like he was starting to get the hang of things. "Total confidentiality's all very well," he said, and his voice was just a little bit louder and more confident. "But it must be possible to find and retrieve people's stuff when they need it. So, we have *just one* employee who knows what stuff we've got and where it is; the lowest of the low ... " (Mr Pecheur's mighty head moved up and down just a little bit) " ... so lowly that, naturally, senior management are barely aware of his existence. He memorises everything; only he knows."

Mr Pecheur cleared his throat. "There are excellent precedents for doing it that way," he said. "Take Iceland. Back in the Middle Ages they had the most sophisticated and extensive legal code in Europe. Never wrote a word of it down. One man was elected every few years to learn it all by heart, and if you wanted to know the law about something, you trotted along and asked him and he'd tell you. Apart from him, though, nobody else in the entire country had a fucking clue. And," Mr Pecheur added, "building on that foundation, in time Iceland grew to be one of the most adventurous and innovative players the world of investment banking has ever seen. So there you are."

"Quite," Maurice said. "Then, as soon as this employee's grasp of what there is and where it's at reaches a point where it poses a confidentiality threat, we promote him to a supervisory or executive grade and hire another minimum-wage oik to replace him. That's why we've got forty-odd people who do next to nothing. Each time we replace him, everyone else gets promoted a grade, with a corresponding wage hike." Mr Pecheur nodded again. "Since we can charge what we like for our hyper-confidential service, we just stick the fees up a bit to cover it, and everybody's fine."

Mr Pecheur was smiling. "And Dave Nacien reckoned you were stupid," he said. "Just goes to show, nobody's right all the time. Though you do do an excellent impression of an idiot. Protective mimicry, I guess."

Maurice was on a roll now. "Morning coffee is essential because that's when we do all the supervision, which is an essential and much-hyped part of our service. So you ask me 'Is everything OK?', and I nod. Mr Nacien asks you, 'Everything OK?' and you nod. And so on, up to board and CEO level, and nobody has to ask questions that could actually yield meaningful answers and thereby jeopardise confidentiality. This didn't happen yesterday, of course, because I'd only just started."

Mr Pecheur clapped his hands together slowly three times. "That's good," he said. "You know what, it took me six weeks before I figured that out, when I was your age. And I'm *smart*."

"Thank you. Truth serum—"

"Yes, thank you. I can see you've got the gist of it."

"Truth serum," Maurice said, politely but firmly, "is to weed out industrial espionage spies sent in to infiltrate Carbonec, which happens a lot because we've got such an amazing reputation, so other players in the industry are desperate to find out what we're actually doing here. When I went for my interview, all the other applicants turned out to be spies, so I got the job." He stopped, and looked at Mr Pecheur, whose face had hardened since he'd last looked at it. "Or not," he added quickly. "Maybe I'm completely wrong about that."

Slowly and deliberately, Mr Pecheur lifted his coffee-cup to his lips and drank two swallows. "The thing about truth serum is," he said, "after a while – twenty years, maybe, something like that – you can grow immune to its effects. Not everyone," he added with a sly smile, "just some people. It's a matter of individual biochemistry. Of course," he added pleasantly, "not all of us know that. Good if it was to stay that way."

Maurice looked down at his own untouched coffee. "Actually," he said, "I'm more of a tea drinker myself. Do you think it'd be all right if—?"

"No."

"Right. Thanks. I'm guessing that sugar counteracts the effect or something."

"Yes."

"Ah."

"Also," Mr Pecheur went on, "it turns the mixture into a hypervolatile high explosive, something like nitroglycerine but a tad more frisky, if you get my meaning. We don't encourage it."

"No, of course not." Maurice stood up quickly. "Well, I'd better be getting on with some work," he said. "Lots to do, time is money and all that. Thank you ever so much for—"

"Yes."

It took him three days, working through his lunch hour, to find the last two boxes, during which time other boxes arrived and two more notes were Sellotaped to the Omskium door. He didn't mind. For the first time in his working life, he felt motivated, empowered, corporate, happy. This surprised him. The work itself was ninety-nine parts futile tedium and one part exhausting manual labour, the sub-basement was dark and gloomy and the only time he saw other human beings was the morning coffee ritual, on which occasions he stayed as far away from the others as he could manage and only spoke, reluctantly, when spoken to. No matter. Outweighing such minor irritants was the glorious sense of wellbeing that came from knowing what was going on, combined with the moderate certainty that he was doing tolerably well and his job was reasonably secure. True, he spent a great deal of time walking up and down the rows of shelves not finding what he was looking for; but so what? It wasn't his time he was wasting, it was Carbonec's, and there was nobody competing with him, checking to see if he was thirty seconds late coming in or trying to make him look stupid in front of the boss. If he'd wanted to, he could've strolled out at twelve noon and not come back in till three, or spent an entire afternoon sitting with his feet up playing games on his LoganBerry. Oddly enough, he didn't want to do either. Knowing he could was far more rewarding than actually doing it, and meanwhile there were boxes to be found, and forty-odd bone-idle colleagues relying on him to keep the wheels of industry turning. One day, he told himself, one day in the not-too-distant future, so long as I play my cards right and keep my nose clean and to the grindstone, I'll be one of the bone-idle supervisors, and won't that be nice?

When he woke up on Saturday morning, he felt a strange sense of disappointment. He wasn't going in to work today. Oh.

Crazy. After all, work is the price you have to pay for fun, and fun only happens in the evenings and at weekends. Nevertheless. Far away, across the rooftops of London, he thought he could just hear the faint voices of the boxes calling him; come and sort us, and we will take you to the promised land. Well, the promised floor, anyhow: three storeys up, where the work stopped and the offices began.

Get a grip, he ordered himself. Today is *Saturday*, when I can laze around all day, do things at my own pace, without being at someone's beck and call every moment; when I can watch TV or read a book, go out for a coffee or a nose round the shops. More realistically, based on my usual behaviour patterns, I can laze around contemplating reading, going out or nosing round shops but never actually get round to any of it. And then he thought, Yes, but that's basically what I do all week, and I get paid for it.

In which case (he tipped himself out of bed, like someone emptying a trash can) on Saturday I ought to get out and *do* something. Define something. Rock climbing. White-water rafting. Paragliding. Fair enough, none of the above. But how about cultural activities: galleries, theatre, gigs, the whole vibrant scene that's going on all around me? Quite. Even so. There's got to be more to life than sloughing around in a dressing gown all day. I could, um . . . I could improve myself: take up something, join a society—

He winced. There are two categories of people who join things: nerds, and men who want to meet girls. He toyed with the possibility that he might be both, then decided not to think about it anymore. Instead, he'd, let's see, he'd, well now, he'd—

Go out. That had to be the starting point, because nothing that could happen in this flat could possibly broaden his mind, enrich his soul or electrify him with fascinating new possibilities. In fact, he was getting heartily sick of his little home. Dragons materialised inside it, valued friends vanished from it, and the rest of the time he sat around in it slowly devolving into an amoeba. Out.

He asked himself, as he walked down the street, if this sudden access of vitality was connected with his new job, and came to the surprised and reluctant conclusion that it had to be. It was, by any objective criteria, a rotten job, though actually the money (which he'd forgotten to ask about at the interview, for some reason, but which had come as a pleasant surprise when a packet of paperwork had appeared on the sub-basement floor on Friday morning) was rather more than he'd been getting at Overthwarts, and the holiday was a week more. It wasn't about the money, though, not even the joyful thought that before long he'd be able to pay George what he owed him and thereby redeem the mortgage on his soul. It was (he stopped dead, because this wasn't something you could think about and walk at the same time) the most strange and unaccountable sense of belonging, of being in the right place. I once was lost and now I'm found.

Crazy as a passionfruit-and-mynah-bird milkshake, but there you go.

He'd reached the end of the street. That way, the convenience store and the DVD rental. This way, the Tube station, gateway to the world. He hesitated.

"Excuse me."

He looked round. There were two women facing him. His first thought was, either market researchers or Jehovah's Witnesses; in either of which cases, his suddenly woken glands told him, yes I'll buy it, or yes, I want to be saved. But they had no clipboards or pamphlets. One of them was about thirty-five, dark, classically beautiful in a severe grey suit; the other was probably just too young for him, in T-shirt and jeans, with a cascading waterfall of white-blonde hair that made him wish he was a salmon.

"Um?"

"Allow us to introduce ourselves," the dark one said. "I'm Duty, and this is my colleague, Fun."

"Hi there," said Fun, with a smile and a tiny fluttering wave of her fingers.

"Though you don't know it," said Duty, "you're about to make a choice that will fundamentally affect not just your life, but the lives of untold millions. So, before you commit yourself one way or the other, we thought we'd like to take this opportunity, assuming you can spare us a minute or so of your time, to discuss the issues with you and maybe offer a few thoughts which might guide you in making your momentous decision. Would that be all right, do you think?"

There was only one thing he could say. He said it. "Um."

Fun was looping a strand of hair round her index finger. He found it ever so difficult not to look. "Of course," Duty went on (and he was so preoccupied with not watching what Fun was doing with her hair that he realised he'd been staring at Duty's awesomely perfect mouth for three long

seconds) "we are precluded from applying any undue influ-
ence whatsoever. We're not here to lobby for our particular
viewpoints, simply to explain and advise. I trust that's perfectly clear."

"Oh yes."

Duty's eyes were a sort of deep, glowing green. You could
die of eyes like that and probably not even notice. "Specifically," she said, "it's incumbent on us to point out that
although we appear to you as attractive, urgently desirable
human women we are, in fact, abstract concepts entirely
devoid of physical substance; therefore, you should entirely
disregard any physiological responses that our apparent
appearance may trigger in you. If you wish, you can close
your eyes at this point."

"Um, no, that's fine."

"Very well." Duty paused and glanced at Fun, who
nodded. "With my colleague's permission, I'll go first. Duty,
Mr Katz. May I ask you what you understand by the concept
of Duty?"

"Um."

"I invite you to consider—" She'd lowered her voice just a
little, and Maurice could feel a buzz running the length of his
nervous system. If he'd been a wine glass at this point, he'd
most likely have shattered. "Excuse me, are you listening to
me?"

"What? Oh, right. Yes."

"You appear to be in some discomfort."

"No, I'm fine, really."

"Very well. I invite you to consider the purpose of your
existence. Are you here simply to exist, like lichen or seaweed
or plankton, to feed, aimlessly reproduce, ultimately take your
place in the food chain as prey to some higher species? I ask
you, Mr Katz, are you merely Darwin's cannon fodder, or is
there possibly more to you than that?"

"Um."

"If so," she went on, and for an abstract concept she had the most amazing scent; like vanilla-flavoured woodsmoke mixed with brandy. "If so, if you are to elevate yourself above the meaninglessness of the genome, the template, the helical bars of the prison of your DNA, it can only be through the selfless, implacable pursuit of me. Of Duty," she clarified, as Maurice nearly swallowed his Adam's apple. "You must embrace me, submit to me, allow yourself to be consumed by and utterly joined with me in a union that transcends the flesh and the individual will. Only through me can you break free from the fetters of Schopenhauerian nihilism. You do want that," she whispered hoarsely, "don't you?"

"Oh yes."

"Very well. In that case, you must be sure to do *the right thing*. Do you understand?"

"Um. No."

She frowned at him, and the thought he might have offended or disappointed her made him want to cry. "You do know the difference between right and wrong, don't you?"

"Yes. Well. I think so."

"There you are, then. Do the right thing." She gave him a look you could've smelted iron ore in. "You wouldn't ever knowingly do the wrong thing, would you?"

"Me? Gosh, no."

"You are, of course, firmly and implacably opposed to evil in any form."

"You bet."

"You agree that the sole justification for your existence is to improve the lot of your fellow human beings and make the world a better place."

"Sure." A tiny thought struck him. "Although—"

"Altruism in its highest form is, and should be, your sole motivating—"

"Du," Fun interrupted quietly, "I think he wants to say something."

"What?" Duty frowned. "Oh, very well. What is it?"

Maurice blushed. "I'm very sorry," he said. "Only, it did just occur to me, when you were saying all that—"

"Well?"

"It's just," Maurice gabbled, "if all everyone did was spend their time doing things to help other people—"

"Yes?"

He shook his head. "Well, that's silly, isn't it? I mean, it's a bit like everyone doing each other's ironing. I spend all my life doing things for you, you spend all your life doing things for her, she spends her life doing things for me—" At that point, Fun giggled, which made him lose his thread completely for a moment. "What I mean is, wouldn't it all be much simpler and less *messy* if we spent at least some of the time doing things for ourselves, so other people wouldn't have to do them for us? Just a thought," he added quickly, as Duty gave him a terrible look. "Stupid, really, I shouldn't have mentioned it."

Duty waited about three seconds, then said, "Have you finished?"

"Um, yes."

"Good, I'll continue with what I was saying. Duty," she said, lifting her head magnificently, "is the meaning of the Earth. If, as has been argued in some quarters, in the beginning was the Word, that word was Duty, and I put it to you that it's inconceivable that, once you've been made aware of this, you could possibly choose any other path. Well?"

Maurice looked furtively to either side. To the right, the kerb. To the left, Alphamax Heel Bar & Shoe Repairs, Keys Cut. "Um," he said.

"You keep saying that."

"Sorry."

She clicked her tongue. The sound made him think of a

firing squad disengaging their safety catches at dawn on a cold winter morning. "Well," she said, "that's my pitch. I imagine my colleague would now like to say a few words."

Fun smiled. "A few," she said. "Not nearly as many as you."

"Get on with it, will you?"

Fun's eyes – pale blue, they reminded him of Stephanie – were fixed on him. "It's pretty simple, don't you think?" she said. "I mean, don't you want to have me? Fun, I mean? All the fun in the world, for ever and ever. If you think you can handle it."

"And if you say Um," Duty interrupted, "I'll personally brain you."

"Can't, you're an abstract concept," purred Fun.

"It's an expression," Duty snapped. "Well? Is that it?"

"I think that's all I've got to say," Fun said quietly. "Less is more, right?"

Maurice's mouth was open and moving; he managed to choke back Um at the very last moment. Duty might be an abstract concept, but he wasn't taking any chances.

"He can say Um if he wants to," Fun said. "That's the trouble with you; you're always bossing people around."

"People don't always know what's good for them," Duty said firmly. "I do."

"Whatever." Fun was smiling again. "Well? Made your mind up yet?"

Maurice thought for a moment. "This choice."

"Yes?"

"It's whether I turn right or left at the end of the road, isn't it?"

Duty frowned. "That information is classified," she said, but Fun just nodded.

"Fine," Maurice said. "So what'd happen if I turned right round and went back the way I just came?"

"You'd die," Fun said sadly.

"Excuse me?"

"She's quite right," Duty said. "A car would run you over, or a wall would collapse on you, or you'd be killed by an exploding gas main. Sorry, but that's how it's been set up."

Maurice had gone quite pale. "Oh."

"It's important, you see," Fun said. "You really do have to choose."

"Right or left?"

"That's it."

"OK. So, which is which?"

Neither of them spoke, though Fun blew him a little kiss.

"Oh come on," Maurice said. "How can I choose if I don't know?"

Duty looked mildly embarrassed. "Heroic intuition," she said. "As a hero, your instincts should – will you stop that *right now*?"

Fun was nudging her head sideways, pointing left. Duty closed her eyes and sighed. "You do realise," she said, "you may have ruined this whole exercise? In which case, the destiny of millions yet unborn—"

"I never said a word."

"Yes, but you—"

"I had a crick in my neck," Fun protested. "From standing here while you made your very long speech. I was just wiggling it a bit."

"I must ask you," Duty said grimly, "to disregard any apparent attempts by my colleague to suggest or imply anything, and make your choice on the basis of your instinctive reaction *prior to* her entirely misguided and ill-advised fit of wiggling. Otherwise – Stop! Where do you think you're going?"

Maurice had sprung sideways, in through the door of Alphamax Heel Bar & Shoe Repairs, Keys Cut. He turned and looked back. Through the glass he could see the two of them, arguing with each other. Then, quite abruptly, they vanished.

He breathed a long sigh of relief. Just for once, he told himself, I've outsmarted the weirdness. They thought they could force me to play along, but—

"But instead," said the old man behind the counter, "upon being asked to choose between duty and pleasure, you instead opted to follow the path of budget footwear maintenance. You know what? I wouldn't want to be you when them upstairs catch up with you."

Maurice winced and turned slowly to face him. "Wouldn't want to be *in my shoes*, you mean."

"Exactly." The man smiled evilly. "But when that dreadful moment comes," he said brightly, "you can at least face it with a brand new heel and crisply stitched seams. Now get out of here while you're still able."

"And if I don't?"

"This building will collapse, and we'll be squashed so flat, they'll take us down the morgue in envelopes."

Fair enough. "Sorry," Maurice said, and left the shop.

So: right or left? Microwave pizza and a DVD, or adventure and infinite possibilities? Put like that, there could only be one choice.

In the end, he opted for a deep-pan Meat Feast with extra salami, though he was sorely tempted by a slightly out-of-date Margarita reduced to just 79 pence. But his heroic intuition seemed to be telling him that this was a situation that called for a heavy protein boost, where mere mozzarella and tomatoes just weren't going to get the job done. The DVD dilemma was rather more broadly based; in the end, he went with *Harry Potter 8*, on the grounds that any film based on the premise that magic is only real in an escapist fantasy world was all right by him. In any event, it was just something to have on while he did the ironing.

Bearing in mind what Duty had said about the perils of retracing his steps, he went home the long way, just in case the supernatural bureaucracy that handled these things was as efficient as its real-life counterpart. He was just about to cross the road when a motorcade of armoured Land Rovers with motorcycle outriders roared across his path. He stopped to let them go by, and realised that they were escorting a single cyclist, in T-shirt, spandex shorts and an Imperial Storm-trooper crash helmet. Also, they'd slowed down and stopped. The cyclist climbed off his bike, lifted his helmet onto the back of his head and yelled, "Maurice!"

He blinked. "George?"

"There you are." He handed the bike to a black-clad para-military and stalked over to join Maurice on the pavement. "Where the hell have you been? Why aren't you answering your phone?"

"It hasn't rung."

"What? Oh hell." He snapped his fingers, and a stormtrooper handed him a latest-model LoganBerry Vector. He held it out and pointed to a string of figures on the screen. "That's your number, isn't it?"

"No."

"Oh." George frowned. "But that's the number I've been ringing."

"Yes, well—"

"It's the number they've got in your MoD file."

Maurice made an impromptu gurgling noise. "There's a file on me at the Ministry of *Defence*?"

"Sure, why not? Oh well, mystery solved. Pity they couldn't have got a simple thing like a phone number right; it'd have saved me dragging out all this way just to see you."

Maurice was contemplating the motorcade, which was filling twenty-five yards of the road, engines purring softly, like angry lions. It was well known that George bicycled everywhere, because of his carbon footprint. "Um, what did you want to—?"

"Message for you," George said. "From Steve. She's been trying to get hold of you too, but you aren't there during the day."

"No. Well, I wouldn't be. I, um, got a job."

"Congratulations." George slammed him on the back, not quite rupturing his spleen. Maurice jerked convulsively forward, his hand inadvertently brushing his jacket pocket. Thirty security people stiffened, but George signalled that it was OK. "That's brilliant. Well done."

He made it sound like Maurice had just swum the Atlantic. "Thanks," he muttered. "George, what was the—?"

"So, tell me all about it."

"Sorry?"

"The job. What field are you in? Marketing? IT? Manufacturing?"

"Data retrieval."

George nodded sagely. "Good choice," he said. "We're looking for a bigger presence there ourselves. We must talk sometime. What's that you've got there?"

"What?"

"That sort of disc thing."

Maurice looked at him. "It's a frozen pizza."

"Do you actually eat that stuff?" George shook his head sadly. "I didn't think anyone ate that junk anymore."

"I do."

"You should be eating locally sourced, sustainably packaged organic produce. That sort of thing's not just killing you, you know, it's killing the planet." He took hold of the DVD and tilted the box so he could read the title. "Haven't you seen it yet? I caught a preview at the studio with Dan and his people. Of course, it's much darker than the—"

"George," Maurice said patiently. "What was the message?"

"Excuse me?"

"From Stephanie."

"Steve." A traffic jam about a hundred yards long had built up behind the motorcade. Nobody was revving their engines or leaning on the horn. Presumably they thought it must be a foreign president or something. "Right, yes. She wants you to know she's perfectly all right and she'll call you sometime."

"That's it?"

"Mphm." George nodded.

"You came all this way just to—?"

"Got to go," George said, "we're holding up the traffic, and you know how bad that is for emissions. Did you realise that 32 per cent of vehicular carbon is released from stationary vehicles? Always remember, you've got to think green to be green. Take care of yourself, Maurice. Bye."

George got back on his bike and waved his arm, like a cavalry officer signalling the advance. With a roll of thunder like a tropical storm breaking, the motorcade roared into life and surged magnificently away, leaving Maurice standing alone on the kerb, coughing his lungs out in a cloud of diesel fumes.

The hell with it, he thought. Weirdness, then George. I need a drink.

There was an off-licence on the corner. He bought a bottle of lager and walked slowly back to the flat. So much for the great escape.

So; why would Stephanie feel the need to reassure him about her safety and wellbeing after all this time; and why would she route the message through George? He'd noted the point about him not being in during the day, and for all he knew the godforsaken place where Stephanie was playing around with explosives and razor wire might be ten hours ahead or something, so that his evening was the middle of her night. Fine. He couldn't have found that line of reasoning less convincing if he'd read it in a political manifesto. The only possible explanation was—

The hell with it. He couldn't think of one offhand, and he really didn't want to dwell on it. He went home, ate the pizza, drank the beer and slept through the movie.

On Sunday, he cleared up a bit of the mess in the flat, ironed his shirts for the week, polished his shoes and made himself cheese on toast. He filled two black plastic sacks with Styrofoam pizza trays and hamburger boxes, separated his cardboard (think green; George would've approved) and put yesterday's beer bottle on the kitchen windowsill, ready for an expedition to the bottle bank. All this domesticity made him feel uncharacteristically grown up, but it wasn't exactly his idea of having a wild time while he was young enough to enjoy it. Not fun; more like duty. That thought gave him a nasty jolt, and he resolved to spend the rest of the day having fun, if it killed him.

Some kinds of fun you can have on your own, but most of the recognised forms call for the company of others. That gave him pause. Lately, he'd rather got out of the habit of being sociable. The quest for Stephanie had involved talking to people but only at a distance, on the phone or by email. Before that, he'd been staying late at Overthwart & Headlong, to try and save his job. And before that – well. Turning into a bit of a hermit, he told himself; that won't do at all. He called up his address book.

Maybe he'd been out of things a bit too long, or perhaps the changes in his character wrought by his brief time at Carbonec went deeper than he'd realised; he looked at the names of his friends and thought, I'm not sure I want to see any of these people particularly. Nice enough people in their way: Kevin, Darren, Mike, Tony and Liza, Shaz, Baz, Gaz and Maz, the usual suspects, the regular crowd. If he saw them, he'd hear about their lives, talk about telly and football and electronic gadgets; work, of course, they'd all want to tell him how ghastly their jobs were and how well they were doing in spite of it. He carried on down the list until he got to S.

She's perfectly all right and she'll call you sometime.

OK, try this. She's talked to one of the old crowd and heard that he'd been asking around after her. She wants to reassure him, but whenever she's phoned during the day, there's been no reply, and for some reason, maybe to do with combat training and blowing things up, she can't phone in the evenings. So she asks George to pass on the message. George has got the wrong number for him; being a determined, do-it-now, attention-to-detail kind of guy, he leaps on his bike, falls in the 4th Panzer Division, and pops round to deliver the message in person. Well. It could happen like that. Stranger things have been known.

Then why was his intuition – his *heroic* intuition; yes, well, we won't let ourselves get side-tracked with all that right now – why was his gut feeling screaming at him that something was appallingly wrong, and he ought to be out there doing something about it, instead of wasting time *ironing*? Maybe because he couldn't get his head around the idea of George-and-Stephanie; and maybe that was because, deep in the coal-seam of his subconscious, he'd been rather hoping that one day it'd be Maurice-and-Stephanie (though that was, if not denied, then most strenuously not admitted). Or maybe it felt all wrong because it *was* all wrong. Well? Decide.

Multiverse theory; how about this? In a version of reality so bizarrely at variance with normality that Maurice could not only get a job but fit in reasonably well and not mind terribly much going to work every morning, it'd be perfectly reasonable for Stephanie and George to be in love; and, by the same token, for personifications of Fun and Duty to accost him in the street and demand that he make high-level policy decisions affecting the future of the human race. Meanwhile, back in the boring old default reality where two plus two insists on making four, and a coffee cup dropped on a stone floor smashes instead of sprouting wings and flying away, Maurice is still working late every night at Overthwarts, Stephanie would rather be eaten alive by lemmings than go out with George, dragons don't just appear in people's bedrooms, and doughnuts—

Doughnuts don't just float up off the palm of someone's hand.

Screw multiverse theory. He went to switch off his computer, and saw he had mail in his inbox. 5,976 items.

He called them up.

From: Max Bernstein. Subject: HELP!!!. 5,976 copies.

He sighed and deleted the lot, promising himself a new spam filter when the technology budget could run to it. Then he checked to make sure they'd gone. They were still there.

Bloody Microsoft. If he was going to have to go through deleting each one manually, there'd be an extra few pins in his Bill Gates doll later on. He called one up at random and opened it.

Maurice, you clown, I'm still here. Why do you never answer your phone? Why don't you check your voicemail? Why don't you do something instead of just sitting around like a small shelf of sedimentary rock?

You've got to get me out of here, now, and then we've got to find Theo and rescue him. Have you got it yet? If not, why not??? Is this really what passes for heroic conduct in that rathole reality of yours?

Do you have any idea of the lengths I have to go to in order to get a message out to you?

Pull yourself together, man, for crying out loud. I expect to hear from you within the next twenty minutes.

He read it again carefully. Maybe, he told himself, it's a new angle; plausible, since he couldn't help but think that the traditional there's-twenty-billion-dollars-frozen-in-the-First-National-Bank-of-Fasimba-and-I-need-your-help approach was probably not quite as effective as it had once been. On the other hand, explicit references to money seemed to be lacking. Also, he realised, there was no return address. From: Max Bernstein, but no email.

He chose another one and opened it.

Maurice, you're a total disaster. I have to confess, I've never had a particularly high opinion of the human race, but you've got to be the laziest, most stupid, least gormful entity that a misguided Providence ever wasted sentience on. Why don't you get off your bony Anglo backside and get me out of here? It's not even as though it'd inconvenience you terribly much. I mean, I'm not asking you to do anything challenging or liable to stretch your reserves of ingenuity, like blowing your nose.

You must have got it by now. Come on. Please. I'm not sure I can stand much more of this.

He looked at the dates. All the emails had apparently arrived on the same day. He clicked on the one at the top of the list:

All right, Maurice. I give up.

Obviously, for some reason I can't begin to understand, you hate me, or Theo, or both of us so much, you're prepared to leave us stranded for ever, rather than lift a finger to help. So be it. You've made your decision, obviously. I won't be bothering you again.

I don't know how you can live with yourself, though. Two perfect strangers; yes, I can see how someone as selfish and cold-hearted as you are could simply turn a blind eye. But when it comes to someone you grew up with, one of your closest friends – ah well. No point saying any more.

Anyway, it's too late now. They tell me they can only keep this line open another hour or so, and then that's it. I just hope you're

A cold shiver ran down his spine. No address, but what the hell. He clicked on Reply, and a box appeared. He typed:

Hello?

—and hit Send. The little just-wait-there-till-we-can-be-bothered-with-you hourglass flickered for a second or so, and a Reply-sent box came up. He waited.

Someone you grew up with. One of your closest friends. She's perfectly all right and she'll call you sometime.

1 new message. He scrabbled with the mouse and clicked Inbox. There was a bang like a firework and a bright flash of light, the screen went dead and a plume of grey smoke streamed out of the USB ports.

When he reached the sub-basement door on Monday morning, Ms Blanchemains was there waiting for him. She was sitting on the bottom step of the staircase, reading the *Financial Times* and eating a—

"Hello," she said with her mouth full. "Good weekend?"

—Doughnut. "Not particularly," he said. "You?"

She shrugged. "So-so. On the one hand, I split up with my boyfriend – actually I threw him out – and the washing machine exploded. On the other hand, I fixed my car without any help from anyone and I won a hundred pounds in a raffle. What was so bad about yours?"

She'd changed her lipstick colour. "Well, it was dull and my computer's broken down. What can I do for you?"

"Ah, right you are. Can they mend it, do you think?"

"No idea."

"I hope they can. It's always such a pain if you lose all your stuff. I've got everything on mine. If it went wrong, I'd probably cease to exist."

"What was it you wanted, exactly?"

"Of course I back up regularly, like they tell you to, but—"

"Please?"

"What? Oh, yes, right." Her face changed, and suddenly she looked like someone getting ready to put a suffering animal out of its misery. "Here's a list of some stuff they want." She handed him a piece of paper. "Top priority. Urgent."

"Thanks."

"Well." She'd just pushed the plunger of the syringe all the way down, and was watching him for the first tell-tale droop of the eyelids. "Nice talking to you. We haven't really had time to get to know each other, have we?"

"Um."

"So long." She moved past him, then, as quick and neat as an Olympic fencer, she dipped her head sideways and kissed him on the nose. "Bye now," she said, and darted away up the stairs.

Maurice stood perfectly still for five seconds. Then he shrugged and opened the Omskium door.

Inside, the place was total chaos. Boxes had been dragged off the shelves and scattered all over the floor. One section of shelving in MORE STUFF had been ripped away, and the framework was bowed and twisted, like a collapsed suspension bridge. The derelict computer in the corner was a sad heap of broken glass, smashed plastic and exposed circuit boards.

He stared at the mess for a moment or so, then turned and ran up the stairs into Reception. It was deserted, as usual. He realised that he had no idea where anyone worked. He'd been in Mr Nacien's office, once; likewise, Mr Pecheur's. He hadn't paid any attention to where they were; he couldn't even remember which floor they were on (but Carbonec was an inverse pyramid hierarchy, right? So Mr Pecheur would be on the first or second floor. But it was a huge building, and he couldn't very well trek the whole length of every corridor on the first and second floor, knocking on each door he came to. Could he?) He scanned the Reception desk for a bell or a buzzer he could press, but there wasn't anything like that. Effectively, he was as conclusively alone as if he was on a desert island.

Fine, he told himself. Not my fault. Why not just wait till half past eleven, when everybody will be congregated in the back office? Meanwhile, he could go back downstairs and make a start on tidying up the appalling mess—

No, bad idea. What if the police had to be called? Fingerprints, disturbing the evidence. Oh *God*.

Think, he ordered himself. He thought. Then he looked around on the front desk until he found a sheet of Carbonec letterhead, located the company phone number, tapped it into his mobile and waited.

"Hello, Carbonec Group, Elaine speaking, how may I help you?"

"I'd like to speak to Mr Pecheur, please."

"Certainly. Who shall I say is calling, please?"

"Maurice Katz."

He waited. An orchestra played Vivaldi at him, which was nice of them. Then Mr Pecheur's voice, deep as the Mariana Trench. "Maurice?"

"Oh, hello. Um. I'm in Reception."

"That's all right, I'm broad-minded. Be where you like, so long as the work gets done."

"I think you'd better come down here."

Pause. "Why?"

"I really think you ought to come down here right now."

Another pause. "Can't it wait till coffee time?"

"No."

Sigh. "Fine. I'll be there in five minutes."

End of call. He put his phone away and sat down. Did it really take five minutes to get from Mr Pecheur's office to the front desk? Maybe. It was, after all, a pretty huge building—

Quite. And forty-three people worked there, not counting Maurice Katz. Only forty-three, in a place this size. You could fit at least eighty-six good-sized offices in on the ground floor alone.

A reckless urge gripped him, and he went through all eight drawers of the front desk. All empty, apart from four paperclips, a hole punch and a very, very old Cadbury's Creme Egg.

He heard movement behind him and looked round. Mr Pecheur was limping towards him across the front office, trailing one leg, his face screwed up with pain. That would explain the reluctance to come down, of course.

"Well?"

"I'm really sorry to drag you down here," Maurice said. "But I think there's been a break-in. Down in the basement."

Mr Pecheur frowned. "When?"

"I don't know, I only just got here. Well, about ten minutes. The basement door was unlocked."

"Well, it would be. I unlocked it this morning when I got here." He shrugged. "Let's go and take a look," he said.

Mr Pecheur had terrible trouble getting down the stairs; he had to turn sideways and lift his bad leg from one step to the next with his hands. Eventually, they got there and Maurice opened the door. Everything was how he'd left it.

Mr Pecheur looked round. "What makes you think there's been a break-in?"

Maurice looked at him, then pointed out the split boxes, trashed shelving, wrecked computer.

"Oh, that," said Mr Pecheur.

"It wasn't like this when I left on Friday," Maurice said firmly.

Mr Pecheur frowned again. "Mice?" His eye rested on the shelves in MORE STUFF. In one place, the steel struts had been twisted into a corkscrew. "No, maybe not. Is anything missing?"

"I—"

"Well." Mr Pecheur hadn't waited for an answer. "This morning, 8.51 a.m., the door was locked. There's just the one key." He reached in his pocket and produced a tiny gold key, like something off a charm bracelet. "Get this mess cleared up and we'll say no more about it."

"But Mr Pecheur—"

"Leroy. Call me Leroy."

"Shouldn't we *do* something?"

Mr Pecheur shrugged. "Like check all the boxes off against the inventory, you mean?" He smiled. "The door was locked; there's only one key. You know about the door. Tell me how it'd be possible for anything to have been taken out of here."

"Well, I—" Maurice made a hopeless gesture. "I don't know. But—"

"If it's impossible, it's impossible. So, nothing to worry about."

"But the mess," Maurice said. "The damage—"

"Seismic activity," Mr Pecheur said. "A minor earth tremor. Something like that."

"But wouldn't that have damaged the rest of the—?"

"Doesn't seem like it," Mr Pecheur said briskly. "So I guess we can count ourselves lucky, right? I mean, it could've been so much worse. Was there anything else?"

"Well, um, no, that was about it, really. I just—"

"Fine. Carry on. Oh, and did you get that special requisition I sent down? Make sure you get on to that right away. *Top* priority." He paused, then smiled again. "You did right to fetch me down here," he said. "I mean, we need to know if there's something you think is wrong. However slight it may seem."

"Um."

"Well done, Maurice," Mr Pecheur said, as he picked his way up the stairs, like Sir Edmund Hillary in a blizzard. "You're doing a grand job."

Maurice went back through the Omskium door and took another look. Boxes everywhere. He picked one up off the floor. As usual, it was painfully heavy; he'd wondered about that, because the boxes were only cardboard, and you'd have thought they'd have split or torn when you lifted them. He heaved it up onto a shelf, getting his knee under it to achieve the last few inches of lift. The label read *i*. Ah well.

There was, of course, absolutely no way of telling if there were any boxes missing, but at least he felt confident that none of them had been opened. He thought about it some more as he set about restoring some form of order. If someone had broken in here with intent to steal – well, now. If they were just ordinary thieves, surely they'd have tried opening a box or two, just to see if the contents were of any value. But if they'd come to steal something specific . . . he laughed out loud. Bloody good luck to them, finding anything in this lot. Besides, Mr Pecheur's point was hard to ignore. The door hadn't been forced. It was still locked at ten to nine, and there was only one key. True, that left ten minutes unaccounted for, between Mr Pecheur unlocking and his own arrival – ten minutes, in which to find one specific thing in among all those boxes and lug it up the stairs. No, less than ten minutes, because Ms Blanchemains had been waiting for him when he got there, and presumably she hadn't seen anything or anyone, or she'd have mentioned it.

Yes, but seismic activity—

He remembered the list he'd been given. Top priority. He pulled it out, glanced at the five lines of jumbled numbers and letters, did his by-now-well-practised memorising trick, and committed the bit of paper to the flames in the usual way. Then he embarked on stage one of the box-finder's prowl, a manoeuvre he was proud to have developed.

The trick was, he'd found, to stroll slowly and comfortably down the rows of shelves, not really looking at the boxes, letting his peripheral vision do all the work. It was much quicker and less tiring to notice something out of the corner of his eye than painstakingly scan each label head-on. There was probably a sound scientific explanation for this, something to do with the mechanics of the rods and cones, or the electromagnetic communications between the retinal ganglion cells and the orientation-selective receptor fields in the cerebral cortex. Anyhow, it seemed to work, and after a whole week in the job he was too set in his ways to change.

Today, it seemed, was a good day. He found three of the five boxes on the list in just under twenty minutes. The fourth practically jumped out at him a quarter of an hour later. He hauled them down and walked them corner-to-corner across the floor to the door, asking himself (not for the first time) how whoever collected the bloody things managed to get them up the stairs to the ground floor without slipping a disc. That just left the fifth and last: *8896431976N/6428914404W/3947582919W/9012348746W.*

Should be relatively easy to find. It was quite a distinctive shape, which he ought to be able to recognise at quite some distance. He walked up and down two rows. Nothing as yet, but there were plenty of shelves to go. It was bound to be somewhere – *ah!*

There it was: *8896431976N/6428914404W/3947582919W/ 9012348746W.* He scowled at it. He was sure he'd walked past this exact same spot ten minutes ago. He looked hard at the box, which just sat there looking innocent; butter wouldn't melt in its flaps. He carefully counted the digits. Something about them was curiously familiar, but he couldn't think what it could be. But anyway, yes, right box. Excellent. Job—

He froze. There was a noise.

You're imagining things, he told himself, but without any real conviction. There was quite definitely a noise, and it was unmistakably a voice, muffled, far away, shouting, accompanied by the drumming of fists on some hard surface. The question was, was it coming from inside the box, which was impossible but also what his ears were insisting on telling him, or from somewhere else? He looked carefully round the room; maybe someone – the hypothetical breaker-and-enterer, maybe – had got himself buried under a pile of boxes, passed out and had just this minute woken up. That would be more—

Thud thud *thud.* Sound of someone head-butting a wall. Feeling utterly wretched. Maurice knelt down and put his ear to the side of *8896431976N/6428914404W/3947582919W/ 9012348746W.* The voice was saying, quite distinctly, *Mwah-wa-mwa-wa-MWA-wa-wa.* Maurice was no linguist, as his French teacher would cheerfully testify on oath before any tribunal in the world, but he had an idea that that lot translated as, Will you get me OUT of here?

Without turning round, he quickly retreated five long paces. Oh no, he said to himself, not me, not again. Besides, can't open the boxes – against the rules, set that bloody alarm off, more than my job's worth. It could be – he grabbed at the idea like a lifebelt – it could be a management test, to see how obedient he was. They put a tape recorder in the box, and trigger it with a remote. Unsuspecting employee opens the box, and next thing he knows he's standing in line at the Job Centre, disgraced and without references. Or maybe it was just a practical joke, a rite of passage for the new kid, in the grand old tradition of left-handed screwdrivers and universal industrial humour. What it wasn't, what it couldn't be, was a sentient being trapped inside a cardboard box. Honestly. Do I look like I'm that stupid?

Don't answer that. From where he was standing he could still hear it quite clearly; thud-thud, mwa-mwa-MWA. Or it could be one of those reality TV shows, where they extract a few shreds of dubious humour from making an innocent man look like a prune. Any number of explanations, any one of them considerably more plausible than the one he knew, deep in his heart, to be the truth.

"All right," he said wearily. "Hold your water, I'm coming."

He looked round for something to open the box with.

Actually, it was perfectly logical. They don't want you to open the boxes, therefore box-opening equipment is not supplied. He searched his pockets, but the nearest thing he carried to a short, sharp knife was a two-pence coin. The current round of thud-thuds from inside the box was so fierce that the box itself was visibly vibrating. He jumped up and scampered round the room, looking for an improvised scalpel, but there wasn't anything. Even the bits of glass from the scattered computer monitor were too small to get a grip on.

At this point, he suddenly became urgently aware that he needed a pee. "Sorry," he yelled at the box, "I've just got to— Be back in a minute." He raced to the door and scrambled up the stairs to the upper basement, where the toilet was.

There are few moments of clarity more profound than those that follow the emptying of an overcharged bladder. The world slows down. The focus sharpens. The brain comes back online. Huge nebulous difficulties prove, on close, calm examination, to be mere cloud-giants, no big deal. He zipped up his fly, pressed the flush handle and moved away to wash his hands. He heard the cistern sigh and gurgle, cheerful as a highland stream. He turned on the hot-air hand-dryer.

Suddenly, out of the toilet bowl, there reared up a human arm. It was clad in some white, diaphanous fabric, almost certainly samite, and in its long, slim hand it held a shiny letter-opener in the shape of a knightly sword. Three times it brandished the letter-opener, slow and solemn, as the hand-dryer finished its cycle and fell silent.

"Oh come *on*," Maurice pleaded, but it was no good. The hand was still there.

You remember how it was at school, when the teacher said that the whole class would have to stay behind until whoever did this owns up; and slowly, reluctantly, feeling every eye in the room watching you, you raised your hand and said, Please, miss, it was me. Thus Maurice, reaching out and taking the letter-opener. The samite-clad hand let go, quivered for a second or two in silent acknowledgement and sank back into the toilet bowl, which flushed again and then was still.

Maurice looked at the blade in his hand. It was thin and mirror-polished, and on the spine of the blade he could just make out lettering, engraved in an elegant Gothic script.

The X-Calibre Novelty Corpn, Chicopee Falls, Mass.

Brilliant, he thought. And even I can take a hint, when it's rammed so deeply up my bum it comes out through my ear.

He stuffed the X-Calibre in his pocket and slouched back down the stairs to the sub-basement.

The box was still where he'd left it, still making the noises, still shaking. Bracing himself against the wailing of the alarm, he knelt down, pricked the point of the X-Calibre into the brown parcel tape in the exact centre of the main seam, and plunged the blade home.

Nothing happened. No alarm. Oink.

All *right*. With a gentle sawing motion he cut the parcel tape, first up the seam then back down again. The thuds and muffled noises had stopped; *I've killed it*, he thought wildly, and then his nose detected a whiff of stale air, like drains or a neglected public lavatory. He cut the tape on the sides of the flaps, pocketed the X-Calibre and slowly peeled back the flaps.

Nothing continued to happen. No genie, imp or goblin leapt out. As far as he could tell, the box was empty. He sat up and leaned down into it for a closer look.

It was like peering down into a mineshaft, or a very deep well. He shuffled a bit so he could get his head right down inside the box. There was nothing in it, except vintage air and that horrible musty smell. So, it had all been a figment of his imag—

He hadn't seen it at first, because it was wedged way down in the far left-hand corner; but there was something. A box. He stared at it, and, as he did so, it seemed to grow. Not just one box, but a row of boxes. Lots of rows of boxes. Lots and lots and lots—

It reminded him of pictures he'd seen of battery chickens or American prisons: seemingly endless rows of boxes or cells or whatever they were. He could see inside them and there were no bars, so maybe they were glass-fronted, or closed in with invisible forcefields. He was prepared to bet good money they were closed in with *something*.

Looking at them was making his head swim, and he wanted to look away, but he couldn't. There was something there that he was supposed to see; he was convinced of it. He peered harder. There was nothing at all to give any idea of scale or perspective. The boxes could be inches away, or miles. He closed his eyes and opened them again.

In a box a long way away to the right, something moved. It took him a long time to find it. There was a man in the box, a man in a heavy winter overcoat, with a long Tom Baker scarf wrapped three times round his neck. He was sitting on a – well, on a box – and his arms were crossed over his chest, his hands tucked under his armpits for warmth. The man turned his head, as if he'd heard a noise. He was looking straight at Maurice.

Hang on, he thought. Hang on just a minute. Those numbers, the numbers on the box. He jammed his hand in his pocket and fished out the scrap of paper on which he'd jotted down the coordinates from his hypnosis session. *8896431976N/6428914404W/3947582919W/9012348746W.* Bet you anything you like that those Ns stand for North and the Ws mean West. Oh boy.

"Max?" Maurice said.

"What?" The voice was faint but just audible.

"Over here," Maurice called out. "Are you Max?"

"Yes. Who wants to know?"

"I'm Maurice."

"Maurice Katz?"

"That's right."

The man swung round so fast he nearly fell off his box. "You *arsehole*. What took you so long?"

"I'm sorry, I don't—"

"Did you get my emails?" The voice was getting fainter.

"Yes."

"Why the hell didn't you answer them?"

"My computer blew up."

"Was that before or after the dog ate your homework? No, forget it, you're here now. Look, get me out of here. Right now."

"Um."

"What? Speak up, can't you? I can barely hear you." Maurice's neck was killing him. "How do I do it?"

"What?"

"How do I get you out of there?"

"*What?*"

"How do I get you out?"

"Stop *mumbling*, for crying out loud. This is not a public library. You're allowed to raise your voice above a low whisper."

"HOW DO I GET YOU OUT OF THERE?"

"Simple." So faint now, he could only just make out the words. "All you have to do is whamble murble wurble wham."

"*WHAT?*"

"I said, all you have to whumble—" No good. All he could hear was the sound of words, not words themselves; the same noise, in fact, as he'd been hearing before he opened the box. "SAY AGAIN," he bellowed. "PLEASE."

No use. The man and the boxes, the whole thing, seemed to be moving slowly away from him, as though he was a camera panning back. He tried pushing his head even further inside, but that just made the boxes retreat quicker, triggering a burst of vertigo that made him moan out loud.

He heard a noise behind him. Someone was coming.

Without thinking, he pulled his head out of the box and sat up. His head swam, as though he'd been caught by the feet and held upside down. He could feel blood pounding behind his eyeballs. And he remembered—

At the very last moment, as he was just starting to move, he'd caught sight of another box, way out at the far end of a row. He'd only glimpsed it out of the corner of his eye, on the edge of his peripheral vision, the way he'd been training himself to do. He'd seen another inhabited cage, another figure sitting hunched and miserable on a cardboard box. Stephanie.

Footsteps approaching, in the real world. He could barely see straight, but he scrabbled the flaps of the box back into place and pressed down with the palm of his hand to keep them flat. There was a roll of brown parcel tape about the place somewhere, but he had no idea where, and there wasn't time to go looking. He looked round wildly, saw another box, grabbed it and heaved it on top of the box he'd just been inside. That took the last of his strength, and he flopped against the short stack he'd created, holding on to the top box to keep himself from sliding to the ground.

"Hello." Ms Blanchemains appeared in the doorway. "Can I come in?"

"Sure." Maurice waved a hand in vague invitation, then quickly grabbed at the box. "What can I—?"

"Have you found the last – well, you know? For that rush job."

Maurice grinned feebly. "What? Oh, that one. No, not yet."

She frowned. "Well, you'd better hurry up about it. They're getting all sorts of flak upstairs, apparently, and it's bothering them. Apparently, someone's been on the phone to the board. They're not used to being talked to by outsiders." She looked round. "Don't take this the wrong way, but this place is a mess."

He nodded. "I know," he said. "Mr Pecheur thinks it must've been an earthquake or something."

"An earthquake?" She didn't sound convinced. "Well, if that's what he says, he must be right. But it looks just like my room at college, third year." She was peering at box labels. Maurice had a strong feeling she wasn't supposed to do that. "You want a hand?"

"No, really." He grinned idiotically. "Everything's under control."

"You don't say. Under control of what? A poltergeist?"

"Everything's fine, really. In fact, you're seeing it on a good day."

"Apart from the earthquake."

"Apart from that, yes."

She frowned some more, then shrugged gracefully, like a trout slipping through a hole in a keep-net. "Well, it works for some people, I guess. Like, my uncle's office was pretty bad. So much paperwork piled up on the floor, we used to say he was growing his own diamonds, but he always said he knew exactly what was going on and where everything was. And he ran the fourth biggest bank in Ireland, until the crash."

"There you are, then."

She narrowed her eyes. It suited her. Mind you, most predators are beautiful. "You sure you don't want any help? I don't mind."

"It's no—"

"Ah, go on. What's the number?"

"Sorry?"

"The number on the box."

He knew in his bones that that was a bad question. He went slightly cold all over. "I don't think I'm allowed to tell you that, am I?"

He'd been guessing, but for once he'd guessed right. Her face changed just a little; the smile sharpened, the eyes were assessing him carefully and reporting that he wasn't going to be quite such a pushover as originally anticipated. "You know, strictly speaking that's probably true." The smile widened. What a lot of teeth you have, grandmother. "But who the hell's going to know, eh?"

He tried to mirror the smile. "Better not."

"Ah well." The smile was up somewhere around the

melting point of tin, but the eyes were furious. "Suit yourself. I expect you're right. But they want that box found before coffee." She lifted her wrist so he could see her watch. "Ten minutes. Happy hunting."

She left quickly, as if she'd just spotted a big crack in the roof. As soon as he was sure she'd gone (three-inch heels on the concrete stairs; he counted the taps) he pushed away the decoy box and stared down at the violated flaps, where he'd cut the parcel tape.

Ten minutes to get it fixed so no one would know it had been opened, and get it out through the door.

Stephanie's in there.

Stephanie's in this box, somehow, and I've got to send it on in ten minutes. I can't. I must.

He issued a general pull-yourself-together order to all departments. Stephanie couldn't be inside the box, because she was over six feet tall and robustly constructed from quality components. What he'd seen inside the box was either a weirdness-induced vision or the result of bending over with his head down for rather too long. Also, he'd only seen what he'd thought was Stephanie for a fraction of a second, so it could easily be some other impossibly compressed girl whose wellbeing was none of his concern. In any event, for all he knew, the box had been sent for by someone who was going to release her, and the enigmatic and obnoxious Max too most likely, so if he refused to obey the order he'd be screwing everything up and causing endless suffering and misery. And it was more than his job was worth. And his job was worth a *lot*, because of its rarity value.

He saw the roll of parcel tape on the floor a few feet away. He made himself stay perfectly still and quiet for a moment, and listened. No thuds, muffled voices, and the box wasn't shaking. I must've imagined it, he told himself.

He'd always been a bad liar. Never mind. He glanced at his

watch. Make that six minutes. He grabbed the parcel tape and scrabbled for the end, which for the first time in his life came up easily and in one piece. The tape made a screaming noise as it unwound from the roll, but it always did that.

Two minutes later, he stepped back and examined his handiwork. Not bad. You'd hardly know, if you weren't looking. Clearly, he had a natural talent for burying people alive in cardboard boxes. He threw the tape aside, grabbed the sides of the box in a bear-hug and lifted. It was incredibly heavy, and he nearly dropped it, which would've spelled disaster for his toes. But he managed to shift his grip just in time, straightened his back with an enormous effort and staggered to the doorway, nudging the Omskium door with his foot so he could get the box through. Once he was outside, his fingers gave up without having to be told. He stepped back nimbly, and the box thudded to the ground like a falling tree.

Another look at his watch. Coffee time. He was going to have to run. He ran.

They were all there as usual, except for Mr Pecheur. He looked wildly round the room, but there was no sign of him. Instead, Mr Nacien walked up to him, gave him a faint smile and said, "Everything all right down there, is it?"

He nodded. "Where's Mr—?"

"Leroy's not feeling a hundred per cent, I'm afraid. Nothing to worry about," Mr Nacien added soothingly, "he'll be good as new tomorrow, I'm sure. That last box—"

"Ready and waiting. Um, what's wrong with—?"

"Oh, the old trouble." Mr Nacien nodded gracefully and withdrew, and nobody else seemed to want to talk to him.

As soon as he could he left the back office and scampered down the stairs to the sub-basement. The box had gone. So, apparently, had the parcel tape. Also – he couldn't be sure, but he had a feeling that someone had been in there while he was away and put back a load of the displaced boxes on the shelves.

Hardly a criminal offence if they had (and if it was a crime, what would it be? Breach of the mess? Breaking and tidying? Mind you, his mother had been known to do that, and if it wasn't criminal it was certainly offensive). Even so, he didn't like it. Right, then. *What do I do now?*

It was weirdness, he told himself sternly, and we have a clearly defined policy on weirdness. We ignore it completely, because paying attention to it only encourages it. We refuse to recognise it, as if it was an illegal or oppressive regime in a far-away country. In which case, nothing just happened here, and we should get on with tidying up after the earthquake.

Yes, but it was Ste—

No it wasn't.

Yes it was.

No it wasn't. *Physically impossible* (and the first inner voice that so much as whispers 'multiverse theory' is going to get frogmarched to the nearest ear and given a flying lesson). That wasn't Stephanie he'd seen in there, just as the attractive brunette in the smart suit hadn't really been Duty. Just weirdness, that's all. Just another floating doughnut, among so many.

(He thought, *Guess I must've chosen the path of duty after all, because I haven't exactly had much fun since Saturday morning. Instead, I've put my duty to my employers ahead of my personal feelings. That's good, isn't it? Like hell it is.*)

The rest of the day merged with the rest of the week, and drained away into the past like gasoline poured on a flower-bed. He didn't bother getting out of bed at all on Saturday; odd, since he'd barely slept at all that week, and yet didn't feel particularly tired. In fact, he didn't feel anything much. It was as though he was waiting for something, and until it happened, nothing he did could possibly have either value or meaning. On Sunday he got up at 6 a.m., got dressed, sat in his chair more or less motionless until eight o'clock, then went for a walk. He got home shortly after 9 p.m., and couldn't remember where he'd been.

9 a.m. Monday morning. There was an envelope taped to the Omskium door. He opened it, memorised the enclosed list and burned it. Six boxes; he'd found them all by lunchtime. He dragged them out to the foot of the stairs, closed the Omskium door, then tried to figure out where he could hole up and watch the boxes from without being seen.

The ideal place – it could've been put there especially for the purpose – was the basement toilet, the one where the white samite hand had given him the X-Calibre letter-opener. He put the toilet lid down, thought about it, remembered where he'd seen a pile of bricks sitting in a neat stack in his sub-basement (what were they there for? God knows), fetched four of them and piled them on the lid just to be on the safe side. Then he sat on the floor, opened the toilet door just enough so he could see anyone going up or down the stairs, and settled down to wait.

Maurice Katz wasn't one of Nature's passive observers. A cat can spend a whole day watching a mousehole. Sentries presumably find a way of coping with the tedium as they stand outside public buildings. Maurice hadn't been cast in that mould. Under any other circumstances, he'd have given up after ten minutes and found something to do. Not this time. Every time he felt the urge to fidget, even when the pins and needles set in, converting his left leg into an instrument of diabolical torture, he forced himself to keep still and quiet. *It's important*, he told himself, and for once he listened.

It was around four thirty when they came. He heard footsteps, and saw two pairs of feet go past: one pair of steel-toe-capped workboots, size ten; one pair of Adidas trainers. He counted footfalls on the stairs going down to the sub-basement – easy, because the workboots squeaked. He heard a distant grunt and moan, then the feet coming back up, rather more slowly. Now, he thought. He jumped up, winced as the cramp caught him, forbade it to hinder him (amazingly, it worked) and strode out onto the landing.

Coming up the stairs towards him were two enormous boxes. Behind each one, a man. He took position on the top step, legs astride.

"'Scuse me," said a voice from behind the leading box. "Coming through."

"No you're not," Maurice said, in a voice he barely recognised.

The box wavered, then dropped to the ground, as the very old man who'd been holding it lost his grip. Behind him, a very tall, thin young man lowered his box in a rather more controlled way.

"You," Maurice said.

The old man blinked at him through bulletproof-glass-thick spectacle lenses. "Would you mind stepping aside, please, sir? Can't get past, you see, with you stood there."

"It's you," Maurice repeated. "The dragon-remover."

The old man (it was definitely him; once seen, never forgotten) frowned. "Not quite sure I follow, sir. Look, if it's all the same to you—"

"You came round to my place," Maurice said firmly. "You and the half-wit. You took away a dead dragon. Well, you vanished it, anyhow."

The old man nodded. "That's right," he said. "I remember you now, sir. Got to excuse me, terrible memory for faces."

"You kidnapped my friend."

The old man smiled and shook his head. "Not really, sir. Just our little joke. Tradesmen's humour. Not very funny, but it brightens up our lives, you know?"

"You weren't joking," Maurice said. "You meant it."

"Hardly," the old man said. The young man was unwrapping a slice of clingfilm-wrapped fruit cake. "All due respect, sir, but it was just a joke. Now, if you really wouldn't mind getting out of the way, we're on a schedule here."

Maurice glared at him, then sat down on the top step. "No one's going anywhere," he said. "Not until I get some answers."

The old man gave him a very sad look, then nodded. "If you insist," he said. "But keep it short, can't you? We got to get these back to the depot by half five."

"Right," Maurice said (and the young man swallowed the last of the fruit cake, took out his mobile and started texting). "For a start, what are you doing here?"

"Collecting boxes," the old man said. "It's our job."

"No it isn't. You clear up dead dragons."

"Removals and deliveries," the old man said. "Specialising in specialist commodities, which I'm afraid we are not at liberty to discuss. Sorry," he added. "Rules."

"What did you do with my friend?"

The old man blinked at him. "Nothing, sir. Honestly."

"I don't believe you."

The old man just gazed at him, patiently, like a horse.

"Fine," Maurice said. "Where are you taking those boxes?"

"Just down to the depot, sir. Like we always do."

"Where's the depot?"

The young man put his phone away, as if he'd just noticed Maurice was there. For a moment he looked at Maurice, a slow, calculating look, as if he was working out, quite dispassionately, the most ergonomically efficient way of getting rid of him. Then his hand went back in his pocket and produced a Snickers bar, which he ate.

"Not supposed to say, sir, sorry. Confidential."

Maurice tried staring at him, but the old man's glasses seemed to deflect him, like the shields of a starship. "Do all the boxes go there?"

"Yes, sir, that's right."

"Splendid," Maurice said. "Now, tell me where the depot is, and nobody's going to get hurt."

The old man sighed. "Really, sir, you shouldn't be asking that. Not allowed, see. Need-to-know basis."

"I'm asking."

"Please don't. Otherwise, I'll have to get young Arthur here to thump you, and I really don't want to do that."

"Him? He doesn't scare me. Now if I was a sandwich it'd be different, but I'm not. Where's the depot?"

"Oh dear." The old man shook his head sadly. "Art, move the gentleman out of the way, would you? Gently."

The young man stood up – there really was rather a lot of him, far more than was necessary – popped the stub of his Snickers bar in his mouth and edged past the old man, heading up the stairs. Without thinking what he was doing, Maurice stuck his hand in his jacket pocket. His fingers closed around something and he pulled it out. The letter-opener; he must've been carrying it round with him all week without realising.

The young man froze, his eyes wide, his jaws no longer moving. "I've got a—" What had he got? Good question. He paused and rephrased. "I've got this," he said, "and I'm not afraid to use it."

The old man looked worried. "Please be careful with that, sir, if you don't mind. I promised the lad's mother I'd look after him, see. Look, if you wouldn't mind very much putting it away."

What's so terrifying about a cheap pot-metal letter-opener? "No chance," Maurice said. "Not until you tell me where the depot is."

"Really, sir, if you could see your way to not pointing that thing at me." The old man seemed genuinely worried, which Maurice found mildly terrifying. "Excuse me," the old man went on, "but you do know what you've got there, don't you?"

"Yes, of course. Well," Maurice conceded, "not exactly. What is it?"

The old man pursed his lips, then gave him a humourless grin. "Exactly what you want it to be."

What a strange thing to say; but as soon as he'd said it, Maurice got the strangest feeling. He was holding an aluminium-alloy paperknife, yes; but he was also, and simultaneously, holding a sword, a crossbow, a shotgun, a rocket launcher, a fleet of nuclear submarines, a rigorous program of economic sanctions and a neutron blaster. He looked down at his hand. He was holding a paperknife. "Um," he said. "What *is* this?"

"You mean you don't—"

"Obviously not. Well?"

The old man nodded. "What you've got there, sir," he said, "is a constant object. Very sought after," he added eagerly, "very rare. Only about forty of them ever made in the whole of the multiverse, and only four of them was weapons. Of course, with you being a hero and all—"

One word had hooked into his brain and stuck fast. "Multiverse?"

"That's it, sir. Multiverse theory. A constant object stays the same no matter which universe it's in. Well, not the *same*, naturally. But it *retains its identity and function*, see. Like, if it's a door, it works as a door no matter where you are. And if it's a weapon – what I just said about not pointing, sir, if it's all the same to you."

The only thing keeping Maurice from dropping it like a red-hot coal was the thought that if he did that, it might go off. "All right," he said desperately. "I've got a whatever-it-was-you-said . . . "

"Constant object, sir."

"Yes, right, and I'm *still* not afraid to use it. Well, I am, but what the hell. I'm afraid of *everything*, but I manage to cope."

"Course you do," the old man said politely. "That's what true heroism's all about, isn't it? And now if you'd *please* put that thing away—"

Maurice nodded, and put the Thing back in his pocket, but he kept his hand on it. "I'm still threatening you," he explained. "I'm just doing it safely, that's all."

"That's a very responsible attitude, if I may say so. If more heroes was like you, there'd be less bloody stupid accidents, excuse my language, and we wouldn't have all this regulation we're getting in the industry these days. Get him, Art."

The young man could move surprisingly quickly when he wanted to. He was almost quick enough to reach Maurice before he got the letter-opener out of his pocket. But not quite. There was a horrible moment when the young man was rearing up in front of him like a psychotic ent; then there was a dazzling green flash, and the young man slumped and fell down the stairs until he came to rest against the nearest box.

"Oh." The old man was staring at him. "Oh, you shouldn't have done that, Mr Katz, sir. You killed Art."

Maurice gawped at the letter-opener, which wasn't a letter-opener anymore. It was now a grey plastic thing, sort of a cross between a Dymo tape dispenser and a water pistol. It was faintly warm against his skin.

"Um," he said. "Actually, I think it's all right."

"It's *not* all right," the old man wailed. "He's dead; you killed him. That was *very wrong* of you."

"I think it's got different settings," Maurice said anxiously. "Look, you see? This switch thing here."

He pointed with his other hand. There were three posi-
tions: KILL, STUN and ANNOY. The little lever was
opposite the middle one. The old man peered down at it,
took off his glasses, put on a different pair and leaned forward
till his nose was almost touching the plastic. "Stun," he said.
"You set it on stun."

"Well, not— Yes, I did," Maurice corrected. "Naturally,"
he added, "I don't want to hurt anyone. I just want you to tell
me where the depot is."

"He's breathing," the old man said, as the young man let
out a ferocious snore. "Thank God for that. I promised his
mother—"

"The depot," Maurice said, and he clicked the switch audi-
bly (from STUN to ANNOY, but the old man wasn't to know
that). "Take me there. I really do mean it, you know. And you
shouldn't have told him to attack me."

"Oh, he wouldn't have hurt you," the old man said. "He's
completely useless, bless him. Always tripping over his own
feet, for one thing." He straightened up and looked at the
plastic gadget in Maurice's hand. "We did have the not-point-
ing conversation, didn't we?"

The young man groaned and stirred; his right hand lifted
feebly, groped for his pocket and tugged out an individual
pork pie. "He's feeling better," Maurice said, as the young
man stuffed the pie in his mouth and discovered it was still
wrapped in cellophane. "Soon as he's ready to move—"

"Sorry, sir, I can't take you to the depot; it's more than my
job's worth," the old man wailed. "And if I get the sack, so
does Art, and he's not going to find another job any time
soon, not without me to look after him. There's no harm in
him, sir, it's just that he's—"

"Useless."

"That's right, sir." The old man nodded vigorously. "So
please don't ask, sir. Please."

Oh for crying out loud. "All right," Maurice said. "Just tell me where this depot is. And I promise, if I get caught or anything, I won't tell them you told me."

"Promise?"

"Promise."

The old man sighed, glanced down at the young man, who'd half opened his eyes and was checking his phone for messages, and nodded once. "You're a hard man, Mr Katz, very hard. All right, then. You carry on down to the bottom of the road, first left then second right, three hundred yards you come to a T-junction, turn left, follow your nose about two hundred yards, left then sharp right, should bring you out opposite a big grey building; immediately after that you look for a sharp turning on your left, fifty yards then you turn right, then second left, then right again just before you get to DVD World, carry on straight two hundred yards then third left, second right, over the railway bridge – that's the second railway bridge, but if you're at the third railway bridge you've come too far – across that and you come to a big roundabout, take the third exit then carry on for about six hundred yards, then first left, second right, which sort of bends you back on yourself, straight on half a mile past the old tyre factory, under the railway arches, then third left, carry on three hundred yards and there you are. You can't miss it."

"Sorry?" Maurice said.

"You take the first left then the second right— Tell you what," the old man said, pausing for breath, "I'll draw you a map. Got a pen?"

"Um."

"I've got a pen," the old man said, unclipping one from his top pocket. "Now, something to write on." He turned out his pockets and eventually found a crumpled till receipt, which he smoothed out against the wall. "All right, we're here, see—"

The map, when completed, looked rather like Picasso's lost masterpiece, *Still Life With Spaghetti*, reduced to a sixteenth of its true size, but Maurice had the feeling that it was the best he was likely to get. "Thanks," he said, stowing it carefully in his inside pocket. "And look, I'm sorry about the—"

"It's like they say," the old man said. "Might is right, and a polite enquiry backed up with deadly force generally gets you what you want in this life. He's going to have an almighty headache when he comes round, poor kid. Look, he'd hardly touched his cheese and ham slice."

Maurice helped them get the boxes up the stairs to the ground floor. He felt it was the least he could do. Then he went back down to the sub-basement, shut the door and reached in his pocket. The letter-opener-ray-gun was now a small plastic tape measure. He positioned it carefully on a shelf and stared at it for a while, then wrapped his handkerchief tightly around it and put it away.

He spent the rest of the working day mooching around the sub-basement, just in case anyone came down there; they didn't, and at five thirty sharp he left the building with the map in his hand. It took him an hour and a half, and when he got there it was just starting to get dark.

He was standing outside a large, utterly nondescript brick building, the sort you barely see. If you do happen to notice it, your brain tags it as *warehouse* and you forget it instantly; which is odd, because if you believe in all the TV cop shows and thrillers, 97.46 per cent of all murders take place in buildings like that, and 76.19 per cent of people who go inside them come out in a plastic bag.

He made himself look at it carefully, from a tactical

viewpoint. There were big steel sliding doors at the front, high windows he couldn't see anything through, a side door at the top of a flight of stairs, which he guessed might be a fire escape or something. He had no experience whatsoever with buildings like that – no owner's manual, user's guide or *Large Brick Buildings For Dummies*. Presumably, if you had legitimate business there, you went to the big sliding doors, which would be open during normal business hours; if you worked there and wanted to get in or out when the main doors were shut, you went up the stairs to the little door. He could only see the front, of course; there could be all manner of architectural delights, including but not limited to French windows, a portico and a colonnaded cloister out back, but unless he could find a way over the razor-wire fence, he had no way of knowing.

There were lights in two windows; one in the third floor, right-hand side; one roughly central on the fifth. Someone, therefore, was in there, though it could simply be the cleaner. He waited half an hour; no lights went on or off. He had the feeling he wasn't making any significant progress.

I haven't thought this through, he told himself. I haven't got a Plan. I've committed acts of violence and intimidated two innocent strangers to find this place, and now I'm just a member of the public standing on a pavement. Maybe I should go home and get a grip. True, I'm probably under a moral obligation to do something, having possibly seen Stephanie inside a cardboard box that's presumably somewhere inside that great big building, but people like me don't do breaking and entering. In fact, now I come to think of it, I'm not sure what people like me are supposed to do in situations like this. Write to my MP, presumably.

People like you don't kill dragons, or walk around with constant objects in their jacket pockets. That's the point. *You aren't a person like you. You're a—*

He shuddered away the H word. No I'm *not*, he told himself angrily. And suppose, let's just suppose for the sake of argument that I am. In which case, I ought to know about this sort of stuff: how to scale walls and jemmy windows, how to move noiselessly in the dark, how to find one cardboard box in a large warehouse in less than a month. There should've been at least some degree of vocational training, instead of which, I got maths, English, geography and computer studies. And I'm *not* a hero. I'm not even a plucky and determined hobbit. I could get killed trying to break into a place like that. Worse still, I could get *arrested*.

He waited another half hour, then made a mental note of the street name and went home.

The depot didn't show up on Google Street View; the viewer jumped like a frog over the place on the street where he'd stood and stared at it, and squirmed and wriggled when he tried to make it go back. He found it on the satellite view, but there was an impenetrable black shadow masking it, presumably from the office block opposite. When he tried again later, the computer froze. He left it for an hour, came back and switched it off at the mains.

A week later, at the end of the eleven-thirty coffee ceremony, Mr Pecheur caught his eye just as he was about to leave.

"You're wasting your time," he said.

"Excuse me?"

"Not here. This way."

He followed Mr Pecheur down a long corridor to a tiny,

windowless room with one plain wooden table and two plastic chairs. "Sit down."

He sat. Mr Pecheur lowered himself painfully into the other chair, folded his arms and looked at him for a while.

"You're wasting your time," he repeated.

"I'm sorry," Maurice said. "Um—"

Mr Pecheur leaned forward a little. "All right," he said, "I'll go through it with you step by step. What do you do most days, after work?"

"Um."

"No answer required," Mr Pecheur said. "I know exactly what you do. You take a 67 bus to Sarras Road, then walk to Sangreal Street. Then you stand about for between thirty minutes and an hour and a quarter, staring at a brick building." He shook his head. "Give it up," he said. "Find something else to do. Watch TV. Join a male voice choir. Go out and get pathetically drunk. You'll thank me," he added kindly, "in the long run."

Maurice gave him a blank look. "I'm sorry," he said. "But what I do out of office hours—"

"Fine." Mr Pecheur mimed washing his hands. "This is not an official interview. I'm talking to you as one human being to another. Listen to me. There's no point to it. You're barking up the wrong tree. You've got the wrong end of the stick. You're crying over spilt milk, adding two and two and getting five, playing with fire, putting the cart before the horse *and* locking the stable door after the horse has bolted, you can't see the wood for the trees, you've thrown the baby out with the bathwater, you've put the telescope to your blind eye and you're making bricks without straw. Do I make myself clear?"

"No."

"*You're wasting your time.*" Mr Pecheur took a deep breath, then counted to five. "You're seeing a grand mystery where there isn't one. You think there's something going on, and there isn't. Also, you're risking our cast-iron reputation for confidentiality by drawing attention to a particular building you aren't supposed to know about. Oh, and there's been a formal complaint from our shipping contractors. Apparently you intimidated two of their people, causing them psychological trauma. The only reason you haven't been fired is that we don't fire people, ever."

Maurice nodded. "Because I know too much."

Mr Pecheur scowled at him. "Because, believe it or not, we're too soft-hearted. Once, a good many years ago, the firm did give an employee three weeks' notice, but then they decided they were being too harsh and gave him a second chance. That employee was me, by the way, thirty-two years ago. That's why I haven't mentioned any of this to Dave Nacien. I'm running a serious risk, not telling on you."

"Really?"

"Sure. I'm still on probation. So, for my sake if for no other reason, give it up. You've got nothing to gain by it and quite a lot to lose." He smiled. "The goodwill of your employers. Your job. Your mind. There's nothing in there, Maurice. Just a lot of cardboard boxes that are no concern of yours. You do see that, don't you?"

Maurice looked straight at him. For some reason, he wasn't scared a bit. "I understand," he said. "I won't do it anymore. I promise."

Mr Pecheur gave him a crooked smile. "Because you can see the merit of my argument."

"Because it isn't working, so I'll have to try something else." Maurice replied. "But thanks anyway." He stood up, walked to the door, then hesitated and looked back. "What did you do?"

"Excuse me?"

"That nearly got you fired. What did you do?"

Mr Pecheur's face froze. Then, like a grenade exploding, he laughed. "Oh, that," he said. "No big deal. I fell in love."

"Ah."

Mr Pecheur nodded slowly. "With a beautiful girl I saw in a glass ball inside a cardboard box that split open when I dropped it. Shouldn't have looked, should I? Of course, that was way back when. The firm was still in Battersea in those days."

"Um."

"So," Mr Pecheur went on, "I tried and tried and tried not to think about her, but it wasn't any good, so I cut the box open – set off all the alarms, but what the hell – and asked her, How can I get you out of there? Simple, she said, all you need to do is burn down the building." He lifted his head and smiled. "That's why we're not in Battersea anymore."

Maurice stared at him. "And they didn't fire you?"

"Ah well." Mr Pecheur grinned at him. "The boss in those days, Mr Pelles, he felt sorry for me. You see, the roof fell on me, and I got squished up a bit. Also, I kind of got the impression he *understood*; like something of the sort had happened to him once, maybe? In fact … well, I've never asked, because you don't, but I get the impression it's not exactly uncommon, in this line of work. You see something in a box, and for a while you act a little crazy. I think the boxes … " He paused and frowned. "There's something about them, I don't know. Maybe it's what's inside them, or having so many of them crowded together in one place. They do something to your head." A curious look crossed his face, and his manner was unusually intense. "Sometimes the boxes seem to tell you things," he said. "When you're alone with them down there. They tell you things, or suggest things, or they make you think you've seen something. The important thing is, don't believe them. They aren't necessarily telling the truth."

It was a while before Maurice could speak. "So that's why they didn't sack you."

"Partly," Mr Pecheur replied. "Also, the building was insured for four times its value, and they owned the freehold. Luck isn't a wheelbarrow, Maurice; it works better if you don't push it. Stay cool, you hear?"

So he stopped going to Sangreal Street. Instead, he spent the evenings sitting in his chair with the constant object sitting on a shoebox on the table in front of him, looking at it. Sometimes it was a tape measure; other times it was a can-opener or an iPod or a tin of furniture polish; sometimes it was a small pewter statue of a leaping dolphin; for a constant object, it changed shape rather a lot, but never into anything particularly interesting. Just once, when he took his eye off it for a split second, he could've sworn it turned into a dough-nut, but when he turned and looked straight at it, it went back to being a tube of superglue.

One afternoon, while he was searching for a spectacularly elusive box, Ms Blanchemains came by. She'd brought a sealed envelope, another rush job. He took it and went back to his search; it wasn't until he'd found the box he'd been looking for that he realised she was still there.

"Can I help you?" he asked.

She sat down on the box he'd just found and offered him a Polo mint, which he refused. She shrugged, and ate one her-self. "I've been asking myself that question," she replied. "But on balance, probably not." She crunched up the last of the mint and looked at him for a moment, her head slightly on one side, as if trying to see if he was properly aligned with the wall. "You like it here?"

"It's all right."

"All right."

"There's worse places. Overthwart and Headlong, for instance."

She frowned. "They're that import/export firm, aren't they? Very big in coffee."

"I never really figured out what they did. I just kept a computer company. It did all the work; I just ... " He shrugged. "Not quite sure what I did, really. Anyhow, here's much better."

"Mphm. I like it here too. It's good to know you're doing work of real social importance, rather than just stirring the money around."

He had no idea what that was supposed to mean. "Been here long?" he asked.

"Seven years." She looked at the wall for a bit, then asked, "What are you doing here?"

"Excuse me?"

"I'll rephrase that. What is it that you do here?"

"Um." He thought for a moment. "I look for things."

"Ah." She made it sound like he'd said something clever. "So that's your job, is it? Looking for things?"

"I guess so, yes."

"And when there's something you can't find straight away, do you just give up and try and put it out of your mind, or do you keep on looking till you've found it? Come on," she added. "Simple question. No need to show your working or draw a diagram."

"I keep looking."

She stood up. "Is that right?" she said, and left the room.

He thought about what she'd said for the rest of the day. When he got home, he fired up his computer and started doing some research. It was time, he'd decided, to find out a bit about heroes and heroism.

Heroism, he discovered, is really nothing more than a means to an end, a way of getting things done. Your country is infested with monsters? You need a hero. The princess has been abducted by an evil sorcerer? Reach for the Yellow Pages and thumb through the pages beginning with H. Heroism is there to deal with the narrow but significant tranche of issues that lie between the purviews of the environmental health authorities and the military. It's designed to tackle straightforward but strenuous problems, the sort that can be dealt with by young men of superior physique, moderate intelligence and above-average testosterone. You don't send in a hero to clear up an impending catastrophe on the fixed income derivatives market, or grapple with the implications of peak oil. A hero's role is to kill something or find something or retrieve something or get rid of something. In nearly all cases the job could be done some other way, but a hero is cheaper, quicker and more efficient. Heroes are for when you want the cat out of the tree, but without deploying helicopters or cutting the tree down, on a budget not exceeding $49.95.

Heroes, he discovered, were the simple souls recruited to do these rotten but necessary jobs; and the most striking thing about heroes was that, almost without exception, they could only exist within the framework of one of a limited number of narratives. These narratives were as fixed and inflexible as Inland Revenue procedural directives; they had to be, presumably, to keep the heroes from wandering off and getting lost, which they'd almost certainly do if allowed any latitude for initiative or creative thinking. Thus: the hero has his destiny revealed to him at an early age; he proves his true worth by battling with some supernatural creature; he seeks or has thrust upon him a quest, usually a task that at first sight appears to be impossible or at least exceptionally difficult, very often involving the rescue of a young female royal; despairing of being able to perform the task, he gets spoon-fed the necessary help by a wizard, minor deity or other supernatural nanny; in many cases, he's also cosseted by being supplied with superior kit in the form of weapons or other advanced technology that give him an entirely unfair advantage and make his success practically a foregone conclusion; nevertheless, he still manages somehow to get himself into the most frightful mess, at which point the same or other supernatural helpers show up and bail him out, leaving him to complete the task and get all the glory.

Hm, he thought. Rings a bell.

Well, the weird people keep telling me I'm a hero, and you could make a case for my life having many of the elements of a heroic narrative. Is it possible that it's all a case of mistaken identity? No, not that, as such; more a case of the wrong man in the wrong place at the wrong time. Like, for example, a kidnapping, where the ransom's left in a plastic bag in a trash can on a street corner at 2 a.m., and some drunk just happens to come along before the kidnappers can get there and collect, and the drunk takes the bag and the money? Only, in my case, I lucked out and got the life of Sir Lancelot rather than two million in used notes.

He'd heard weirder explanations. Once, a friend of his who did something nebulous and antisocial in the City of London told him that the credit crunch of 2008 was caused by the Bank of the Dead (the venerable institution in which a thousand generations of pious Chinese had made provision for themselves in the afterlife by burning huge quantities of paper money), which had caught the most frightful cold in the sub-prime soul bond market. According to his friend, the bank had bundled together parcels of sub-prime souls – naughty without being clinically wicked – into dubious and complex financial instruments and sold them to the Evil

One. This all came badly unstuck when Gary Suslowicz, twenty-six, of Portland, Oregon, dived into a freezing river to rescue a nine-year-old girl's schnauzer puppy from drowning. So moved were a hundred million news viewers by Mr Suslowicz's heroism that they resolved to turn away from their selfish, egocentric lives and instead live for others and the common good. As a result, they were Saved, which meant massive defaults on the bonds, leaving the Bank of the Dead in dire straits, which in turn infected the major banks in the Sunshine world who were in trading relationships with the BotD. All right, his friend had added, when Maurice expressed a degree of scepticism, it's a tad far-fetched. But it's a damn sight easier to believe in than what we're told actually happened.

All right, how about multiverse theory? Let's see. Somehow or other, without realising it, at some point in my youth I got lifted out of the universe where I belong and dumped in a different version of reality in which I'm a hero and the world is waiting impatiently for me to crack on and get the job done so that destiny can unfold according to the schedule pinned to God's bulletin board. It'd have to be a pretty goofy, far-out version, of course – one in which there really is such a thing as destiny and fate and so on, and narratives, stuff like that. But there's a case to be made that the universe I'm living in *is* pretty goofy: as witness (examples chosen purely at random) self-levitating doughnuts, dragons in the bedroom, the fact that someone gave *me* a *job*, George from school ending up a multi-billionaire, Stephanie in a cardboard box. None of those ought to be allowed in a universe you'd feel happy about sending your kids to school in. On the other hand, everyone around me seems to feel that it's OK, more or less. There haven't been questions in Parliament, or articles in the broadsheets. Egocentric fool that I am, I've assumed that the eye of the weirdness whirlwind is centred on me, and by implication everywhere else is perfectly normal. Query that. Maybe what I've experienced is symptomatic of this *not being the real reality*; and that I'm the only one who's noticed—

Sure. Actually, quite a few other people have come to the conclusion that the universe is crazy and they're the only ones who are sane, but luckily for them there have been giant strides in medication and occupational therapy, so at least some of them may one day be allowed out on their own further than the end of the lawn. Meanwhile, it's probably not a good idea to go around publishing such findings to a wider audience.

But let's just suppose, for the sake of argument (actually, it'd call for something a bit more extreme; let's suppose, for the sake of a blazing stand-up shouting match) that I really am a hero, that my job is to find Stephanie and rescue her, and that right now she's somewhere in that big brick building in Sangreal Street—

Caution, my young apprentice. Think about what Mr Pecheur said, after his experience with a girl from a box. *Sometimes they say stuff that isn't necessarily the truth.*

Yes, but I won't find out for sure unless I go there and actually look. And, if I get there and Stephanie gives me a big smile and a can of gasoline and a box of matches, I'll know Mr Pecheur was right. And if she doesn't—

Get a grip, he urged himself. Nothing's going to happen unless you can figure out a way of getting inside that building. And you can't, can you?

Well?

The old man was troubled. He looked at the box and scratched his head. There was something about it that bothered him.

His nephew, supremely indifferent to his concerns, was eating a corned-beef sandwich. "Art," the old man said, "I don't like this."

The young man chewed at him. The old man shook his head. "This box," he said, "is the wrong size."

The young man's jaws stopped moving for half a second, then started again.

"How long we been collecting boxes here? That's right, a long time. And all that time, all the boxes've been the same size. Identical. And now here's this great big one. Know what I think? There's something funny going on."

The young man swallowed the last of the crust and felt in his pocket for the next sandwich.

"On the other hand," the old man said, "there's nothing in the contract says anything about how big the boxes got to be. And it's in the usual place at the usual time. None of our business, is it? I mean, they don't pay us to ask questions – they pay us to shift boxes. Am I right?"

If eating a sandwich can be taken as agreement, the young man was right behind him.

"And it's not like there's anyone we can ask," the old man argued persuasively. "That's the deal. We pick up the boxes, we take them down the depot, we don't ask questions. Confidentiality, see. Absolute security. Name of the game, right?"

The young man frowned, scratched his ear and ate a Maryland cookie.

"Right," the old man said decisively. "That's it, then. Get that—" He looked round. The young man had got his phone out and was squashing keys with his enormous thumb. "Fine," he said, "I'll do it. You hold the door for me."

The weight of the box actually reassured the old man, as he took the strain, lifted and staggered back. The boxes they were used to collecting were ridiculously heavy. So was this one. Therefore, this box was all right. Basic, fundamental logic.

"I just hope," the old man gasped, when he'd finally wrestled the big box up the stairs, out through the front door and into the back of the van, "there aren't too many more like that. Nearly bust a gut, I did, shifting that. All right, Art, settle down. Off we go."

The rest of the run was pure routine: drive to the depot, stop at the gate in the wire fence, ring the bell, wait for the gate to open, back the van up to the massive steel doors at the side of the building, input the security code, stand well back as the doors whoosh open, unload the boxes, leave. The steel doors sighed shut behind them and clanged together like teeth.

In the loading bay, pitch darkness and dead silence, as usual, for about ten minutes. Then, something very unusual, though of course there was nobody there to see or know about it. A scrabbling noise, coming from inside the abnormally big box. Then a flash of light, a tearing sound, a loud thump and the single word *fuck*, spoken with true feeling.

For about fifteen seconds, Maurice couldn't really feel anything. Then all that changed, and he could feel *everything*: every part of his body shrieking pain at him, accusing him of torture, false imprisonment, culpable negligence and weapons-grade stupidity. He hadn't the heart to argue with himself, because all the charges were true.

Still, he thought, as the pins and needles in the back of his head (now there's a collector's item) slowly began to subside, I'm here now, so I might as well get on with it. Yes indeed. Get on with *what?* For a further seven seconds, during which he made the mistake of trying to flex his left knee, he couldn't actually remember. Then memory seeped back, drip by drip: *you packed yourself in a great big box so they'd bring you inside the depot so you could look for Stephanie.* Really? I did *that?* Yes, apparently I did. Jesus wept.

He rolled onto his side and gradually extended his arms and legs. Each increment felt as though his tendons were ripping like old, frayed cloth, but gradually he felt each joint and sinew agree to forgive, if not to forget. You're not entirely to blame, they told him. It wasn't your fault that the old man couldn't read, or didn't think the words THIS WAY UP in big black capital letters applied to him, with the result that Maurice had endured the entire journey head down and feet up, with most of his body weight bearing down on the nape of his neck. On the other hand, he really shouldn't have added FRAGILE, which every haulage contractor in history has chosen to construe as a hypothesis in need of trial by destruct testing rather than as a statement of fact.

Another question, one he'd been shying away from tackling since emerging from the box, was whether his experiences inside the box had irreparably damaged his optic nerve, or whether it was just dark. He'd actually had the foresight to bring a small flashlight, which had somehow survived the journey; he fished it out and flicked it on. Light. Oh good.

He switched it off again, just in case, and considered his next move. A bit late for that; but since he'd never imagined that his lunatic idea for getting inside would actually work, he hadn't bothered formulating any plans for Phase Two. Just get in there and it'll all be plain sailing. Yeah. Right.

His first outburst of illumination didn't seem to have triggered any alarms or attracted any killer dogs, so he risked another, longer view, playing the flashlight's pale-yellow beam around the immediate area. Boxes; loads of boxes, stacked on top of each other. That was all. If there were walls in this place, they were a long way away, or behind the box-ramparts.

That in turn suggested he was in a very large room indeed – a warehouse or depot, to take a possibility entirely at random.

Even to a Carbonec employee in good standing, there did appear to be an awful lot of boxes. On the other hand, he had an advantage: he knew the box code, *8896431976N/ 6428914404W/3947582919W/9012348746W.* Finding it among all these other identical boxes would be an uphill task for an ordinary mortal, but not perhaps as daunting for someone who did that kind of stuff for a living. If only he could find a light switch . . .

More research with the torch; no joy. It wasn't so much trying to find a needle in a haystack as trying to find a cloaked needle in the intergalactic void between the Milky Way and Andromeda. He tried again and kept going for about three minutes, at which point the battery gave out and left him in pitch darkness.

Oh, he thought. Not that he was scared of the dark, good heavens, no. Perish the thought. It was just a dreadful, dreadful shame that the flashlight had given out, because unless the lights went on in, say, the next six seconds, he was going to start screaming and yelling, and—

A gentle blue glow welled up all around him. He swung round and saw that it was coming from a small plastic object, lying on the floor next to the mangled carcase of the box he'd just escaped from. Ah, he thought. To get out of the box he'd used the constant object. When he'd slipped it into his pocket that morning, just before leaving home, it had been a pair of nail scissors. When he'd found it by feel a few minutes ago, it had felt bigger and squarer and sort of plastic-y; he'd pressed it against the side of the box, hoping it would somehow know what to do, and then there had been the flash of light, and then he'd been too preoccupied with pain to give it any more thought. Now, bless it, it was lying there in the shape of a chunky, mildly late-series-Star-Trek ray-gun thing, and a sort

of bulb arrangement on the butt end was glowing delight-
fully blue.

He looked around. The space he was in – describing it as a
room would be like calling the Second World War a difference
of opinion – was a bit like a giant version of his sub-basement
at Carbonec. There were rows and rows of shelves, on which
sat thousands and thousands of boxes, each one with a label
where a label should be. He walked up to the nearest row and
let his peripheral vision brush along it, like a cat rubbing up
against a leg – the special technique he'd invented. A lot of the
labels were familiar, ones he'd memorised. A lot of them
weren't. That didn't help terribly much – it could mean that
boxes came here from more than one source, or they could be
boxes that had been shipped out before he had joined the
firm. He wasn't really interested in that. More to the point,
they didn't seem to be in any sort of obvious order. Not
alphabetical or numerical; not date order, because a box he
remembered shipping the day before yesterday was right
alongside another box from his third day on the job, while
next to that was one whose designation rang no bells at all.
Finding the Stephanie box, *8896431976N/6428914404W/
3947582919W/9012348746W*, would therefore be a matter of
pure fluke.

Yes, but he did that sort of thing all day every day; he
strolled down rows until the number he was looking for just
happened to catch his eye. There were thousands of boxes in
his sub-basement – not nearly as many as here, but still more
than enough to make a normal, methodical person believe
that finding one would be impossible – and yet he found them
easily enough. The same principle might well apply here. Or
it might not. Only one way to find out.

He concentrated. He concentrated on making his mind a
complete blank, which is a difficult thing to do. He took the
bucket of blankness and bailed out the floodwater of thought,

until his vacuity level was roughly that of a delegate at a party conference. Then he stuck his hands in his pockets and began to stroll.

8896431976N/6428914404W/3947582919W/9012348746W. It practically jumped out and mugged him. He stopped dead. A little voice inside his head was urging him, Stay calm, don't rush, no sudden movements or you'll scare it away. Personally he thought that made no sense at all, but what the hell. He was getting used to his subconscious being rather better clued up about what was going on than he was.

Accordingly, he stood for a minute or so just looking at the box, like a man admiring a view. The box stayed perfectly still and quiet, so he moved towards it – not directly, bull-in-a-china-shop fashion, but obliquely, as though he was going to walk right past it without noticing it was there; then, at the last moment catching sight of it, like when you're out shopping and you see someone you know and you'd really rather not have to talk to; you scuttle away but, at the very last moment, they see you, give you a cheery wave and call your name, and you're lost.

He stopped. He was six inches or so from the box. Hello, box.

Gently, now. This is a situation that calls for empathy and understanding rather than haste and brute force; the box-whisperer rather than the stevedore. Very slowly he reached out with his left hand until it rested lightly on the cardboard. He gave it a gentle pat. Maybe it winced ever so slightly, but he was probably imagining it. OK so far. Here goes.

When he pulled the constant object from his pocket, it had turned back into the X-Calibre letter-opener; great. Like a surgeon preparing for the first incision, he readied the tip against the packing tape, and—

Wham. Something hit his shoulder like a sledgehammer. He heard a tinkle, as the X-Calibre hit the floor.

"About *fucking* time," roared a voice in his ear. He spun round, and found himself nose to nose with a man he was sure he recognised.

He was tall, spare, big-eared, curly-haired, mid-thirties, dressed in a long tweed overcoat with the collar turned up, and a Tom Baker scarf wound tightly round his neck and tucked in for maximum insulation. Apart from his mother, Maurice had never seen anyone angrier in his entire life.

"Max?" he said.

"At last." Max was twitching, as though only an invisible security guard pinning his arms to his sides was keeping him from immediate violence. "Thank you *so* much for eventually deigning to turn up. It's so very, very kind of you to find the time in your hectic fucking schedule."

There are times in every life when you know you're just about to say precisely the wrong thing, but you still go ahead and say it. On these occasions it's like you aren't actually involved; you're more like an observer, watching from a safe distance through binoculars. "Um," Maurice said.

"What?"

"Sorry."

"*Sorry*." Max's fingers flexed and balled into fists. "You're *sorry*. Well, that makes everything all right, then, doesn't it? Just so long as you're *sorry*, we can forget all about me being stuck here in this shithole for the best part of a thousand years. I mean, we can put it all behind us and move on."

"Excuse me."

"We can— What?"

"Did you say you've been here for a thousand years?"

Max frowned. "Well, maybe I'm exaggerating just a teeny bit."

"Ah."

"A more precise figure would be nine hundred and sixteen

years, three months, four days and nine and a quarter hours. You *bastard*."

"But—"

"Relative local time," Max added. "Probably only a few months where you come from, but that's not the *point*. You should've realised. You should've *done something*."

"Um—"

"What?"

"I'm sorry."

It was a bit like a nuclear weapons test, where they evacuate all the neighbouring islands, build the massive concrete blast walls, hold off on a warship twenty miles out to sea and press the button, only to discover that someone neglected to install the warhead. For a moment Max looked like he was about to disintegrate from pure rage. Then he sagged, shrugged and said, "Well, you're here now. Let's get on with it, shall we?"

"Yes, right." Pause. "Get on with what?"

Or maybe they fitted it after all. "*What?* Finding my brother, of course. My brother," he repeated, as Maurice did his impression of a blank sheet of paper. "Theo Bernstein. The man you've come to save."

"Um."

Yes, he'd said the wrong thing again. Curious, how such a little word could have such a big effect. Max stood up on the points of his toes, as if gathering himself up for a colossal Ali-Frazier punch, then staggered, caught himself just in time and leant heavily on Maurice's shoulder to keep himself from falling over. "Theo Bernstein," he repeated. "Oh come *on*. Theo *Bernstein*."

"I'm very sorry," Maurice said. "I don't know who you—"

Max screamed, right in Maurice's ear. Maurice hadn't been expecting it; he jumped like a salmon, barging into Max on the way down and jolting him to the floor. Max sat up quickly and wriggled backwards away from him. "All right," he yelled, "calm down, will you, for crying out loud? There's no call for *physical violence*."

Under other circumstances, Maurice would've been the first to agree. But his ears were still ringing, and Max was starting to get on his nerves. He bent down, retrieved the X-Calibre and showed it to Max. "Know what this is?"

Max had gone a funny colour. "Yes."

"Wonderful. I'm so glad one of us does. Look, I haven't got a clue what this thing is or what it does, but I'm not afraid to use it, right? So, no more yelling."

"OK."

"Splendid. Now, I'm just going to open this box here and have a look inside. When I've done that," he added, as Max let out a pitiful whimpering noise, "you can tell me all about your brother and why he's so important. Agreed?"

"Look, would you mind pointing that thing somewhere else? Like, they call them constant objects but that's just marketing-speak, like Wonderkleen actually means, *with any luck it won't leave your clothes any dirtier than they were when you started.* Actually, they're pretty damn unstable, so if you wouldn't mind—"

"Agreed?"

Max nodded. "Yeah, fine. Do what you want. But as soon as you're done—"

"We'll look for your brother," Maurice said nicely. "Promise."

All of Max's attention appeared to be focused on the X-Calibre. That was actually pretty scary, but Maurice didn't have time to worry about that. He pricked the point of the knife into the parcel tape, took a deep breath and—

"I'm forgetting my manners," Max said. "Have a bagel."

"What?"

"A bagel. Fresh this morning. Go on."

Maurice gave him a look that would've stripped paint, but Max just stood there, holding out a paper bag. Maurice sighed. Easier to accept than to argue. He took a bagel, then paused. "I thought you said you'd been trapped here for nine hundred years."

"Nine hundred and sixteen years, three months, four days and nine and a quarter, no, make that nine and a half hours. So?"

"How come you've got freshly baked bagels?"

Max shrugged. "Well, it wasn't *that* bad. You can order in."

Maurice clamped the bagel between his teeth, found the point where he'd made his tiny incision and pressed down on the handle of the X-Calibre. There was a tiny moment of resistance, and then the tape gave way, the knife passed through, and—

As he walked in through the door, they all stood up to greet him. They were singing:

For he's a jolly good fellow
For he's a jolly good fellow
For he's a jolly good fellow . . .

He looked at them. They looked at him. He smiled.

. . . *And so say all of us.*

He laughed. They gave him three cheers. He took off his coat and hung it on the hook behind the door. "That'll do," he said loudly. "Now, get on with some work, before I fire the lot of you."

Chorus of exaggerated groans and hisses; then the group dissolved. They went back to their desks, phones and photocopiers, and soon the front office was its usual humming, vibrant self. He was still smiling as he stepped into the glass lift and said "Thirty-seven."

A thought struck him.

On the thirty-seventh floor, opposite the lift, was a men's room. He went inside and looked at himself in the mirror. *I'm me,* he told himself. The reflection agreed with him. And then he thought, *Why am I holding a bagel in my left hand?*

He remembered. No time for breakfast, busy day, early start; so he'd bought a bagel from Max on the street outside the front door. Good old Max. Always a cheery smile, and the bagels freshly baked that morning.

He pushed through the fire doors into his office, and stood for a moment admiring the view. At the time, he'd been in two minds about using three-quarters of an entire floor as his own personal space, given what they were having to pay per square metre just to be there. It was recklessly extravagant, and, although he could easily afford it, he was uneasy about the conspicuous consumption aspect. It was a bit too Gordon-Gecko-Goldman-Sachs for his taste, and, besides, did he really need it? After all, he'd started the business and grown it into a multi-billion-dollar corporation in his parents' garage, with his first laptop balanced perilously on cardboard boxes full of books and china they'd brought from the old house and never got around to unpacking. Now his office was longer and wider than their entire street; if his carpet was grass, he could graze a flock of sheep there all winter without having to feed them hay.

True; but he wasn't the same man he used to be. Nowadays, he needed room to think in; and although you could argue that the Wiltshire estate and the New Mexico ranch and the private Alp and the forty-thousand hectares of protected

Brazilian rainforest served that function pretty well, the fact was that he was still always at his best and brightest when he had his team, his people, around him. They'd probably put up with jumping on a jet and going with him whenever he felt the need to brainstorm, but it wouldn't be fair on them or their families, not to mention the carbon issues of having three 747s constantly shuttling across the globe. Seen in those terms, the office wasn't so bad after all. And besides, he liked it like this. He worked best when he was happy. The team worked best when they were happy, and they weren't happy unless he was happy – happiness, he'd discovered, really was the key to success in business – so, well, there you go. It's the assets that don't show up on the balance sheets that really make the difference.

He wandered across the room to his desk – well, sort of desk. Really it was three planks of wood resting on two substantial tea-chests, with a seat salvaged from a Renault Clio and welded to a frame, the one thing (apart from a certain attitude) he'd brought with him from the old garage days. But he simply couldn't imagine working anywhere else; and if bank CEOs and heads of state and captains of industry thought he was eccentric – well, yes, they were perfectly right. In fact, it was a pretty fair litmus test. The ones who got the desk were the ones he could do business with. The others . . . well, perfectly pleasant people in their own way – most people were all right when you got right down to basics – but some people were more on his wavelength than others, simple as that.

"Maurice," said a disembodied voice.

He looked up. "Talk to me, Charlene."

"Your nine fifteen's here."

Ah. He smiled. "Get him a coffee and a slice of carrot cake," he said, "and tell him I'll be right down."

He used the back lift, the one they called the Teleport: a

single stainless-steel disc set into the floor, with a tube of his patent invisible glass surrounding it; you stood on the disc and said where you wanted to go, and three seconds later, there you were. The ground-floor exit was just behind the front desk in main Reception, which meant he could suddenly appear out of thin air to greet his guests. Silly, really, but fun; and if there's no fun, why the hell bother with any of it?

"George." He stepped out of the invisible tube, hand outstretched, a huge unforced smile on his face. "How the devil are you?"

Nothing special, if his appearance was anything to go by. George was thinner than he'd been the last time they'd met, and he'd never been particularly substantial at the best of times. His suit was shiny and too big for him, and the sole of his left shoe was attached to the upper with silver gaffer tape. "Fine, Maurice," George mumbled, "how are you? Amazing place you've got here."

As always, Maurice felt mildly embarrassed by the compliment. "I know what you're thinking," he said. "Disneyland. I guess I should never have let my inner child approve the drawings. Come on up, and we can talk properly. How long's it been? Must be eighteen months since Kieran and Shawna's wedding. Can you believe it, by the way? Eighteen months, they're still together and nothing worse than minor cuts and bruises."

George laughed nervously, and Maurice felt a flood of compassion. Dear old George. Something really would have to be done about him, before his entire life slipped down the back of the sofa of entropy and was lost forever. He stood back to let George go past him into the lift.

"So," Maurice said, as cheerfully as he could, "how's it going? Still living with your mum and dad?"

George shook his head. "No, I had to move out."

Ting. The doors swooshed open, and Maurice led the way. "My office is just through here. *Had* to move out? They're all right, aren't they, your parents?"

"I wouldn't know," George mumbled bitterly. "Haven't seen them since they moved."

"Oh. That doesn't sound so good."

He opened the door. George stood in the doorway, staring, which made Maurice feel ashamed of himself. "Come and sit down," he said, leading the way to the balcony. George hesitated, then sank into the right-hand milk-white sofa. "I should've guessed," George was saying, "when they paid for me to have a fortnight in the Greek islands. You need a break, they said, take you out of yourself. And when I got back, I found they'd gone. Sold the house – the lawyers wouldn't give me their new address. All my stuff was in a container at a storage depot."

Maurice was appalled. "George, that's dreadful. What a mean thing to do."

George shrugged. "Can't blame them, I guess. I mean, they'd been dropping hints long enough, and we weren't exactly getting along. Still—" He looked away. "And now I've lost my job, which doesn't exactly help."

Right, Maurice said to himself, enough's enough. Destiny's had things her own way for far too long. It's time I took a hand. "I see," he said. "And where were you working?"

"Overthwart and Headlong. They're a firm of sort of importy-exporty people in—"

"I know who you mean. Did you like it there?"

George shrugged. "It was all right, I suppose."

"Fine. Charlene."

"Yes, Maurice?"

"Get Paul in here, would you?"

"Right away, Maurice."

Paul came up on the Teleport. "Paul," Maurice said, "I

want you to buy Overthwart and Headlong. You know, the import-export brokers in Breunis Street."

Paul frowned. "No disrespect," he said, "but if your heart's set on a cowboy outfit, wouldn't you be better off with Levis and a Stetson hat?"

"Deal with it, Paul. Oh, and George here is going to be their new CEO. Got that?"

"I'm on it."

Paul vanished with the usual *whoosh*, and Maurice turned and gave George a friendly smile. "That's all right with you, is it?"

George was staring at him as if he was the Second Coming, with lighting effects by Steven Spielberg. "Maurice—"

"That's all right," Maurice said shortly. "Actually, it's enlightened self-interest: they're a decent little business at core, it's just the tossers running it that are dragging it down. You'll do a much better job, I know you will. I've always said you've got what it takes, if only someone gave you a break. Now then, how about pancakes?"

"What?"

"Pancakes. With maple syrup and cream. I always have pancakes when I buy a company." He grinned. "Charlene. Pancakes."

"What, *again?*"

"Pancakes," Maurice said firmly. "I don't know, staff nowadays. You wouldn't believe what I have to put up with, George, really you wouldn't. I suggest you take a firm line with them at Overthwarts when you're in charge."

The sugar rush was good for George; it helped him pull himself together and stop saying thank you, eventually. To change the subject, Maurice decided to show him the R & D wing. After all, George had always had a bit of a geekish streak. "Oh, by the way," he said, as they got out of the lift at the fourteenth floor. "Steph sends her regards."

"Right."

Maurice looked at him out of the corner of his eye. It would always be a ticklish subject, what with George and Steph having had that brief thing while they were all still at school. For Steph it had been one of those things you grow out of, like spots. For George, he suspected, it was rather different; and when it came to carrying a torch, George would have no trouble getting top billing at any Olympic opening ceremony. Another flash of pity; he put it firmly back where it had come from. Someone like George didn't need pity, the same way the Atlantic doesn't really need more water. "She's doing wonders over at Valkyrie Industries," he went on. "She's designing a new main battle tank for the Americans."

"That's nice."

Quite enough of that. "Here we are," he said, stopping in front of the big steel door. "Now this is something I'm really quite excited about. I think you will be, too."

At that precise moment, in exactly the same place, but at ninety-one degrees to that time and place in the D axis, the dark-haired man in the glass tank in the exact centre of the room was thinking: Hang on.

Far away – but distance didn't exist; it was a delusion, like Zeus or Santa Claus, something the terrified mind needed to believe in, to make sense of its context – he could see a human entity, and he perceived that the human entity was looking at him. It wasn't the female entity; it was a significantly different shape, with short hair and no bumps and wiggles. He concluded that it must be a male entity. I'm a male entity, he thought, so presumably I look like that. Oh well.

The male entity's face was arranged in such a way as to express some emotion. The man in the tank studied it for a while, then did his best to reproduce it. Then he asked himself, Wearing this expression, how do I feel? Answer, puzzled. Confused, bewitched, bothered and bewildered. Therefore, the male entity is looking at me and thinking, Uh?

Curious. The male entity stopped pulling the face, then realised that he'd resumed it automatically, presumably because he too was now confused, bewitched, bothered and bewildered as a blenderful of ferrets. Why, he wondered, does the sight of me cause the male entity such intense perplexity? It's like he doesn't know what I am, or why I'm here, or where here is. True, all of these are very good questions, answers to which I haven't quite figured out yet. Maybe he's wondering why I'm not partially covered in fabric, like him and the female entities. Perhaps being partially covered in fabric is the norm among human entities, and I'm some sort of aberration. In which case, *why* am I not partially covered in fabric like everybody else? Was it something I did wrong? If so, when? In the past, presumably. I can't remember the past. Why can't I remember the past? What is going *on* around here?

The human entity was still staring at him. He thought, Perhaps he recognises me, and he's wondering what I'm doing in this glass bottle (assuming what I'm in is a glass bottle, though so far that particular hypothesis is holding up pretty well). If so, it can only mean that he encountered me at some stage in the past, which I can't remember, and that we interacted in some way, which he can remember and I can't. Oh—

He hesitated. There really ought, he felt, to be some means of expressing rage and frustration verbally, some word or phrase or words or phrases you could use to signify sheer anger and despair, preferably with overtones of hostility, displeasure with the status quo and general lack of respect for the world as it's constituted. Ideally, such word, words, phrase or

210 • TOM HOLT

phrases would, in and of themselves, constitute an act of deliberate offence, because that's how I'm feeling right now and I'm pretty sure, if this is the way things are around here, I'm not the only one. All right, let there be such a word. Let it be—

He considered. It'd have to start with a suitably projectile labial, followed by a vowel you could really put your heart and soul into, and terminating in a throaty guttural you could practically *spit*. Also, one syllable would be best. Anything longer would dissipate the effect.

Oh *fulk*, he thought.

The male entity was still standing there, gawping at him, and he felt a powerful urge to apprehend the male entity and subject him to percussive force, presumably using hands and/or feet, since you could bash someone with those real good without hurting yourself in the process. To be precise, he wanted to grab that fulking fulker by the throat and smash his fulking face in. Curious, he thought. Why exactly do I want to do that? Is it because I somehow choose to attribute to him the blame for my current confinement and lack of memory? Does that in itself imply that confinement and lack of memory are bad things, and that I am, consequently, suffering? And if so, if I am suffering, why doesn't that fulking fulkwit *do* something, instead of just standing there?

Maybe there's nothing he can do. After all, I'm a male entity, and I can't do anything. Maybe only female entities have the capacity to exercise control over environments and conditions. In which case—

He was finding it hard to concentrate. Curious. Hitherto (as far as he could remember; grrrr) he'd had no trouble directing the full force of his intellect towards solving the questions that teemed in his mind; because, after all, what could be more important than making sense of the universe? Now, though, ever since fulk-for-brains over there had popped up and started staring at him, he could feel his attention wandering, as if trying to point him in the direction of something even more important than pure empirical enquiry. What could that possibly be? He considered the possibilities. Something, perhaps, directly relevant to *me*, as opposed to the universe at large or all human entities or all male entities or all male entities not partially covered in fabric. Me. Just me, myself—

Which brought him back to an earlier question, which he'd shelved for lack of data: *how many of us are there?* He'd got as far as *more than just me*, which stood to reason once he'd figured out the workings of genetics and the need for a gene pool rather than just a gene puddle. But *how many* was still very much unquantified. More than twelve. All right, yes, but how many more than twelve? Fifteen? A hundred and fifty? Fifteen hundred? Fifteen *thousand*?

Steady on, he told himself. Fifteen *thousand* human male entities; getting a bit wild here – whatever would be the point of there being fifteen thousand of us? But more than twelve, definitely, because otherwise the species would die out through interbreeding. So; here's me and there's him. Where are the other more-than-ten?

And quite suddenly he thought, I wish I could remember the past. I wish I could obtain access to further and better extraneous data. I wish, I really really wish I could get *out of here*—

"Is he all right?" George asked anxiously.

Maurice smiled. "Oh, you don't need to worry about him. He's just fine."

"He looks a bit upset about something."

Maurice laughed. "He doesn't actually exist," he said. "At least, not yet."

George frowned. "You tell him that."

"It's a bit more complicated than that," Maurice said kindly. "What you're looking at isn't a real human being."

"Ah."

"Well, of course not. You don't think we'd keep a human being locked up in a glass tank with no clothes on, do you?" He grinned. "I don't think even old Fisher-King would've done that, or at least not for more than an hour. No, he's a construct."

"Ah."

"Meaning," Maurice went on patiently, "he's artificially generated. We built him. Out of pure logic."

There was an awkward pause. "Sorry," George said. "I think you just lost me."

Maurice laughed. "Don't worry about it," he said. "This is absolutely *the* ultimate final-frontier cutting edge of theoretical multiple-state particle physics. All right. You know about multiverse theory?"

George gave him a helpless look. "Sort of. Bits and bobs."

Maurice explained about multiverse theory. "So you see," he concluded, "the only way you could possibly move from one reality to another is if you could somehow construct a stable multidimensional portal. A door, if you like, between our universe and a different one."

George nodded slowly. "Right."

"And he," Maurice went on, "might just be that portal."

"Ah."

Maurice chuckled. "It's like that old joke," he said, "*when is a door not a door?* Answer, when it's a paradigm. Or, to use the buzzword that's going round all the top physics boys these days, a constant object. Something that stays the same, no matter which version of reality you're in. If you could somehow manage to get your paws on one of them, you'd be away. See?"

"Well, sort of. But—" George frowned. "I mean, do they even exist?"

"It'd be nice if they did," Maurice replied. "Also – multiverse theory – somewhere in some version of the world in the infinity of possibility, yes, of course they do, because everything exists, because in the multiverse everything is possible. So, the trick is to find a way of getting to the universe where constant objects exist, get hold of one and bring it back."

"I see," George said. "But if you haven't got one, how do you—?"

Maurice smiled at him. "Quite," he said. "So, alternatively, you make one yourself. Which is what we're trying to do here. Him," he added, with a nod towards the glass tank.

"Ah."

"What we thought was," Maurice went on, "how'd it be if the constant object was a *person*? Not just two birds with one stone, a whole *flock*. Create a person who's a constant object, send him to the constant-object universe and get him to bring you a truckload of them back. Perfect."

Maurice could almost smell George's brain frying. "Yes," he went on, "I know it sounds utterly, utterly crazy and quite probably it is. I imagine the electric light bulb sounded like the ravings of a demented loon when Edison was first explaining the idea to his mates in the pub; you get a bit of wire and you stick it in a glass bottle and you pump all this invisible magic stuff through it and it catches fire. Sure, Tom, now why don't you go home and take it easy for a day or so? But if you actually sit down and do the maths—" He shrugged. "Not quite as crazy as it first appears. I do believe we can do this, George. You see, we're not inventing him – him in the tank, I mean. The thing is, *he's* doing it for us."

George gave him a blank look. "He's—?"

"That's right." Maurice paused for a moment and looked at the man in the tank. "You know where it says, *in the beginning was the Word*? Well, that's how he started out. Just a word. Well, four, actually. What, how, why and when. We programmed a really, really hot computer, linked it up to a particle collider inside a totally null EM field, and ... well, three days later we came back and there he was." Maurice paused again. He still didn't understand it himself. "It's sort of like the questions *needed* him, to answer them. So they—" For some reason, he faltered a little. "I think they kind of *pulled him in* from somewhere. And there he's been ever since."

George was wearing a stunned look, as if his brain had been painlessly extracted and replaced with pink blancmange. "He's not—"

"Real? No." Maurice decided it was important to press his point home. "We'd hardly leave him in there if he was, would we? But he's not. He doesn't eat or drink, he doesn't pee or anything. We ran an infra-red sensor over him, and there's no body heat whatsoever. It looks like he's breathing, but we rigged up a monitor, and when he breathes in there's no decrease in the ambient oxygen level, and when he breathes out there's no CO_2. We considered the possibility that he's some kind of highly advanced android, but when you shine a beam of light at him, it comes out the other side, which means he's just not *there* in any meaningful sense. Or at least," Maurice corrected, "*here's* not *here*. If you can grasp the difference."

George didn't look like he was grasping anything very much. Still.

"What we think," Maurice went on, "is that he's actually *somewhere else*, and that what we're seeing—"

"A hologram?" George suggested.

"Mmm." Maurice pursed his lips. "No, we don't think so, because a hologram would show up some residual energy traces, and this fellow doesn't. But sort of like a hologram, in a way. Well, more like a shadow, only in 3D. We think he's the shadow cast in this reality by a real human being in another one."

"Ah." George looked thoughtful for a moment. Then he asked, "Why are you doing this?"

What an odd question. "Excuse me?"

"Why? What's the point? How are you going to use this to make money?"

Well, that was George. But never mind. "Actually," Maurice said, "I don't see why we shouldn't. Make money, I mean. Just think of the possibilities. Like, it stands to reason. Out there somewhere there's got to be, say, a universe where they didn't fight the Iraq war but instead used all the money they'd otherwise have spent on bombs and stuff on finding cures for diseases. If we could go there and get those cures, we'd save millions of lives back here and make a fair profit on the pharmaceutical patents. But it's not really about *money*, is it? It's about—"

"Yes?"

Maurice could feel himself getting tense. He relaxed. "It's about time we had a cup of tea and some cheesecake," he said. "And then you'd better make a start on reading the Overthwart and Headlong company reports for the last ten years, if you want to be up to speed when you start work on Monday."

After George had gone, weighed down with printouts and glossy corporate literature until he could barely stagger (so he'd called down and had them drive him home) Maurice sat down at his desk and tried to get on with some work, but his mind couldn't find a way into it; very strange, for someone who sang snatches of computer code to show tunes in the shower each morning and regularly dreamed in binary. It was something George had said – well, two things: *he doesn't exist/you tell him that*, and *how are you going to use this to make money?* The first one; well, they'd been into all that. Every test they could think of, and all of them had produced the same answer. He's not alive. He's not a living, breathing human being. We can see him and hear him, but there's no actual atoms and molecules there, so he can't be *suffering* – he's got nothing to suffer *with*. And the other one; good question. Very good question. He hadn't looked at the figures for a day or so, but last time he'd seen a detailed analysis, the project had cost slightly more than the GDP of Honduras. The money was there, of course – there was plenty of money, and if the program carried on much longer and they had to sell something or borrow to finance it, then so what? This was *important*, the way everything else he'd ever done wasn't, in comparison. The project was *key*, it was *core*, it was the *reason why*. Without it, none of the other stuff – the child genius, the breathless, soaring ascent, the success, the money – made any real sense. There had to be a reason, after all. Otherwise, it was all ridiculous, like building the world's biggest ever ship in Lincoln, Nebraska, and leaving it there to rust.

Yes, quite. But what was the project—?

(He frowned. He'd just had a sharp pain right between his eyes, and his fingertips were slightly numb.)

—For? What was it trying to achieve? *Why were they doing this?*

A fair question (he massaged his fingers; for some reason, it made his head feel better), and one that'd have to be answered sooner or later, because, otherwise, how would they know if they were winning or not? If they didn't know what the project was for, how would they know when it was finished, and when to stop?

A fair question – he was much better now – to which he realised he didn't know the answer. Yes, it was the most exciting area of scientific discovery at this time. Yes, they were poised on the edge of the most amazing discovery since Newton realised that fruit hurts. But what were they poised to discover, exactly? We don't know; we haven't discovered it yet.

The phone rang. He sighed and pressed the button on his desk to put the call onto the sound system. "Hello?"

"Your wife called," the room told him. "While you were with your friend."

He scowled. "Why didn't you tell me?"

"Didn't think you'd want to be interrupted."

"Charlene." He tried to stay patient. "I'm never too busy for Steph; you should know that by now. Get her for me. Now."

He waited, drumming his fingers on the desktop. Rather a long time later, the room said, "I'm sorry, she doesn't seem to be answering her phone."

Maurice felt a sudden spurt of anger. "What? She always answers. Try again."

"You're the boss."

He waited. It was something he'd got out of the habit of doing. Eventually, the room said, "Sorry, no answer. We tried five times."

"Are you sure you got the right number?"

"Good heavens, we never thought of that. Yes, of course we did."

"All right." Why was he feeling so jumpy all of a sudden? No idea. "What's her last known location?"

"Huh?"

"Where was she calling from, when she called?"

"Just a second." Infuriating delay, lasting a whole five seconds. "That's funny."

"What's funny?"

"Ran the GPS on her phone, and there's no trace. She must've been in a railway tunnel or something."

He realised, much to his amazement, that he was panicking. Don't *do* that, Maurice, you know it never solves anything. "Charlene," he said, slowly and firmly. "I want you to find out where she is, then get in touch with her and ask her to call me."

"Sure."

"Urgent, Charlene. Like, if she's in the middle of a field somewhere, send someone in a helicopter. You got that?"

"Sure. Maurice."

"What?"

"Don't you think it's maybe possible that you're ever so slightly overreacting just a teeny tiny bit?"

"Yes. Now get on with it."

He picked up his LoganBerry Ultra Plus, then slammed it down again. Overreacting. Well, quite. He hoped to God he was overreacting, but for some unfathomable reason he had a horrible feeling he wasn't. Steph *always* answered her phone, no matter where she was, or what she was doing, or with whom. They'd had their one and only really bad row over that very issue.

He drummed his fingers on the desk a hundred and ninety-six times. Then he shouted, "Well?"

"Well what?"

"Have you found her yet?"

"Not quite."

"Not—?"

"Last known location," Charlene said, "the Ministry of Defence, London. She—"

"That's just down the road."

"I know. Shut up for a minute and let me finish. She had a meeting there at ten fifteen. I imagine they make visitors turn their phones off, or hand them in at the front desk. You know, security and stuff. And that'd probably explain why we couldn't track her signal when she called. They've probably got some sort of jamming—"

"They have," Maurice remembered. "We sold it to them. All right, get the defence secretary for me, right now. Tell him to find out where she is, and get her to call me."

"Um."

"Well?"

"Do you really want to talk to the *defence secretary*? I mean, there are several other people working there. I'm sure one of them could—"

Maurice sighed. "You're right. I'm losing it, I'm sorry. Only, it's so unlike her."

"You're worried."

"Yes."

"That's so sweet."

Four minutes later, Steph called. "What?"

"Hi, Steph. Your phone wasn't answering."

"No."

"That's not like you."

"I had—" Pause.

"You had what, sweetheart?"

"Technical problems."

"Ah, right."

"If you must know, I shot my phone."

"You shot your phone, kitten?"

"Accidentally. I'm helping them evaluate a new concept in rapid deployment individual fire platforms, and my phone was in my coat and I hung my coat behind the door and—"

"I see. Don't you just hate it when that happens?"

"Right. Was there anything?"

"No, that's fine. Just a bit concerned, that's all."

"You're an idiot, Maurice."

"I know, precious. See you this evening."

So that was all right. He breathed out, long and slow. No idea why he'd got in such a state. There was absolutely no reason why he should worry about Steph – people in her immediate vicinity, yes, but not Steph – and he couldn't remember ever having done so before. But, when he hadn't been able to get through to her – well, it had been the way he imagined it'd be when you're drowning, and you try and breathe in air but instead you get water, and he was extremely glad it was over and he could get back to what he was supposed to be doing.

I'm hungry, he realised. It had to be a reaction to the panic, because he'd already had pancakes and cheesecake with George. The body's need for food to reassure it that it's still alive, after a brush with what it had perceived as mortal peril. Silly old body. Still, a nibble of something wouldn't hurt.

In his in-tray, he noticed, lay the bagel he'd bought from dear old Max that morning and hadn't got around to eating. Probably stale by now; on the other hand, it was here, well within arm's reach, and so why not? He picked it up and looked at it, turning it over in his fingers until the central hole was exactly aligned with his eye—

"Well?"

Maurice blinked.

"You idiot. You stupid fucking *idiot*."

He was back. Where he was back from he had no idea, but he was once again standing in the vast storehouse on Sangreal Street, staring at the box walls by the pale-blue light of the constant object. In which case—

"No," he yelled. "*No!*"

"You left him there." Max was shouting at him again. "You did, didn't you? You left him there, stranded. You know what you are? Well?"

Sadly, Maurice thought, yes. I'm me. Or at least, I'm this me. But just now—

"I'm going back," he said. "Get out of my way, I'm—"

"No you're not." Max grabbed his wrist and lifted it to eye level. "Not through that, you clown. What did you have to go and do that for?"

The bagel was no longer a perfect circle. There was a bite-sized chunk missing from it at about three o'clock. "I didn't—"

"You must've done. Dear God, how could you be so *stupid*?"

Maurice scowled and flung the bagel away. "You've got another one, right?"

"No. Why should I? This isn't exactly Supersize-me City, you know. Rations are, like, rationed. That was supposed to be my breakfast. And my lunch. And my dinner."

Maurice looked round to see where it had landed. "Couldn't we—?"

"Mend it somehow? I don't think so. I mean, if it was just a simple matter of cutting you open, retrieving the bitten-off chunk and gluing it back, I'd be, like, go for it. Unfortunately, I need you alive. Always something, isn't there?"

"But I've got to get back there," Maurice shouted. "You don't understand. Suddenly it all makes sense. I don't belong here; I belong *there*. That's my *home*."

Max stared at him for a moment, then burst out laughing. "You know," he said, "for an idiot, you're *smart*."

"Thank you."

"But for a smart guy, you're really dumb. Actually, you remind me a lot of my brother."

"Oh." Maurice wasn't sure what to make of that. "Is he, um, dumb?"

"No, he's smart. He won the Nobel Prize, for crying out loud. But he goes about being smart in a very stupid way. Like you do." Max was calmer now, a steady burn rather than an explosion. "Do you want me to tell you about my brother?"

"No."

My brother (Max said) is the smart one in our family, which is saying something. Also the biggest idiot and the one who's done the most damage, and that's saying something too. He won the Nobel—

Sit *down*, for Pete's sake. There. That's better, isn't it? No, don't do that. Don't—

(The room was completely dark. Maurice had grabbed the constant object with a view to threatening Max with it and making him shut up. Obligingly it had turned into an Uzi. There's no built-in lantern on an Uzi, unless you go for the deluxe exclusive collector's limited edition. Accordingly, it was now pitch dark, so Max couldn't see that he was being threatened. Totally pointless and counter-productive, Maurice thought: the story of my life. He put the gun down on the floor and silently implored it to be a lantern again. It must've taken pity on him.)

—the Nobel Prize (Max went on), which is pretty damn impressive, but then he blew up the Very Very Large Hadron Collider, which also made an impression, but not in a good way. Actually, it wasn't his fault entirely. It was needed so the multiverse could begin. But try telling that to the VVLHC oversight committee.

Well, after he'd done that he was out of a job, for some reason, and he got mixed up in some dumb scheme involving his old professor. Now there was a guy, Pieter van Goyen, the man who finally cracked multiverse theory and invented YouSpace.

Yes, calm down, I'm coming to that. YouSpace was this way of crossing between alternate universes, and actually I know quite a bit about it, because I was in on it from an early stage. Well, Pieter – he was my professor too – Pieter needed someone to try the thing out, and I volunteered. Sounds pretty brave, huh? Actually, I had my reasons. The thing was, I was sort of on the run from some unpleasant people from Vegas, on account of a disagreement we'd had about some experiments I'd been doing into probability theory. So it suited me to be somewhere very far away for a while. Anyhow, Pieter's gizmo worked just fine as far as getting me there was concerned. Getting me back, though . . .

Well, long story short: Theo, that's my brother, came and got me and we made it back to here, meaning our home reality; and then, just as I thought we were starting to get along, build bridges, repair our hitherto fraught and fractious relationship, he got all flaky and decided he was going to take YouSpace and go sit on a mountaintop somewhere and be serene for a while. To be fair, I think it was partly because he'd found out he created Creation when he blew up the VVLHC, which kind of made him God, in a sense. Anyhow, he reckoned he needed to get his head together, so off he went, and off I went, and that's where you came in.

(Maurice looked at him. "Me?"

"You." Max nodded. "You arsehole.")

That you, anyhow – the version of you that you were just now.
The rich, successful and powerful you, somehow got wind of
what Pieter van Goyen had been doing just before his death,
and you decided to pick it up and throw money at it; and the
result was, my poor dumb brother got sucked in off his mountaintop and trapped, in there, in that *jar* you've got in your
laboratory. And now it's up to *you* (here Max pulled a very
serious face indeed) to get him out again.

"Me?" Maurice said.

"You."

"But that's not me," Maurice said bitterly. "I mean, it
should be. I'm absolutely, definitely sure that should be me –
I mean, it felt so *right*. It was so much more me than I am."
He paused. "Does that make any sense?"

"Amazingly, yes," Max said. "I think you're trying to say
that you've spent most of your life in the wrong version of
you. Think back. When did it all start to go horribly wrong?"

"That's easy," Maurice replied immediately. "Mr Fisher-
King's study, me and Stephanie. When we were kids, at
school."

Max nodded slowly. "Tell me something. I don't know a
whole lot about what passes for an education system in this
country. You do exams, right?"

"Sure. GCSEs and A-levels. I did—"

Max was looking at him. "Go on."

"I was *going* to do physics, maths and chemistry," Maurice
said. "I was quite good at all that stuff, though I didn't do a
hell of a lot of work. But that's what I'd made my mind up I
was going to do. Until—"

"Yes?"

Maurice took a deep breath and told him about Mr Fisher-King. "And after that," he went on, "there didn't seem to be any *point*. I mean, what use was there studying a rational Newtonian universe governed by immutable laws of physics when I'd just seen a doughnut levitate off the palm of a man's hand? Obviously, all the physics and chemistry and maths stuff *wasn't true*. So I changed my mind and did IT and media studies instead."

Max raised an eyebrow. "Media studies?"

"That's right. It's like doing nothing at all, but you get a certificate. And I guess—" The full force of it closed in around him, like earth filling a grave, and he closed his eyes for a moment. "I guess that's where our paths forked; him in the box there and me. *He* went on to be a billionaire before he was old enough to vote. And here I am. A total—"

"A hero," Max said.

"A weirdness-haunted victim of circumstance who spends his days looking for things."

Max grinned. "That's what I just said."

"And that man in there—"

"My brother," Max reminded him. "Your mission in life. Your *quest*."

Maurice frowned. "You mean to tell me he's been stuck in there like that for eleven years?"

"It doesn't work like that," Max said, with as much patience as he could muster. "You know, you've really got to do something about this cockamamie linear approach to cause and effect. It's most definitely not your best friend."

He'd chosen his words badly. "My best friend," Maurice shouted at him, "is in that box. In there, I'm *married* to her; she's my *wife*. Out here, she's—"

"What?"

"Missing. Or, just possibly, shagging the obnoxious turd

who's got *my* life in this—" He stopped. There was no way mere words could keep up with what he needed to say. "It's so *unfair*," he mumbled. "Why me? What did I ever do to deserve all this?"

Max shook his head. "There you go again," he said reprovingly, "linear approach to cause and effect. Monodimensional thinking, leading to a chip on your shoulder you could terraform and build colonies on. You clown," he added, not unkindly. "You *did* get what you deserved. You did your maths and your physics exams, you founded your corporation, you made your billion bucks, you married your childhood sweetheart. You know you did. You just saw yourself having done it."

"But that was—" Something broke deep in Maurice's heart. "That was *him*," he said feebly. "That's no bloody use to me, is it? That's like saying, it doesn't matter me having a truly shitty life, because my brother's now the chairman of Unilever."

"Quite," Max said quietly. "Or a Nobel laureate. Or even, just possibly, God. You have no idea how little comfort that can be when you're looking back on a distinguished career in the abject failure sector. And it's even worse, believe me, when, just when you think you can relax, come to terms and have a good time, your stupid, quasi-divine, sun-shines-out-of-his-anal-aperture brother gets himself stuck in a jar, and you've got to drop everything and get him out again. And so you do that, and you find *you've* got stuck yourself because some dumb jerk of a hero can't be bothered to check his email. You know something? That can go beyond trying and into the realms of tiresome."

Maurice looked at him. "You got stuck?"

Max nodded. "Theo gave me this bottle," he said. "A YouSpace bottle. Kind of like a portal. So, when he got lost, I used the bottle to try and go find him. Only—" He shrugged and smiled. "I think I may have done something wrong, because suddenly there I was in this cave, with no heating and not enough to eat, and an invisible sound system playing 'I Need a Hero' on a continuous fucking loop. Oh, and a cell phone, with one number in its address book. That's where I've been for—" He paused and frowned. "Nearly as long as I can remember. Or longer; I'm not sure which anymore."

If you could have connected up a basic hydro-electric system to the surge of pity rushing through Maurice's heart at that moment, you could've lit Scotland. Even so. "I still don't see why it's anything to do with me," he said. "I didn't—"

Max's face was as cold and hard as stone. "Yes you fucking did. You just saw it. *You* sucked my brother into that jar. *You're* keeping him there. So you're the one who's got to make it right. Which," he added crisply, "is why you're here. Destiny, I guess. That's the basic OS of heroes, isn't it? Clearly what's happened is that destiny shifted you from your home reality into this one, when you were a teenager. In this reality, destiny shapes the lives of heroes. So, here, you've gotta do what you've gotta do. Do you understand, or do you want me to run something up using PowerPoint?"

Maurice blinked. "Destiny?"

"Sure. In your reality, destiny's just a crock; there's no such thing. Here, though, it's the mainspring of the cosmos. And, when in Rome . . . " He grinned. "And there you go."

A tiny light flickered in Maurice's head. "But that's all wrong," he said. "*Here*, it's not me holding your brother prisoner in a jar, it's George."

"George?" Max scowled at him. "Who the hell is George?"

"Guy I was at school with. Total jerk. Always has been. In there—" Maurice pointed at the box, "as far as I can gather, he's me; at any rate, he's an unemployable, no-hoper wimp—"

Maurice nodded. "He's you."

"But in *this* reality," Maurice went on, "he's the billionaire industrialist and technological wizard I should've been, and *he's* the one who's got your brother banged up in a Kilner jar. So in *this* reality it's *not* my fault, so it *can't* be up to me. Right?"

Max sighed. "Sorry," he said. "You've just proved my point. In this reality, he fits into the pre-ordained traditional narrative conventions like a brick in a wall. He's the villain. The bad guy. The wicked sorcerer in his tower. If it was any more perfect, it'd fold up on itself and disappear up its own axis of symmetry. Gee, I'm glad you mentioned that. You've convinced me that my hypothesis is one hundred per cent correct. Thank you. Also," he added with a sly grin, "I'm prepared to bet good money he's got your girl locked up in his tower as well. Am I right or am I right?"

"I—" Maurice shook his head, as if it was suddenly full of water. "I think so," he said. "That's why I came here. I saw her, you see, in that box. And before that she disappeared. And then George said the two of them are— But I couldn't believe that. So I came here."

"Bingo." Max clapped his hands together. "There's your narrative dynamic. You're basically Jack and the Beanstalk, adapted for the twenty-first century. Can't you see it? It's so obvious it should be visible from orbit."

"But—" Maurice stared at him, and felt his throat clog up. "I don't *want* to be Jack and the Beanstalk."

"Jack never does," Max replied gently. "If he did, he wouldn't be Jack, he'd be ... I don't know, Theseus or Beowulf or Captain frigging America. But where there's a beanstalk, there's got to be a Jack. And it's your destiny, so you're it. Sorry," he repeated, "but them's the rules. And anyway," he went on seductively, "I don't know where you're coming from with all the hostility. We're on the same side, basically. What we both want is through there, right? My redemption is your redemption."

"You what?"

"Think," Max said smoothly. "You go back through, OK? You take a stroll over to wherever it is they're holding my brother, you say, Sorry, guys, change of plan, we let the prisoner go, or words to that effect. What happens?"

Maurice thought for a moment. "Your brother gets out of the jar."

"Out of the jar," Max said, "out of that whole reality, back to where he wants to be. And what've you done?"

"Um." Trick question? "Let him go."

"*Exactly*. Or, in heroic terms, fulfilled your destiny. Achieved your quest. And what happens to heroes when they do that?"

"Um."

"*They live happily ever after*." Max's eyes were burning. "They marry the princess and settle down to rule the kingdom. OK, afterwards, presumably, they've got to deal with inner-city unemployment and negative macroeconomic trends, but the story's not interested in that sort of thing. The story just wants them out of its hair. They get to live *normal lives*. And what life could be more normal," Max added with a grin, "than your own? The one you should've had all along."

Maurice blinked three times. "You mean—"

"*Yes*. You go in there, you let my brother go, you've *done it*. What you were *abducted* for. The obvious and inevitable result will be, you'll stay there. You'll be married to your girl, you'll have your business empire, it'll all be the way it was supposed to be. As far as this reality's concerned, you'll just vanish, and since nobody gives a damn, who'll care? And over there ... "

Maurice was having difficulty breathing. "You really think—"

"Of course. It's obvious. Use your brain, for crying out loud. There was a screw-up, which caused a . . . I don't know, a disturbance in the flow, ripples in the Force, whatever – and you got dragged out of your reality and dumped in this one, which shows all the signs of being tailor-made to enable you to fix the screw-up you caused—"

"Inadvertently caused."

"Whatever. Soon as the screw-up's fixed, *obviously* everything will then go back to how it should be. And then . . . what are you pulling that face for?"

Maurice shook his head. "It won't work," he said.

"Won't work? Are you nuts? I just explained—"

"I won't remember," Maurice said sadly. "When I get back there. Like, when I was there just now, I had no memory whatsoever of being me here. I'd always been *him*, you know, the rich-happy-successful me. So, if I go back, how the hell will I know to set your brother free?"

Max looked as a man might look if he'd finally got to the front of the queue only to be told the last ticket had just been sold. "You didn't remember anything?"

"Nothing."

"That's weird. Whenever I've jumped realities, I've always stayed me."

"How wretched for you."

Max gave him a not-now-I'm-busy look. "I guess," he said, "it could be because the version of you over there, in the box there, is the *real* you, and over there's where you really belong. Or maybe it's just the difference between doughnuts and bagels; I really don't know. Shit," he added succinctly. "That's—"

"The constant object."

"Huh?"

"That thing." Maurice pointed at the source of the blue glow. "It stays the same no matter which reality you're in, right?"

"Its *function* remains the same, yes." Max frowned. "Yes, but it's a weapon, not a personal organiser."

"Couldn't we, I don't know, write something on it or pin a note to it? I mean, I think it sort of knows how to make itself useful. Hence the light."

Max raised his eyebrows. "It's worth a try, I guess. When you say pin a note to it . . . "

"I don't know, do I?" Maurice made a vague impatient gesture. "All right, let's think about this. If you're right and I'm in a narrative, what would happen?"

Max considered the point. "I think the weapon would know what to do of its own accord. Like, the sword would know to come out of the stone. Of course, if I'm wrong we'd be wasting our time, but I don't see where we've got any options. We'll just have to trust it."

They both peered at the constant object, which carried on belting out eerie blue light.

"Trust that," Maurice said.

"Well, yes. Actually, that's quite plausible. Like when the two lost hobbits are forced to trust the little creepy guy to get them through the marshes. It's a standard; it's classic. I think I'm supposed to say something like, Yes, but can we trust him? And you say, I think we can. Heroic choice, see. You follow your heroic intuition. That's core."

Maurice shrugged. "Fine," he said. "So, all we need now is a doughnut."

They looked at each other.

"We could try ordering in," Max said.

A suggestion best ignored. "How about you?" he said. "You got the bagel. Can't you—?"

"Sure, if you feel like waiting around here for anywhere

between twenty-four and forty-eight hours. And then it could be pastrami on rye or ravioli or semolina pudding. I have absolutely no control over the catering arrangements. Or," he went on, "you could go out and get a doughnut."

"And get back in again." Maurice shook his head. "That could be difficult. In fact, I haven't got a clue how to get out of here, let alone get back in again. No, there's got to be a simpler way." He looked round and found the discarded, bitten-into bagel. "Maybe we *could* fix it," he said. "After all, it's only missing a little bit."

Max shook his head. "I don't think that'd be a good idea," he said. "I have no idea how these things work, but I have a gut feeling that this isn't one of those areas where a bold and imaginative approach is called for."

But Maurice had picked up the bagel and was gently squeezing it in his hands. "I think all we have to do is just gently squidge it like putty," he said, "until the two ends meet, like *this*, and then it's just a simple matter of— See if you can get some of that parcel tape off the box lid."

"You're going to fix a damaged transdimensional interface terminal with *parcel tape*?"

"Only because I haven't got any glue."

Max threw his hands up in the air. "What the hell," he muttered. "I guess this is where I say, It'll never work and you say, Trust me. Only don't," he pleaded, "please."

Maurice grinned at him. "Won't that screw up the narrative?"

Max was stripping tape off the box flaps. "Let's risk it," he said.

Maurice had massaged the two severed ends of the bagel together so that they were just about touching. "Tape," he said.

"I still think we should call out," Max said. "There was this pizza place in Newark I used to know – they were quite incredibly persistent. If you'd called them from Alcatraz, all they'd have wanted to know was if you wanted extra cheese."

"Tape."

"Tape," Max sighed. Maurice held out the bagel, and Max wrapped the tape firmly round the join, applying gentle but steady pressure. "That ought to do it," Maurice said. "Now, am I right in thinking that all I have to do is—?"

On the desk in front of him was a small plastic rectangle.

It had seen better days. It was smashed, shattered, twisted and squashed, but most of all it was cut. Some sharp-bladed instrument had left a deep diagonal gash right across it.

Maurice sighed. "Gruz," he said.

"Boss?"

Maurice closed his eyes. By and large, he enjoyed his job. He'd always wanted to be a journalist, and the five years he'd spent working for the *Horrible Yellow Face* had been the best time in his life. He was proud of having clawed, scratched and backstabbed his way up from the print room to the editor's office. Even so, there were times when he despaired of his chosen profession.

"Gruz," he said gently, "when I said it might be a good idea to hack into her mobile phone, this wasn't quite what I had in mind."

"Boss?"

That was one of the things he found hardest about working with goblins: that way they have of looking up at you with those great big round red eyes, and you know they haven't understood a single thing about what you wanted them to do, but they went and did it anyway. The sublime alchemy that results when you bring together extreme stupidity and unquestioning obedience. "Forget it, Gruz," he said. "And, um, take that thing away and bury it somewhere, OK?"

The senior arts and media correspondent shuffled away, and Maurice sat down in the big chair and tried to decide what they were going to lead with today. He was, he admitted to himself, still having trouble coming to terms with the takeover. When King Mordak had staged his leveraged buyout of the *Beautiful Golden Face*, the reaction of the paper's High Elven owners had been sheer blank horror. They'd taken the money, of course. The two things High Elves do best is elegant distaste and cashing cheques. But they'd prophesied. In six months, they said, the *Face* will be unrecognisable. It'll be a dumbed-down, knuckle-dragging tabloid gutter rag catering to the lowest common denominator, utterly devoid of redeeming social importance, pandering to the basest instincts of the Goblin 2 and Orc 3B demographics. It might even end up as the sort of thing a lot of poor people might pay money to read. The sound of them washing their hands of it was like the roar of a mighty river emptying into the sea. They'd been right, of course. One year on, gone were the ecological crusades and the opera reviews, the corruption exposés and the elegantly phrased editorials bitching about every aspect of government policy. Instead—

Well, that was the problem. King Mordak frowned on in-depth political coverage, particularly with the Coalition in such a fragile state. Since goblins' reproduction involved a large vat of beige goo heated to precisely 78 degrees Celsius and a small army of technicians in hazmat suits, celebrity sex scandals were more or less out. Usually, a goblin newspaper was 95 per cent war reports, suitably improved to give an impression of constant victory, but thanks to Mordak and the Coalition, that was out too; likewise sport (see above, under war). That just left—

What?

And that, essentially, was why Maurice, as the paper's token human, had got the big chair. Celebrity gossip, Mordak had rasped at him, during that fateful video-conferencing interview twelve months earlier, I want celebrity gossip. You people know all about that kind of stuff. Well, don't you?

The memory made Maurice wince. What he should have said was, Yes, but goblins have no real concept of celebrities, apart from wanted posters, and you don't give a stuff about the other species, except when you're killing them, so really I honestly believe you're scrabbling up the wrong tree here. Instead he'd tried very hard not to stare at the splintered ends of the three yellow tusks sticking up out of King Mordak's lower jaw and said, Yes, great, no problem, I'll get on it straight away. Give me six months and I'll drag this paper kicking and screaming into the Third Age.

Fool. He sighed, reached instinctively for his coffee mug, then remembered that before it was a coffee mug it had been the skull of his predecessor, and pulled his hand away sharply. Some goblin customs he'd been able to get used to – bowing instead of shaking hands, not walking on the cracks between paving stones and giving dried fruit rather than flowers on Mother's Day; easy-peasy. But whenever his subordinates made coffee-cup jokes (two heads are better than one; hey, latte-for-brains; won't be long before we see his ugly mug down the print room) he just felt sick.

Tomorrow's lead story, for crying out loud. He picked up the sheaf of papers on his desk and shuffled through them, in the hope that something wonderful had crept in there since he last looked, a quarter of an hour ago. Productivity down 0.7 per cent at the Central Weapons Factory. Ereth Morzul Arts & Literature Festival: three dead, one critical but stable. Financial crisis: heads will roll, promises bank chief. He took a second look at that one; but no, Mordak wouldn't like it.

The party line was, *what financial crisis?* and he'd run it as a headline the day before yesterday. Besides, heads rolling at the bank was hardly an unusual occurrence (see above, under sport). Global warming: catastrophe inevitable if immediate action not taken. Yawn. Who the hell would possibly want to read about *that*?

No, he needed a celeb story, and he needed it now. Taped to his wall was the goblin A-list. There were just five names, all decorated war heroes, all (by goblin standards) of unimpeachable integrity. Nothing inherently bad about that; the further up the moral high ground they are, the harder they tumble when skilfully pushed. Trouble was, goblins *loved* their few heroes. Say something nasty about Azog or Gnazhk or One-Eared Zug, and there'd be no trouble finding next morning's front page: *Face Editor Disembowelled By Furious Mob*. Not a bad story, but some great leads come at too high a price. There were always positive celeb stories – *Gogor saves comrades from burning house* had been a sellout; they'd had to print a special edition – but goblin heroes weren't really like that. They simply didn't do warm-fuzzy-feeling stuff. Heroism was simply shorthand for *kills elves* or *massacres dwarves*; and thanks to Mordak and the wretched Coalition—

He stopped, and turned his head. There was a sixth name on the A-list that hadn't been there yesterday. He peered at it.

Not a goblin name. Theo Bernstein. Not elf or dwarf either; unmistakably human, but he was quite sure he'd never heard it before. Not that it'd have mattered a damn if he had. Goblins weren't interested in humans, not even as prospective enemies. As far as goblins were concerned, humans were irrelevant, inhabitants of a faraway country of which they knew little, contemptibly unwarlike, philosophically and ethically incomprehensible, and (according to leading TV chef G'rd'n R'mzarg) unpalatably stringy and with a distinctive bitter aftertaste that no spices could effectively disguise. No, it was pointless even considering—

He looked at the name again. Theo Bernstein. Who the hell was Theo Bernstein? He leaned back in his chair and took a doughnut from the paper bag beside the phone.

And then it happened. Suddenly, spontaneously and with dazzling clarity, he saw the front page. In the same moment, he also saw a computer screen showing record sales figures, a block-long queue besieging a news-stand, Mordak grinning happily, a printing press spewing out copies of a third special edition; it was as though he was standing outside time and space, watching an entire sequence of events, beginning to end, all happening simultaneously. He dropped the doughnut, scrabbled for a pencil and drew the front page.

It was to be completely blank, apart from the *Face* logo and four words:

WHERE IS THEO BERNSTEIN?

The receptionist looked up and grinned at him. Grinning is something goblins naturally do well, the same way that fish are accomplished swimmers. "You can go in now," she said.

He tried to stand up, but his legs had unaccountably turned to pasta. He jammed a fixed smile on his face and used his arms and the arms of the chair to raise himself to his feet. Ah well, he thought. It's been a short life, but a miserable one.

He'd never actually met Mordak in person, only via video conferencing (though the Great King's voice in his ear was a regular feature of his working day), and although there were pictures of him everywhere – posters, the official portrait on the money and the stamps, the omnipresent authorised action figures – he guessed they were stylised and probably designed to flatter, or at least terrify (in goblin terms, much the same thing), so he wasn't really sure what to expect when he nudged open the door to the inner office and teetered through. Certainly not an elf.

"Mr Katz?"

"Um."

The elf smiled. "My name is Glorfangel," he said. "I'm Mr Mordak's executive assistant. Mr Mordak's been held up."

Inside Maurice's head, a fanfare of trumpets, son et lumière, massed choirs. "Ah."

"He sends his apologies," the elf said. "Do please take a seat."

The chair was, of course, pure goblin. Typical in that it was crafted from the leg-bones and tanned hide of some long-dead adversary who'd won the silver medal in a power struggle with the king. Goblins made most of their office furniture out of other goblins; when you joined a major goblin corporation, it wasn't just for life, it was *for ever*. The chair was also typical in that when he sat down in it, it creaked horribly and sagged under his weight, so that he was practically sitting on the floor.

"I know what you're thinking," said the elf.

I bet you do, Maurice thought. "Um."

"You're thinking," the elf went on, "an elf, personal adviser and administrative assistant to the Great Goblin. What is the world coming to?"

You were wrong, then. What I was thinking was, I'm so terrified I really need the bathroom. "I, um—"

"But times are changing, Mr Katz," the elf went on. "That's what the Coalition's all about. Peace in our time, Mr Katz, an end to centuries of bitter, bloody, pointless war between elf and goblin. That's Mr Mordak's dream, and I'm proud to share it."

"Um."

"It's basically a confidence trick, of course," the elf went on. "Mordak spun it to the goblins by saying, Well, do you

want the dwarves back in? And we said exactly the same thing
to our people. Lesser of two evils – the most compelling
argument in politics. We hate A but we hate B more." He
stopped, and smiled the unique elf smile: ethereal beauty and
utter contempt. "But you're an outsider," he said. "Which is
what gives you your unique perspective. You're human. You
hate all of us equally. That's why Mr Mordak gave you the
job."

Maurice wanted to say, No, you're wrong, actually I don't
hate anyone, not even the dwarves. Yes, the violence of the
goblins appals me, but I admire their straightforwardness and
loyalty. Yes, the dwarves are powered by greed the way a
boat's driven by an outboard motor, but they make the most
amazing works of art. And elves – well. Um. But not *hate*. But
an elf wouldn't understand that.

"Right," Maurice said carefully. "Got that. Yes. Um, what
did you want to see me about?"

"This." With a movement of pure poetic grace, the elf
reached down and picked up that morning's *Face*. He turned
it round and laid it on the desk, so that the headline was
aimed at him, like a weapon. "What the hell is it all about?"

Good question. I will not say Um, Maurice promised himself, I will *not*—

"Well?"

"Er."

The elf smiled. "Mr Mordak," he said pleasantly, "was
rather taken aback when he saw that over his pixie eggs and
pan-fried liver this morning. He's curious to know what you
think you're playing at. I confess, so am I." The elf looked at
him for two eternal seconds. "Hm? Who exactly *is* Theo
Bernstein?"

Oh well. "I don't know."

"You don't know."

"No."

"Ah." The elf's eyes sparkled. "You do realise," he went on, "seven million goblins read that today—"

"Seven point six two five. Three special editions. Our best sales ever."

The elf frowned. "Yes, very good, well done. Seven point six two five million goblins, seven point six two five million and one including Mr Mordak, are asking themselves, who is Theo Bernstein and why are we being asked to concern ourselves about him? Is he a threat? Is he the saviour of goblinkind? What does he look like, and where might we expect to find him?" The elf leaned back a little in his chair and ran an elegant fingertip over the point of his left ear. "They all assume," he went on, "that there are answers to those questions. Can you imagine what their reaction's going to be when they find out that *you don't know*?"

Quite suddenly, Maurice felt completely calm. "You don't know a lot about the newspaper business, do you?"

"What makes you say that?"

Maurice smiled. "The public memory," he said. "Absolutely wonderful thing. I call it collective amnesia. It's like when you lead with a health scare or a disaster story. The headline says, we're all going to die the day after tomorrow. Well, the day after tomorrow comes along, and we're all still here, and nobody *minds*, because nobody *believes*. Oh, they see the headline and they buy the paper, but they don't think anything bad will ever actually happen. You can't live that way; life would be impossible. People love to be scared, but only if they know it's not really real. So, they read, and then they forget. Which is exactly what'll happen here. Trust me," he added, "I'm a journalist. Journalism is just one of many stages in the life-cycle of a tree: seed, sapling, tree, lumber, pulp, earth-shattering revelations, fishwrap. Its function – " he was enjoying himself – "is to insulate people from the truth by making them think they know what's going on. Really, it's anti-news, like matter and anti-matter. I mean, if you read about it in the paper, you can be pretty well certain it's not really important, because the really important stuff—"

He dried up. The elf was looking at him, and his face was alight with barely concealed joy; such joy as an oil executive might feel on discovering a vast, untapped new oil field. "What?" Maurice said.

"You believe that?" the elf said.

"Yes."

"Bless you. That's so *sweet*."

Maurice withered and died a little. He was face to face with the Look, the subtle but unique facial expression that only elves can do. *"What?"*

"You're a newspaper editor," the elf said, "and you don't *know*."

"Know what, for crying out—"

The elf smiled. He was happy. "You don't know," he said, "what newspapers are for. Really, I'd never have believed it possible. It's like being a fish and having no concept of water."

Maurice waited patiently, while the elf savoured the moment. When he reckoned the elf had had as much fun as was good for him, he said, "Well?"

"Well." The elf relaxed into his chair, making it look beautiful. "Has it ever occurred to you to wonder why my people, the Elder Race, got into the newspaper business in the first place? We invented them, after all. We founded all the great pillars of the Fourth Estate – the *Tides*, the *Bystander*, the *Warder*, even the dear old *Face* – long before your King Mordak was even thought of. Haven't you ever thought it was odd, the Elders sullying their hands with something so unspeakably *commercial?*"

"That's easy," Maurice replied. "You did it so you could talk down to millions of people at a time and let them see how incredibly superior you are."

"That was just an incidental benefit," the elf replied. "No, the real function of newspapers is to mark the passage of time." He smiled, and went on, "You know what the real heart of a newspaper is? The only bit that matters, though it's the bit that nobody ever actually reads?"

"Um. The wine column?"

"Close, but no. It's the date." The elf's face changed. "On the front page, top left or top right, in small print, usually the only statement of unassailable fact in the whole production."

"The—?"

The elf nodded. "Newspapers exist to mark the transition from one day to the next. Before that, people had to rely on things like the sunrise, but that's not much good, if it's cloudy or foggy. There has to be *publication*, you see – it has to be *written down* somewhere: yesterday was the fifteenth of June, today is the sixteenth, it is now, officially, today. The world has moved one small step. The machinery of time is *working*. Oh, it seems like such a small, silly little thing; and it is, of course. It's mundane, simple, unexciting – an everyday sort of thing, if you'll pardon the expression. You could, of course, say exactly the same about the beating of the heart. It's so commonplace it's boring – until it stops." The elf shook his head. "But it's important, vitally important. So, of course, we saw to it. We kept the clock wound. Well, who else? Humans would forget to wind the clock, goblins would smash it, dwarves would carve it a stunningly ornate case and then sell it. But we're patient, responsible people who understand about things." He frowned slightly. "And then Mordak came along. But that was fine. We saw that Mordak, with his dreams of peace and reconciliation, was just slightly more evolved than your average goblin. We decided he could be trusted, so long as we kept him firmly under control."

Maurice said, "That's your job."

The elf dipped his head in mock salutation. "Of course.

I'm here to control him, which is best done from a position of absolute power. A busy man like King Mordak relies absolutely on his trusted, efficient second-in-command, the man who actually does things, gets things done. It's a subtle distinction, but a vital one. He makes decisions; I decide what decisions he makes. It's a little bit like the difference between a bronze-caster and the man who owns the foundry. Any fool can be trained to make things. Especially decisions."

Maurice looked at him. "He doesn't realise—"

"And wouldn't believe it, if told." The elf studied him for a moment. "Anyway," he said, "now you know. I can't quite believe I told you all that." A quick flash of anger in his deep green eyes. "You provoked me," he said, "into showing off. Ah well, never mind. I think we're drifting away from the purpose of this meeting. I'm supposed to tear you off a strip for your somewhat ill-judged front page. You can see my heart isn't in it."

"Ah."

"But your heart will be in *something*," the elf went on, "if you irritate Mr Mordak. I have no idea what, but I can guarantee it won't be your chest. Think on, human."

Maurice thought. Then he said, "Is that really true? Just the date?"

"Just the date. Everything else is merely salad, pine kernels and a bed of wild rice. But then," he went on, "as a great elven philosopher once said . . . "

"Yes?"

"It's a funny old world. I'm so glad we've had this little chat, Mr Katz. Please don't let me detain you any longer."

All hell had broken loose when he got back to the office. Phones were ringing, goblins were running about shouting, and the art director had eaten the sports editor. He ignored them, wedged a chair under the handle of his door and sat down to get his head together.

When he felt a little better, he checked his in-tray. As well as the usual junk, there was a thick sheaf of Theo Bernstein sightings, which made him smile. He winnowed them down to six and put them carefully to one side. Screw the elf. Rest the story for three days, then a couple of sightings on page 2; two more days, then lead with *Theo Bernstein Seen At—*. Properly handled, he could make it last for months.

Now then; today's lead. But for once, he didn't have to worry. It was there waiting for him. Catastrophic fire at the GorgorSoft HQ, right here in the capital; dozens feared dead (the report on his desk said *confirmed no fatalities*, but you can't stop people being scared, can you?), chaos as networks frozen, heroism of goblin fire crews, the works. He smiled happily, picked up the phone and yelled for his ace reporter.

"What?" she said, dropping into the chair and scowling at him. "Make it quick, can't you? I'm just on my way out to this fire."

"Ah." Of course. He should've known she'd be on it straight away. "Why aren't you there already?"

"Because some fool said he wanted to see me in his office right away."

Maurice nodded. "All right," he said. "I want full coverage. Stories, pictures, angles—"

"Well of course you do. Can I go now?"

"Also," he said firmly, "there's the nameless dread aspect. What really goes on inside the dark towers of GorgorSoft? Make it sound like they're up to something sinister and horrible in there."

"Of *course* they're up to something sinister and horrible. They're goblins."

"Something *goblins* would consider sinister and horrible."

Stephanoriel frowned. He liked it when she did that. It made her look not-ravishingly-beautiful, just for a moment; you could almost believe she wasn't an elf. "What, for crying out loud? They're stockpiling toothbrushes and bath salts? Blast caused by accident in top-secret deodorant research?"

Maurice shook his head. "Steady on," he said, "we don't want to spark off a riot. You'll think of something."

She shrugged, then nodded. "Leave it with me," she said. "Just a moment. GorgorSoft isn't a part of MordaKorp, is it?"

Maurice grinned. "Not yet."

"*Ah.*"

"Got there in the end," Maurice said. "Now go away."

An elf, yes, but she was a damn good reporter. *Horror Blaze At Doomsday Plant*: the perfect headline. He knew he didn't have to read the rest of her copy – it'd be just fine – but he did anyway. And stopped. And frowned. And lifted the phone.

"Get her in here *now*," he barked.

She arrived ten minutes later, looking slightly singed and grubby; it suited her. "Now what?"

He pointed to the relevant paragraph. "What's all this?"

"What's all— Oh, that." She smiled and sat down. "Exactly what you wanted," she said. "Happy?"

"You've made it up, though. Haven't you?"

Something dangerously resembling humility flickered across her face. "Actually, no," she said. "That bit's – well, you know. Practically the T word."

Maurice pursed his lips. "Fearlessly heroic goblin fire-fighters were unable to enter the top-secret sealed lab on the seventh floor, believed to be where the blaze started. That's true?"

"About them not being able to get in there? Yes, actually. Not that they tried too hard – they were having too much fun smashing windows. Anyhow, there wasn't much point. The head geek told them, don't bother with that, there's no one in there and besides, it's one-hundred-per-cent fireproof."

"I see. I don't suppose you've got any idea what's in there?"

"The fire chief did ask. The geek said, Nothing much, just a load of old cardboard boxes."

"Right. And in your view, it's perfectly normal to build a sealed, fireproof facility and use it to store old boxes in."

"Well, I—" She paused. "Yes, that is a bit odd, isn't it? Mind you, Gorgor's off his rocker anyhow; he's well known for it. Always doing crazy stuff."

"He's always doing crazy stuff," Maurice repeated slowly. "You mean, the CEO of a vast and powerful corporation with links to pro-dwarf extremist groups habitually acts in a deranged manner and you haven't got me the story?"

She blinked at that. "Links to—?"

"Oh grow up," Maurice snapped. "Everybody's got links to everything – first rule of journalism. Presumably some pro-dwarf nutter's got GorgorSoft Portals 6 on his laptop somewhere. That's a link. Seriously, though. Why haven't you done anything on this? It's a story. A real one."

She proceeded to say the unthinkable. "You're right."

"It could be huge. We can crucify him. And Mordak hates him, so it's wonderful." He hesitated. "Mordak does hate him, doesn't he?"

"Oh, I should think so. He's rich and successful, and Mordak failed to buy him out eighteen months ago. You know, that's weird. Why haven't we gone for him before? Correction: why hasn't Mordak ordered you to get him? Doesn't make sense."

Maurice thought about that. "I guess I'd better check with Upstairs before we print anything," he said. "But don't let that stop you doing the story. Soon as it's been cleared, I want to get right into it."

"Sure." She stood up. "It'll be strange, though, doing a real story."

"Don't get used to it," Maurice replied. "This time next week we'll be back to making stuff up."

She walked to the door, hesitated. "Of course, if you're into multiverse theory—"

"What?"

"Multiverse theory. Oh, do excuse me. For a moment there, I thought I was talking to an elf."

(There you go. A rather nice compliment all bundled up with an insult. Elves.)

"Thank you," Maurice said. "What the hell is multiverse theory?"

She told him. He looked at her. "That's just silly," he said.

"There's definitely something nasty in there," she reported back. "They've got an elf in charge of R and D, so I asked around. Turns out he works for GorgorSoft because no elven corporation's prepared to touch him with a ten-foot pole. A morbidly unhealthy interest in metaphysics, is how his old tutor described him. Coming from an elf, that's *bad*."

Maurice tapped his fingers on the desktop, which made her scowl at him. "We need to get inside," he said.

"Don't be ridiculous. It's a fortress. Everything else is a heap of smouldering ashes, but the paint on the door of the top-secret bit hasn't even bubbled."

"Good-quality paint?"

"It's on the *seventh floor*."

Maurice thought about that. "Ah."

"I talked to an elf in the fire department," she went on. "As far as he can tell, the seventh floor is what's holding the rest of the building up. *All* of it."

"That's—"

"Yes. There's clearly something seriously weird going on over there." She hesitated and bit her lip. "You know, we ought to tell someone."

"That's the general idea," Maurice said gently. "We're a *newspaper*. Telling people things is definitely part of our remit."

"No." She glared at him. "Not like that. We should go to the proper authorities."

Maurice stared at her for a moment, then burst out laughing. He stopped when he was sure she was about to hit him. "Sorry," he said. "It's just, I don't think you quite understand the *realpolitik* of the Coalition. It means, basically, goblins in charge." He hesitated, as an image of Glorfangel's smile flitted through his head, but he let it go. "In which case, the proper authorities—"

"Would be the goblin military. Yes, fine." She scowled horribly, but it was herself she was angry with. "Bad idea."

"And if you go to your lot," he went on, as kindly as he could, "and if they were to take you seriously—"

"Which they wouldn't. They're a snotty, toffee-nosed lot in Elf Intelligence."

"Um. Anyway, just suppose the elves decided to take it into their own hands. Unilateral use of force against a goblin corporation. That'd be the end of the Coalition, and we'd be at war again. A bit of a high price to pay for a story." A thought struck him. "Do we have any idea what caused the fire in the first place?"

That earned him the oh-come-*on* look. "GorgorSoft Consumer Electronics," she said. "We're talking about an enterprise which places goblins and electricity in close proximity on a regular basis. The question should therefore be: how come it lasted as long as it did."

"Yes, but you said yourself, there's elves working there. In charge of R and D, you said. Therefore, I'm assuming there wasn't the usual cheerful goblin attitude to health and safety. You know what your lot's like when it comes to regulations."

"Valid point." She lifted her head and looked at him with – well, it was as close as an elf could come to respect: roughly as close as Sydney is to Newfoundland, but on the same planet. "I'll see what I can find out. The very fact they spent all that money making sure it was fireproof—"

Maurice hadn't thought of that, but he smirked in such a way as to imply that he had. One advantage of working closely with elves—

With one particular elf—

"We need to get inside," he heard himself say, though his mind was suddenly occupied with other thoughts. "That's where the story is. We need to get in there and see for ourselves."

She gave him a startled look. "Steady on," she said. "It's just a story."

"That's where you're wrong." The sudden passion in his voice was fuelled by other, more complex emotions, but hopefully she hadn't realised that. "This one's different. It's a *real* story. Also, it's one we'll be allowed to tell. Better still, if we tell it, Mordak will love us to bits and pieces. This could be our big chance, don't you see?"

"Yes, but—" She was looking at him oddly. "You're talking as though we have to prove something to somebody; you know, actual unassailable facts, evidence, that sort of thing. Whereas all we really need to do is make up something nasty and print it. Job done."

Which was, of course, perfectly true. But deep inside his head, a little voice was telling him there was another way, a better way: the way we do it back home—

"Sure," he said. "We make something up, we print it,

people read it. And then what? They forget all about it. After all, it's just news." He was talking to her, but also to another elf he'd met recently, one whose philosophy of journalism had also been somewhat at odds with his own. "But if we write a story with *evidence*, a story that might even be at least partially *true* ... " He paused. "True news," he said, with a touch of awe in his voice. "An entirely new and different approach to the newspaper business."

She was frowning, but not sneering. That suited her, too. "You think people'd go for it?"

"No idea." He shrugged. "Maybe they will, maybe they won't. But it's got to be worth a try. And we couldn't have a better opportunity to try it out, don't you think? A genuine shock-horror story about one of the proprietor's main business rivals. It's *beautiful*."

"Even so. Sending round a bunch of goblins to burgle the place ... they're bound to get caught by the security guards, and then there'll be a bloodbath, for sure. True, they're only goblins, but—"

"Who said anything about sending goblins?"

Later, thinking back, he was almost certain that the words came out before he thought the thought, as if someone else hiding inside his body had said them. But, when he heard them, his immediate reaction was: yes, right, go for it.

"You *what*?"

"I couldn't agree with you more," he said cheerfully. "We can't send goblins, they'd make a total mess of it and start killing people, and then we wouldn't get the story."

"But you said—"

"So what we need," he went blithely on, "is a reporter who isn't a goblin. Fortuitously, we happen to have one on the staff. And a very good reporter she is too."

"Have you gone stark raving mad?

Coincidentally, a question he was asking himself at that

very moment. His answer was a qualified no; he had a feeling he wasn't in total control of himself, almost as if something or someone else was prompting his actions, but that wasn't the same as being crazy. Actually, he couldn't remember ever feeling saner in his life. Admittedly, there were some distinctly odd and disturbing things going on inside his head, all of them to do with her, but that was different, and he'd deal with them later, when he had five minutes. Right now, though, he knew what had to be done. Unfortunately, he realised, he didn't have a clue how to do it. "You're an elf," he said. "You're smart, and you people keep telling the rest of us how you know everything. What's the best way to break into a high-security building?"

She was thinking, a symphony in compressed eyebrows and high cheekbones. Later, he had to tell himself, not now. What she was thinking, he had no idea. He was, therefore, surprised on a number of levels when she suddenly grinned at him.

"With a clipboard," she said.

The clipboard was for him – also the tape measure, the gadget with buttons (later she told him it was the remote from a TV that had packed up eighteen months earlier), the video camera and the black attaché case. All she needed, she told him, was a set of fake ID, a haughty expression and pointed ears.

"Agent Tintaviel," she snapped at the security guard, a short, massive-necked goblin with the biggest tusks Maurice had ever seen. "Specialist Cooper." Maurice nodded and tried to look like a Specialist, whatever that was. "And this," she went on, with a respectful gesture towards a particular patch of thin air, "is Chief Director Gr'zog. We need access to the damage zone." She waved a plastic wallet under the goblin's snout. It contained an out-of-date Moviezone season ticket, but her thumb was strategically placed. "It's all been cleared with Division," she said briskly, "but you'll need to file a PZ88C with Area."

The goblin stayed firmly in front of the door. "Hang on," he said.

She sighed perfectly. "What?"

"You said there's three of you."

"Yes. Well?"

"But there's only two."

She gave him the Look. "Chief Director Gr'zog is on a need-to-see basis," she snapped. "Now, if you don't mind, we're on a schedule."

But the security guard didn't move. Instead, he wrinkled his flat, scallop-shell nostrils and sniffed. "And a need-to-smell basis too, of course," she added quickly, but it was obvious she'd got it wrong and they were maybe half a second away from disaster. So Maurice hit him over the head with the clipboard, which, being goblin-made out of ten-gauge sheet iron, got the job done just fine.

"I can't believe I just did that," Maurice said, looking down at the sleeping guard.

"*I* can't believe you just did that," she said, stepping over him. "We're going to be in so much trouble."

"No we're not," Maurice replied crisply. "Think goblin. It's exactly what a senior goblin officer would've done. Come on, will you? This isn't exactly a happy place."

The door they were facing was massive. Maurice had read about it in the file; it was made out of some weird stuff mined from a shooting star that had landed somewhere in the Ice Country, and it was reckoned to be proof against anything known to goblin science. But it had a handle, and when Maurice turned it, the door swung open. "Need-to-see basis, for crying out loud," he muttered, closing the door after her. "That's the trouble with you people. Always got to be *clever*."

"Think goblin," she repeated, mimicking his accent into a whine. "You know perfectly well, all task forces have to be headed by a senior goblin. We haven't got a senior goblin. So—'

They were in a long, white corridor. She tried to overtake him, but Maurice quickened his pace. "And *you* know perfectly well that goblins go by scent more than eyesight. What you should've done was say need-to-smell *first*, and then we'd have had no bother at all. Next time—"

"There isn't going to be a next time. And whether or not there'll be a *this* time is still pretty moot."

They'd reached the end of the corridor, a white door in a white wall. They stopped and looked at it. After about twelve seconds, she said, "Well?"

"After you."

"Why?"

"You're an elf. You have a significantly higher pain threshold and redundant cardio-pulmonary systems enabling you to sustain high levels of physical trauma without sustaining debilitating shock and injury."

"You mean you're scared."

"Yes."

"Fine." She glared at him, opened the door and went through. "Oh wow."

"What?"

"You want to see this."

Shivering a little, he followed her, and found himself in a huge vaulted chamber, lit by fluorescent tubes running horizontally along the bare white walls. He saw a ring of desks and monitors, like settlers' wagons drawn into a circle, surrounding a shimmering glass jar that was somehow very difficult to see. And inside the jar—

At exactly the same time as Maurice opened the door, in exactly the same place, but at ninety-one degrees to that time and place in the D axis, the man in the jar lifted his head and thought, Gosh, a human male entity and a female entity, not quite human. Presumably, she must be one of the Elder race whose existence I deduced just now. Good heavens. And I was right about the ears.

—In which case, this must be somewhere in the *Third* age, because here we've got humans and the Elder folk apparently acting in harmony, or at least together, so presumably they've reached their uneasy rapprochement with the short, grumpy lot with the teeth and formed an alliance against the short, grumpy lot with the beards, assuming I was right about the beards, though surely it stands to reason, because it must be really tricky shaving in the dark. In which case—

The two entities were approaching his jar, and he thought, Oh *snot*, they've come to wipe my memory again, which is a real nuisance, because in about an hour's time I should be ready to prove the existence of the Higgs-Sauron. Oh well. Never mind.

"Hello?" he said.

"It's talking," she whispered.

"Yes," Maurice whispered back. "And it's not an *it*. He's human."

"Shh."

Nobody shushes like an elf. They have the upper lips for it. Maurice listened, but he couldn't hear anything.

But maybe she could. "Say again?"

The man's mouth moved. No sound.

"Yes, hello to you too," she said. "What are you doing in there?"

"You can hear him?"

"Yes, of course. Can't you?"

Maurice shrugged. He'd always known that there was more to elf ears than simply a convenient spike for cleaning under your fingernails with. "What's he saying?"

"Hello."

"Ah, right," he whispered, and waved at the man, who waved back.

♪

"Yes, hello to you too," said the female entity. "What are you doing in there?"

He thought for a moment. "Thinking," he said.

"Thinking?"

"Yes."

"What about?"

"Oh, lots of things." He smiled. He rather liked her. She had a kind face and she hadn't wiped his brain, or at least not yet. "For instance, would I be right in thinking that we're all standing on a big ball of rock perpetually circling around a much bigger ball of incandescent gaseous plasma?"

"What? I mean, yes."

"Oh *good*. I thought we must be, but it's so nice to have it confirmed. What does it look like?"

"What does what look like?"

"The big ball of burning gas."

She thought for a moment. "Like a white sort of blob thing in the sky," she said. "I suppose."

"Only it's not good to look straight at it, because it can damage the optic nerve?"

"Yes."

"*Thank you.*" He gave her an enormous smile. "And what about atmospheric precipitation?"

"What about it?"

"Does water—' He felt rather shy about asking. After all, what if he'd got it completely wrong? "Does water really fall out of the sky sometimes?"

"Well, yes. It's called rain. Almost always happens during major lawn tennis championships."

"Rain," he repeated. "That's a very beautiful word. Did you choose it?"

"No."

"Ah well, never mind. If you happen to meet the person who did, tell them I like it a lot." He hesitated. "You don't mind me asking you things, do you?"

"Um, no. No, that's fine."

"Splendid." He really did like her a lot. "In that case, could you please explain to me exactly how sexual reproduction in humanoid mammals actually *works*, because I've sort of figured out the basic principles, but the actual mechanics of it—"

"Um."

He'd said the wrong thing, obviously. "Sorry," he said quickly. "Are you going to wipe my brain now?"

"Huh?"

Maybe she wasn't. "If it's all right," he said, "I'd quite like it if you didn't, not just yet anyhow, because I'm onto a rather interesting thing about light. You see, if I'm right and light really is the fastest thing in the multiverse, then it sort of stands to reason that if you accelerate matter to light speed in the vacuum of space—"

"Just a second." She was giving him an odd look. "You make it sound like you've thought of all this stuff for yourself. You know, from first principles."

"Yes?"

"That's—"

"I know," he said sadly. "Completely pointless, because just when I think I'm actually getting somewhere, they come along and wipe my brain, and then I've got to do it all over again from scratch, which I can't help thinking is a bit of a waste of time and effort. Still, I guess you've got a perfectly good reason for it, though I have to admit, I haven't been able to figure out what it could be." He looked at her hopefully. "I don't suppose you'd be prepared to give me a hint, would you? It's so frustrating not being able to figure it out for myself. Makes me feel such a fool."

Maybe it was contagious; "Um," she said.

"Fair enough," he replied, "I understand. For some reason I've got to work it out for myself." He frowned, then looked at her again. "If I do work it out, do I get to keep my memories?"

("What's he *saying?*" Maurice hissed.

"Quiet."

"Why's he telling you to be quiet?")

"It's not me," she said.

He took a moment to parse that one, because, self-evidently, she was definitely her, or who else could she be, unless he'd got something drastically wrong in his chain of reasoning. "I'm sorry," he said. "What's not you?"

"It's not me doing this to you."

"Oh." He frowned. A whole new concept had just burst into flower inside his head: good and evil. "Just to clarify," he said. "It's not you."

"No."

"And, from the way you said it, you don't, um, approve. Of me having my mind wiped and everything."

"No, of course not. It's barbaric."

"Ah." His brain was seething, as though it had just switched from monochrome to full colour. Right, he thought, and wrong: fascinating idea. "Dualism."

"You what?"

"A dualistic moral system."

"What? Well, the goblins do that sort of thing, of course. Always fighting duels, goblins, but what else can you expect from people like that?"

"A fully dualistic perspective," he said excitedly, "resulting in value judgements and blind prejudice. Gosh." He pursed his lips. "Isn't that a bit dangerous, though? Ah well, not to worry; I'm sure you've got all that sort of thing completely under control. I mean, you must have, or how could society function?" He stopped and grinned. "Sorry," he said. "Carried away there. So, you don't approve of me being inside this jar?"

"I just said so, didn't I?"

"Yes, of course you did. They haven't just wiped your memory too, have they?"

He could tell she was struggling to stay patient. "Who's been doing this to you?"

"Entities."

"Mm." She nodded. "You couldn't be a bit more precise, I suppose?"

"Not really," he said sadly. "Really, you see, it's just logical extrapolation on my part. Because, well, obviously, I must have been in existence for more than one hundred arbitrary time units; I know that, because I figured out how biochemistry works, and that involves growth and ageing, and I'm fairly sure I'm quite grown up. Well, in a hundred arbitrary time units I've done quite a bit of figuring-things-out, though obviously I'm not all that good at it, because for the life of me I can't seem to prove the existence of the Higgs-Sauron, and I hadn't even tumbled to dualism until you came along – probably I'm just a bit thick or something. But anyhow, one hundred arbitrary time units and I'm this far along from an absolutely clean start; but I've been alive rather longer than one hundred arbitrary time units, so why haven't I figured out loads and loads more stuff? And as far as I can see, the only possible explanation is, every so often someone comes along and wipes my brain clean. Naturally I assumed there was a perfectly good reason for it, so I didn't mind, but now you come along and say it's not right, so I don't know what to think."

She was looking at him. "So you don't have any idea who you are, or why they're keeping you in that jar thing?"

"Well, no," he said apologetically. "I suppose I really should've worked it out by now, because it must be pretty fundamental, don't you think? I mean: who am I, why am I here? I bet everybody else knows that except me."

"Um," she said. "And you just stay in there, and think about things?"

"Yes."

"And when you've thought for a bit, they come and remove your memories."

"That's right, yes."

"Why would anyone want to do that? For crying out loud stop prodding me."

"Sorry," Maurice said. "But look, what's going on? Who is he, and why are they—?"

"Shut *up*."

d

"Sorry," he said.

"Not you. Oh hell, I've forgotten what I was asking you now."

"'Why would anyone want to do that? For crying out loud stop prodding me.'"

"Yes, right. Well? Why *would* anyone do that? I mean, it's not just nasty, it's pointless. You sit there conceptualising the universe—"

"Multiverse."

"What?"

"I think there's probably more than one universe. Actually, I have a shrewd suspicion there's lots of them."

"You sit there conceptualising the universe," she repeated, "from first principles, to an amazingly advanced level, which is, um, amazing; and then someone comes along and scrubs it all out. It gives a whole new sinister penumbra of meaning to the term think-tank. And it's *stupid*. It's no use to anyone. They can't possibly make any money out of it."

"Money?"

"Circulating medium of exchange assigned a token value to facilitate economic activity."

"Cool." He pulled a dubious face. "But hang on, though. Actually, it's not such a good idea, surely. I mean, if you had something like that, isn't there a risk someone might start speculating in overextended synthetic credit derivatives and trigger a global economic crisis?"

"Don't be silly."

"Quite," he said humbly. "Who'd do such a thing? Sorry, I interrupted you."

"Listen to me." She leaned forward until her nose touched the barely perceptible wall of the jar. There was a sizzling noise and a smell like seawater, and she shrank back. "It's all

right," she said, "just a minor electric shock, that's all. *Listen.*
They're holding you in a— Oh hell, how am I supposed to
explain when you can't understand? All right, try this. The
situation you're in is *not normal.*"

"Isn't it?" He stared at her. "Oh."

"Absolutely not. There are millions and millions of people
in the world – elves, goblins, dwarves, even humans – and
very, very few of them are kept in jars and have their brains
messed with. And of that very small number, the majority are
being tortured to find out what they know. But nobody seems
to want to find out what you know. Quite the reverse." She
pulled a puzzled face. "Do they feed you?"

"Ah. You mean regular intake of nutritional biomatter."

"I suppose I do, yes."

"No." His eyebrows furrowed. "I was wondering about
that. I'd got this theory about how organic life operates, but
obviously it's completely wrong, because—"

"We've got to get you out of there," she said.

"Gosh."

"Well, obviously we've got to; we can't just leave you in
there indefinitely." She paused, took a step back, looked up
and down. "Trouble is, I don't see how. There doesn't seem
to be a door or anything."

"What's a—?"

"There's got to be one," she went on. "Otherwise, how did
they get him in there in the first place? Unless this jar thing
was somehow built round him, but I don't see how—"

"Excuse me."

"Not now. And there's definitely some sort of low-yield,
high-resonance EM field, which means we can't use conven-
tional cutting tools, so—"

"Listen."

"What?"

Maurice was trying really, really hard not to grin. "I think you're missing the point," he said.

"*What?*"

"Think about it. There's no door, right?"

"Well, duh."

"That's because," he said kindly – all his life he'd wanted to patronise an elf – "you're not asking yourself the right question."

"Oh really. And what would that be?"

"When is a door not a door?"

"When it's a— Oh."

"Yes."

"But that's *ridiculous*," she exploded. "It's a *joke*, for crying out loud."

"Nominally, at least," he agreed. "Let's just call it wordplay, shall we?"

"All right, *wordplay*. It's still just ... well, words. It's not coherent matter, atoms and molecules. It's not *real*."

Maurice frowned. "I think he wants to tell you something."

"What?"

"Sorry," he said. "But I couldn't help overhearing. When you were saying, 'It's still just ... well, words. It's not coherent matter, atoms and molecules.' And that made me—"

"Well?"

His face was a study in bewilderment. "Remember something."

"Oh. But I thought—"

He nodded. "Yes. It's the first thing I've remembered. You know, it's a very odd sensation, like having someone talking to you inside your head. I guess you get used to it after a while, but I'm not sure I like it. Sort of creepy."

"What," she said firmly, "did you remember?"

"In the beginning was the Word."

"What?"

"In the—"

"Yes, I heard you. But—"

"And it sort of makes sense, doesn't it? I mean, you just said, 'It's still just ... well, words. It's not coherent matter, atoms and molecules.' But if in the beginning there was just the Word, then it sort of follows that coherent matter—"

"It's just a metaphor," she said. "Imagery. Poetry. Not actually *true*."

"If you say so. But I seem to remember that it is true. Well, sort of trueish, anyway. I think it was terribly important to me at some earlier stage in my existence, though quite possibly not this stage I'm in now. Which implies, doesn't it, that—"

"Oh be quiet."

*

"Think about it," Maurice said. "We're looking for a door, right?"

"Yes."

"But there isn't a door, there's just a jar."

"Yes, but—"

"Well, then."

"You can't just say, *Well, then* and expect everything to be— Oh."

He reached out his hand. There was a sizzle and a flash, and he landed on his back, as a private firework display that would've cost thousands played out in front of his eyes.

"Told you so."

"So you did," he replied from between gritted teeth.

"Bugger," he added. "I was so sure it'd turn out to be something simple and obvious."

She had that faraway look that elves get sometimes, that ineffable blend of delicate spirituality and smugness. "It may well be," she said. "Find something to occupy yourself with for a minute or two. I need to think about this."

Maurice was no lawyer, but he'd read about the landmark case of *All Sentient Life On Earth vs Tarturiel*, in which it was argued that killing an elf who spoke to you like that wasn't murder or even homicide; it was justifiable pesticide and abating a public nuisance. The trial had foundered on a technicality, so the actual point of law remained a grey area, needing to be clarified in a further test case. For two pins, Maurice thought.

"All right," she said abruptly, "let's do this step by step. When is a door not a door?"

"When it's a jar."

"Correct." She nodded. "Therefore, when a door is a jar, it's not a door, yes?"

"Um."

"Yes. By syllogistic extrapolation, we accordingly find that a jar is not a jar when it's a door. Agreed?"

"Syllogistic what?"

"This," she went on, pointing, "is a jar. A jar being a jar. Therefore it's not a door."

Maurice rubbed his elbow, which was still a bit numb. "I think I sort of proved that already."

"So you did. Clever old you. It's a jar being a jar, not a door being a door, so when you tried to use the jar as a door, it zapped you and gave you a nasty jar." She waited, then shrugged. "But," she went on, "acting on the hypothesis that the jar/door equivalency is in some degree valid, it must therefore follow that at some stage, induced by some process, this jar was at some point not a jar but a door. With me so far?"

"I think we should go home now."

"Now then," she continued, giving him the bent eye, "the jar/door equivalency only makes sense in the context of multiverse theory, which posits that there are points of bifurcation at which a continuum divides into separate parallel continu*a*, effectively duplicating any given object or person and thereafter subjecting it to two or more different sets of events, influences and environments, which might tend to alter that object or person—ouch, that *hurt*."

"It was meant to," Maurice said grimly, massaging the finger he'd prodded her with. "But I had to make you stop, before it became unbearable."

She scowled at him, then made a visible effort. "Maurice," she said, "this is *important*."

"You just called me—"

"Let me put it," she said, gently but firmly, "another way. Multiverse theory, yes?"

"All right."

"Every time something happens, a new universe branches off from our one, OK?"

"Go on."

"And the branched-off universe is a carbon copy of ours except for the one different thing."

"If you say so."

"Will you stop *sulking*? There, that's better. All right. Carbon-copy-except-for-one-different-thing. But the different thing means the branch universe develops in a different way. Yes?"

"Yes."

"Splendid. So, you've got two versions of what was originally the same thing. Like evolution, really. One fish decides to grow legs and walk up the beach; one fish decides it's perfectly happy being a fish and stays in the water. Time passes. The fish that grew legs is now a bird. Result; you've got a bird and a fish. But originally they were both fish." She beamed at him. "Don't you *see*?"

"No."

She sighed. "If we apply multiverse theory, a door in the mainstream universe can be a door in one post-bifurcation branch universe and a jar in another, and *still be the same door*." She paused, wrinkled her nose and added, "Or jar. Whatever. You do see that, don't you? You don't, do you?"

"No."

"All right," she said. "It's magic. Better?"

"Much. Thank you."

"The difference being," she went on, "that evolution is a one-way process and irreversible. But what if there's a way of reversing multiversal bifurcation, or at least arcing across from one branch to another? Using, I don't know, some kind of interface or portal." Her face suddenly lit up. "Some kind of *door*."

"Or jar."

"Shush. No, actually, not shush. Some kind of *jar*."

Maurice made a soft whimpering noise.

"No, really," she assured him, "it's like embassies."

"I thought it was like evolution."

"No, you clown, that was like evolution, *this* is like embassies. Like, you know, an embassy is nominally the soil of the country it represents. What if the inside of that jar's like an embassy for a different reality? It's here in this one, but it's a little bit of another one, hermetically sealed? A non-permeable interface." She gave him a beautiful smile, so that he very nearly forgave her for frying his brain. "A *locked* door."

"Of course," Maurice said. "Suddenly it all makes sense. *Now* can we go home, please?"

"I told you, didn't I? I said it'd turn out to be something simple and obvious."

Two more seconds and the lawyers would've had their test

case. Before Maurice could make legal history, however, the door flew open and a dozen goblins burst into the room. They were armed with a wide variety of Weapon-Of-The-Month Club selections, and their faces bore the look of quiet joy goblins only wear when they're about to get paid for doing something they love.

"That'll do," snapped a voice behind them. The happy faces immediately went sad and droopy, and the goblins fell in at attention on either side of the doorway. A man walked in. A—

She was staring at him. "Human?"

The man smiled pleasantly. "Yes," he said. "By birth," he added. "But I've been a naturalised goblin for the last ten years. My name's Gorgor. I own this place. I don't know who you are."

"A naturalised—"

"Goblin, yes, and I'm sorry, but you're starting to annoy me. Would you mind explaining what you're doing here?" His smile levelled out a bit. "A good answer buys you lunch. A bad one gets you a trip to the roof and a flying lesson. No pressure."

She blinked, then smiled. "Lunch sounds good."

Maurice, who'd opened his mouth, closed it again. *She never smiled at me like that,* he thought; and then, hang on, *you're being threatened with death by armed goblins and you're doing qualitative analyses of* smiles? *Yes, because it matters. Maybe. But not now—*

"I'm having strips of pan-fried duck on a bed of roast artichoke hearts with parmesan and dark chocolate sauce," Gorgor said. "Not very goblin, I know, but the raw liver of my mortal enemy gives me heartburn. What are you doing here?"

"We're journalists," she said.

"Good heavens."

"That's right," Maurice broke in. "We were doing a follow-up story about the fire, and I guess we must've got lost wandering around the building, and—" He stopped. Nobody seemed to be listening to him.

"I always thought that must be a fascinating job," Gorgor was saying. "I mean, you must get to meet the most remarkable people."

Hang on, Maurice thought; hang on just a moment, this isn't right, they can't be—And then he caught sight of the notched blade of the sword one of the goblins was holding, and he thought, Priorities. And then he thought, Well, of course. She's only schmoozing him to save both our skins; it's a purely tactical schmooze, after all, she'd never— Tactical, he repeated firmly, and realised that nobody, not even a seasoned newspaper man, can ever lie convincingly to himself.

"Maurice." She was smiling brightly to herself. "I think I can handle things here OK, if you want to get back to the office. You want to get back to the office, don't you?"

"Um."

"You want to get back to the office," she said grimly, "because it's nearly one o'clock and you've still got pages four and five to see to, and weren't you expecting that very important call?"

"What call?"

"*That* call." Furious eyes and a fixed beaming smile. "The important one, remember? The one you said you had to be back in time for."

It is better to have loved and lost, the ancients said, than never to have loved at all. Indeed. This from the same people who brought you *the earth is flat and the sun revolves around it,* and *the urine of a red-headed virgin will cure malaria.*

Gorgor was also smiling at him. "Thanks ever so much for dropping by," he was saying. "Sorry you've got to rush away. The lads will see you out."

The goblins snapped to attention. They blamed him, he could tell. The hell with it. Time to go.

"Don't be too long," he wasted his breath telling her as the goblins escorted him to the door. "Remember, I need a thousand words by four o'clock." A goblin accidentally trod on his foot and he moved briskly. As he did so, he glanced back at the jar, where the man was now sitting cross-legged on the floor, his eyes closed, his face completely blank, as though his mind had somehow been wiped clean. But before that, he'd been moved to breathe heavily on the jar wall, and, in the resulting condensation, had fingertip-traced—

MY NAME IS THEO B

—only back to front.

*

"Oh." he said. "It's you."

Quarter to six. He'd spent the afternoon shouting at people and not getting much useful work done. Tomorrow's lead story was going to have to be WEATHER CONTINUES MILD, but he wasn't sure he cared anymore. And now she was back, standing in the doorway of his office with a ridiculous and totally non-elven grin on her face.

"Yes," she said.

"Well?"

"Oh, I had a marvellous afternoon," she said. "First we had lunch; did you know the whole of the top floor is like this amazingly cool staff canteen? Well, the goblin bit is pretty gross – you really don't want to hear about the mixed grill – but there's a balcony overlooking the river, and—"

"Yes, thank you. What a great story that'll make."

"Anyway," she went on, "he had the duck and I had a

really nice goats' cheese and dandelion-leaf salad, and then we went for a walk on the roof; he's got this beautiful sort of formal garden laid out, with—"

"You interviewed him."

She giggled. Elves just *don't*, but she did. "In a sense, yes."

"Get anything?"

"Oh yes."

"Did you find anything out?" he corrected grimly. "About the man in the jar?"

"What? Oh him. Yes, Gorgie explained all about that. Apparently this poor man was in a dreadful accident, fell off a building or something, horrendous brain damage – it means he can't remember anything for more than an hour and then it's gone again. So Gorgie's medical team are trying to help the poor lamb, but there isn't much hope, I'm afraid. I think it's really sweet, the way Gorgie's using his own money and all those resources to try and help a perfect stranger, because you know what the goblins are like – *they* couldn't give a damn, though Gorgie says he's right behind Mordak's new medicare proposals; even though they don't agree about a lot of things, still, he's fair-minded enough to see that—"

"Right," Maurice snapped. "Got that. So there's no story there, then."

"Oh, I think it'd make a marvellous story. Philanthropist backs Mordak on health reforms. Mordak'll love it. I said, we'll put it on tomorrow's front page, because it's a bit late for today's edition. What're you leading with, by the way?"

"Weather continues mild."

"Mphm. Anyway, we can lead with that, and we can have a follow-up human-interest story on page four – you know, the man behind GorgorSoft—"

"I think our readers will find *human* and *interest* something of a contradiction in terms."

"Ah, but he's a goblin now." She smiled. "We can make a big thing out of that. I used to be human but I'm better now, says GorgorSoft founder. The goblins'll love that."

She was right; that was the horrible irony of it all. And Mordak'd be happy too. True, he'd have preferred an excuse to employ Gorgor in an advisory capacity (advisory as in *pick your brains*), but support for his floundering and deeply unpopular flagship welfare program from a totally unexpected ally would probably do almost as well. And it'd sell papers – absolutely no question about that. All in all, she'd done brilliantly well. Only—

"Oh, by the way," he said. "He's Theo Bernstein."

"What?"

"The man in the jar. He's Theo Bernstein."

She gave him an indulgent smile. "Don't be silly."

"But he *is*. He breathed on the side of the tank and wrote it."

She shook her head. "He may *think* he's Theo Bernstein," she said kindly. "But he can't be, because you made Theo Bernstein up, just to sell a few papers." She clicked her tongue. "Probably the poor, confused man heard people talking about it and decided that's who he is. It's all very sad, but at least he's getting the best possible care. Don't you think that's rather wonderful?"

Oddly enough. Maurice didn't. Nor was he entirely convinced by her account of Gorgor's explanation, though he was prepared to admit that he might be somewhat prejudiced. What surprised him most, though, was that she seemed to believe what Gorgor had told her. After all, she was the one who'd talked to the man in the tank, to Theo B—

I made him up, she'd said. But I didn't. I saw his name, on the A-list.

Entirely true; but now he came to think of it, he couldn't remember having added Bernstein's name to that list, which he'd written out himself. He got out of his chair and went and looked at it. His handwriting, for sure, and five names, all goblins. Theo Bernstein wasn't on there.

Oink?

He sat down again. I saw the name on the list. I *thought* I saw the name on the list. I wrote the frigging list, and I don't remember adding him to it. Think carefully; when was the first time I can remember coming across the name Theo Bernstein?

He thought. Hard.

When I saw it on the list. But that's—

Oh boy. Things, he couldn't help feeling, were rapidly slipping out of control. It was now fairly clear that he was in love with Stephanoriel, just as it was pretty blindingly obvious that she was besotted with Gorgor the human goblin. Furthermore, he appeared to have invented a fictional character he himself had firmly believed in, who'd then turned up in a mysterious glass jar (which was also, in some sense, a door; oooh, let's not go there) in the high-security research facility, *seventh-floor* research facility that was apparently keeping the rest of the fire-ravaged building from collapsing in a heap of ash and rubble. Add to all that multiverse theory, and a very remote but still material possibility that in the beginning was some sort of Word, and you had what? A mess, is what you had; see also under shambles, pig's ear, goblin's all-day breakfast and pain in the bum. Still, he reminded himself, he also had tomorrow's headline. That made up for a *lot*.

But not, he realised, enough. He chased the problem through his mind for a bit, and kept coming to the same conclusion. The man in the jar: he was key, possibly even core. Because if the man in the jar really was Theo Bernstein, that meant—

—he hadn't invented him;

—Gorgor was lying; therefore—

—Gorgor was sinister and up to no good, in which case—

—She wouldn't love him anymore, the *Face* could do a really vicious exposé and get loads of good headlines and extra sales, which would please Mordak almost as much as destroying his hated rival, the CEO of GorgorSoft, and—

—he could round off the Theo Bernstein story with Bernstein being rescued from unspeakable torture (actually, there was precious little that goblins found unspeakable; unspellable, yes, practically everything more than one syllable long, but not unspeakable), with loads of kudos for Mordak and the forces of law and order, and a huge headline announcing the discovery and rescue along the lines of IT WAS THE FACE WOT TRACED HIM.

Yes, he thought. I like that.

Fine. That just left the question of how. Well, he'd have to go back, on his own this time – no, *not* on his own, but definitely without her; and sneaking in pretending to be someone else was out, because he'd be recognised, so good old-fashioned aggravated burglary seemed to be called for. In which case, he'd need muscle. Not goblins, though. The goblin idea of going equipped for burglary was siege towers and a battering ram. What he needed, he decided, was two highly skilled and experienced private investigators, the sort of men every tabloid editor turns to when the going gets tough—

"Um," he said.

"And this is my nephew, Art," the old man went on. "Don't judge him by how he looks; he's a good lad, and I promised his mother I'd look after him. He's got a real gift for the covert surveillance and information-gathering business, haven't you, Art?"

The young man shrugged and ate a lamb samosa.

Maurice frowned. "Do I know you two from somewhere?"

"It's possible," the old man said, "very possible. I mean, we been in the business three years now, and before that I was forty years in clawmarks with goblin CID, followed by fifteen years as a hired assassin and soldier – oops, excuse me, one of my giddy spells – of fortune. So yes, our paths may well have crossed, sir, given the nature of our respective callings. Quite possible."

"Or maybe not," Maurice said firmly. "Not to worry. Listen," he went on, lowering his voice. "Have you ever heard of—?"

"Say what?"

"Have you ever heard," Maurice shouted quietly, "of a human called Theo Bernstein?"

"Oh yes."

"You have?"

"Course. Read about him in the *Face*, didn't we. Art? Always read the *Face*, we do."

Maurice sighed. "Yes," he said. "But before that."

"No, can't say I—" The old man paused. The young man had tugged his sleeve and was whispering in his ear. "Yes, that's right," he said. "Now you come to mention it, I think I do. The lad says, Mr Katz, wasn't Theo Bernstein that chap who blew up the Very Very Large Hadron Collider a year or two back?"

"The what?"

"And then went on to complete the late Pieter van Goyen's work on the YouSpace multiverse portal before disappearing in mysterious circumstances. Would that be who you were thinking of?"

"Um."

"Is that who we're going after, then, sir? Theo Bernstein? Only young Art here was saying just the other day, bet you anything you like that bloke they got in the glass jar up GorgorSoft is that Theo Bernstein. Didn't you, Art?"

The young man nodded with his mouth open and full. Maurice closed his eyes for a moment, then said, "Something like that. Of course, we're going to have to break into the building."

"Leave all that to the boy and me, sir. There isn't an electronic surveillance device on the planet young Art can't outwit. Infra-red beams, underfloor pressure pads, air-displacement monitors, one-thirty-six-bit encryption – might as well not bother when the lad's on the case, sir."

Maurice blinked. "*Him?*"

"They call him the Wizard," the old man said simply.

"Do they really? And what about the rest of it? Scaling sheer walls and abseiling off rooftops and stuff?"

"Oh, I handle that side of it. We're a team, see. He's the brains, I'm the brawn, you might say."

There was a soft crackle, as the young man stripped the cellophane off a meat and potato pie. "Fine," Maurice said. "I love it when a plan comes together."

In the event, it went pretty well. There were a couple of anxious moments: when the old man was hanging by his foot from a piton hammered into the eighth-floor balcony and his hearing aid fell out; when the young man paused in the middle of winching himself down from the ceiling on a titanium-framed collapsible crane to check his text messages; when he unscrewed the cap of his Thermos of hot soup without first neutralising the heat-detection circuit. Other than that, the proverbial walk in the park.

Surprised, therefore, but enormously relieved, Maurice found himself standing in front of the glass jar in the secret laboratory, looking at the man inside. He was asleep, his head resting against the wall of the jar, eyes closed, mouth open. He rapped on the jar wall with his knuckles. "Hello," he said. "Can you hear me?"

The man opened his eyes, blinked, frowned, and Maurice realised he was looking at a completely empty mind. He banged on the jar with his balled fist. "Can you hear me?" he yelled, but the man carried on gawping.

"Can we hurry it up a little, please?" the old man was saying behind him, but he couldn't be bothered to answer. The man, he somehow knew, was Theo Bernstein. All he had to do was get him out of the jar, and—

"Only I think I can hear someone coming," the old man went on. "About ten of them, at a guess, and probably goblins, so if you could start thinking about leaving."

Maurice swung round. "Can you get this thing open?"

The old man looked sad. "Doubt it, sir, doubt it very much. That's a multiversal static inversion chamber, see, and they don't strictly speaking actually exist in this reality, so getting it open would be rather difficult. Also, it might set off a chain reaction and bring about the end of all universes everywhere. Don't know how you stand insurance-wise, but you might want to check and make sure you're covered before you—"

"I don't care. Get it open."

"Right you are," the old man said. "Art. Get that chamber open, son, and don't take too long about it. Definitely goblins, sir, headed this way."

The young man stuffed the rest of his sausage roll in his mouth and loped over to the jar. He scratched his head, peered up and down, picked his nose, ate an individual pork pie and frowned. Then he prodded the jar with his finger. There was a faint *ting!* like the jingle of a slightly bent bell, and a door slid open.

The man in the jar jumped to his feet, staggered, stood up straight and drew in a vast lungful of air. That made him stagger again; he slumped against the jar wall, bounced, and hurled himself through the open panel. The moment his foot hit the floor outside the jar, the whole building started to shake.

The old man grabbed Maurice's sleeve. "Got to go *now*, sir," he said. "Fissures in the interdimensional walls, leading to a potential multiphasic implosion. Oh *crikey*."

Maurice pushed him away. The man from the jar stumbled towards him, his face red with sudden, unlimited rage. An alarm went off somewhere. The floor under Maurice's feet bubbled and rocked. "What the *hell*," the man was shouting, "is going on?"

Maurice lunged towards him, but a tremor sent him sprawling sideways. He blundered into the old man and knocked him down. "Are you Theo Bernstein?" Maurice yelled.

"What?"

"Are you—?"

"Yes. Who are you? Where am I? Why aren't I wearing any clothes? Why's the building shaking like that?"

The door flew open. Three goblins with crossbows stumbled into the room. The young man picked up two of them, one in each hand, and banged their heads together with a clang that made Maurice's teeth hurt. The third goblin—

"Theo Bernstein? Really?"

"I just said so, didn't I? Where is this? And what are those horrible *creatures*?"

Pausing only to stuff an iced doughnut in his mouth, the young man lunged at the third goblin, just as he was about to loose an arrow at Maurice. The floor shook again. The goblin tripped and fell on his knees, dropping the bow. The young man swung at him with his fist but missed, and the unexpectedly unblocked momentum carried him off his feet; he crashed into the old man, who was just getting up, and choked, spitting out the doughnut, which hit Maurice in the eye. He caught it without thinking. The third goblin had crawled to his crossbow and was aiming again, not at Maurice this time, but at the man from the jar. "*No*," Maurice heard himself yell, and without knowing why, he sprang forward, putting himself between Bernstein and the goblin, just as the goblin pressed the trigger—

Oh, Maurice thought.

The arrow flew. He watched it. He noticed how it bucked slightly as it left the bowstring, fishtailing for a moment before stabilising and flying straight at him. In that fraction of a second, he'd lifted his hand in a fatuous attempt to shield himself from the arrow. He was still holding the doughnut. The arrow came on, went straight into the hole in the middle of the doughnut without touching the sides, and vanished.

"Hey," the goblin screamed, "that's cheating!"

The young man was on his feet again. He looked longingly at the doughnut, then back at the goblin, who was frantically reloading. "Get him, Art!" the old man screamed, but the young man hesitated, maybe because he was weak from lack of food. The goblin swung up his newly spanned crossbow and levelled it at Bernstein, who had stepped out from behind Maurice and was waving his arms in fury. Maurice tried to stop him, but Bernstein shoved him out of the way; Maurice staggered and fell backwards, in through the opening in the jar. As his head hit the glass he heard a twang and saw, through the hole in the doughnut in his flailing left hand, the arrow hit Bernstein squarely in the chest—

"What in *God's name*," Max was shouting, "do you think you're playing at?"

Maurice opened his eyes. He was looking at a box. There was a short arrow sticking out of it, the head buried in the cardboard up to the socket. He was lying on something. He shifted, and found the squashed remains of a doughnut under his right knee.

"He's dead," Maurice said.

Max froze. "You what?"

"He's dead," Maurice repeated numbly. "A goblin shot him with a crossbow. I saw it."

Max sagged. He sort of came apart, like a badly put-together flat-pack chair when you sit on it for the first time, and slid into an untidy heap on the floor. "That's not possible," he moaned. "He can't be."

"I saw it," Maurice said quietly. "He was in a sort of jar, just like in George's place, only where we were, George was a goblin called Gorgor, except he was human, and Stephanie was an elf. I broke in to rescue him, but a goblin shot him. I'm sorry," he added. "But there it is. He's dead."

"Don't say that," Max said, his voice angry and weak. "That's my *brother* you're talking about."

"Sorry. I tried to save him," Maurice remembered. "I jumped in front of the first shot, but he reloaded. I can't see how he could've survived."

"You *idiot*." There were two tears running a crooked race down Max's face. "And what do you mean, goblins? That's just *stupid*."

"Where I was, the goblins are in charge," Maurice said. "I was the editor of a newspaper, and Stephanie—" He got the impression that Max wasn't all that interested. "Anyway, that's what happened," he went on. "If you don't believe me, you could ask the lad who eats a lot. He and his uncle bring the boxes here. He saw the whole thing."

Max gave him a just-don't look, but he ignored it. He was listening to what he'd just said. It didn't sound quite right. "The old man and the kid who's always eating," he said. "They were there. How could they be there? I don't understand."

"Hold it just a second." Max was back. "Two guys from this reality were over where you just were."

"That's right," Maurice said. "And the boy managed to open the jar. *I* was in the jar," he recalled suddenly. "I fell into it when your brother shoved me out of the way. Then I looked into the doughnut, and—"

"What jar?"

"The jar that's a door. Sorry," Maurice added quickly, as Max glared at him. "They had your brother in this glass jar, like the one at George's. Stephanie thought it was some kind of interdimensional portal thing. When the boy opened it, the building started falling down."

"Then it can't have been an interdimensional portal," Max snapped. "You can't open those things. Well, maybe you could if you had a constant object, but you left it behind." He pointed at the plastic ray-gun, which was lying on the floor still glowing blue. "And if you did open it, that'd be *it*. The end, finito. Goodbye universe."

Maurice shrugged. "Maybe that's what happened after I left," he said. "Don't suppose it matters terribly much. It wasn't a very nice universe anyway. There was a goblin called Mordak who owned nearly everything." He shook his head. "Anyway, I suppose that's the end of the road. I really am sorry about your brother."

"Screw you," Max said. "Theo isn't dead. He can't be. He won the Nobel frigging prize."

Slight non-sequitur there, Maurice thought, but he didn't say anything. "I think we should think about how we're going to get out of here," he said. "If they find us here in the morning, we're going to be in the most awful trouble. They'll probably call the police. I could lose my job."

Max didn't seem to be listening to him. "You're right," he said. "Maybe you're right," he amended. "Maybe it was an interdimensional portal, so when it opened, the universe *did* end." He twisted round sharply and grabbed a handful of Maurice's shirt front. "When you last saw my brother," he growled, "was he alive?"

"I told you, he got hit by an arrow. Like that one," he added, pointing at the arrow sticking out of the box. "It got him around about there," he added, "where you're holding my shirt."

"Yes, but was he still *alive*? As in not actually dead *yet*?"

"I don't know, do I? I'm not a doctor. Look, I really am most dreadfully sorry, but I don't see how he could possibly have survived getting shot like that. And we really do need to get out of this building if we possibly can." He stopped; a nasty thought had just struck him. "You can leave, can't you? I mean, you're not stuck here somehow, like your brother was."

Max shrugged. "Don't ask me," he said. "I don't know how I got here. Not all that sure where here is, now I think about it. Last time I looked, this was a cave, but you seem to think it's some kind of warehouse—"

"Cave?"

"Yeah, cave. A long, deep hole in the ground. Where I've been for the last— For a very long time. Look, stop it, will you, you're confusing me." He looked so very sad that Maurice couldn't help feeling sorry for him. "Jesus, I don't know. I've been centred on finding Theo for so long, I haven't really noticed much else. And now you've gone and got him killed."

"I did *not*—" Maurice stopped. If he hadn't burgled the GorgorSoft building, Theo Bernstein would still be alive. Oh, he thought.

"I guess you're right," Max went on. "We should get the hell out of here. After all, there's not a lot of point sticking around anymore, and you've got a life to go back to, and— Well, *you've* got a life. Me, I'm legally dead. I suppose I'll have to go scrounge some money off my sister. That'll be a gas – she's a total flake – but what else am I supposed to do, for Christ's sake?" He stood up, caught sight of the clothes he was wearing and shuddered. "I've really let myself go, you know? I'm going to have to put some serious work in. Well, you coming or what?"

He set off, and Maurice followed, and they came to a huge steel door. It was fitted with a fiendishly complex system of sliding bars and bolts, operated by cams and connecting rods. There was also a plain brass handle, which Max turned. The door opened.

Max hesitated and turned his head. "So long, then," he said. "You were worse than useless, but I guess you did try, for what that's worth. Not a hell of a lot, but—" He shrugged. "Fresh air," he said. "Been a long time. Is it *supposed* to stink like that?"

"I can't smell anything."

"Yes, but you live here, God help you." He frowned. "Hey," he said. "What country is this?"

"England."

"Oh boy. Never mind," he added graciously, "I assume they have aeroplanes in this reality. Talking of which, give me a thousand dollars."

"Um."

"Sorry, forgot. Give me, say, seven hundred pounds. My sister'll pay you back," he added hopefully. "At some point."

"I haven't got—"

"No, of course you haven't. How much have you got? Cash," he added, "no cards or cheques. I'm dead, remember?"

Slowly, Maurice took out his wallet. It held two ten-pound

notes. He handed them over. Max looked at them as if he'd just been given a dead baby bird, then stuffed them in his top pocket. "England," he said. "Well, look on the bright side: it can only get better. So long, loser. If anyone asks, you haven't seen me." And he stepped through the door and was gone.

Maurice stood for a while looking at the door, then turned away, looking at the opened box. He frowned, then walked over and peered down into it. Empty, of course. He knelt down and taped it up again, then he prised the arrow loose, wrapped his handkerchief round the needle-sharp point – no way on earth Bernstein could've survived – and dropped it in his pocket. Then he picked up the plastic ray-gun. It felt different somehow: more plastic, less ray-gun. What the hell, he thought; he looked round until he found the squashed remains of the iced doughnut, then backed off ten paces and aimed the ray-gun at it. There were no sights, of course, so he squinted down it, using the slight raised line of flashing left behind by the moulding process to align it as best he could. Then he pressed the trigger. The ray-gun made a vague and wholly unconvincing roaring noise, the blue light flickered and a tinny machine voice said "*EXTERMINATE!*" Nothing else happened.

Ah, he thought. Then he stooped and picked up the squashed doughnut and walked out into the night, slamming the door behind him.

He walked to the nearest bus stop. It was raining.

He half expected to be fired the moment he walked through the door the next morning, and he spent the rest of the day waiting for a summons from Management, but it didn't come. Morning coffee was the same as usual, except that, just possibly, Mr Pecheur was reluctant to meet his eye. Or, more likely, Mr Pecheur wasn't particularly interested in looking at him. Reasonably enough; after all, it wasn't like there was anything worth looking at.

The next day, after he'd put out the boxes to be collected, he lay in wait with the Omskium door just a crack open (ajar, not a door, ho bloody ho). Two men came to collect the boxes. He'd never seen either of them before in his life.

So he tried pushing his luck. He went back to the McDonald's where the weirdness had taken place, but the worst that happened to him was a Filet-O-Fish with regular fries and a vanilla shake. He spent one evening riding the Underground, but his experiences, though varied and not particularly pleasant, were depressingly normal. He rang round the old crowd for news of Stephanie, and all he got was, Hadn't you heard? She's getting married. To George.

The plastic ray-gun resolutely stayed a plastic ray-gun, until he got sick of the sight of it. One night he left the blue light on, and when he woke up the next morning it had gone out. Battery flat. He couldn't be bothered to replace it. Then, one lunchtime, he happened to pass Forbidden Planet, and saw it in the window; one just like it, anyhow. One sale, clearance, marked down from £16.99 to £1.99. He went inside and asked, Is it real? I mean, will it really vaporise things? They were used to that sort of question and answered kindly, No.

Back in his sub-basement, he sat on a box and thought, It's over. No more weirdness. It's been, what, three weeks since my trip to, the time I spent in, since I killed Theo Bernstein, and nothing remotely weird has happened to me. So, let's see.

From his pocket he took a small, grease-transparent paper bag, and from the bag he took a single doughnut. He weighed it in his hand, then held it up and deliberately looked through it. He could see the angle where the walls met at the top left-hand corner of the room. That was all.

He ate the doughnut. Yum.

So; it really was over, finally, conclusively, now lettest thou thy fall guy depart in peace. He frowned, trying to figure out what that might mean.

Max had reckoned that he'd been drawn into this universe because the real Maurice had trapped Theo Bernstein in a jar – the real him being the super-cool, super-rich technology wizard currently played, in this reality, by Horrible George. Accordingly, the powers that were had snatched him away from all that and dumped him here, in the role of hero, to put things right. But he'd failed; in the goblin reality, which he'd ended up in, presumably through trying to use a damaged or defective bagel as a portal, he'd been responsible for the death of the man he'd been tasked with retrieving. At that point, he hypothesised, reality had stuck like it, the way his mother had warned him he'd do if he persisted in pulling faces. Stuck like it, stuck here, forever and ever: this is now officially and definitively real. You are now you. Tough.

Well, he thought; not so bad. After all, this is the life I've always known, and this is the me I've reluctantly grown to accept. True, this me's life was warped at an early age by weirdness, which I now know to be part of a failed attempt to rescue Theo Bernstein, deceased. Presumably I'll have to live the rest of my natural lifespan like this, and it wouldn't be reaching too far to see in that an element of punishment. He couldn't quite see the justice in that; it was unless-the-guilty-party-owns-up-the-whole-class-gets-detention justice, which had always offended him on an instinctive level. But that approach does seem to inform the legislative philosophies of nearly all liberal democracies, so what the heck; better thirty innocents should suffer than one guilty man go free and all that, and you're notionally complicit in that because you voted in the last election, albeit for the other side, who never stood a chance anyway. The hell with all that. Too big and too remote to worry about. Not really his fault.

So; on a map of the multiverse, You Are Here. In a way, there was some slight consolation in knowing a little bit of the backstory, a privilege not extended to 99.9999 per cent of humanity, who get no sort of clue whatsoever. And, when he came to think about it, it *wasn't so bad*; he had a roof over his head, a job that he didn't actively hate, tolerably good health, a certain limited degree of freedom of speech and association, not that he had anything he wanted to say or anybody he was particularly keen to associate with. If he was arrested for a crime he hadn't committed, he had a right to see a bored and relatively badly paid duty solicitor. He couldn't be beheaded on the whim of a baron; he couldn't even be mistakenly shot dead by the police without several newspapers making a fuss about it. If he was starving, he'd be fed. If he got toothache, he could see a dentist within a week. Compared to the vast majority of human beings over the course of history, he was unbelievably well off and had absolutely nothing to complain about. In a multiverse crammed with unspeakable horrors, he was sitting pretty. So—

And Stephanie was going to marry George. Big deal; see above. Whatever love is, it's notoriously not hereafter (he wasn't quite sure what that meant, not having paid attention in English when they covered that part of the course), and what you've never had, you don't miss. Now he came to think of it, he couldn't see any way in which being in a long-term relationship with Stephanie could be *fun*, or tolerable, or even survivable; she was so *her*, and he was so *him*. The other him, of course, the one with the helicopter pad on the roof, was a different story; that him and Stephanie could quite easily have lived happily ever after. But the road had forked, the cell had divided, and therefore it was all for the best that George, the him he should have been, should end up with her. He had half a mind, in fact, to send them a wedding present. Towels, maybe, or a nice clock.

It could be worse. I may be stranded on a desert island, but at least I didn't drown when the ship went down. Not like Theo Bernstein.

So he made an appointment, and went to see George. The pretext was paying back the money George had lent him, which he was now in a position to do. That'd be one small piece of rusty shrapnel dug out of his soul, at any rate.

There was a framed photo of her in his office; well, there would be, wouldn't there? But it wasn't the usual paperback-sized effort perched on his desk. Instead, she occupied a whole wall. It was a head-and-shoulders shot, which made the pupil of her eye substantially bigger than Maurice's head. She wore combat fatigues and her default expression: slightly bored, mildly contemptuous, a tad resentful. It was some sort of attempt at 3-D technology, but clearly George's people hadn't quite cracked it yet, because all it did was make her shimmer slightly, as though she was being projected onto a thick bank of fog. Very occasionally, when you were least expecting it, she flickered.

"You needn't have bothered, you know," George said, as he double-checked that the cheque was signed and dated. "You sure this isn't leaving you short?"

"I'm fine," Maurice replied, a little bit too emphatically. "The new job's working out really well; they're very pleased with me. I think I've fitted in straight away, so everything's great." He smiled, a thin sheet of ice over shallow water. "How about you? Oh, congratulations, by the way."

"Thanks." George grinned at him. "No hard feelings, right?"

George, of course, was sitting with his back to The Wall, which meant Maurice got the full blast of it, right in his face. "Absolutely not," he said. "I hope you're both very happy. It's the right thing, I'm sure of it."

"Yes," George said; statement of fact, with which only a fool would disagree. "It's a dreadful cliché to say some things were meant to be, but this is definitely one of them. I'm so glad you see it like that. I know Steve will be pleased. She thinks a lot of you, you know."

He wished George hadn't said that. Somehow, *she couldn't give a damn about you* would've been better. Still, there it was. Served him right for killing Theo Bernstein.

"So," he said, with a brisk let's-change-the-subject clip in his voice, "how's that special project coming along? The one you showed me last time I was here."

George frowned. "I'm sorry, I don't quite remember—"

"There was this man," Maurice said firmly, "in a sort of jar made out of your extra-special invisible glass. He was key, I think, or was he core? Something like that."

"Ah," George said, and he didn't quite meet Maurice's eye. "That project."

"Yes. You were going to buy up billions of dollars of junk bonds and sell them to alternate realities."

George smiled, but it was only a pale imitation of his usual feral grin – still a sabre-tooth tiger, but a vegetarian sabre-tooth tiger with sabre-toothache. "Well, you know," he said. "I initiate a lot of project, um, initiatives, and some of them pan out and some don't. That's the name of the game in R and D: you chuck a handful of gravel at the target and one or two pebbles hit the bullseye. That one turned out to be a complete waste of time, as it happens. Load of old rubbish." He laughed, a sound like a chair leg grating on a slate floor. "I bet you realised that when I was telling you about it, only you were far too polite to say anything. I mean, the very idea. Multiverse theory. Reality-hopping. How wacky can you get?"

"I thought it sounded really interesting," Maurice said. "It set me thinking. I went away and read all about it on Wikipedia."

"You did?"

"Yes. And I'm absolutely convinced it could work."

George gave him an elf smile. "All due respect," he said, "but I've got some of the finest minds in the world on retainer here, and they say it's pants. Great pity, good idea at the time, cut our losses, move on. That's always been our philosophy."

"I read up on that, too. Philosophy, I mean. I think, therefore I am. And the bloke in the jar was doing an awful lot of thinking, wasn't he? What happened to him, by the way?"

"Him? Oh, he went home."

"Really? I thought he just appeared out of nowhere."

George shook his head. "Saffron Walden," he replied. "That's where he was from. Got a bump on the head, lost his memory, wandered in here somehow. Then one day it suddenly all came back to him: he's a self-employed plasterer from Saffron Walden. So we gave him some clothes and money and a train ticket, and off he went. There's always a perfectly rational explanation, isn't there? Anyhow," he went on, "no point in dwelling on stuff, is there? Let's have some lunch. Roderigo's doing flash-fried escalopes of glacier-frozen woolly mammoth in breadcrumbs with a rocket, nettle and guava-rind salad, with roly-poly pudding for afters."

"I'm not hungry, thanks," Maurice said. "But I do need to use the toilet."

Mercifully, it was one of the few rooms in the building with solid, non-transparent walls and a solid door. Maurice went inside, counted to two hundred, then crept out again.

He couldn't see anyone, though presumably everywhere was CCTV'd and monitored. He probably wouldn't get very far. Still, it'd be interesting to see exactly how far he could get.

He found one of the horrible no-visible-walls-or-floor lifts. Of course there were no buttons. "Seventh floor," he said firmly, and the invisible box shot upwards like a mortar shell.

Of course, he was only guessing it was on the seventh floor, because that's where it had been in Goblin World. There was a musical *ting*, an invisible door slid back and he stepped out onto a carpet so lush and thick that hitherto undiscovered tribes could easily be living in the depths of the pile. None of it looked familiar from his last visit, but nevertheless he had a feeling he'd been somewhere quite like it before, with an old man and his perpetually hungry nephew. So; first left then second right then third left—

He was standing in front of a door. It was a plain grey monolithic slab. Very tentatively, he pressed the tip of a forefinger against it – a slightly cold, greasy feel. Omskium, like the sub-basement door at work. There was a handle. He let his fingers rest on it, applying no pressure, while his other hand crept to his jacket pocket and touched the roll of soft lavatory paper in which he'd carefully wrapped a single, fresh, pristine, perfectly round doughnut. No intention whatsoever of using it, of course; perish the thought. Also, he had every reason to believe that it no longer worked, now that he'd found his true place in the multiverse and normality had been restored. Still, it was comforting to know it was there, just in case. Shifting his hand to his inside pocket, he tapped his fingernails lightly against the butt of the plastic ray-gun. It was just a cheap nerdish toy, like the doughnut was only a doughnut, and the man he'd seen in the jar was merely an amnesiac plasterer from Saffron Walden. Perfectly normal, mundane, rational. Quite.

He tightened his grip on the door handle and pressed down. The door glided open on frictionless hinges. He walked forward; one small step for a lemming, a giant leap for lemmingkind.

Nothing was remotely the same, but it was all very familiar. A huge empty white space, and in the exact centre – draw diagonal lines from the corners of the room and here's where they cross – a glass jar. He couldn't see it, of course, but he knew it was there. Inside the jar, a hospital bed: stainless-steel frame, cantilever adjustment for raising and lowering, small thick-tyred wheels. Next to the bed was a bank of monitors and a complicated rack sort of thing for hanging drip bottles from. Tubes from the bottles fed into the arm of the man in the bed. His eyes were open, fixed on the ceiling. At the foot of the bed, a clipboard with a chart.

Maurice walked towards him, taking care to be as quiet as possible, although there was no need; the hard white floor seemed to soak up all noise. He stopped about three feet from the end of the bed and peered at the chart, at the top of which was the patient's name:

THEO BERNSTEIN

Well, of course.

Maurice cleared his throat. "Hello?" he said. "Mr Bernstein. Can you hear me?"

The man didn't move, except for one eyelash.

"You don't know me," Maurice said, "I'm Maurice Katz. I think it's my fault you're here. Um, is it all right, me talking to you? One blink for yes, two for no?"

Blink.

"Thanks, that's really nice of you. I was wondering. How you got here. Would it be all right if I just sort of ran a theory past you? You wouldn't mind that?"

Blink blink.

"You see," Maurice went on, "when we were in that other reality, with the goblins— You remember that?"

Blink.

"Great. All right, then. We were in that other reality. I guess you're in all realities simultaneously. That must be—"

Blink.

"Yes, quite. Anyhow, there you were, and I came blundering in, and I opened the jar. Not a good idea."

Blink blink.

"Because opening the jar breached the interdimensional whatsit and caused a multiphasic thing, and, um, basically, blew up the universe."

Blink.

"Thought so. And then you got shot."

Blink.

"Mphm. Actually, it was your brother Max who set me thinking. Max is fine, by the way, or was, last time I saw him. He's here, in this reality. Bet you're pleased to hear that."

No eyelid movement whatsoever.

"Well, anyway. Max asked, were you dead when I left that reality, or just dying? I couldn't see what possible difference that could make, since the wound was, like, really bad, but Max seemed to think it was really important. He's smart, your brother."

Blink. Long pause. Blink.

"Anyway," Maurice said, "I got to thinking; if the universe ended while you were mortally wounded but not actually dead—"

Blink.

"And so you sort of got cut off in the goblin universe, but you'd still be here, and in all the seventh floors of all the other buildings like this in all the other realities in the multiverse—"

Blink.

"With a bloody great big hole in you, of course, but not actually dead."

Blink.

Maurice paused. He hadn't really thought it through past this point, not having imagined he'd get this far. But still.

"My old head teacher, Mr Fisher-King," he said. "And my boss, Leroy Pecheur. Which is like medieval French for fisher king. Like in the Arthurian myths."

Blink.

"They're, um, you, aren't they?"

Blink blink. Pause. Blink.

Maurice waited for a moment. "Sorry," he said, "but I need to press you on this one. Yes or no."

Blink. Pause. Blink blink.

"Fine," Maurice said. "Only, on Wikipedia it said that the king of the disordered land gets wounded by the knight of the dolorous stroke, and as long as he's ill the land stays a right mess, and he can only be healed by the knight who hurt him in the first place. Look, am I barking up completely the wrong tree, or—?"

Blink blink.

"Only it all sounds so—"

Blink blink blink.

"I'm sorry," Maurice said anxiously, "I don't understand. Three blinks—"

Blink blink blink blink.

"What does that mean? You agree?"

Blink blink blink,

"You disagree?"

Blink blink blink blink.

"I've got it all completely wrong? You want me to go away?"

Blink blink blink blink *blink.*

"You've got something in your eye?"

Blink.

"But it's gone now."

Blink.

"Fine. So—" He sighed. "I've forgotten what I was saying now."

Blink blink blink.

"Oh, I see. One blink for A, two blinks for B—"

"Look," the man said. "Wouldn't it be easier if I just talked to you?"

Imagine the man who goes for a quick pee in a field, only to discover, as he unzips his fly, lifts his head and sighs contentedly that the bushes he nipped behind back onto an open-air theatre staging *Coriolanus* to a packed audience. That, more or less, was how Maurice felt. "You can talk."

"Yes."

"But I thought— Why didn't you say something?"

"You told me to communicate by blinking."

"Yes, but I thought— No. Time to take a deep breath and move on. "You can talk. That's good. How's the memory?"

"Which memory?"

"You can remember things."

"Well, yes."

"Such as."

"Um. Well, I was in this sort of glass jar thing."

"Yes?"

"And then—" The man frowned. "You were there. And a very tall, plain girl with pointed ears."

"Yes."

"And a— A *goblin*?"

"Yes."

"A goblin shot me with a crossbow."

"Yes."

"It hurt."

"Yes."

"And then I guess I must've passed out, because suddenly I was here, with all these tubes sticking out of me and that thing there going bleep-bloop." He hesitated, then asked, "Am I all right?"

"Um."

"Am I going to get better? Or—?"

"You'll be fine," Maurice said quickly. He said it with a degree of confidence, because of multiverse theory; because somewhere in an infinite multiverse there had to be a version of Theo Bernstein living in a universe with a real functional Valhalla, where goblin-shot heroes were eligible for free board, lodgings and entertainment in perpetuity. Stretching the definition of *fine*, maybe, but he needed to get on. "Can I just clear up a point or two?"

"I don't know. Can you?"

"I think," Maurice said, "that the jar was both inside and outside all the universes in the multiverse. Like," he remembered, "an embassy; you know, native soil in a foreign country. But when the jar was opened—" He closed his eyes and opened them. "Which was possible because when a jar isn't a jar, it's a door, and *please don't ask me to explain that*; when I opened the jar, it pulled you out of the embassy into the goblin reality, which I then left through the eye of the doughnut, and because we happened to collide at that precise moment, you came too. Look, I know that makes no sense whatsoever—"

"You can travel through doughnuts too?"

Oink. "Excuse me?"

"I can do that," Theo Bernstein said excitedly. "You just reminded me. I did that. Several times. Oh, and bagels and Polo mints work, too."

"Oh." Maurice gave him a startled look. "So you think I'm right about all that?"

Theo nodded. "Sounds pretty reasonable to me."

"My God. All right, then, so that's what happened. And here you are, and—" He stopped. "Your brother Max."

"Oh. Him."

"You remember him."

"Oh yes."

"He's been looking for you."

"Has he really."

"Yes. Well, he made me look for you, but I guess it's the same thing. Listen, we've got to find him and bring him here. He'll know what to do."

"Max? Are you kidding?"

Maurice nodded slowly. "I take it you don't get on."

Theo laughed. "You could say that."

"Ah."

"And I definitely don't want his help. If I was stranded in an alien universe, destitute and defenceless and surrounded by evil enemies with nobody else to turn to, I still wouldn't want anything to do with him."

"Um. But you are stranded in an alien—"

"There you go, then. Max can go to hell, though if I was the Devil I wouldn't let him in."

"I see." Maurice paused for a moment. "So I guess it's up to me, then. You see, I got you into this mess."

Theo blinked at him. "You did?"

"Afraid so, yes. I got you trapped in the jar thing, and I got you shot."

"Oh. Why?"

"No idea," Maurice said sadly. "It just happened. Destiny and stuff. And I sort of get the impression that I stay stuck here in this universe, which is all wrong for me, unless I sort out the mess."

"You."

"Yes."

"Ah."

"But that's all right," Maurice said, "because I'm a hero."

"Yes?"

"Mphm. A woman in McDonald's told me. And the head teacher at my school sort of hinted. And there were these other women on a train. Anyhow, that's what I am, and I got this plastic ray-gun out of a toilet bowl, except that it seems to have stopped working. So you see, there's nothing for you to worry about. It should all be fine."

"Of course. Why shouldn't it be?"

"Absolutely." Maurice took a step back and thought for a moment. "Of course, it complicates matters that you're seriously injured and moving you right now would be extremely dangerous."

"I suppose it does rather."

"But we won't worry about that," Maurice said. "Now, let's see, how do you release the brakes on these things?"

"I imagine there's a little lever."

"You saw that when they brought you here?"

Theo shook his head. "Worked it out from first principles."

There was a little lever. Maurice pressed it with his foot. The bed moved slightly. "You know what?" he said. "You're smart."

"Am I?"

"Fairly."

"Wow."

"Definitely smarter than average," Maurice said firmly. "For someone who's had his brain wiped a zillion times. I mean, let's see. Suppose you wanted to work out the area of a circle. Assuming you knew the diameter, of course."

"Gosh." Theo frowned. "No idea. I suppose I'd probably multiply the radius, no sorry, scratch that, the *square* of the radius by 3.141592653589793238—"

"There you are, you see. Quite smart."

"—46264338327950289—"

"Yes, thank you."

"Sorry, that should be 950288—"

"Yes."

"Forgot to carry the six," Theo said sheepishly. "Dumb mistake."

"Nobody's perfect." Maurice grabbed a big handful of IV bags and draped them over his left arm. "Off we go."

The bed moved quite freely when he pushed it, though one of the wheels squeaked. "Where are we going?" Theo asked.

"Not sure." Maurice nudged the foot of the bed carefully against the door, then remembered that it opened inwards. "Just a moment." He dumped the IV bags on the bed, nipped round, opened the door, went back, got the bags, pushed the bed through the door. "Anywhere rather than here, really. You see, I think the man who runs this place is up to something bad."

"Good heavens."

"Yes, because when I asked him—"

"Dualistic morality. Each act takes on an ethical dimension. The possibility of evil. Hold on, that rings a bell."

"Because when I asked him," Maurice ploughed on, "about you, he said you were an amnesiac plasterer from Essex and you'd got better and gone home."

"Oh. And am I?"

Nobody in the corridor, at the end of which was the lift. "I don't know, do I?"

"So he could have been telling the truth."

"About you being a plasterer, maybe. But not about you getting better and going home. He definitely lied about that."

"I guess," Theo said doubtfully. "Except I've got memories now. Loads of them."

"Yes, but—"

"And I'm not in that place with the goblins, where I'm fairly sure I didn't belong, so arguably I am indeed home."

Maurice stopped dead. "Look," he said. "Do you want me to rescue you or not?"

"Is that what you're doing?"

Maurice suddenly felt very, very tired. "Listen, you," he said. "I'm putting myself in grave danger here, I had to pay George back all his money, which leaves me short for the week, I've taken a day off work, and if we get caught George will probably have me killed. Therefore, I am rescuing you. Got that?"

"Um, no."

"Then you're not nearly as smart as I thought." He pressed an apparently free-standing button in an invisible wall. "Look, take it from me, you're being rescued. All right?"

"Why?"

"*Because.*" Ting; the lift had arrived. Maurice nudged the bed inside and said, "Ground floor. No, hold it. Goods entrance."

"As in goods and evils, presumably."

"Something like that." *Ting.* "We're here. All right, let's think."

"Sure. What about?"

Maurice peered round the invisible door of the lift. They were in a part of the building with solid, non-transparent walls, which was a relief. A large room full of cardboard boxes, with a few sack trucks and empty pallets for good measure. Directly opposite, a big steel door. "That way, I think," he said. "And then, I think, screw the expense, we'll take a cab."

"Hold it right there."

Maurice swung round, nearly dropping the bags. George was standing in front of the lift. To his left, a very old man holding an Uzi. To his left, a tall young man with a slice of fruit cake and a pickaxe handle.

"Sorry, Mr Katz," the old man said sadly. "Get him, Art."

The young man stepped forward, chewing grimly. Maurice's hand (left hand – his right was holding the drip bags) flew to his pocket and closed around the grip of the plastic ray-gun. He drew it and pointed it at the young man's head; then, remembering whom he was up against, he changed his aim and pointed it straight at the chunk of cake. "Don't do it, Art," he said. "One more step and the cake gets it."

Art stopped dead. George sighed. "Grow up, Maurice, for crying out loud," he said wearily. "Oh come on, you two, it's a *kid's toy*. You think it'd have got through the security sensors if it was real?"

Maybe the young man knew something George didn't. He stayed exactly where he was, his jaws barely moving. George made a furious grunting noise and grabbed the Uzi out of the old man's hands. "Maurice, you're being colossally stupid," he said. "That man is *sick*; he needs specialised medical treatment, and if you take him outside this building he could *die*. I have no idea what's going on in that ten-watt brain of yours, but I can't allow you to endanger the life of this poor, sick, vulnerable man. So stop pratting about and step away from the bed."

"You know what, George?" Maurice could hear a voice just like his own. It was coming out of his mouth. "I don't like you. I never liked you, even at school. *Nobody* at school liked you, George. They all thought you were a—"

"I'm going to count to five, Maurice," George said. "Please don't make me shoot you."

"And as for Stephanie—"

"Steve. One."

"No way in hell," Maurice said passionately, "would she

ever do it with you. Not for a billion pounds. Not if it'd solve global warming. So what've you done to her, George? Well?"

"Two."

"You." The young man looked at him, terrified. "Here. Put that down, and grab a hold of these." He offloaded the IV bags onto the young man's outstretched arm. Then he dipped his right hand into his other pocket and pulled out—

"Four."

—the doughnut. It was a bit squashed, but the plastic bag had kept the worst of the lint and fluff off it. "You or me, George," Maurice said, and turned the ray-gun on him.

"*Get him, Art!*" the old man wailed, but the young man just stood there, his arms festooned in intravenous drip tubes. George swallowed and lifted the gun. "Five," he said. "Sorry, Maurice."

But Maurice had already pushed the muzzle of the ray-gun through the hole in the doughnut. He could feel raw energy pulsing through the plastic, as a digital readout on the top lit up a brilliant green. *Setting: vaporise.*

What the hell do you think you're doing? he asked himself, and pressed the trigger.

There was a high-pitched shrieking noise and a dazzling blue flash, and George wasn't there anymore. No scorch-marks, smoke, burned-flesh smell; nothing. Dead silence, except for the crinkle of crisp-packet cellophane.

"Mr Katz?" the old man said. "What did you just—?"

"Me? Nothing."

"But you just shot him. He's—"

"Balls," Maurice said kindly. "I haven't shot anyone. This isn't a real gun. Look," he added, pulling the ray-gun out of the doughnut and showing it to the old man. "Kid's toy. You can buy them in Forbidden Planet. See?" He pointed it at his own head and pressed the trigger. It moaned *Extermin ...* and glowed a feeble blue. "Battery's flat," Maurice explained.

"Definitely non-lethal. Therefore, I can't have shot anyone, can I?"

"But Mr George—"

"Yes? What about him?"

"He's not *here*."

Maurice smiled. "Quite," he said. "And if I haven't shot him and he's not here, he must be somewhere else. That's logic, that is."

Theo stirred slightly. "Actually—"

"Besides," Maurice said quickly, "even if I had shot him, it'd have been self-defence, so really, there's nothing to get excited about, so why don't you just take your nephew somewhere and feed him, before he starves to death? After all," he added, "you promised your sister you'd look after him, didn't you?"

The old man shook his head. "You shouldn't have done that, Mr Katz, sir. You really shouldn't."

"Oh, I don't know." They looked round. "What?" Theo protested. "It's no big deal. All he did was relocate that man back to his default reality. I think that's what he did," he added. "Assuming I'm right and that blue flashing thing's a transdimensional stabilising cathode. I'm only guessing, mind."

"A transdimensional—"

"There's probably a proper name for it," Theo said. "But logically it's got to be something like that; it stands to reason. Well, hasn't it?"

Maurice took a deep breath. "He's feeling better," he said. "I think we'll go now."

The old man was looking mildly stunned, as if he'd just cut into a Victoria sponge and a dozen chorus girls had jumped out. "Mind how you go, Mr Katz," he said, not unkindly. "Thanks ever so much for not shooting our Art. He's a good lad."

"Really?" Theo said, puzzled. "It seems to me, all he does is stand there and eat. Does he actually need all that food? Because I'd have thought, a human being that size would really only want around 2,550 calories a day, and he's just—"

"Theo."

"Yes?"

"Shut up." Maurice took back the IV bags from the young man, who grinned sheepishly; then he looped them over his arm, took a firm hold of the bed and propelled it forward. "Would someone mind getting the door for me?" he asked. The young man sprang forward and opened it. On the other side it was dark, which seemed odd, but what the hell. "Well," Maurice said, "goodbye for now. And, um."

"Same to you too, Mr Katz, sir."

He went through the door, which immediately slammed shut behind him. It was pitch dark – not just nocturnal-absence-of-sun but the sort of darkness someone had spent effort and money creating. With a certain level of misgiving, Maurice pushed the bed forward. After a couple of steps, it bumped up against something and would go no further.

"We've stopped," Theo said. "Are we there yet?"

Maurice felt in his pocket for the plastic ray-gun and pressed its trigger. There was practically no juice left in the battery, so all he got was a very brief sputter of blue glow; enough, however, to shock him so much that he dropped the ray-gun on the floor. "Yes," he said.

"Oh good. Now what?"

"Now," Maurice said, "I turn on the light."

He knew exactly where to find it, even in the dark. He pressed the switch, and a landlords'-special light bulb slowly began to gleam overhead. Maurice looked round to make absolutely sure there was no mistake, then said, "Shit."

"Oh. Have I got to?"

Absolutely no mistake at all. It was exactly as he'd left it, when he finished work the previous afternoon. He looked down the long rows of shelves, each one lined with innumerable identical cardboard boxes, then across to the ruined computer, on which sat the half-eaten roll of chocolate digestive biscuits he'd brought in yesterday morning. Just to be sure, he walked over and counted them. The drill was, he allowed himself one biscuit per box found, as a reward. There were nine biscuits left, which was exactly right.

"Is this really a medical facility?" Theo asked. "I have to say, it's not quite what I'd expected."

Maurice rushed to the door and tried it, but it wouldn't budge. Omskium, the toughest material known to Man. Oh boy. He glanced down at his watch. The hands were spinning so fast they were just a blur.

"Excuse me," Theo said.

"What?"

"Where is this, exactly?"

Maurice spun round and glared at him. "Exactly," he said, "this is the sub-basement of Carbonec Industries plc, Evelake Street in the City of London. I should know, I work here."

"Ah," Theo said. "That's all right, then."

"No it's *not*." Maurice slumped against the wall and dribbled down it, ending up in a sort of huddled crouch on the floor. "Because this can't be the *real* Carbonec, because two minutes ago we were in George's building, and that's half a mile from here. On the other side of that door, there ought to be a staircase leading to the front office. Also," he added bitterly, "the bloody door shouldn't be locked."

"Oh. Is that bad?"

"Yes." Maurice lifted his head. "It looks just like my subbasement – even the biscuits are right – but obviously it's not.

And we're trapped in it. Absolutely no way out. We're stuck here."

"Ah." Theo hesitated, then said, "I think I'm hungry."

"You think."

"Well, I've never been hungry before. At least, not that I can remember. Is there any food?"

"Nine digestive biscuits."

"Is that enough?"

"No."

"Oh." Pause. "So what happens next?"

"I think," Maurice said, "we starve to death. Well, I do. You'll probably die long before me, when the stuff in the drip bags runs out. It's just possible that we stay in here like this for ever and ever, but I wouldn't bank on it. Also," he added, "no offence, but I think death would be better."

"I'm inclined to agree," Theo said solemnly. "I have a vague recollection of being stuck in a little bare room for five years with my brother Max. Of course you're much nicer than him, but—"

"Death would be better."

"I think so."

"Well, we'll find out soon enough." Maurice got up, went to the packet of biscuits, broke one in half and offered a half to Theo, who looked at it. "That's food, is it?"

"Broadly speaking."

"What do you do? Theoretically, I assume it goes in through the mouth, and I'm guessing the teeth are for breaking it up into small bits for swallowing, but I've never actually—"

"Watch and learn."

Theo watched. "I think I see," he said. "It's more or less what the young man was doing."

"He was better at it than me, but yes."

He slid the half biscuit into Theo's mouth, like posting a

letter, and watched as he closed his teeth on it. "Harder," he advised. "There, that's the idea."

"Mm. Mmm mm."

"Sorry?"

"Mm mm mmm mm."

"Now you swallow," Maurice replied. "Like this. Watch. All right," he added later, once Theo had stopped coughing, "biscuits probably aren't a good one to start off with. Not that it makes much difference in your case, I'm afraid. It doesn't look like you'll get a chance to try anything else."

"I'm not all that bothered, to be honest with you," Theo rasped. "I didn't enjoy that at all."

"Just as well, really." He sat down against the wall and munched his half of the biscuit. "So," he said. "What exactly do you remember?"

"Not a lot," Theo replied apologetically. "At least, I'm fairly sure there's quite a lot of stuff in there somewhere, but I can't seem to get at it, somehow. Little bits sort of float to the surface from time to time, but they're not connected to anything, if you follow me. Like, I can distinctly remember how irritating my brother Max is, but I can't remember growing up or being a kid." He paused. "I think I may have blown something up at some point."

"The Very Very Large Hadron Collider."

"Yes, that's the one. But I can't remember what it was, or why I did it. And I *think* I may have created the multiverse."

Maurice frowned. "You mean multiverse theory."

"No, the multiverse," Theo replied. "But that's all really fuzzy. I'm just going by what I think I can remember people telling me. Oh, and I think I won the Nobel Prize, for something or other. I can remember a lot of standing about in tight shoes, and someone called the King of Norway, and I do believe it rained."

"Ah."

"Apart from that, though, it's all just conjecture, stuff I've figured out as I've gone along, just by looking at things and trying to work out what's going on. I mean, take this cellar, for instance."

"Sub-basement, actually."

"I stand corrected. You said it shouldn't be here. Not next door to the other place, I mean."

"Definitely."

"Ah yes," Theo said, "but in multiverse theory, it stands to reason that there must be a universe which is exactly the same as the one you're used to, except that the Carbonec building's next door to the place we just came from. Therefore, that's where we are."

"Um."

"Which in turn begs the question," Theo continued earnestly, "how did we get there? How did we shift from one universe to another without a YouSpace device?"

"I've heard that name before," Maurice said. "Didn't you—?"

"You know, I do believe I did. Or rather, Pieter did, and I—" He stopped. "I think the term would be, *got lumbered* with it. Anyhow, I think I got it to work sort-of-reliably."

"Reliably?" Maurice asked. "Really reliably or Microsoft reliably? What I mean is, every fifth time you used it, did you get blown to pieces?"

"Fairly reliably," Theo said, after a pause. "You need a dimensional transit chamber. I used bottles. But any glass vessel would do just as well."

"A jar, for instance."

"I don't see why not. And then you had to have an activating interface portal."

"Let me guess," Maurice said. "Doughnuts."

"Or bagels or Polo mints. Naturally, the activating interface portal only works in conjunction with the dimensional transit chamber. I think that's why, when the jar was opened and the field got broken back in the goblinny place, things didn't work anymore."

Maurice nodded slowly. "Except just now."

"Excuse me?"

"When I shot George," Maurice explained. "Something told me, put the ray-gun inside the doughnut and it'll work. And it did. And something, *stuff* must be working, or we couldn't have reality-hopped from where we were to here when we came through that door. In which case—"

Theo beamed. "We must now be inside the active field of another dimensional transit chamber," he said. "Not the one I was in when I kept losing my memory, because that one failed when it got opened. Therefore, there's got to be another one. Another bottle." He stopped, and frowned. "There were six," he said thoughtfully. "Yes, I'm sure there were. Five brown ones and a green one. I made them, just before I—"

"You what?"

Theo shook his head. "I don't know," he said. "I really wish I could remember, but I can't. But I'm as certain as I can be that at some point I made six YouSpace bottles, any one of which would create a stable YouSpace field which could be activated using a simple doughnut. So, if the ray-gun turned real when you stuck it through the hole in a simple doughnut, you *must* be within the active locus of a stable YouSpace field, and the only way I know that that would be possible would be if *you* had one of my six bottles." He stopped, frowned and asked, "Does that make sense?"

"No." Even as he said it, a picture appeared in his mind: two beautiful, bewildering women on a street corner. Duty and Fun. And he'd chosen—

"What did you do with these widgets after you'd made them?"

"I don't— Yes I do." Theo leaned forward, eyes wide open. "I gave them to people. *Max*. I gave one to my brother Max."

Maurice frowned. "Can't be that one," he said. "He was trapped. He said so."

"You don't want to go believing anything Max tells you," Theo said, suddenly ferocious. "Not if he drenches you in gasoline, strikes a match and tells you you're burning. Which is an entirely possible scenario, I might add. Look, didn't you say Max kept turning up in places?"

"Well—"

"Max has got the bottle," Theo said firmly. "He's been using it to screw me around. Just wait till I—"

"No, it was me," Maurice insisted, but Theo didn't seem to be listening. "I knew I should never have given him one, the treacherous little creep," Theo went on. "Oh, I loaded it with safety protocols so he couldn't do anything bad with it, but he's crafty, Max is, he must've figured out how to disable them. And then he used the bottle to strand me in that jar thing. The *bastard*."

"You're wrong about that," Maurice insisted. "That was George, or me. Both of us. Max has been trying to rescue you. Or trying to get me to rescue you, which is more or less the same thing, I suppose. He told me; he came looking for you using *his* bottle, and got stuck."

"No." Theo's face had set hard, like a neglected paintbrush. "If something horrible is happening to me, it'll be Max. Everything bad is Max, always has been."

Maurice drew in a long, deep breath, but before he could put words to it, he heard a very faint but nonetheless irritating jingle, coming from inside his jacket. Theo heard it too. "Your clothing is singing to us," he said. "That's—"

"My phone." Maurice started clawing at his front. Suddenly his inside pocket was harder to find than Lord Lucan.

"That's not possible," he said. "My phone can't work, we're in a—"

"Universe where your phone works," Theo said. "What's a phone?"

Maurice hauled it out, flipped it open and said, "Yes?"

"Maurice? It's Kieran."

For a moment, Maurice couldn't make any sense of that at all. Then he thought; Kieran. Kieran I was at school with. Kieran-and-Shawna, otherwise known as the Fight Club. "Kieran?"

"Yes. How's things?"

"Um, fine. How's Shawna?"

"Don't ask. Listen, there's a bunch of us getting together for Darren's birthday, nothing special, just meeting up at Wetherspoon's and having a few jars. Shawna wondered if you'd fancy—"

"A few whats?"

"Jars." Kieran sighed. "A few drinks. Beer. Brown stuff that makes you fall over. Anyway, if you fancy coming along, it's seven thirty on Fri—"

"A few *whats*?"

"Maurice? You sound a bit funny, mate. Are you—?"

"Call you back." He snapped the phone shut and lunged forward, until he was practically in Theo's face. "Listen," he said urgently. "When is a door not a door?"

"Excuse me?"

"When it's a jar. When is a jar not a jar?"

"I'm not sure I—"

"When it's a *beer*." He smacked his forehead in self-rebuke. "It's so *obvious*, I must be really stupid.," he said. "What sort of bottle?"

"Excuse me?"

"What sort of bottle did you use to make your space things?"

"YouSpace modules." Theo frowned. "I don't know. I think five of them were green and one was brown. About yay high." He held his hands roughly a beer-bottle-length apart. "And about so wide."

"You sure about that?"

"Sureish. Possibly sure."

Maurice forgave him for that. "Now then," he said. "What comes in brown and green bottles about that sort of size? Say, a third of a litre."

"A third of a litre."

"No, it's an *expression*. Well?"

Theo shrugged. "I don't know."

"*Beer*," Maurice roared. "You made your gadgets out of beer bottles."

Theo blinked. "You know what," he said, in a soft, almost awestruck voice, "I do believe you're right. In a café, in Rio de—"

"*Beer bottles*." Maurice's eyes were shining. "Now, I really need you to remember. You said you gave them to people. One to Max, yes. Who else?"

An agonised look crawled across Theo's face. "Sorry," he said.

"All right, not to worry." He felt as if he'd just been shot out of a cannon: rushing at enormous speed, not under his own control, but definitely going somewhere. "What happens to old beer bottles, do you think? Once they're empty, I mean."

"Um." Theo frowned. "Well, they could just get thrown out in the trash, but that would be environmentally irresponsible, so nobody in his right mind would do that; so, presumably, they're taken back to the beer-making place, washed out and refilled. Obviously."

"Obviously," Maurice repeated. "So, just suppose one of your YouSpace bottles got accidentally dumped in a bottle bank, taken back to the brewery, just like you said. They wash it out and put beer in it. Would that stop it working? As a YouSpace thing, I mean."

Theo shrugged. "I wouldn't have thought so. I mean, it's not as if transdimensional correlative algorhythms are going to rust if they get wet."

"And then the brewery ships the bottle out again; for export, maybe – it could have ended up pretty well anywhere. Couldn't it?"

"Well—" Theo nodded. "I suppose so."

"In which case—"

"But you'd need to activate it before it'd start working."

"Activate it?"

"Yes. Set it going. Turn it on."

"Fine. How would you do that?"

"Can't remember."

Maurice closed his eyes. Painfully slowly up the ladder, dizzyingly fast down the snake. Never mind. "But presumably it's something that could happen accidentally. Well?"

"I suppose so," Theo said. "I mean, multiverse theory—"

"Whatever," Maurice said firmly. "Here's the scenario. One of your beer bottles got thrown out and recycled and accidentally switched on. Therefore, the doughnut now works. Therefore, we can use it to get out of here. Well?"

Theo looked thoughtful. "Define *out of here*," he said.

Oh come *on*. "Not in here," Maurice shouted. "Not stuck in a locked room with no food or water. Not stuck in a locked room with no food or water that *shouldn't be here*. Anywhere's got to be better than that, right?"

"Um."

"*Not* Um," Maurice said furiously. "Take it from me; I'm an expert on Um and this is one case where it doesn't apply. If we stay here, we die. Got that?"

"If you say so," Theo replied meekly. "I just think we ought to be a tiny bit careful about—"

Too late. Maurice had pulled out the doughnut. It was starting to look a little bit sad, what an antiques dealer would call distressed, but it was still in one piece, with a clearly defined central hole, through which—

𝓭

"Um," said Maurice.

A tall man in a white jacket with brass buttons handed him a beer. He looked at it.

"You know about these things," Theo said, about two feet to his left. "Does this kind of stuff happen very often?"

Maurice looked round. The first thing that registered with him was the huge crystal chandelier, glistening like a galaxy seen far off from deep space. Then the gleaming polished wood floor; then the hundred or so six-seater round tables, with their snow-white tablecloths. Then the bizarre assortment of people sitting around those same tables. Then the stage and rostrum at the far end of the room. "What stuff?"

"One moment we're trapped in a cellar—"

"Sub-basement."

"Sub-basement, then, with no food and no way out, and then a fraction of a second later we're here, wherever this is." He pulled a sad face. "It wasn't like this when I was in my jar. I knew where I was."

"Not for very long," Maurice pointed out. "They kept erasing your brain, remember?"

"Well, no."

"I think," Maurice said, "that we've been YouSpaced. Come on, you invented the stupid— Hang on."

"What?"

He stared. "You're better."

"Excuse me?"

"A moment ago you were lying in bed with about a million tubes stuck in your arm."

"So I was." Theo looked down. "Now there's a weird thing."

"What?"

"You and I are wearing practically identical clothes. Two black garments, one white one and some kind of strange black noose thing around our necks. Is that a coincidence, or what?"

"Black tie. Formal wear." He considered trying to explain, but when you come right down to it, there is no rational explanation for the tuxedo. "Don't worry about it," he said, "it's, um, a thing."

"All those other people—"

"Yes. Like I was saying. You invented this YouSpace stuff. What just happened?"

Theo shrugged. "Assuming what just happened actually was a YouSpace event, you decided we should come here."

"*I* decided?"

"Well, I didn't, so it must've been you. What instructions did you give the interface?"

"I didn't."

Theo gave him a look. "Well, you must've wanted it to do *something*."

"I— Well, I just thought, Get us out of here. And—"

"Here we are." Theo nodded. "I have a vague recollection that the YouSpace device is sort of mildly telepathic. You think what you want it to do, where you want to go, and that's how you program it. Of course, if you aren't pretty damn precise, there's a margin for misinterpretation."

A margin for— Maurice reckoned he understood. Unless YouSpace was infinitely more sophisticated than any form of technology he was used to, it operated on more or less the same sort of logic as, say, the Windows spellcheck. All in all, they were extremely lucky not to have rematerialised at the bottom of the sea. "Oh well," he said, sipping his beer, "no harm done, I suppose. All we have to do is take another trip through the doughnut, this time being a bit more careful about—"

He'd been fishing in his pocket for the doughnut. He'd found it. He drew it out and put it on the plate in front of him, whereupon a large black bird swooped down out of nowhere, snatched it up in its beak and flapped away, struggling to gain enough height to clear the heads of the party at the next table. Mildly stunned, he watched the bird make its laborious way across the room, until it eventually flopped down on the shoulder of a tall, grey-ponytailed, eyepatch-wearing man in the far corner, who took the doughnut from the bird's beak, brushed it off against his sleeve and ate it.

"Did you see that?" Maurice asked. "That bird stole our doughnut."

"Yes. Is that normal at this sort of occasion?"

"I don't know. I've got no idea what this is." He studied the room again, aware of the faint tinkling of the bell of memory. "If I didn't know better I'd say it was the Oscars or something."

"The . . . ?"

Another thing you couldn't possibly explain. (Well, go on. You try.) "But that makes no sense," Maurice went on, "because why would my subconscious mind tell the YouSpace thing to take us to the Academy Awards? So it can't be—"

A PA system made one of those extraordinary twanging noises. Instinctively, Maurice looked at the rostrum, and saw a man in glasses and a tux and a woman in evening dress. The woman handed the man an envelope. "Actually," Theo said, "thinking about it logically, I can sort of reconstruct a possible subconscious train of thought that might've led you to bring us here. If I'm right . . . "

"... Nominations for the Best Thunder God award are ..." The man pushed his glasses up onto the bridge of his nose. "Jupiter, for the Roman Empire, 776 BC TO AD 326."

There was a roll of applause. "Ah," Theo said. "Thought so."

"Unkulunkulu, for Southern Africa ..."

"You *what*?" Maurice hissed.

"Well," Theo said, "it's really quite simple. When you thought, *Get us out of here*, what you actually meant was—"

"And finally," boomed the man on the podium, "Thor, for Dark Age Scandinavia. And the winner is—"

"*I don't deserve to be here, so take me to where I ought to be*," Theo went on, raising his voice to make himself heard over the applause for Thor. "And clearly, deep down you've got such a high opinion of yourself—"

"Thor, for Dark Age Scandinavia!" The room erupted into clapping, cheers, rolls of thunder and the opening bars of *Also Sprach Zarathustra*. A huge man in a white tuxedo got up from a table about ten yards away and lumbered towards the podium, waving as he went.

"—that you reckon you deserve universal recognition for your selfless and heroic acts," Theo shouted, as Thor shook hands with the man with glasses, who doubled up with pain and snatched his hand away. "Not that I'm saying you don't, of course, but—"

"Shh!" A stern-looking woman with an owl on her shoulder at the next table was glaring at them.

"I'm just saying," Theo whispered, "clearly, your view of yourself casts you in a stereotypically heroic mould, so when the YouSpace—"

"No," Maurice protested, "that can't be right, I don't—"

"*Shhh!*"

"... To Ymir," Thor was saying, "for creating the world out of the Void of Gunningagap, and to Audunla the Cosmic

Cow, for licking the primal salt block into the shape of the first humanoid, and to Dasher, Dancer, Prancer, Vixen, Comet, Cupid, Donner and Blitzen, the very special goats who pull the Chariot of Thunder and of course a very, *very* special thank you to Odin—" (the grey-haired man with the big black doughnut-stealing bird smirked happily) "—for building Valhalla—"

"If you say so," Theo whispered meekly. "It's just that it does sort of fit all the known facts. And if not, what the hell are we *doing* here?"

"And finally and last of all," Thor went on, "a really big, big thank you to my worshippers, for believing in me." Thunderous applause, flashes of forked lightning; the woman on the podium handed Thor a little silvery statuette the size of an egg-cup, which he lifted two-handed over his head and brandished all the way back to his seat.

"I don't know, do I?" Maurice snapped, whereupon a waiter brought him another beer. He looked at it. The glass, but no bottle.

Theo shrugged. "Ah well," he said. "I suppose it's better than being stuck in that cellar. Why do they keep giving you things to drink, by the way? Are you thirsty?"

Maurice massaged his face with the heel of his hand, as if he'd just woken up. "I think you could be right about the subconsciously giving it instructions thing," he said. "I mean, that does sound like the sort of thing that could happen with computers. But all this . . . " He paused, while the man with glasses read out the nominations for Best Bull-Headed Monster. "No, this isn't really me. All I ever wanted was a quiet life."

"Ah. Fair enough. Me too, presumably. After all, who in his right mind would want a noisy one?"

"In which case," Maurice went on, "what *did* I tell the stupid thing? I'd have thought it'd have been something like, take me somewhere safe—"

Theo looked around. "I think this is *fairly* safe."

"—where we could get something to eat and drink—"

"Talking of which," Theo interrupted, looking at the plate on Maurice's side of the table, "are you going to eat that sort-of-pink-thing with leaves all round it? Only it looks much nicer than the biscuit."

"—where we might stand a chance of finding out what's really going on—"

The man in the glasses had just been handed an envelope. "And the winner of the Most Obscure Esoteric Mystic category is – Zoroaster, for the Zend-Avesta!"

"All right," Maurice muttered, as Theo looked at him. "Point taken. But what I really *really* want most of all is to go home, so—"

"In the Difficult Return Journey category: Ulysses, for the *Odyssey*—"

Maurice turned his head and glared at the podium, but nobody was looking at him. "I suspect what happened," Theo said kindly, "is that when you looked through the doughnut, you were thinking all sorts of different things, and YouSpace was just trying to do them all at the same time. Bit of a tall order, I guess. So it chose this place because it's a sort of—"

"Unfortunately," the man with glasses said, "Ulysses isn't able to be here with us tonight, so collecting the award on his behalf—"

"—compromise," Theo said. "But with definite mythic-heroic overtones nevertheless, so I think I was probably right about that side of it. What do you reckon?"

Maurice scowled at his beer. "If it wasn't for the fact that I'd just shot him, I'd assume George was behind it some-how," he said darkly. "Just the sort of thing he'd think was funny."

"In the Most Evil category, the nominations are: Mordred,

for the Morte Darthur; the Serpent, for the Garden of Eden; Captain Hook, for Peter Pan. And the winner is . . . "

"But he's dead," Maurice said. "So it can't—"

"*Shhhh!*"

"—be him, can it?" Maurice hissed. "After all, I saw him—"

"Only in that universe," Theo said.

At that moment, the room erupted in deafening cheers and applause, leaving Maurice to contemplate the implications of what Theo had just said. "Hang on," he shouted. "Does that mean—?"

A man walked up to the podium with a huge snake draped around his neck like a Tom Baker scarf. "That he's still alive in some other part of the multiverse?" Theo nodded. "Almost certainly. When I was looking for Pieter – that's Pieter van Goyen, my old professor – I saw him get blown to bits by space aliens, but—"

The snake was telling the audience they were all wonderful, wonderful people and it loved them all. "So you're saying he's probably still alive? Here, say, in this—?"

"Almost certainly, yes."

"Hellfire." Maurice scowled. "In that case, it's definitely George. After all, he was the one who was keeping you locked up in that jar thing. He had some insane scheme about making money on the stock market or something. Bet you anything you like he's the one who's got your bottle."

"It's possible," Theo said politely. "Only, I'm not quite sure how this particular universe would be to his advantage. You've got to admit, there's nothing particularly bad about it."

"Yes, but—"

"Nominations for the Greatest Hero category," the man in the glasses read out. "Siegfried, for the Volsung cycle; Hercules, for the Twelve Labours—"

"Actually, "Theo said, "it's rather—"

"And Maurice Katz, for the rescue of Theo Bernstein. And the winner is . . . "

Maurice's jaw dropped like BP shares after an oil spill. "Oh for crying out loud," he moaned.

" . . . Hercules," the man with glasses boomed out, "for the Twelve Labours!"

The room exploded with noise. A huge man with a lion's skin draped over his tuxedo jumped up and shook his fists in the air. "Oh," Maurice said.

"Never mind," Theo said kindly. "There's always next year."

"But I didn't—"

"Which goes to show," Theo went on, "you were right. It wasn't your overblown ego that brought us here, or else you'd have won."

"Not that I give a damn," Maurice said, in a slightly strained voice. "I mean, fair play to the man; he did strangle those snakes in his cot. Even so—"

Hercules had grabbed the microphone and was launching into an impassioned tirade about the plight of endangered Emperor penguins on Coulman Island. "You're upset," Theo said.

"What, me? God, no. I mean, it's just a silly little tin statue, and everyone knows it's all a great big fix anyhow; I expect the Disney people've got some movie in the pipeline—" He stopped and shook himself, like a wet dog. "I am *not upset*," he said firmly, "because this *isn't real*. It's just—"

"Oh, it's real all right," Theo said. "That's the whole point of YouSpace. But on the day, the better man won, so—"

"Here, you." Maurice waved furiously at a passing waiter. "I want a plate of doughnuts, this table, *now*."

The waiter bowed slightly and withdrew. "So if it's not your friend George," Theo said, "and it's not you wanting to be the greatest hero ever, that still leaves us not knowing what all this is in aid of. Unless, of course—"

The security people had finally got the microphone back from Hercules, and passed it to the man with glasses. "And finally," he said. "Nominations for the Best Creator award are as follows. Vishnu, for creating the universe; Amon-Ra, for creating the universe—"

"Oh *goodness*," Theo muttered.

"And Theo Bernstein, for blowing up the Very Very Large Hadron Collider. And the winner is—"

Maurice's face was like thunder. "Bet you," he hissed savagely. "Bet you a million dollars—"

"*Theo Bernstein*, for blowing up the Very Very Large Hadron Collider."

The loudest cheers yet. Clapping so intense that it welded itself into a solid wall of noise. A spotlight, bright as a supernova, bathed Theo in blinding white light, and he rose to his feet, like a man in a dream.

Sit down, Maurice yelled, *you can't go up there; it's a trick, it's a trap, it's not real.* But the noise was so loud he couldn't hear himself, so there was no way of knowing whether he'd actually said the words or merely thought them. Made no odds. He was wrong anyhow. Not a trick or a trap. As Theo arrived at the podium and reached out his hand for the silly little statue, Maurice finally understood. Pretty obvious, actually.

The subconscious command he'd given the doughnut—

Theo cleared his throat and grinned feebly. He was going to make a speech. Oh well.

The subconscious command—

"As a very good friend of mine would say," Theo said, "Um."

The subconscious command (they were laughing and cheering) must have been: *Get Theo Bernstein to where he needs to be.* Your actual basic selfless, altruistic act.

"First of all," Theo said, "I'd like to—"

Now he came to think of it, Theo had mumbled something about being God, or having created the world, or some such nonsense, at some point. Blowing up the Very Very Large Hadron Collider obviously came into it somewhere. If he could be bothered, he'd ask to hear the full story sometime. Meanwhile, the doughnut had brought Theo here because here was where he was supposed to be: to collect his award, receive the recognition of his peers, all that kind of stuff. By the same token, Theo would never have brought himself here—

"—apologise," Theo went on. "Because, if I really did create the multiverse, I can't help feeling I didn't do a particularly wonderful job. So, to everyone out there whose lives aren't exactly the way they'd like them to be: sorry."

—Because, unlike every other candidate for the Best Creator award, the one thing Theo didn't go around looking for was praise, adulation, worship, sacrifices, burnt offerings, choral evensong, any of that stuff. Far too modest and self-effacing. Which, presumably, was why he'd won, and why it'd never have occurred to him to tell the doughnut to bring him here. Which was why—

"Next, I'd like to say a really big thank you to my friend Maurice Katz, who rescued—"

—Some other poor sod had to be lumbered with the job of doing it. Which sort of answered one question, but begged a whole hatful of others. Why me, for example; now there was a question. Because it was my fault, because in the life I ought to have had I was George, and George inadvertently trapped Theo in the beer bottle that was the jar that was the door between the dimensions, so I had to be shunted back into a parallel universe where I could make good the damage I'd done, which has now happened, and I got nominated for Best Hero, even though I somehow ended up losing out to a lion-skin-draped club-toting monster-botherer, and how was that fair, exactly?

Someone moved behind him and he felt a hand clobber his shoulder. He jerked his head round to see who it was, and found himself nose to nose with Max, who grinned at him and slid into the chair Theo had been sitting in.

"What the—?"

"Shh," Max said, nodding towards the podium, where Theo was thanking the junior deputy assistant under-managers in the stock control department of the VVLHC project gift shop. "The boy done good, yes?"

"How the hell did—?"

"*Shhh!*"

Maurice had never felt less like shhhing in his entire life, but Max clearly wasn't going to answer questions while Theo was still on his feet, so there was no point in making a big thing out of it. Accordingly he clenched his teeth together hard and looked away, and caught sight of more familiar faces sitting at the table directly behind: Mr Pecheur, a sullen-faced woman who somehow managed to look strikingly like both Theo and Max, Stephanie and—

"But that's not—" he mumbled. "That can't be—"

George, who was lifting a black attaché case onto the table and flipping the catches.

"Finally," Theo was saying, "I'm reminded of the words of Gottfried Wilhelm Leibniz, who said, 'All is for the best in the best of all possible worlds.' Now I don't know if Gottfried is here tonight" (at which point a short, fat man stood up and bowed solemnly towards the podium) "but, ladies and gentlemen, I reckon I'm uniquely qualified to assure you that this is the best of all possible worlds, and—"

George took a shiny black tube out of the case and screwed it onto the end of a longer, thinner shiny black tube.

"If it gets any better than this, well, all I can say is—"

George fitted the long, thin black tube into a chunky black rectangular box thing and gave it half a twist; it clicked into place.

"Anyhow, that's quite enough from me, so I'd just like to add that this award isn't just for me alone, it's for all the incredibly talented and dedicated men and women at the Very Very Large Hadron Collider—"

Resting his elbows squarely on the table, George pointed the assembled thing at Theo and squinted carefully down the length of it.

"—but for whose passion, determination and sheer unrelenting hard work there'd have been nothing for me to inadvertently blow up—"

Hang on, Maurice thought, that thing George is pointing at Theo – doesn't it look uncommonly like a gun?

"I have great pleasure in accepting this truly wonderful award—"

Some little part of a greater mechanism clicked into place in Maurice's head, releasing a spring that activated his legs and would've shot him out of his chair and onto his feet, if Max hadn't grabbed him firmly by the elbow and dragged him down again. "Shh!"

George was taking aim. Stephanie was pouring wine into Mr Pecheur's glass. The sullen-faced woman was lighting a cigarette. A waiter approached with the doughnuts Maurice had ordered earlier.

"Thank you!"

Deafening applause; more than enough background noise to drown out the muffled thud of the silenced rifle. In that split second, with a quite exceptional degree of clarity, Maurice knew exactly what he ought to have done. He should've pushed Max's hand aside, jumped up, put himself between George and Theo and taken the bullet himself.

Then he looked down at the two-dimensional red rose on his shirt front, and realised he'd just done exactly that.

Sod it, I'm dead, he thought. Then he opened his eyes. No, apparently not.

"Theo?" he called out, and his voice echoed off the stone walls of a huge, empty room. Stone floor, too: ceiling very high, supported by massive oak beams. Freezing cold. "Theo? You there?"

No reply. He looked down again, and saw he was still wearing his bloodsoaked dress shirt. He frowned. A waiter had been heading his way with a pile of doughnuts on a silver salver, but he'd got shot before the man had reached him. But there had to have been some kind of YouSpace event, snatching him from the jaws of death in roughly the same way as Theo had been saved from the goblin's crossbow, or else he'd have bought the farm for sure. Gingerly he touched the reddened cloth: wet and warm. But he couldn't feel any pain. Couldn't feel anything.

So how—? He looked round. Footsteps – boot heels on a slab floor – coming his way.

So how come he wasn't dead? No doughnut; and the bullet had definitely hit him. At that range it must've gone clean through him—

Aha. He grinned feverishly. At the moment of impact he'd looked down, looked at the wound, the hole in his tummy. In the split nanosecond before the hole that the bullet had blasted through him closed up with blood and relaxing tissue, he must've *looked through it*, as through a doughnut or a bagel; and that, apparently, had been enough to trigger a YouSpace event and bring him here, wherever here might be. A bit grisly, he decided, and not maybe in the best possible taste, but what the heck. Better gruesomely alive than the other thing, any day.

A door at the far end of the hall opened, and a young woman entered the room. For one heart-stopping moment he was sure it was Stephanie, but it wasn't. Same height, same build, quite similar face, remarkably similar default expression, but it wasn't her. The woman looked at him, frowned, overcame whatever doubts or misgivings she'd been troubled by and said, "This way."

"Hi," he said. "I'm Maurice—"

"Katz, yes, I know. Follow me."

He stayed where he was. "Excuse me," he said. "Where is this, exactly?"

She looked at him. She was, he realised, wearing what looked like a chainmail nightie. "Say what?"

"This place. I don't know where I am."

Slight sigh. "A certain degree of confusion is perfectly normal," she replied. "Now come on, for crying out loud. He gets really pissy if he's kept waiting."

"Who's—?" Maurice said, but she turned on her heel and walked away so fast that he had to break into a trot to keep up with her.

"You were about to tell me," he said, breathing hard, "where this is."

"No I wasn't."

"Who gets pissy if he's kept waiting?"

"You'll see."

They'd reached the door. Something about it reminded Maurice of something or other, and as he walked through it – on the other side, the foot of a stone staircase – his hand brushed against it and immediately he recognised the feel: cold, hard, alien, so smooth it very nearly wasn't there at all.

"You've got an Omskium door," he said.

"Yes."

"That's funny. There was an Omskium door where I used to work."

"Really."

"That's right, yes. Only, I sort of had the impression it was the only one anywhere in the universe."

"Well," she said briskly, not looking round, "there you go. Keep up."

Easier said than done; the steps of the staircase were steeply raked, and it seemed to go on for ever. It occurred to him to wonder why he'd suffered no apparent ill effects from the bullet wound. Theo Bernstein, shot with a goblin cross-bow, had needed IV drips and a bank of monitors. But maybe the universe he'd YouSpaced into had advanced medical technology or ambient bacteria with amazing curative properties. In which case, yippee; and what a pleasant change it made, landing somewhere nice, even if the locals were annoyingly uninformative.

"Through here." They'd reached the top of the staircase. Maurice looked round. It was as if someone had rebuilt the front office of the Carbonec building in rough-hewn granite blocks, ten times larger; the layout was roughly the same, but vast and horribly bleak. First chance I get, he promised himself, it's a one-way doughnut to civilisation. This place gives me the creeps.

They crossed the wide floor of the front office. The woman stopped in a corner and just stood there for a while. "Excuse me," Maurice said, but then he heard a by-now familiar *ting*, and a door in apparently nothing slid open. The question was: is it a jar or a lift? When is a lift not a lift? Of course: when it's a—

"Get in."

They rode the invisible lift for what seemed like a very long time. Eventually, when Maurice had more or less made up his mind that it must be a jar after all, they stopped and the door slid open. The woman hesitated just a moment before getting out.

"Look," she said. " I— Um. Oh, this is difficult."

Maurice wasn't sure he liked the sound of that. "What's difficult?"

She gave him a look that seemed to go right through him to the sub-atomic level. "The fact is," she said fiercely, "I like you. You're not like the rest of them round here. And you remind me of someone I used to know."

"Funny you should say that—"

"Shut *up*. Anyhow," she went on, her face slightly red, "I shouldn't be saying this, but—"

"But?"

She lowered her voice to a rasping whisper. "*Be careful*," she said. "Got that?"

"Um."

"Right." She grabbed him by the arm and hauled him out of the lift. "Straight ahead down the corridor, then second on your left, you can't miss it. And, er—"

"*What?*"

"Good luck," she mumbled; then she turned on her heel, stepped into the lift and vanished.

Be careful. In isolation, possibly the most useless piece of advice one sentient being can give another. I'm always careful, Maurice protested to himself. And a fat lot of good—

The corridor, although built from the same brutally monolithic stone slabs as everything else, was achingly familiar, as was the bench opposite the door he didn't miss. It couldn't be, and it wasn't; but when he looked at it he knew it instantly – not the thing itself, but its perfect *equivalent*. It was the bench outside Mr Fisher-King's study at school.

Um, he thought.

Be careful, he told himself, as he knocked on the (Omskium) door. All *right*; I'm being careful, already.

The door swung open, and he walked through.

The room was enormous – so big, in fact, that he couldn't see three of the walls. He just had to assume they were there, because the ceiling (which had to be up there somewhere) must be resting on something or else it'd have fallen down. It didn't help with the scale/perspective issue that someone had seen fit to whitewash all the surfaces. Light, a lot of it, was coming in from somewhere, but he couldn't see its source.

Directly in front of him, a man sat in a chair. He hoped very much that the chair wasn't made out of human tibias and femurs expertly dovetailed together, but it sure looked that way. He recognised the man instantly.

"Oh," the man said. "It's you."

He wasn't wearing his tux, but he still had the eyepatch, the grey ponytail and the huge black bird (the one that had stolen his doughnut at the awards ceremony) perched on his shoulder. He was tapping the fingers of his left hand on the arm (no pun intended) of the chair.

"Excuse me," Maurice said, "but—"

"Yes," the man said; and although Maurice wasn't quite sure which question the man was answering, he decided not to press the issue. "Anyhow, here you are, at last. There's a meet-and-greet speech, but we can skip it if you'd rather."

"Um."

The man made a vague gesture. "Well," he said, indicating the amorphous vastness all around them, "this is basically it. What you see is what you get. Have a really great time."

"Excuse me," Maurice repeated. "You were at the awards—"

The man nodded. "Hard luck about the Best Hero thing," he said, "though I think you ought to know, I didn't vote for you. Not because you didn't deserve it, but because I don't like you very much. Well, that's that got out of the way. Any questions?"

"Yes," Maurice said. "Where is this?"

"You what?"

Maurice took a deep breath. Yes, he was overawed and intimidated, but there are limits; and a man who's just missed out on Best Hero by a whisker shouldn't take that sort of thing from anyone. "This place," he said. "What and where?"

The man narrowed his eyes. "Are you serious?"

That didn't sound terribly good. "Well, yes, as a matter of fact. I've only just got here, but you know who I am – it's like you were expecting me – but for the life of me I can't—Sorry," he said. "Did I just say something funny?"

The man was grinning. "Yes. Oh for crying out loud," he went on, "you don't get it, do you? You're dead."

That gave him a nasty turn for a second, but he knew it wasn't true. "No I'm not."

"Yes you *are*. You got shot, remember? In an act of selfless if rather ostentatious heroism."

Maurice actually smiled. "Ah," he said, "let me just explain about that. You see, there's this thing called YouSpace – it's horribly complicated and I don't really understand about it myself, but—"

"I know all about YouSpace."

"You do? Gosh. Anyway, when I got shot, I looked down at the bullet-hole, and it must've acted like a YouSpace dough-nut, because instead of dying, I found myself . . . "

He tailed off. The man was shaking his head.

"Yes," Maurice protested, "but here I am. I'm quite obvi-ously alive, so—"

"Sorry." No he wasn't, or he wouldn't be smirking like that. "The good news is, the universe in which you got yourself killed is one of a tiny handful in the multiverse that has a fully functional, operational afterlife." He paused and widened the grin. "That's the good news."

"Um."

"The bad news," the man continued with quite uncalled-for relish, "is that you died as a consequence of a voluntary positive act of conflict in a combat situation, with," he added spitefully, "unmistakable heroic intent. All of which, I'm truly sorry to say, makes you one of mine. I know, neither of us would've chosen it like this, but that's what you get for being a goddamn show-off."

"One of—"

"Indeed. My name is Odin. Welcome to Valhalla."

It was the classic walking-through-a-plate-glass-door moment: the shock, the surprise, the feeling of utter foolishness. His mouth fell open and his mind went completely blank.

"I'll just give you a quick overview of what we do here," Odin went on, in the bored-automatic tone of someone who's given the speech a million times before. "Valhalla is the eternal home of heroes who die in battle. That's you. Breakfast is at six sharp; be there or miss out. Six twelve to twenty fifty-eight hours, should you survive that long, mortal combat. Twenty-one hundred hours, the dead come back to life and there's boisterous feasting and macho drinking games in the Great Hall. Lights out at zero four hundred until breakfast at six. Your personal valkyrie or wish-maiden is Stefhilda, whom I think you've already met – best of luck with that one, or better still, just don't bother. I think that's everything, unless you've got any questions."

"Mortal combat?"

Odin nodded. "You fight. People fight you. The loser dies. Quite simple, once you've got the hang of it."

"Yes, but—"

"Talking of which," Odin said, looking over the top of

Maurice's head at someone he couldn't see, "I'd like you to meet one of your fellow guests, Eric Bloodaxe. Eric, Maurice, Maurice, Eric. See you this evening for dinner."

"But—"

Directly behind him, someone or something was growling. He looked round and saw a huge man casually dressed in bearskins. He held a long, wide-bladed axe.

"Excuse me," Maurice said.

"*Defend yourself!*" the axeman yelled, but only for form's sake. If he'd really meant it, he'd have given Maurice a split second more time—

He opened his eyes.

He was sitting on a hard bench, drawn up to a long wooden table. The noise in the room was deafening: off-key singing, mostly, though there was also the clatter of metal crockery and the distinctive chunky noise of competitive head-butting. A plump arm appeared on the right side of his head and slammed down a wide wooden dish on the table in front of him. He looked at it.

"What's this?" he asked.

"Boiled pork," said a harsh female voice overhead. "What does it look like?"

"I'm Jewish."

"Tough."

He scowled at the plate. Not even any greens or mashed potatoes. He nudged the man sitting next to him. "What else is there?"

"Boiled pork," the man replied. "It's always boiled pork. It's what there is."

"I can't eat this."

"Don't, then."

"But—"

The man hit him in the face with a fist the size of a large melon, and he went straight to sleep.

◗

He opened his eyes.

He was lying on the floor of the room he'd been in last night, except that there were no tables or benches. Someone dressed head to foot in camouflage gear was standing over him, pointing a rifle at his head. He blinked. "When's breakfast?" he asked.

"You missed it," the man replied, and shot him.

◗

That night, at dinner, he attracted the waitress's attention by grabbing her hand and twisting the index finger back as far as it would go. "Excuse me," he said.

"What?"

"No pork for me, thanks. Instead—"

"There's pork. That's it."

"Instead," Maurice said firmly, "I'd like a nice bagel and a plate of doughnuts. Now, please."

The waitress grinned at him, pulled her hand away and smacked him across the top of his head. It hurt like hell. "No doughnuts," she said. "No bagels. House rule. Forbidden. Just pork. Eat."

"Yes, but—"

The waitress hit him over the head with a wooden tray, and he went straight to—

◗

"Don't tell me," Maurice said, as the Napoleonic grenadier levelled his bayonet and prepared to lunge. "I missed breakfast again."

"*Oui.*"

"Sod. Look, is there anywhere you can buy sandwiches or something, because I'm absolutely *aaargh!*"

He looked at the slab of boiled pork and winced. If I had a knife, he thought, I could cut a hole in it and maybe—

"Excuse me."

"What?"

"Could I have a knife, please?"

The waitress gave him a mocking grin. "Forbidden at table," she said. "House rule."

"Yes, but—"

Whack.

He woke up.

Dining hall. That meant he'd come back to life again, for the, what was it now, seventeenth time? Eighteenth? No idea. The disjointed nature of his existence, the fact that he only spent a few minutes alive and conscious each day, and the frequent savage blows to his head had left him with an unreliable memory and recurring bouts of double vision. He was so hungry he even considered eating the boiled pork, for a moment or so.

Eighteen days? Nineteen? Forty-six? A thousand? He simply couldn't be sure anymore; and besides, what possible difference could it make? It was slowly starting to sink in: this sort of thing, every day, for ever and ever and ever. Eternal life – or, as his fellow inmates called it, Paradise.

Um.

As the plate of boiled pork swooped down from overhead he felt like a rabbit in the shadow of an eagle. He cowered; the waitress accidentally-on-purpose clonked the side of his head with her elbow, making his teeth rattle. She had the knack of catching him on exactly the same spot every single time. He thought: for ever. Even after the last star's gone nova and entropy's devoured every last erg of energy in the universe, we'll still be here, killing each other and noshing boiled pork. And, apart from me, everyone seems to be enjoying it.

The bloodstain on his shirtfront was a sort of milk-chocolate brown now, and the left armpit seam of his tux had split; apparently, the daily resurrection didn't apply to property, only flesh and blood. The pork, he'd gathered, was actually the same pig, over and over again. One admirable thing about Valhalla – it was carbon neutral, 100 per cent recycled and infinitely, infinitely sustainable.

Any minute now, he'd do something to offend one of his neighbours at table and get his face smashed in, so if he wanted to do any thinking, it had to be now. He thought, hard. For a while, nothing came. Then, just as Big Olaf to his left swung his fist back for his trademark right cross, he remembered—

He woke up. He'd missed breakfast. Ah shucks.

Today, the enemy du jour was a colourfully dressed hussar from the era of the Franco-Prussian war. As the bastard charged him, sabre uplifted ready for the killing downstroke, he reached in his jacket pocket, pulled out the plastic ray-gun and hoped very much that he'd figured this out right.

The hussar was within arm's length. He pointed the ray-gun and pressed the trigger. There was a blinding flash of white light, and no hussar.

Maurice smiled. One down, untold millions to go. Still, it wasn't as if he had anything else to do.

A couple of hours later, he found out that the ray-gun had a wide-beam maximum-dispersal setting. It was way cool. Get the angle just right and you could take out a whole battalion of American Civil War zouaves or the entire Zulu contingent at Rorke's Drift. He pressed on. That evening at dinner, he knew, he wasn't going to be popular with his fellow residents, but he couldn't help that. If this was going to work, he was going to have to zap them *all*.

Round about tea-time, by his best estimate, he stood alone in the Great Hall. The battery was showing signs of being on its last legs, but he hoped he wasn't going to need more than one more shot, if that. He twiddled the dial on the top of the ray-gun across to minimum beam, maximum output, and waited.

Not for very long. Boot-heels on the stone stairs, and then Odin appeared in the doorway. He looked at Maurice and smiled.

"Evening," Odin said. "Nice to see you're entering into the spirit of things."

Maurice raised the ray-gun and took careful aim. "This is a constant object," he said, trying to be Dirty Harry but coming out a quarter to Christopher Robin. "Do you know what that means?"

Odin just grinned.

"There comes a time," Maurice went on, "when a man, even if he's English, gets so pissed off he demands to see the manager. That's you, right?"

Nod.

"When I was a kid," he went on, "my aunt Jane bought me

a load of 'Myths and legends of the ...' books. I seem to remember, Norse gods aren't actually immortal. They chuff along pretty well indefinitely under optimum conditions, but if you kill them, they die."

"Hypothetically," Odin replied, a trifle too casually. "Can't say it's actually true, because it's never been tried."

"I have a scientific turn of mind," Maurice said. "Let's give it a go."

Odin shrugged. "Why not?" he said. "I've always wondered what it'd be like. Of course, the Valhalla Effect would bring me back to life in, let's see ... " (a glance at the Rolex Oyster on his wrist) "three hours and seventeen minutes, at which point I'd come back to life seriously annoyed with you. But by all means, go ahead."

"Seriously annoyed," Maurice repeated. His arms were hurting from holding up the ray-gun for so long. "You might even do me physical harm, or kill me." He smiled. "Yawn."

Odin walked up to him, gently took the ray-gun out of his hand and tucked it back in his pocket. "You're pathetic," he said kindly. "You wouldn't shoot me, for the same reason I wasn't all that keen on getting shot; neither of us know if the Valhalla Effect works on gods. You know what? You really shouldn't be here."

Always nice to know you agree with the Supreme Being on *something*. "Fine," Maurice said. "Send me home."

"Sorry, can't." Odin looked at him; half annoyance, half compassion, one vivid blue eye. "Follow me," he said. "I have a private dining room."

"Private—?"

"Mphm. Oh come on," he added. "You don't think I make do with boiled bloody pork, do you?"

It was through another of those tiresome invisible doors. Inside—

Maurice stared. The colour scheme was daffodil yellow and Delft blue. The cooker was *magnificent* – straight off the set of the most fashionable TV chef. Burnished copper pans hung from hooks; a complete set of Le Creuset crowded the hobs. The spice rack had more shelves than the British Library. The most ravishingly amazing smell—

"*Filet de chevreuil roti avec sauce aigre-douce dauphinoise,*" Odin said proudly, "my signature dish. Grab a plate and park your bum. Just give me a couple of minutes while I sauté the artichoke hearts."

For a moment . . . just for a split second. But, "Not for me, thanks," Maurice said (and his heart broke as he said it, but what the hell).

Odin opened the oven door. The perfume of roasting juices filled the universe. "Sure?"

Maurice nodded. "In my myths-and-legends book," he said, "if you eat anything in the Underworld, you've got to stay there forever."

Odin laughed. "You're a smart boy, Maurice Katz," he said. "Maybe I misjudged you. That's genuine hero thinking, that is." He put the casserole dish back in the oven and slammed the door. "How about a frothy coffee instead? That's allowed," he added. "Promise. Gods' honour."

"Thanks."

For two minutes or so, Odin fooled about with a machine of unbelievable complexity and sophistication, which eventually granted him a triple espresso and a gingerbread latte. He sat down on the opposite side of the red-and-white chequerboard tablecloth and lifted his cup in genuine respect. "Right," he said. "What can I do for you?"

Maurice licked the crests off the petrified froth-breakers. Cinnamon sprinkles. Maybe he'd been wrong all along, and this was Paradise after all. "Simple," he said. "Thanks ever so much for having me to stay, but I want to go home now, please."

"Can't. Sorry."

"All I need," Maurice said, "is a simple doughnut. I bet you've got a recipe."

"Loads," Odin replied. "There's plain and simple, or with jam, Dutch style, New Orleans style, yeast batter doughnuts Polish style, doughnut babas with rum, Greek honey doughnuts, creme fraiche doughnut balls—"

"Any of them got a hole in the middle?"

"No."

"In that case, I'll settle for a nice bagel. You can do bagels, can't you?"

Odin shook his head. "Can't seem to get the right flour. And before you ask, onion rings in batter are also a big double negative. House rules. Look," he went on, smiling gently, "I wish it wasn't this way. We both know you don't exactly fit in here, and that's sad. I respect where you're coming from. I believe you've got character, integrity and a whole lot of guts—"

"You ought to, you've seen them often enough."

"But unfortunately there's nothing I can do – my hands are tied. Death is *death*; there's no going back."

Maurice glowered at him. "Multiverse theory."

"Ah, well." Odin spread his hands in a vague, ambiguous gesture. "Exactly so. All across the multiverse, in countless billions of alternative realities, there are versions of you walking around alive and well, in some cases even *happy*, and I'm sure that's a tremendous comfort to you. Here, though—" He shook his head. "No dice. Sorry. Look, here's what I'll do, given that you're probably one of the most heroic heroes we've ever had the privilege of hosting. You give me the constant object, and I'll see to it you get chicken noodle soup every third Friday. Just for crying out loud don't tell anyone or I'll have riots on my hands."

Maurice shook his head. "In my myths-and-legends book," he said, "there was this man who wrestled with Death and won."

"Hercules. He beat you for Best Hero."

"Quite," Maurice said. "Thank you, Mister Tactful. The point is, it can be done. Right?"

Odin gave him a cautious look. "Are you suggesting that you and I *wrestle*? Only, forgive me, there's definite overtones there, and I have to say, no offence, but—"

"What I mean is," Maurice said firmly, "there are ways and means round the rules. Yes?"

Odin looked at him.

"And you don't want me here, and I really don't want to be here. Well?"

Odin smiled. "It's really got to you, hasn't it?" he said. "Missing out to Hercules, I mean, for the Best Hero gong. Listen, just being nominated is pretty hot stuff; you should be satisfied with that."

"I couldn't give a damn," Maurice said, like he really meant it. "I want to get out of here *now*. You can fix it, if you really try. Otherwise, I guess I'll just have to go on blowing everybody away, forever and ever. And I really don't think you want that. All those bruised heroic egos—"

Odin scowled at him; then, quite abruptly, his face went blank. "Did I tell you," he said, "about the Equal Opportunities program?"

"Don't change the—"

"You may have noticed," Odin went on, "that the guests we have here are exclusively male."

"Yes. So what?"

Odin shook his head. "Such an outdated attitude," he said. "Particularly now that so many of the major warmongering nations are putting women into front-line combat as well as men. I ask you, is that right? Of course not. I'm fully committed to a chauvinism-free Valhalla. Naturally, to start with there'll have to be a quota system—"

"What's this got to do with anything?"

"Think," Odin said, beaming at him. "Naturally, we can't rush things, I mean, there's accommodation issues, changing-room facilities, the whole nightmare realm of redoing all the plumbing, but—"

Maurice took out the ray-gun. "Stop *drivelling*," he said. "What are you up to?"

"Quite simple," Odin replied. "To begin with, naturally, we'll be looking to recruit the brightest and the best from the female military community. We want the first intake of women in Valhalla to be of the highest possible calibre, no pun intended. To which end, I've drawn up a shortlist of Fighting Women of Today whom I want to see coming here in, say, the next six months. Now, would you possibly care to hazard a guess as to which name is right at the top of that list?"

Maurice stared at him. "You wouldn't."

"Bet?"

"But she's—"

Odin grinned. "Your one true love. Just think. You'd be together, for ever and always, the ultimate romantic resolution. The first thing you'd see every morning for all eternity would be her smiling face, just before," he added with a pleasant twinkle in his eye, "she blew your head off. Now, isn't that your actual honest-to-goodness *Liebestod*? I ask you. What more could a heroic lover possibly want?"

"You bastard," said Maurice.

"I think it was Richard Nixon," Odin said cheerfully, "who said that once you have them by the balls, their hearts and minds will follow. Well?"

There followed a long, awkward silence. Then Maurice said, "Chicken noodle soup?"

"Every third Friday. In here, on your own, no waiting. Best offer you're going to get," he added. "Ever."

"Chicken noodle soup with dumplings?"

"Don't push it," Odin advised sternly.

"OK," Maurice said. "But I get to keep the constant object."

Odin shook his head. "Sorry, no. I'm afraid that's a deal-breaker. This place basically functions on the basis of the consent of the governed, and if a miserable little runt like you were to go around winning all the time, the consequences would not be desirable. So, you give me the ray-gun, I'll see to it that you get your chicken soup." He hesitated, then added, "With dumplings. Well, dumpling. And that's a promise. Well?"

Maurice thought about it for a long time. Then he said, "Deal. Except, I get to keep the ray-gun, so long as I promise not to shoot more than fifty people a day, and then only in self-defence. I just want a peaceful life," he added. "Nothing wrong with that, is there?"

"Of course not," Odin said, smiling. "Personally, I abhor gratuitous violence." And then he hit him over the head with a sauté pan.

d

The first thing he did when he woke up was check that the ray-gun was in his pocket. Yes, fine. So that was all right.

For some reason, nobody wanted to sit next to him at dinner that evening. Also fine – suited him perfectly. He stared at his dish of boiled pork until it was time to go to sleep, and woke up in time for breakfast. It was, needless to say, boiled pork.

A few hardy souls did try to kill him during the course of

the day, but, as he'd hoped, the Valhalla Effect worked on bat-teries, and he zapped them easily. He made a sort of base camp in the corner of the room, where nobody could sneak up behind him, and sat down, and waited. To pass the time, he tried to make sense of—

Let's see, he said to himself. Multiverse theory (he heard someone scream, and realised it was him) means that some-where there's a universe where I took the right subjects at school, founded a multi-billion-dollar company, got together with Stephanie and lived happily ever after. But, at some point in my research work for some project, I accidentally created a portal into the YouSpace thing and trapped Theo Bernstein in a jar. This wasn't supposed to happen, so my memory was wiped and I was shunted across into a parallel universe where I took the wrong GCSEs and ended up as a serial underachiever, but where I was also destined from birth to be a great – second best, but still great – hero, who'd rescue Theo Bernstein and set everything to rights. Which, god-dammit, I did. Well, then.

When in hero-world, do as the heroes do? Done that. Let's see: his destiny prophesied twice; kills dragon; enters the mysterious castle of the fisher-king; confronted with a whole load of annoying tests, passes tests; rescues the FK and heals him of his wounds (well, he's better now, isn't he?); gives his life—

Um, yes. Heroes do that. At least, the top one per cent, the real high-fliers do; it's the second-raters, the supporting cast, the straight-to-video heroes who survive, marry the girl and live happily ever after. But they don't get their footprints on the Walk of Fame, they don't win the big gongs. Only the ones who snuff it do that—

Um.

And there's a subset of that top one per cent who get sent down to the Underworld and *make it back*; they steal the guard dogs, or they wrestle or play chess with Death (I can't play chess; would Ludo do instead? Probably not), and because they're so very exceptionally cool, so exuberantly uber-uber, they die *and* go on to live happily ever after. Which, presumably, is why Hercules won the Best Hero award, and I didn't.

Bastard.

Yes, but you've got to hand it to the big guy. He busted out of Hell *and* he wrestled with Death – that's two for two, while I'm stuck here. Stuck here because if I force Odin to let me go – *which I can* – he'll kill Stephanie and she'll end up down here, and there's an outside chance she might actually like all this garbage, well, more than an outside chance, but I can't bring myself to do that to her. True heroism, see. Catch twenty-bloody-two.

Think about it, will you? Do you really honestly believe Odin *wants* women in Valhalla? Hell as like, no pun intended. It's a threat – one I can't risk him carrying out, true, but let's think about this. To keep me here, given that I'm at least a nominee for Best Hero, maybe; to get his own back on me if I escape, probably not. Like he said, the aggravation of installing separate toilet facilities alone would outweigh the cold joy of vengeance any day.

And then it came to him, in a blinding flash of clarity: the word of God, or at least, the word of the winner of the Best Creator award, which had to count for something, surely. *There's always next year*, Theo had said. Or, loosely paraphrased, it ain't over yet.

Ex cathedra? Well, he'd been sitting down when he said it, and the lack of a burning bush was probably just something to do with the fire regulations. One of these days, if ever he had the time and the opportunity, he felt he'd quite like to know precisely how Theo Bernstein had created the multiverse by accidentally blowing up the Very Very Large Hadron Collider; until that time, he was, however, prepared to accept it as an act of faith. He'd met Theo, talked to him, rescued him, even; no doubt whatsoever in his mind that Theo Bernstein existed. So, then; with an explicit mandate from the Creator, how could he possibly go wrong?

Don't answer that. Instead, think about how it might just possibly go right, and put your trust in—

Theo Bernstein. God help us. Well, quite.

♂

The waitress was sullen but guarded. They'd made her put on a white pinafore over her chainmail. She held the bowl at arm's length, as if the contents were corrosive.

"Chicken soup," she said. "With dumplings."

Well, actually dumpling; but that was fine. He waited till she'd gone, leaving him alone in Odin's private dining room. He peered down into the bowl.

As he'd anticipated, the chef had tweaked the recipe slightly to give it that distinctive Valhalla regional twist; instead of chicken noodle soup, it was boiled pork noodle soup, without the noodles. Well, of course. The pig, he knew, came back to life again every morning, was therefore sustainable, equals free. Chicken they presumably had to send out for (he shuddered to think what freight costs were across the border between Life and Death), and once it had been eaten, you had to buy more. A small, understandable deception. The main thing was, it was boiled pork noodle-free noodle soup *with dumpling*.

Well, he thought, I'm entitled. I gave my life, after all, not knowing there'd be an afterlife; I took a bullet for Theo, and that's real heroism. And then, I didn't wrestle with Death, I did something rather less sweaty and more civilised: I *negotiated* with Death. And won. And besides, this may not work, in which case I really am stuck here for ever.

Only one way to find out.

With the handle of his spoon he fished out the dumpling and laid it carefully on the tablecloth to drain. Then he drew the ray-gun and adjusted the beam setting down to maximum output, third-to-tightest beam focus. He patted the dumpling dry with his table napkin, then stood up, backed off two paces, aimed at the exact centre of the dumpling and opened fire.

The beam went through the dumpling, the table and the floor, and presumably downwards and onwards into infinity. He moved close to examine the result. One dumpling, with a hole in it.

The door flew open. The waitress was back, minus pinny, plus battleaxe. She roared as she charged, but when he turned to face her he'd already lifted the holed dumpling to his eye.

"Here's looking at you, kid," he said, and vanished.

He looked up, and saw his own face.

It was on the front cover of the international edition of *Newsweek* magazine, which the passenger in the seat opposite was reading. Behind him, through the window, he saw the distinctive circle-and-crossbar logo of the London Underground – like a crossed-out doughnut, if you're fancifully inclined. The train was just leaving Piccadilly Circus station.

Because of all the dead people, he thought; of whom I'm now one. But he felt all right, more or less. He looked down at his feet, which were encased in thousand-dollar designer trainers, then back at *Newsweek*. The caption read, *Miracle Worker*.

The magazine reader got off at the next stop, leaving his comic on the seat behind him. Maurice leaned across and picked it up. Lead article: world's richest man Maurice Katz

launches revolutionary new games console. True virtual reality now, well, a reality; imaginary worlds so real you'll actually
believe you're there.

Um, he thought.

He felt in his pocket and found his phone. Two new messages: one from George, pleased to report that profits at
Overthwart & Headlong were up 26 per cent on last quarter,
and thank you for believing in me (well, quite; one good turn,
and all that). One from Stephanie; arriving back in the UK
Friday, so will be home in time for our anniversary, love and
XXXX's. Gosh, Maurice thought, I'm back.

He frowned. No, not quite yet.

He got off at Regent's Park and had to search for quite
some time before he found a café selling doughnuts. *I hope
I'm right about this*, he thought, and lifted the doughnut to his
eye.

His flat was pretty much as he'd left it; looking like it had just
been burgled (but it hadn't), lingering smell of vintage
processed foods and long-term unwashed underwear. He
pushed through into the kitchen and, on the windowsill, there
it was.

Very carefully, he picked it up. He thought hard, trying to
remember exactly. He'd met Duty and Fun out in the street,
and presumably he must've chosen the path of Duty, because
by no stretch of the imagination could the sequence of events
thereafter be described as Fun. The next thing you do, they'd
told him, will be the most momentous event of your life. It
will change everything. It will enable you to fulfil your destiny.
And what had he done? He'd bought a bottle of beer, drunk
it, washed out the bottle and put it here, on the kitchen shelf,
to drain.

When is a door between alternate universes not a door between alternate universes? When it's a jar. When is a jar containing a hermetically sealed transdimensional micro-environment not a jar containing a hermetically sealed transdimensional microenvironment? When it's a beer. Of course, he'd soaked off the label, so he was having to rely on his memory here, but it was that Spanish stuff, the treacly one that gives you a headache. One empty San Miguel bottle to bring them all, and in the darkness *et* gratuitously allegorical *cetera*.

He found some brown paper and wrapped it carefully; then he took the Tube into town, and walked down to the Embankment, pausing only to buy a doughnut from a street vendor. He stood on the middle of Waterloo Bridge and looked down into the churning, oxtail-soup waters of the Thames. On the brown paper he'd addressed it *Theo Bernstein, Somewhere*. As he leaned forward and dropped it into the river, he had no doubt at all that it'd reach him. Messages in bottles always do.

He wasn't sure the next bit was necessary, but decided on balance that it probably was. He went into the nearest pub, down the steps to the gents' toilet, into the cubicle. From his pocket, he took the ray-gun. He hesitated; I might still need it, he thought. No, he thought; maybe if I was still a hero, but I'm not, am I? Or maybe this is exactly what a hero ought to do, in which case—

Oh, the hell with it, he told himself, and dropped it into the toilet bowl. There was a loud *plop*, nothing for a whole second; then an arm clad in white samite broke up through the blue-disinfectant-tinted water, holding the ray-gun aloft. Three solemn brandishes – for some silly reason he felt a lump in his throat, like you sometimes do in the movies, when they get something perfectly right – and then it disappeared, leaving not a ripple behind.

That's quite enough of that, he told himself. The doughnut was already in his left hand. He lifted it to his eye, and—

The wall spoke to him. "There's a Mr Bernstein to see you, Maurice."

He looked up. "Bernstein?"

"Apparently."

He caught his breath. "Theo or Max?"

"Just a second." And what a long second it proved to be. "Max."

Ah well. "Great," he told the wall. "I'll be right down."

"What's for lunch?" Max said, as they soared heavenwards in the invisible lift. "I'm starving."

"Chicken noodle soup."

"With dump—?"

"No," Maurice said firmly. "Also, no bagels or deep-fried onion rings, and absolutely definitely no doughnuts. Definitely for sure. I'm through with all that."

"Watching the calories?"

"Like a hawk."

The door opened, and Maurice led the way. "No calls, please, Betty," he told the wall. "Lunch for two in the small boardroom."

Max's head was swivelling in every direction. "Nice place you've got here."

"Designed it myself," Maurice replied. "This is our sixth-generation Now-U-C-Me HardlyThere glass." He swung his fist apparently sideways, and there was a bonging sound. "Virtually invisible and as tough as oak. Tougher, actually."

Max grinned at him. "You invented it, naturally."

"So they tell me. Now, of course, I'm going to be taking more of a supervisory role as far as R and D is concerned.

After all, we've got the best brains in the business working for us, so why keep a pack of ravening wolves and bark yourself? From now on, I intend to concentrate on the executive and managerial side of things."

"Meaning?"

Maurice smiled. "Keeping out of people's way," he said, "not getting under their feet. And living happily ever after, of course." They'd arrived. He pushed open the door. It was only *faux* Omskium, of course, but you'd need a master's degree to tell the difference. Inside, a bare white room, a long, plain pine table, six plastic stackaway chairs. "Right," he said, grabbing Max by the collar and flattening him against the wall. "How the hell did you get away from the Awards Ceremony world?"

Max gently prised open his fingers until he could breathe. "Easy," he said. "You ordered doughnuts, remember? While everyone was crowding round your dead body, we just sort of helped ourselves, and—"

"You left me there," Maurice snarled. "To die."

"Well, to go on being dead. There's a subtle but distinct difference."

"You saw the bastard was going to shoot Theo. You didn't lift a finger."

"Of course not," Max said gently. "No need. You were there."

"What?"

"Don't try and be a have-a-go hero – isn't that what they keep telling us? Leave it to trained professionals. So we did. And," he added, nodding at the room, "no harm done. In fact, everything turned out like it should. If we'd interfered, God knows what might've happened." He eased away from Maurice and sat down at the table. "Did you know, by the way, that Theo actually means God, in Greek? Like in theology and atheist. Funny old world, isn't it?"

Maurice realised he looked pretty silly, standing there fuming while Max sprawled comfortably in a chair. He sat down opposite. "He's your brother," he said. "And you left it to me."

"Yes, well, look at me. Hero material? Hardly. Anyhow, water under the bridge. Theo says thanks for the bottle, by the way. No idea what he means by it, but presumably you do."

Maurice looked at him. "You've seen him?"

"So to speak." Max nodded. "He appears to me in dreams. Mostly he just moans at me, Max, you're a mess, Max, when are you going to pull yourself together and learn to fly straight? That's the gospel according to Theo all right. Still, you can't choose your family. Talking of which," he added, "my sister Janine says she's suing you for twenty billion dollars, mental distress and anguish caused by the disappearance of her brother. She's a laugh and a half, my sister."

"Runs in the family," Maurice said sourly.

"Don't be like that," Max said, picking up a framed photograph: Stephanie, Maurice and (Maurice winced slightly) two infant children, their faces combining the very worst aspects of both parents' appearances. Oh well, Maurice thought; happily ever after. "A nice man from the Board of Control explained it all to us. He said that you had to take the bullet for Theo, because—"

Roughly what he'd figured out for himself. He listened patiently, and then they brought in the soup. No rolls, no bread and butter, nothing you could inadvertently poke a hole through. Done with all that.

"Anyway," Max said, "as far as any of us can tell, we're all together in this reality – you, me, Janine, your Xena-Warrior-Princess doll, even George the Bastard who shot you – and this is the best of all possible worlds, and by the looks of things, all is for the best in it. Great, eh?"

Hard to argue with that. "What about—?"

"Took a look for myself on the way over here," Max replied. "No Carbonec House, no Carbonec plc listed at the Register of Companies, no business of that name advertising in the trade press. Where the building used to be, there's a sort of formal garden thing with benches and a fountain and a pigeon-shat statue of some Victorian guy on a horse waving a sword about. Nobody there but a few people eating lunch and the usual duty druggies and winos. So, my guess is, they're not needed in this reality. So, another box ticked, right?"

Maurice nodded slowly, while Max guzzled his soup like a contractor draining a septic tank. "How about you?"

"Oh, I'm fine," Max said. "The bad guys I owed money to don't seem to exist in this continuum. Also, day before yesterday, I won twenty million dollars on the Ecuadorian state lottery." He smiled. "It's like someone up there's looking after me, except I'm confident that's not the case, because he's my brother and he wouldn't. Just lucky, I guess."

Maurice stared at him for a moment, then shook his head in wonder. "Twenty million dollars," he said sadly. "You'll have spent it all in a year or two."

"Yes." Max nodded solemnly. "It'll be fun. And then I expect I'll get some more from somewhere. Or it could all go horribly wrong and I'll have to be dead for a while – you never know. That's the joy of living in an infinite multiverse, I guess." He peered at Maurice for a moment, and frowned. "It's not a joy as far as you're concerned, is it? Ah well, not to worry. Looking at you, I reckon happily-ever-after's got your name written on it anyhow, and if you want it that way—"

"Yes."

"Your call." He pushed away his empty soup bowl. "Really, I only dropped by to say thanks for saving my brother."

"Excuse me."

"Thank you. For saving my—"

Maurice gazed at him open-mouthed for a moment. "Don't mention it," he said, in a tiny voice. "Any time."

Max stood up and held out his hand, which Maurice shook in a rather dazed manner. "My hero," Max said. "Well, so long." He walked to the door, then turned back. "And I'll probably hold you to that."

"What?"

"Any time, you said. So, next time I screw my life up and I'm in desperate need of rescue, you'll be number one on my turn-to list."

"I was just being polite," Maurice yelled after him, but by then he'd gone.

A month or so later, he got a parcel in the post. There was no sender's name, and it was franked, so no identifying stamps. The postmark was so blurred he couldn't read it.

Inside, he found a little silvery statuette, about the size of a salt cellar. On the base was engraved:

MAURICE KATZ
BEST HERO

"What's that?" Stephanie asked.

He looked at her. She didn't have a clue. "Oh, one of those novelty things. Saw it in a catalogue, thought it was rather fun. Like those *World's Greatest Golfer* mugs, only a bit less—"

"It's horrible," she said. "Get rid of it."

He put it on the windowsill in the downstairs toilet.

extras

orbit

meet the author

Charlie Hopkinson

TOM HOLT was born in London in 1961. At Oxford he studied bar billiards, ancient Greek agriculture and the care and feeding of small, temperamental Japanese motorcycle engines, interests which led him, perhaps inevitably, to qualify as a solicitor and emigrate to Somerset, where he specialised in death and taxes for seven years before going straight in 1995. Now a full-time writer, he lives in Chard, Somerset, with his wife, one daughter and the unmistakable scent of blood, wafting in on the breeze from the local meat-packing plant.

For even more madness and TOMfoolery go to www.orbitbooks .net.

Find out more about Tom Holt and other Orbit authors by registering for the free monthly newsletter at: www.orbitbooks.net.

introducing

If you enjoyed
WHEN IT'S A JAR,
look out for

DOUGHNUT

by Tom Holt

The doughnut is a thing of beauty.
A circle of fried, doughy perfection.
A source of comfort in trying times, perhaps.
For Theo Bernstein, however, it is far, far more.

Things have been going pretty badly for Theo Bernstein.
An unfortunate accident at work has lost him his job
(and his work involved a Very Very Large Hadron Collider,
so he's unlikely to get it back). His wife has left him.
And he doesn't have any money.

Before Theo has time to fully appreciate the pointlessness of
his own miserable existence, news arrives that his good friend
Professor Pieter van Goyen, renowned physicist and Nobel
laureate, has died.

extras

By leaving the apparently worthless contents of his safety deposit to Theo, however, the professor has set him on a quest of epic proportions. A journey that will rewrite the laws of physics. A battle to save humanity itself.

This is the tale of a man who had nothing and gave it all up to find his destiny—and a doughnut.

CHAPTER ONE

"One mistake," Theo said sadly, "one silly little mistake, and now look at me."

The Human Resources manager stared at him with fascination. "Not that little," she said breathlessly. "You blew up—"

"A mountain, yes." He shrugged. "And the Very Very Large Hadron Collider, and very nearly Switzerland. Like I said, one mistake. I moved the decimal point one place left instead of one place right. Could've happened to anyone."

The Human Resources manager wasn't so sure about that, but she didn't want to spoil the flow. She brushed the hair out of her eyes and smiled encouragingly. "Go on," she said.

"Well," Theo replied, leaning back a little in his chair, "that was just the beginning. After that, things really started to get ugly."

"Um."

"First," Theo said, "my wife left me. You can't blame her, of course. People nudging each other and looking at her wherever she went, there goes the woman whose husband blew up the VVLHC, that sort of thing—"

"Excuse me," the Human Resources manager interrupted. "This would be your third wife?"

"Fourth. Oh, sorry, forgot. Pauline dumped me for her personal fitness trainer while I was still at CalTech. It was Amanda who left me after the explosion."

"Ah, right. Go on."

"Anyway," Theo said, "there I was, alone, no job, no chance of anyone ever wanting to hire me ever again, but at least I still had the twenty million dollars my father left me. I mean, money isn't everything—"

"Um."

"But at least I knew I wasn't going to starve, not so long as I had Dad's money. And it was invested really safely."

"Yes?"

"In Schliemann Brothers," Theo said mournfully, "the world's biggest private equity fund. No way it could ever go bust, they said." He smiled. "Ah well."

"You lost—"

"The lot, yes. Of course, the blow was cushioned slightly by the fact that Amanda would've had most of it, when the divorce went through. But instead, all she got was the house, the ranch, the ski resort and the Caribbean island. She was mad as hell about that," Theo added with a faint grin, "but what can you do?"

The Human Resources manager was twisting a strand of her hair round her finger. "And?"

"Anyhow," Theo went on, "it's been pretty much downhill all the way since then. After I lost the house, I stayed with friends for a while, only it turned out they weren't friends after all, not after all the money had gone. Actually, to be fair, it wasn't just that, it was the blowing-up-the-VVLHC thing. You see, most of my friends were physicists working on the project, so they were all suddenly out of work too, and they tried not to blame me, but it's quite hard not blaming someone when it actually is their fault." He grinned sadly, then shrugged. "So I moved into this sort of hostel place, where they're supposed to help you get back on your feet."

The pressure of the coiled hair around her finger was stopping her blood from flowing. She let go. "Yes? And?"

"I got asked to leave," Theo said sadly. "Apparently, technically I counted as an arsonist, and the rules said no arsonists, because of the insurance. They told me, if I'd killed a bunch of people in the explosion it'd have been OK, because their project mission statement specifically includes murderers. But, since nobody got hurt in the blast, I had to go. So I've been sort of camping out in the subway, places like that. Which is why," he added, sitting up straight and looking her in the eye, "I really need this job. I mean, it'll help me put my life back together, get me on my feet again. Well? How about it?"

The Human Resources manager looked away. "If it was up to me—"

"Oh, come on." Theo gave her his best dying spaniel look. "You can't say I haven't got qualifications. Two doctorates in quantum physics—"

"Not relevant qualifications," the Human Resources manager said. "Not relevant to the field of flipping burgers. I'm sorry." She did look genuinely sad, he had to give her that. "You're overqualified. With a résumé like that, you're bound to get a better offer almost immediately, so where's the point in us hiring you?"

"Oh, come on," Theo said again. "After what I've done? Nobody's going to want me. I'm unemployable."

"Yes." She smiled sympathetically. "You are. Also, you're a bit old—"

"I'm thirty-one."

"Most of our entry-level staff are considerably younger than that," she said. "I'm not sure we could find a uniform to fit you." He could see she was struggling with something, and it wasn't his inside-leg measurement. He betted he could guess what it would be. "And there's the hand."

Won his bet. He gave her a cold stare. "You do know it's against the law to discriminate on grounds of physical disability."

"Yes, but—" She gave him a helpless look. "Frankly, I think the company would be prepared to take a stand on this one. We've got our customers to think about, and—"

He nodded slowly. He could see her point. Last thing you want when you're buying your burger, fries and shake is to see them floating towards you through the air. It was an attitude he'd learned to live with, ever since the accident had left his right arm invisible up to the elbow. He wished now he'd lied about it, but the man at the outreach centre had told him to be absolutely honest. "Fine," he said. "Well, thanks for listening, anyhow."

"I really am sorry."

"Of course you are."

"And anyway," she added brightly, "a guy like you, with all those degrees and doctorates. You wouldn't be happy flipping burgers in a fast-food joint."

"Wouldn't I?" He gave her a gentle smile. "It'd have been nice to find out. Goodbye."

Outside, the sun was shining; a trifle brighter than it would otherwise have done, thanks to him, but he preferred not to dwell on that. He had enough guilt to lug around without contemplating the effect his mishap had had on the ozone layer. Cheer up, he ordered himself; one more interview to go to, and who knows? This time—

"Worked in a slaughterhouse before, have you?" the man asked.

"Um, no."

"Doesn't matter. What you got to do is," he said, pointing down the dark corridor, "wheel that trolley full of guts from that hatch there to that skip there, empty the guts into the skip, go back, fill another trolley, wheel it to the skip, empty it, go back and fill it again. And so on. Reckon you can do that?"

"I think so."

The man nodded. "Most of 'em stick it out three weeks," he said. "You, I'm guessing, maybe two. Still, if you want the job—"

"Oh yes," Theo said. "Please."

The man shrugged. "Suit yourself. Couldn't do it myself, and I've been in the slaughtering forty years, but—" He paused and frowned. "What's the matter with your arm?"

Theo sensed that the man probably didn't need to hear about the quantum slipstream effect of the implosion of the VVLHC. "Lost it. Bitten off by a shark."

"Too bad. Won't that make it awkward, loading the guts?"

"Oh, I'll have a stab at it, see how I get on."

"That's the spirit," the man said absently. "OK, you start tomorrow."

In the beginning was the Word.

Not, perhaps, the most auspicious start for a cosmos; because once you have a Word, sooner or later you find you've also got an annoying Paperclip, and little wriggly red lines like tapeworms under all the proper nouns, and then everything freezes solid and dies. This last stage is known to geologists as the Ice

Age, and one can't help thinking that it could've been avoided if only the multiverse had been thoroughly debugged before it was released.

But things change; that's how it works. You can see Time as a coral reef of seconds and minutes, growing into a chalk island sitting on top of an infinite coal seam studded with diamonds the size of oil tankers; and each second is a cell dividing, two, three or a million roads-not-travelled-by every time your heart beats and the silicone pulses; and every division is a new start, the beginning of another version of the story—versions in which the Red Sea didn't part or Lee Harvey Oswald missed or Hamlet stayed in Wittenberg and got a job.

So; in the beginning was the Word, but ten nanoseconds later there was a twelve-volume dictionary, and ten nanoseconds after that a Library of Congress, with 90 per cent of the books in foreign languages. It's probably not possible after such a lapse of time to find out what the original Word was. Given the consequences, however, it could well have been oops.

introducing

**If you enjoyed
WHEN IT'S A JAR
look out for**

HELEN AND TROY'S EPIC ROAD QUEST

by A. Lee Martinez

*Witness the epic battle of the cyclops!
Visit the endangered dragon preserve!
Please, no slaying.
Solve the mystery of The Mystery Cottage, if you dare!
Buy some knickknacks from The Fates!
They might come in handy later.*

*On a road trip across an enchanted America, Helen
and Troy will discover all this and more. If the curse
placed on them by an ancient god doesn't kill them or the
pack of reluctant orc assassins don't catch up to them,
Helen and Troy might reach the end their journey
in one piece, where they might just end up destroying
the world. Or at least a state or two.*

extras

A minotaur girl, an all-American boy, a three-legged dog, and a classic car are on the road to adventure, where every exit leads to adventure. Whether they like it or not.

CHAPTER ONE

The strangeness of a minotaur working at a burger joint wasn't lost on Helen, but she'd needed a summer job. If she'd applied herself, she probably could've found something better, but it was only a few months until she started college, so why bother?

Fortunately Mr. Whiteleaf had been pretty cool about it. He didn't make her flip burgers, and he didn't make her stand out on the curb with a sandwich board as she'd feared he might. She usually ran the register, and while some customers might give her funny looks before placing their orders, that was their problem, not hers.

Full-blown minotaurism was rare in this day and age. Last time she'd checked, there had been thirteen recorded cases in the last hundred years. All the others were male. The enchantment or curse or whatever you wanted to call it usually didn't take with girls. Not all the way.

The last full female minotaur, Gladys Hoffman, aka Minotaur Minnie, had made a name for herself as a strongwoman touring with P. T. Barnum's Traveling Museum, Menagerie, Caravan, and Hippodrome. Gladys had made the best of her circumstances, but that was 1880. The world was different now, and Helen had more options. Or so she liked to believe.

She was still a seven-foot girl with horns and hooves, dozens of case studies in various medical journals, and her very own Wikipedia page. But she'd learned to roll with the punches.

The family waiting to be rung up right now was giving her the Look. A lot of people didn't know what to do with Helen, what category to throw her in. Civil rights had made a lot of progress for the orcs, ratlings, ogres, and other "monstrous" races. But minotaurs didn't have numbers. There had been no protests, no sit-ins, no grand moment in history when the rest of the world saw them as anything other than anomalies, victims of lingering curses from the days of yore carried along rare family bloodlines.

The father squinted at her as if she were a traitor to her kind. She didn't even eat meat. Not that it was any of his business.

Helen rubbed her bracelet. She did that whenever she felt selfconscious. Jewelry wasn't allowed on the job, but Mr. Whiteleaf had made an exception since hers was prescription to deal with her condition.

The little girl stared. Kids couldn't help it.

"Are you a monster?" she asked.

Helen smiled. "No, sweetie. I'm just an Enchanted American."

The mother pulled the girl away. Helen was going to say she didn't mind, that kids were only curious, and that she preferred it when people talked to her directly about her condition rather than pretend they didn't notice.

"I'm sorry," said the father.

"It's OK," replied Helen. "Kids, huh?"

He placed his order. She rang him up, gave him back his change and his number.

"We'll call you when your order is ready, sir," she said with a forced smile. "Thank you for eating at Magic Burger. And we hope you have a magical day."

Helen leaned against the counter, but she didn't allow herself to slouch. Working the register was, from a fast-food perspective, a dignified job, but it also came with responsibilities. Mr. Whiteleaf didn't expect much. Look as if she were happy to be there. Or, if not happy, at least not ready to clock out and go home.

"Helen."

She jumped. Mr. Whiteleaf was like a ghost sometimes. The

small, pale elf was past his prime by a few hundred years. Middle age wasn't a pretty thing for elves, who went from tall, regal figures to short, potbellied creatures with astigmatism in a very short time. And then they were stuck with another six or seven centuries walking this earth as creaky old men with tufts of green hair growing out of their drooping ears. But Mr. Whiteleaf was a good boss.

If only he wouldn't sneak up on her like that.

She craned her neck to peer down at him. As she was very tall and he was short, he only came to her lower abdomen.

"Hello, sir," she said.

He adjusted his glasses. "Quitting time."

She made a show of glancing at the clock on the wall, as if she had just noticed it and hadn't been counting the minutes. "Yes, sir."

Whiteleaf said, "I hate to trouble you, Helen, but would you mind working late tonight? I need some help giving the place a thorough cleaning. Word through the grapevine is that there's a surprise health inspection tomorrow. It won't be a problem, will it?"

"No," she replied.

"Excellent. I'll see you around ten thirty, then?"

"Sure thing, Mr. Whiteleaf."

The sudden obligation left her with a ninety-minute block. It was just long enough to be inconvenient but not long enough to make it worth her while to go home, change out of her work clothes, goof off for a bit, then come back. She grabbed an expired salad (they were free) and went to the break room.

Troy was there. She liked him. He was easygoing, smart, handsome, physically gifted. These qualities should have made him annoying, but whereas most people with Troy's gifts would've considered them a license for arrogance, he seemed to know how good he had it. He was always pleasant, always friendly and helpful. Nice to everyone. He was too good to be true, but with billions of people out there, there were bound to be one or two perfect ones.

Smiling, he nodded to her.

She nodded back. She wondered how many girls would go mad for a chance like this. One-on-one with Him. Him with a capital *H*, though not in a blasphemous way. Although there were whispers of demigod in his family tree.

Helen was never nervous around boys. One of the advantages of her condition was that she knew where she stood from the beginning. She liked to think of her figure as curvaceous. Like Marilyn Monroe's. Except gentlemen preferred blondes, not brown fur with white speckles. She had yet to find a pair of heels that fit her hooves. Troy was tall, with wide shoulders. She was taller, with shoulders just a smidge wider. And then there was the whole cow-head thing.

In short, she avoided butterflies in her stomach by knowing she had absolutely no chance with Troy, especially since he was rarely single in the first place.

"Hey, did Mr. Whiteleaf ask you to work late too?" she asked.

Troy looked up from his book. "Didn't mention it. Why? Does he need help?"

She sat, popped open the plastic salad container, and jammed her plastic fork at the wilted lettuce with little success. Either the fork needed to be sharper or the lettuce crisper.

"Guess not," she said.

"Shoot." (He didn't swear either.) "I really could use the money."

"Since when do you need money?" she asked. "I thought your parents were loaded."

"I'm saving for a car. Dad won't buy it for me because he says I need to learn responsibility."

"Don't you volunteer at the homeless shelter? And the senior center? And the animal shelter? And weren't you valedictorian and prom king?"

"Dad thinks I can do better."

"Well, if that's what Dad says, who am I to argue? I can see now that you're a young man in serious need of personal discipline." She stuffed a few leaves and a cherry tomato in her mouth. "What'cha reading there?"

"T. S. Eliot," he said.

That he read poetry was almost comical to Helen. It was as if he were trying to spontaneously ascend to some higher plane of perfect boyness, some sacred dimension birthed from the philosophical union of Aristotle and *Tiger Beat* editors.

He caught her smile.

"What? Don't like him?"

"Haven't read him," she replied.

"You haven't read him? One of the preeminent poets of the twentieth century, and you haven't read him?"

"He isn't that guy who doesn't capitalize, is he?"

"That's E. E. Cummings."

"My mistake."

He slid the book across the table. "Do you want to borrow my copy?"

She slid it back. "No, thanks."

He pretended to gape.

"I don't like poetry," she said. "I know I'm supposed to because I'm a girl and all that. I tried. I really did. But outside of Dr. Seuss, it doesn't do much for me."

"I've always found *The Lorax* to be a little preachy."

"'Don't burn the earth to the ground' always struck me as more common sense than preachy," she replied.

Troy chuckled. "Well, I'd love to stick around and chat about all the metaphorical implications of *Hop on Pop* with you, but I've got stuff to do."

"Giving blood, saving kittens, running from throngs of adoring young ladies," said Helen.

"I'll have you know I only save kittens on the weekend. Later, Hel."

He bounded from the room like Adonis in jeans. She was glad she hadn't been born five thousand years before, when, instead of being friends, they would've probably had to fight to the death in an arena.

She tried reading the poetry book, but it didn't do anything for her. She hid out in the break room, watching its tiny television, because she didn't want to get stuck helping to lock up. Whiteleaf would get her when it was time to clean up. Or so she thought, but everything was quiet at eleven fifteen.

Helen poked her head into the kitchen. The lights were on, but it was all shut down. No sign of the other employees. Her hooves clomped on the tile. They seemed especially loud with the Magic Burger so quiet. The silence was eerie.

The tables and chairs in the dining area, the ones that weren't bolted down, had been pushed to one side, and boxes of frozen hamburger patties sat in their place.

Whiteleaf spoke from behind her. "Hello, Helen."

She jumped.

"Oh, hi, sir. Should those burgers be out like that?"

He smiled, adjusted his glasses. "They'll be fine."

"Are we cleaning the freezer?" she asked.

He held up a small wand with a chunk of blue stone on the end. "Stand over there."

"By the meat?"

Whiteleaf frowned. "Damn it, this thing must be wearing out. It's barely two hundred years old, but once the warranty expires..." He shook the wand until the barest hint of a glow flashed in its stone.

"Are you feeling OK, Mr. Whiteleaf?"

"Look at the wand," he said. "Feel its power wash over your mind, numbing your will, robbing you of all resistance."

Helen stepped back. "This is getting kind of weird. I think maybe I should go."

He threw the wand aside. "Fine. We'll do it the less subtle way." He reached under the counter and removed a sword. She wasn't familiar with weapons, but it looked like an ornate broadsword with runes carved in the blade. It didn't glow, but it did sort of shimmer.

She didn't freak out. An advantage of being taller and stronger than nearly everyone was that she'd developed confidence in her ability to handle physical violence. She'd never been in a fight precisely *because* she was bigger and stronger than everyone. If someone ever did attack her, she'd probably freeze. She wasn't sword-proof. And the blade could do some damage in the right hands. But Whiteleaf was a frail little creature who was barely able to hold the weapon. He certainly couldn't raise it above her knee, which meant he might be able to nick her shins, which would probably hurt but wouldn't be particularly life-threatening.

"I'm very sorry about this, Helen." His arms trembled, and he sounded exhausted already. "But when the Lost God manifests in this world, he must be offered a sacrifice. Preferably an innately magical virgin. And you're the only one I could find who fit the—"

"What makes you think I'm a virgin?" she asked.

Whiteleaf lowered the blade. The tip scraped a gash in the tile floor.

"Ah, damn. Wait. You're not a virgin?"

"I didn't say that. I just asked why you thought I was one."

"It's just...I guess I just...assumed you were."

"Why would you assume that?"

He chewed on his lip for a moment. "Well, you're a very responsible young lady. It's one of the things I respect about you."

She glared. "It's because of the way I look, isn't it?"

Whiteleaf shook his head. "No, no. You're a very attractive young lady. You are!"

She moved toward him. He lifted his sword a few inches off the floor.

"I don't need this," she said. "I quit."

"You can't quit," he replied. "I need you. For the sacrifice."

She removed her name tag and set it on the counter. "I've never gored anyone before, Mr. Whiteleaf. But in your case, I'm considering it."

The Magic Burger's lights flickered and a low, guttural cry echoed from the center of the room. The aroma of sizzling meat filled the restaurant as the boxes of hamburger patties burst into flames. The ground chuck collapsed in a mound of brown-and-pink cow flesh, and it formed a giant gnashing mouth.

"At last, at last!" shouted Whiteleaf. "He has returned to us!"

Helen studied the twisted meat deity.

"You worship a hamburger god?"

Whiteleaf sighed. "He is not a hamburger god. He is a god currently manifested in an avatar of flesh that just happens to be made up of, for convenience, hamburger. Now, we haven't much time. So I'm going to need you to throw yourself into his jaws. I assure you it will be fast and quite painless."

"No."

"I'm afraid you don't have a choice, Helen." He advanced on her. "In my youth, I was a warrior to be reckoned with."

She used one hand to push him down. He fell on his ass. His sword clattered to the ground. The noise drew the attention of the hamburger god. It probed the floor in their direction with its twisted limbs.

Helen immediately regretted knocking the old elf down. He was intent on sacrificing her, and that was a pretty lousy thing to do to a girl. But his lack of ability rendered him harmless, and she could've handled it better.

He struggled to stand. His knees weren't very good, though, and it was painful to watch. "Please, you must do it. If the god isn't given his sacrifice, he'll never be able to focus and he'll never give me the sacred command. I've waited too long to blow this opportunity."

"I'm sorry, Mr. Whiteleaf. I'm not going to let a monster eat me for minimum wage."

She moved to help him up. He slashed at her with a butcher knife he'd had hidden behind his back. The blade sliced across her forearm. The cut was shallow, but it triggered a rage within her. Perhaps it was the wound. Or perhaps it was something buried in her minotaur id, the collective memory of untold billions of bovine in pain and fear.

She seized him by the collar and lifted him in the air.

"Drop. The. Knife."

He did. It clanked against the floor beside the broadsword.

"You crazy old man," she said. "It would serve you right if I offered you to your own hamburger god."

He trembled. His feet dangled limply. "It isn't personal. It's just that my god only appears once every three hundred years, and this is very important to me."

The Lost God lurched slowly around the dining area. If this blind and clumsy thing was any indication of the gods of yore, no wonder they'd mostly been forgotten. It gnawed on the corner of a table.

The glass door swung open and Troy entered. It took only one glance for him to see something was wrong.

"Hel?"

She had yet to figure out how the god perceived the world, but there was something about Troy that drew its attention. The mound of meat squished its way in his direction.

"Troy, get out of here," said Helen.

But it was too late. The god opened its mouth, and out shot a tongue of the same flesh. It wrapped around Troy's leg and pulled him toward its jaws. Yelping, he latched onto a table bolted to the floor.

She didn't think. She didn't have time. She certainly hadn't rehearsed this scenario in her mind. But by instinct she dropped Whiteleaf and grabbed the sword. A leaping blow chopped the tentacle. The god shrieked and leaned backward.

The meat coiled around Troy's leg whipped and writhed. They pulled at it, and the greasy flesh broke apart in their hands. But it kept moving, crawling on their arms like living snot.

The god charged. Helen drove the sword into the monster's lumpy body. The blade flashed and the thing recoiled. It sputtered and bubbled and squealed, swaying erratically through the room until it fell apart into a smoking pile in the middle of the room.

"What the hell was that?" asked Troy.

"A god of yore," she replied. "But I think it's dead now."

Whiteleaf ran to his broken god's corporeal remains. "What did you do? You destroyed it. Now I have to wait another three hundred years. Do you have any idea how annoying this is?" He stuck his hands in the hamburger, pulled them out, and scowled at the rancid meat. "You're fired. Both of you."

"I already quit," said Helen.

Troy grabbed some napkins from a dispenser and cleaned the burger from his hands. "What the heck is going on here?"

"I'll explain later. But we should probably call the police or something. I'm sure it's against the law to sacrifice employees."